I0634306

POWDERFINGER

Paul Fox

Inspired by the Genius of Neil Young

Copyright © 2014 Paul Fox
All rights reserved.

ISBN: 0692313281
ISBN 13: 9780692313282
Library of Congress Control Number: 2014918595
Paul Fox, Leesburg, VA

HELL

The massive eggs breached the internal walls of the female. Afterbirth melted, dripping from the larvae in the flames of hell. Satan watched over the nest, nurturing their growth and panting at the destruction his brood would bring to man. His mass of matriarchs had positioned thousands of eggs. Within the day, the maggots would break free and crane for the only chilled place in the netherworld: a massive chamber of carrion, feces, and decayed souls where the maggots were nourished. Here, the slime cooled and formed two-meter reddish-brown shells to harbor their growth. Inside the pupae, the evil strengthened. Satan touched them all and whispered narratives of the failure of humanity and the war for his soul. His vile lips pressed against the shell of the pupae, and he sang songs of victory over heaven, which would arise with the annihilation of humankind.

The malevolent would split the shell and emerge, grotesque. Satan monitored the multitude of unrighteous on earth and would plant this evil seed into the womb of the wicked. Humanity's inability to control lust and fornication would fertilize the monster and cause it to be born unto the world an agent of hell camouflaged in the skin of a child.

JANUARY 17, 1994

Los Angeles, California

Adobe slate with sunset-peach hues tinted the stage for wrought iron tables adorned with hand-painted wisteria-covered plates. This once-popular open marketplace, converted from a courtyard into the dining jewel of Westwood, fueled the vanity of its owners. The glass dome over the courtyard provided the crowning touch. Rife with the rich and the famous, La Jardin beckoned diners in this pulse of Los Angeles. Whether one was on business with the talent agencies, attending a basketball game at Pauley Pavilion at UCLA, or taking a peek at one of the movies in the fine retro theaters, Westwood offered an upscale haven in a city that had no heart—just little heartbeats.

The assistant manager, Charles, loosened his tie, hauled his fat ass through the lobby, checked that the back door remained locked, and proceeded to turn the key for the front. "Half past two in the morning is way too long of a day," Charles bemoaned under his breath. The particularly long day ended, and Charles cursed under his breath at the swing manager who'd called out for the Sunday brunch shift. "Most likely the Irish flu," he muttered to himself.

Counting the booze capped the final chore for the evening. Weekly inventory was the bane of the staff. Dan, Geoff, and Charles were the most responsible ones. They cracked open a couple of Budweisers and got to work.

"Point three," Dan called as Geoff counted the coolers.

Bottle after bottle was carefully checked off the list: Jack Daniel's, Maker's Mark, Knob Creek. On and on it went until the last bottle of DeKuyper Crème de Cassis was counted.

"Is that it?" Geoff pondered over his brew. He checked his watch.

"We have to do the wine cabinet," Charles reminded them, dark rings under his eyes surfacing. He opened the cabinet. *The Hollywood crowd sure suffered through these expensive wines,* Charles thought to himself.

He pulled the 1986 Château Lafite Rothschild Red Bordeaux Blend Pauillac and wondered what all the fuss was about. "One," he called, and the bartender recorded the item. He reached for the 1988 Sassicaia Tenuta San Guido. The floor jolted beneath his feet, and the neck slipped from his hands. Charles braced the shelf. The wine smashed and bled on the floor. "Earthquake!" he shouted, and his coworkers crawled under the dining tables.

The first ten seconds were sudden and frightening but manageable. Los Angeles had been through these before. The grid collapsed and light evaporated.

The second ten seconds kicked the shaking into overdrive. Vibrations penetrated into their spines. The wisely chosen art sprang from the wall. The glass dome over the courtyard of the restaurant trembled as the streets roared.

The last ten seconds became white noise. The adobe moved freely below their knees. The wrought iron tables offered little defense against the walls of brick raging beside them. Each painted plate became a sharp mortal enemy. Glass shattered like a grenade, sending ceramic shrapnel all around.

Charles screamed for Dan and Geoff in the dark. The walls wailed, muffling his cries. Mirrors splintered and reflective daggers leaped from the panes.

The dome cracked like ice on a spring pond. Lightning bolts of glass rained across the courtyard, smashing into the tables with the hiss of evil harps. The men covered their faces. The slivers exploded, shredding their hands and arms.

The shaking stopped. Three friends shouted in the black. They followed the voices in the void, glass crackling under their shoes, finding themselves tangled in one another's arms. Terrified and dripping blood, they stepped gingerly toward the glowing red exit sign.

In unison they crouched as new, different explosions rocked the abrupt silence.

Transformers ignited in sequence after the quake, creating the illusion that they were under some type of attack. Car alarms added to the cacophonous symphony of the early morning. Residents began to evacuate their homes with only their cell phones and one another.

A homeless man sat unruffled on the curb outside the restaurant. Charles asked him if he was OK.

The homeless man gazed fixedly at the street. He mumbled, "The doors of hell have opened. He has skulked out among us."

OCTOBER 1, 2013
ATLANTA, GEORGIA

GABRIEL BODY FOUND

The Atlanta Journal-Constitution—Bayleigh Debuchy, Staff Writer

The search for African American college freshman Savannah Gabriel came to a grisly end today as the seventeen-year-old's body was discovered in a shallow grave in Sweetwater Creek State Park. Savannah first disappeared over Labor Day weekend on Sunday, September 2, from the campus of Georgia State University, two days prior to attending her first class.

The Fulton County Sheriff's Office reported that Savannah's remains were discovered by Douglasville resident Rufus Cooper, who was fishing at the time.

Cooper told the sheriff's office that his dog had run off into the woods while he was fishing and started "howling and creating quite a commotion." He said he knew his dog "had found something." Deputy Sheriff Jermaine Silva reported to the media that

Mr. Cooper went to find his black Labrador, Jethro, and found him digging in the dirt. Mr. Cooper noticed a black trash bag and a "horrible smell." Mr. Cooper opened the black trash bag, finding Ms. Gabriel's remains, and called the authorities on his cell phone immediately.

Deputy Silva would not confirm or deny reports that Gabriel's body was dismembered.

The Fulton County Sheriff's Office is expected to officially charge suspect Horace Ford, twenty-three years of age, with murder later today. Ford has been in custody since October 9, when investigators found traces of blood and DNA consistent with Ms. Gabriel's in the back of Ford's 2006 Chevrolet Silverado.

Ford, who is white, was recently released from Georgia State Prison in Reidsville after serving fifteen months for aggravated sexual assault of another African American woman, Breanna Green, in 2010. Ford was originally arrested for rape but struck a plea with the district attorney's office after much of the physical evidence was corrupted and defense attorneys challenged Ms. Green's reputation.

Local civil rights advocate Leroi Stocker issued a statement to the press with regard to the ongoing Gabriel case.

"The NAACP is furious that the legal system has failed once again to protect the rights and lives of the African American community. It is a travesty that the case of Breanna Green disintegrated before our eyes, and the racist and rapist Horace Ford was given a slap on the wrist for the crimes committed against Ms. Green. They said it was her fault. The attorneys destroyed her character. They raped her on the stand, just as Ford beat and raped her in the back of that trailer. Then the wisdom of the penal system let him back onto the street. This is a violent man intent on doing harm to African American women. You have blood on your hands. Savannah Gabriel did not have to die. But now we bring her back to her family dead at the hands of Horace Ford. And America is an accomplice. Who shall pay for this unnecessary tragedy? Who?"

Stocker's strong words were supported by many in the African American community. Organizers are planning a march into downtown Atlanta to voice their anger and concern over the developing case of Horace Ford.

OCTOBER 3, 2013
ATLANTA, GEORGIA

FORD ARRAIGNED IN GABRIEL MURDER

The Atlanta Journal-Constitution—Bayleigh Debuchy, Staff Writer

The news vans filled the parking lot of the Fulton County Courthouse, their satellite discs looking skyward like futuristic sunflowers. Close to a thousand citizens folded together outside the grounds of the century-old edifice to show support of Savannah Gabriel, whose body had been recovered two days prior. The emotional and angry crowd shouted "Justice for Savannah!" and chanted "No justice, no peace!" while carrying DEATH PENALTY signs focused on Horace Ford, who had been charged with her murder and was arraigned today.

Ford was accompanied by his court-appointed attorney, Eva Jo Diamond. Fulton County Sheriff Jermaine Silva whisked Ford into the courthouse inconspicuously, so as not to ignite the already volatile crowd.

Ford was officially notified of the twenty-three charges against him by Judge Charlotte Wilshire, a nineteen-year veteran of the bench. Ford was charged with murder in the first degree, rape, and kidnapping in the case of Savannah Gabriel. Assistant District Attorney Leonardo Gargano vowed to "seek the death penalty."

Ford, not granted bail, was remanded into the custody of the Fulton County Sheriff's Office, where he would await trial. A trial date had not yet been determined.

The city openly mourned the loss of Savannah and the promise she'd held. Representatives of all walks of Atlanta assembled at the courthouse to show support for Savannah's family as well as their continued outrage that Ford had been released from prison for the rape of Breanna Green in 2009.

This much attention has not been drawn to the courthouse since 2005, when Brian Nichols escaped from a sheriff's deputy and killed the judge, the court reporter, and another deputy who had been assigned to his rape trial. Nichols escaped with a prisoner and later killed a federal agent before holing up in a hotel outside of Atlanta.

NOVEMBER 7, 2013
GUAM

Pilot Ben Hodgson placed his hand on his hips, squared his Dudley Do-Right jaw, and assembled his team to brief them on their mission. Typhoon Haiyan still gathered strength and headed north-northwest toward the Philippines. Haiyan had been upgraded to a Category 5 storm—a supertyphoon. Command felt it might become the largest and most powerful storm ever recorded in history.

Hodgson and crew sortied from Keesler Air Force Base in Biloxi, Mississippi, to Andersen Air Force Base near Yigo, Guam, aboard a WC-130J, the reconfigured baby brother of the C-130J Hercules. The crew and its vessel had only one purpose: to drive into the heart of the hurricane and study its behavior and movements.

Guam was the largest of the Mariana islands, and the crew had been treated well since its arrival at 0900 on November 6. The overnight flight had worn down the skeleton crew of five. Aerial Reconnaissance Weather Officer Patti Sue Varkley left behind two baby girls—Joy, four, and Denise, two—with their father, Gene. Hodgson was in charge of the plane, but Patti Sue was in charge of the mission. It was her data that was garnered and calculated to save lives.

Carl Vlaard, the copilot, and Nicholas Ziegler, the navigator, had become fast friends at Keesler, sharing a passion for NASCAR and deep-sea fishing in the Gulf of Mexico when they could coordinate leave together. They'd teamed on several missions, including Hurricane Katrina in 2005. Vlaard would often fill the cockpit with banter about the driving virtues of Jimmy Johnson, and Ziegler would counter with the achievements of Kevin Harvick. And then there were the tall tales about their onshore fishing expeditions and the magnificent catches they had recorded. No one took them that seriously. On land it is the hunter who is often hunted.

Quiet Cleavon Giroud was the loadmaster. If something wasn't on board, it was Cleavon's fault. If something fell over during the flight, it was Cleavon's fault. If something blew up, it was Cleavon's fault. Cleavon had to put everything in just the right spot. Keep the plane balanced. Keep everything working. Cleavon always had everything. His daddy had taught him how to be prepared. "Make a list, Son!" He had heard that echo in his head since he was a little boy. Cleavon was teaching his boy, Xavier, the same virtues.

"Haiyan formed in the central Pacific on the third of November and has been tracking north by northwest in a steady path since," Hodgson informed the group. "She has sustained winds of one hundred forty-five miles per hour, and her lowest-recorded barometric pressure to date is eight hundred ninety-five millibars." Hodgson removed his lid briefly and wiped the sweat from his brow. There was a rain forest inside his uniform. The heat in Guam was stupendous. "The Japanese have recorded ten-minute sustained winds close to the eye wall at one hundred seventy-five miles per hour and two-minute sustained winds at one hundred ninety-five miles per hour." He looked directly at his team. "Folks, this storm is no joke. We leave at fifteen hundred. Let's get to work."

Hodgson watched as the team dispersed, and asked the CO if he could Skype his wife and kids. As the connection patched through, Janine's beautiful face filled the monitor.

"Where are the kids?" Hodgson wanted to say hi to the whole family.

"Ben, it's six in the evening here." Janine laughed. "And you are already in tomorrow...time traveler."

Janine was right. In Guam it was already November 7. They were still in November 6.

"Clint is at football practice, and Sandy is at Sweet Frog with Harmony and Vickie."

Hodgson grinned at Janine. He truly had forgotten he was halfway around the world.

"Janine, we are a go at fifteen hundred our time."

"Ben, that thing has gotten out of control. Why do they need to send you up now? They know what it is. It's a killer." Janine did not like her husband's job.

"Baby, we've done this a thousand times. I've got a great crew, and they are ready. Cleavon will have everything prepared, and Carl and Nick are pros. I don't know Patti Sue all that well, but she is sharp. We will be fine." Ben had to calm her down before every flight. Janine became a wreck with these things. "Can you tell the kids I said hello and that I love them?" Ben smiled. It helped calm Janine down. "And don't forget to mail the cable bill." Ben got the dig in just to get Janine's mind right.

"I'll mail the bill, wise guy. And you won't be watching any cable when you get back." Janine winked. That got Ben's attention. "I love you, Ben Hodgson."

"I love you too, Janine Hodgson."

They pressed their hands to the screen, and it was time to go to work.

Cleavon closed the hatch, and Hodgson received permission from the tower to taxi.

"This bucket is ready to fly." Vlaard winked at Hodgson. Hodgson thrust the throttle forward, and the $62 million aircraft gained momentum down the runway.

The wheels lifted up, and Hodgson banked east. The dark outer edges of Haiyan awaited on the horizon.

"Altitude is ten thousand feet, Ben," the navigator reported.

"Let's hold the altitude and adjust the course setting, Nick."

Patty Sue nibbled on a bag of Peanut M&M's. The turbulence did not interrupt her vice. The turbo-propelled aircraft made communication difficult, even with the headsets. Patty Sue looked out the portside window at the wings and props. The one-hundred-thirty-three-foot wingspan teetered in the hundred-mile-per-hour winds, but the vessel was functioning properly.

"Cleavon, go ahead and free the dropsondes," Patty Sue directed.

"Heard." Cleavon proceeded to loose a series on dropsondes that would record the latitude and longitude of their position in the typhoon.

Winds increased to 130 miles per hour, and the barometric pressure dropped. They drove deeper into Haiyan.

The first readings from the dropsondes were calculated on the onboard computer.

"Dew point depression levels are…" The plane rocked violently, and Patty Sue grabbed whatever she could. Cleavon held his strap but thrashed against the fuslage. Nicholas turned pale.

The WC-130J made a rapid descent as Hodgson and Vlaard worked desperately to regain control of the Hercules.

"Engine four has stopped," reported Cleavon calmly as he wiped his bushy eyebrows.

"Let's go, baby," Hodgson said, pressuring the plane to perform.

"Six thousand feet and falling," Nicholas said.

The plane was not pulling up without engine four. Carl worked furiously. He strained, and the team could see the veins in his neck bulge.

"Five thousand feet! Come on, Ben!" Nicholas blessed himself. Patty Sue watched in a daze as the pilots used all their experience to reclaim control, the plane blasted by the fury of Haiyan.

"I got engine four!" screamed Carl.

Cleavon stretched to look at the starboard wing. The propeller on engine four began twisting up to speed.

Hodgson pulled at the stick and banked the Hercules to port.

"Twenty-five hundred feet," Ziegler reported.

"Twenty-five hundred and stabilizing." Hodgson brought the WC-130J back to a safer altitude. "Peggy Sue? What happened back there?"

"I need to look closer at the data, but Ben, I think we were hit by a very large tornado. Maybe an F4."

"I need to call this in ASAP, but with that number four out of whack, I am taking us all home for the day. We have had enough excitement." Hodgson smacked his knee, deflated.

Cleavon whispered in the pilot's ear, "We were brave enough to fight the beast and try to help those who cannot help themselves. Today we retreat, as we are ill equipped and live to fight another day."

Everyone agreed. From the little data they had mined, the crew would bring news of the worst typhoon ever recorded by humankind.

NOVEMBER 8, 2013

Tacloban lay at the northwest edges of Leyte Gulf in the Philippines. Esther noticed the blackening sky over the bridge that spanned the San Juanico Strait and traveled to neighboring Samar. Esther Perez worked with her new husband, Danilo, to board the windows of their modest home that lay far too close to Cancabato Bay. Haiyan was due to arrive tonight. They scraped together supplies and prayed.

They were young and in love and expecting. A simple July wedding had celebrated their commitment. Esther had a little bump on her tiny frame to show for it. She beamed beneath her long brown hair pulled to the side, a smile that anyone would wake to.

Things happened so quickly. With the abundance of promise life held inside her, the typhoon was not to be trifled with. Esther held Danilo's hands tightly, swearing to meet this challenge. "Good things happen to good people," Esther whispered to Danilo and to herself. "Every cloud has a silver lining." She kissed his cheek. "No one would be mad if I did not attend work at that wretched sweatshop." Danilo managed a laugh as the first rains began to fall.

Danilo and Esther shared their abode with Esther's mother and her two sisters, Igme, a flowering fourteen-year-old, and Bituin, her twelve-year-old tagalong. Bituin fidgeted as the rains became stronger, but Esther consoled her by working diligently to secure the home. She stored the garnered food, hoping it would be enough, but she had competed with thousands for the few random cans. Esther would not loot the stores. Their owners were the citizens of her community.

Sirens beckoned in the neighborhood as the police encouraged people to evacuate to higher ground. But for Esther and her family, there was no place to go. They had no car. What sense would it make to walk away from the typhoon? They would hold one another close as the winds approached.

The night fell upon them, and the water came. The winds ran wild, hurtling over the bay in waves. The roof splintered in patches, and the rains poured into the house. The Perez family moved into the bedroom, but soon Haiyan took that with her. Debris slammed into the walls and smashed through the windows. Between the swells you could hear the screams of others losing the battle. And the final screams of others who had lost the war.

Esther held Bituin tight as Danilo pulled Momma and Igme close in the opposite corner. There was no need to close their eyes. All power had been gone for hours. Soaked and seemingly alone in the heart of the night, they prayed while they shivered.

The northwest eye wall ransacked Tacloban with winds of two hundred miles per hour. Water rose to their chests, trapped in the house from the storm surge. They felt the tingle of electricity in the water. The current sucked at their legs, trying to drag them under. Leaving the dwelling was not an option. They would be exposed to the rapid storm surge, winds, and flying debris. The morning light allowed them to see through the frame of the long-ago exploded window. The grim tales of the night revealed themselves. They stepped out of the house. Dead bodies raced past them like insane kayaks on the rapids. The palm trees tried to stand straight but were forced to the ground by the blasts of wind. Electrical fires sparked, unable to gain a foothold in the torrential whirl of wind.

As the eye passed, they took inventory, knowing more terror lurked. They wondered if it would ever end.

The dawn hours passed. Exhausted and emotionally spent, Esther heard a knock at the door. The winds had subsided, and she could see dots of sunlight through the holes in the roof and the walls. She sloshed through the seawater and what she'd called her living room. She opened the door to a blinding sun and a military soldier. He looked afraid and then relieved. He had found someone alive.

Esther called her family forth and they wept at their fortune. They stepped outside to the unrecognizable landscape and gasped at the devastation. Matchstick homes had been pulverized in the surrounding areas. Fires ignited in the ruins of the street. They turned back on their own home. Little of function remained. The roof had collapsed in several places, and walls had completely caved in on one another. Only the tiny room to which they'd retreated had survived, saving their lives.

Esther and Danilo walked a few yards away from the home. They called out to anyone who would hear their cries. A few called back. The true cost of Haiyan became apparent as Esther saw the naked foot under the remnants of a concrete wall. She reached for Danilo and buried her face in his chest, sobbing at the sight of the dead. He turned away, as unfamiliar with death as she was.

Haiyan had dealt a catastrophic blow to the Philippines and Tacloban, specifically. Over 2,000 died in Tacloban. The toll of 6,340 dead by the final count was staggering. There would still be 1,061 unaccounted for.

In the following days the bodies started to rot. The unbearable stench forced them to wear anything over their mouths and noses to avoid the stench of the carrion.

Hundreds of thousands of homeless scavanged across the nation. Esther and Danilo walked the streets, the tides long subsided. Civic buildings lay in waste. Bridges were gone. Even the local Tacloban zoo had been clobbered. A tale spread that a zoo keeper had unlocked the cages of the animals, giving them a chance to survive. A black panther prowled on the loose in the rubble, adding to the fear and the legend of Haiyan.

The Filipino military brought what they could to the ravaged cities and towns. Esther and Danilo rationed the food and water they had, much of their supplies having been swept away. Esther counted the few cans of food, knowing she and Danilo would have to join the looters to stay alive.

The world watched the carnage on television and responded. Countries across the globe geared up the machines to import medical supplies, food, and water. Average citizens called 800 numbers or texted donations to alleviate the suffering in the Philippines, just as they had for Hurricanes Sandy and Katrina and the earthquake that had mauled Haiti. Just as human beings have done for thousands of years. Help was on the way—including the Seventh Fleet of the US Navy.

NOVEMBER 9, 2013
YOKOSUKA, JAPAN

The commander of the destroyer USS *Mustin*, Matt Kexin, observed the loading of supplies for the relief effort in the Philippines with watchful eyes. Pallets of water, medical supplies, canned food, and mosquito nets were craned aboard with usual navy efficiency.

The Seventh Fleet had been called into its home port in Yokosuka, Japan, due to the threat of Haiyan. Operation Damayan was the mission assigned to the fleet—an endeavor to help the millions affected by the typhoon.

The aircraft carrier USS *George Washington* was to sail along with the *Mustin* and several other components of the fleet at 0600. Kexin made mental notes for his briefing. He had seen video of the Tacloban region. Thirteen million people had been affected, but none worse than in Tacloban. This was a rescue-and-aid mission, pure and simple. Kexin had seen the human cost of Haiyan, a desperation that made Katrina look like a thunderstorm.

NOVEMBER 11TH

Two days passed. Esther wondered why they had been forsaken. People went mad from hunger and fatigue. Sickness found their soaked bodies, and many in the streets became violent. The anger festered. Homelss mothers cried out in despair to find their children, not knowing if they were alive or dead. Bodies piled up in corners, and families rummaged through the heaps like they were rummaging through shirts at a discount rack. The continuous, somber lines at the morgue grew as people shooed the gnawing mosquitoes away like oxen.

Esther foraged for food, celebrating each time she found a random can of soup. She worried about the baby. Danilo consoled her. He was strong. Igme and Bituin were strong as well, but they put up a good front. Their tears flowed when they turned, trying to be strong for Momma. But they were hungry. And thirsty. And they could not stand the smell of the dead another day.

The glow of makeshift fires spotted the city, but the black nights ushered in fear. Bituin heard stories of the panther, an unnecessary nightmare added to the current conditions. Danilo and Esther kept everyone close and sang songs to fill the night. They ate what they could and covered one another with blankets.

The USS *Mustin* arrived along with the caravan of naval ships on November 15. The crew went right to work. Sailors began loading supplies onto the Seahawk helicopters and setting forth a forward command post for distribution.

The Leyte Gulf harbored the ships from the Pacific. The Japanese destroyer *Ise* and the Chinese naval hospital ship *Peace Ark* sailed close. Taiwan was represented by the *Chong Ho*, and Korea lent a hand with the amphibious landing ship *Bi Ro Bong*. The USNS dry cargo ship *Charles Drew* boarded tons of supplies. Countries all over the world poured in. The cavalry arrived. The American Red Cross. UNICEF. The American Jewish Joint Distribution Committee and Catholic Relief Services were on the ground. Mammoth Medical brought surgeons, doctors, and medical volunteers. Doctors Without Borders came with surgical tents, hygiene kits, inflatable hospitals, psychological help, and sanitation kits. Mercy Corps, ChildFund International, Team Rubicon, and Habitat for Humanity were all there from around the globe to help.

From the air the destruction came into clear view. Thousands of refugees looked skyward from the street—their home—and the pilot's could see the relief and smiles from the sky. The Seahawks located the advance crew that had secured the area. They deployed in an open field and put security in play.

Esther saw the helicopters and knew her prayers had been answered. She crossed herself and thanked God. Her mother wept openly, her modest dress soaked from the ongoing rain. They, along with thousands of others, moved toward the open field. They needed water. Many had already started to become sick from drinking the bacteria-laden water or scrounging for rotting food. The dysentery brought infection, and the streets smelled of rotting flesh and diarrhea.

Seaman Bud Lang pressed his boots down into the long reeds of the open field, the draft of the chopper's rotors chewing at the air. The curious locals peered at the swarm of help. Seaman Brandon Lyle shouted at Lang, "Here they come!"

Despite the desperation, the victims and the military worked together. The supplies went quickly, and the mass of people grew. Sailors volunteered to keep working, and many of them, upon returning to their respective ships, volunteered to go straight back to the victims to lend more help. They purchased goods from the ship to hand out from their own pockets. Candy. Bread. Even toys to give to the kids, just to see them smile.

Esther made her way to the Seahawks with her weakened family. At long last she stepped to the front of the line. Seaman Lyle had worked feverishly for hours. As he bent down to hand out bottles of water, his head snapped, and he stared at Esther. She did not notice his interest. She could only say thank you in broken English for the gift she received. Lyle handed her the water and watched as she turned and walked away. He put his head down and went back to work.

Esther and the family sat in the remnants of their home and savored the emergency rations as if they were dining at the Redoña Residence, a presidential retreat blocks away. With a small fire and a full belly, Esther knew that her family and her baby would survive. They were the lucky ones. So many others were not.

Lyle retreated to his rack. He had seen the power of death. He felt strong and noted this in his journal. He would not sleep well. He wanted to go back to Tacloban. He needed to go back to Tacloban.

Weeks passed, and more volunteers arrived from around the world. Makeshift tent villages for both the residents and volunteers grew like spring flowers. The sick were tended to, the dead removed from the streets. The anguish continued for those never given answers as to the fate of their loved ones.

NOVEMBER 25, 2013
JEFFERSON CITY, MISSOURI

LOCAL HIGH SCHOOLER MISSING

Jefferson City News Tribune

L ocal authorities are reporting that seventeen-year-old Celia Nair of Jefferson City, Missouri, has been missing since Friday, November 22. Celia was last seen at the Walmart Supercenter on Stadium West Boulevard. Celia was last known to be wearing blue jeans, Nike running shoes, a gray fleece, and a pink Under Armor toboggan or beanie.

Celia has shoulder-length brown hair and brown eyes. She is five feet six inches tall and weighs 115 pounds. She has a butterfly tattoo on her right shoulder blade and a distinct mole on her neck.

If you have seen Celia Nair or know of her whereabouts, please contact the Jefferson City Police Department at 573-555-2233.

DECEMBER 19, 2013
TACLOBAN

Small segments of the city regained power, and house after house was slowly being pieced back together. Esther knew that it would be years before things would be completely normal again. The shop started business again despite the tenuous conditions of the building. This notion was not feasible to Esther, but she was fortunate to have a job. It was early December, and Christmas was soon. It would be a special night to celebrate their fortunes and give a gift to her sisters, her wonderful mother, and, of course, her light, Danilo.

The draconian shop offered Esther the best opportunity for employment in Tacloban. Esther worked for a few dollars a day, sewing, and grabbed any additional hours available. She refused to take the drugs offered that would help her work through the night. She would never hurt her unborn child. She was strong and could do the extra work. She had seen what the drugs had done to others.

The hollow eyes. Gaunt and emotionless. Esther vowed to escape the factory one day. One goal at a time.

Danilo worked on the fishing boats that ventured into Leyte Gulf, harvesting the food from the sea. His lithe frame scurried about the trawlers, and his stature belied his strength. He hoped to own his own boat someday and teach his son the joy of the waves.

Esther met Danilo at the house after her morning shift. She agreed to pick up some supplementary hours at the shop but made a deal with the supervisor to go home and check on Igme, Bituin, and her momma. Danilo arrived home from the docks, and they shared a quick smile. Igme and Bituin had been to a local community center where the rescue relief provided classes for the students. The schools had succumbed to Haiyan, and the children needed the structure and the lessons.

Esther found Danilo in the bathroom, wiping his face. She explained that she was going back to work. He was disappointed but understood. She didn't want to leave him. Ever.

He was the first boy she had ever kissed. He was the first boy she had ever liked. He was different from the other boys in Tacloban. His eyes were a delightful surprise, full of hope and magic. It hurt her heart to leave him, but she had to return for the night shift at the shop.

Esther headed out after spending too much time with her family, and the supervisor was going to admonish her. There was a shortcut through the jungle. She knew she was late, and she had been late once this week already. There were plenty of girls ready to take her place. Danilo had shown her the shortcut. Her mother said to never take the shortcuts. There was danger in the jungle.

The sun had long sunk into the South China Sea, joining the armada of ships that war had gifted to the deep. Flecks of light spotted the foliage like fading lanterns. Twigs scratched at Esther's ankles as she increased her stride to beat the night, the constant chirping of the birds absent. She focused on the path and began to run. It wasn't as easy without Danilo. Or fun. She never felt alone or scared with Danilo. She wasn't alone this trip either.

The animal could smell Esther, its prey moving closer. It used all its senses. It could hear the increasing pace, and the girl's breathing became heavy. The delicious odor wafted on the breeze. The animal lay patiently waiting for Esther to come to it. It had been an eternity since the hunt, and Esther's heat emanated in the first gray layers of night. Esther worked ever closer like a glowing target. Saliva leaked from the beast's mouth. Crouched in the reeds, its powerful shoulders tensed.

Esther lay on the ground, looking up at the terror in the eyes of the beast. The jaundiced eyes of hate and hunger pierced her soul. She tried to twist, but the claws ripped into her side. Esther screamed for her baby, but the beast tore into her belly. Esther had neither time to pray nor time for pain. The light ceased. Esther lay in the night of the jungle as the beast nourished.

MORNING, DECEMBER 20TH

Danilo paced in the dilapidated home and wondered where Esther was. It was much past when she was supposed to return. He decided to walk to the shop and find her. He left and took the path that Esther always chose. He saw the shortcut but knew that she would not have taken that at night. It was too dangerous.

Danilo arrived at the shop, and the workers applied their craft in the pale, dingy glow of the factory. Dozens of workers slaved away, looking beaten mentally and physically. The supervisors walked the floor with the exacting eyes of prison guards, berating workers who had fallen behind due to exhaustion.

Danilo respectfully entered the remnants of the factory and asked, head bowed, if Esther was still working. The supervisor glared at Danilo and informed him that she had never come to work and would not be allowed to work there again. Danilo did not care that Esther was not allowed to work. He did not want her to work in that hellhole. He knew Esther was in danger.

Danilo ran through the streets calling Esther's name. The people in the tent villages of Haiyan nary turned their heads, immune to the anguish of loss and the madness that comes with death. Danilo stopped a relief worker, and she tried to console him. He was apoplectic with fear, but she did not understand his plight. His English was broken at best, and he could not communicate. Together they sought out an official who could assist.

No one knew quite what to do in the heart of the night. They agreed to look for Esther at morning's light, but her disappearance could be the result of a thousand possibilities. Danilo would not leave the streets or sleep for the night. He waited at the steps of the police station until dawn.

The officer held his promise and reluctantly gathered a team to look for Esther. Tacloban remained a disaster area, and the police had their hands full with the recovery effort and looting. They scoured the area, starting by following the path that Esther would have taken, the same journey Danilo explored at night.

A dozen men found nothing, and the lead officer asked Danilo if there was an alternate route. Danilo mentioned the shortcut but reiterated that it was improbable that she would have gone that way. The officer sent his team to the shortcut.

Impossibly out of strength, Danilo followed along, convinced they were heading the wrong way. Hours passed as the search team combed the quagmire, dense with reeds and trees still bent from Haiyan. The perspiration dripped and soaked their uniforms in the tropical heat. They walked straight lines in organized patterns. Locals joined the exploration to help cover more terrain.

Danilo slogged on knowing that Igme, Bituin, and Momma were at home deep in prayer. He would find Esther and bring her home to the family. Her smile permeated his thoughts, and her sweet kiss inspired his search.

A lone boy stood still in the thickest of the grass, frozen. The officers knew he had stumbled upon something. They surged toward him, and he remained a statue of fear. They called upon him, asking what he had found. He turned to them, insipid and hollow. The officer put his arm around the child and pulled him close into his side. The officer looked to the ground at Esther.

"Jesus Christo," he muttered.

Danilo scrambled in behind the gathering group. He collapsed, filled with sorrow and shock.

The locals circled the body before the officers restricted the area. Several of the youth began spreading the news. "The panther!" they screamed in the streets and among the tent villages. "The panther is here!"

ARLINGTON, VIRGINIA

Halfway around the world in Arlington, Virginia, high school senior Madeline Deschamps woke from a horrible, horrible nightmare. She snapped her eyes open and found herself curled at the edges of her bed, soaked in her own urine. Even awake she could not forget the vivid dream. She removed her sheets and put them in the hamper along with her pajamas. She was mortified to have wet the bed and secretly slunk into the bathroom and cleansed herself with a washcloth. Madeline laid a towel on her bed so she would not feel the moisture when she went back to sleep. But there would be no sleep for the rest of the night as she tried to block the horror from her mind.

DECEMBER 21, 2013

The USS *Mustin* would return to Tacloban but first pulled anchor and steamed west to Yokosuka, home of the Seventh Fleet. So many gave of themselves to help, and the well-earned trip to port for rest and relaxation coincided perfectly with Christmas. Lyle felt the sea roll beneath the behemoth ship, and he wrote in his journal, his cropped head resting comfortably on his pillow. He put the pen to paper:

I praise you. I exist to serve you. I seek the day that my vessel serves its true purpose. As in past campaigns of glory, fire will rain from the skies with obliteration. The night will fill with the candescence of missiles and the death we carry onto Jerusalem. We shall turn person upon person, as genocide and racial hatred prevail. The wealthy shall drown the poor with poverty as greed infects this earthly hive. Go forth the disease of their fornication until all crawl with weakness and demise. Alive! Be the legion. Awake! I have come to you! Know that they will forsake their insignificant creator. The hypocrisy of the mongrels is putrid. Slimy ants scurrying, helpless, weak. There is only one true Lord, one true master. Cast them out! Oh Lord, you shall soon rule, and they shall kneel before you, these bugs they call man and these whores they call woman. I relish the task you have bestowed upon me. Never shall they carry the false hope that these gullible creatures have purchased. I will smother the perverted light and lead them into despair. I have tasted the sweet wine and flesh of your victory. When you arrive, oh Lord, they will bow and beg for your mercy.

Lyle closed the journal and secured it in his locker. He rolled over and faced the wall with open eyes. Lyle never slept, but no one could know that. The USS *Mustin* cruised through the night, the perfect incubator for a demon.

DECEMBER 23, 2013
TACLOBAN, PHILIPPINES

A small part of the community stood over the makeshift casket that contained Esther. Haiyan had depleted any respectable accommodations. The priest spoke softly over the tears of the family and the reverberating mourning of Danilo. Members of the search team blessed themselves as they lowered the box into the ground; a small white rose floated on top, caressed by the earth spilled upon it.

Shoulders rounded, friends walked away, but the family stayed by Esther's side for many hours. Publicly, a search for the panther consumed the city. Citizens forayed into the hills, hunting for the killer. A reward had been posted for the capture or slaughter of the big cat. Privately, local officials could not convince the vigilantes that this death was not at the claws of the panther. The marks left on Esther's body were not those of the animal they sought. They were not positive what type of animal could inflict that kind of damage on Esther. They began the investigation quietly, unsure of the killer among them in the ruins of Haiyan.

DECEMBER 23, 2013
SALEM, OREGON

LOCAL GIRL MISSING

Statesman Journal

S alem, Oregon: Officials have posted a missing-persons report for Aditi Buffon, sixteen years of age. Aditi has been missing since Saturday, December 21, and was last seen at the Salem Center shopping mall near the GNC nutrition store. She was Christmas shopping with friends and went to the bathroom.

Aditi was last seen wearing dark green spandex leggings, an Oregon Ducks sweatshirt, and matching baseball cap. Aditi is five feet nine inches tall and weighs 121 pounds. She has brown curly hair and a medium-dark complexion. She has green eyes. She wears braces and has a noticeable birth mark on her upper right arm.

If you have seen Aditi Buffon, please call the Salem Police Department at 503-555-2945.

CHRISTMAS EVE
YOKOSUKA, JAPAN

Seaman Bud Lang woke, excited. The USS *Mustin* had docked in Yokosuka, and the commander was granting them leave. Lyle was already dressed and packed. Lang noticed Lyle was always up and showered early. He was shy, Lang supposed.

"Got any plans for leave, Lyle?" Lang queried.

"I got a girl in Tokyo," Lyle lied.

"That's awesome! What's her name?" Lang bursted at the seams.

Lyle thought fast. "Chiya. It means 'a thousand nights.'" Lyle hated questions. "What are your plans, Lang?" Lyle felt obliged to return the question, though he couldn't give a rat's ass. Lyle truly hoped he did not mention he was going to Tokyo.

"The Seahawk guys and I are going to get drunk and find a poker game." Lang pulled out a bankroll that would evaporate before tomorrow.

"Well, good luck to you, Lang." Lyle extended his grip as a human formality he did not understand.

"You too, Lyle. See you when you get back!" Lang headed off, the sucker at the table.

In his head Lyle knew it was nearly impossible they would ever meet again, unless it was in hell.

DECEMBER 24, 2013
TACLOBAN

The wild cheers ripped through the morning routine. Locals were quick to pass Danilo's house, hoping he could hear the buzz. Hunters had killed the panther.

Spontaneous crowds gathered as a dozen victorious pursuers carried the black panther upside down on a pole. The crowds gasped and applauded the courageous. They had avenged Esther's killer and saved others from the same fate. The posse sought the acknowledgment and the reward. Authorities had made no progress on finding the truth.

A girl in the crowd began to cry. She had worked at the zoo and had fed the great cat. She knew him as Midnight. She loved him.

USS *MUSTIN*

Commander Kexin called the crew to the deck and addressed what everyone already knew. Lyle and the crew were relieved for seventy-two hours of rest and relaxation after their efforts in the Philippines. Lyle excused himself to his rack and certified that his berthing area was spec. He grabbed his duffel bag and headed toward the ramp. Lyle never looked back, though it would be the final time he stepped foot on the Arleigh Burke–class destroyer USS *Mustin*. A small grin came to his face as he thought of the day the *Mustin* would loose the guided missiles toward a heavily populated area or free the Mark 46 torpedoes to swim into their target, sending ten scores of men to the bottom of the sea.

Lyle stepped off the plank and felt solid ground under his feet. Yokosuka, Japan. Sayonara! Lyle had a date on the Keikyu Main Line leaving Yokosuka-Chūō Station in forty-five minutes. In two hours he would be in Tokyo.

Lyle eyed the gooks. Hordes of them. He boarded the train and found a seat in the corner. A bit of privacy. He reached for his journal and was surprised it was not there. Lyle dug through his duffel but made no contact. He assumed he had left it in his locker. It gave him no worry. No one would be looking for it in seventy-two hours. By then Lyle would be far, far away. Seaman Brandon Lyle would be officially absent without leave. UA. Unauthorized absence. AWOL.

TOKYO STATION

Platform two at Tokyo Station was in a frenzy. Lyle was not. He sauntered through the expanse, looking up at the high ceilings and noticing almost everyone was dressed in black.

Through the automatic doors, he exited into Marunouchi, the business district of Chiyoda. The brick facade evoked the architecture of Europe as opposed to Japan. Lyle took a moment to himself outside the station and bowed his head. He stood in the same spot as the Hitler youth had in 1938 when he exited the station, the moment personal and rewarding.

The Imperial Palace was a short walk away. Lyle thought of Hirohito. He had done a good job as well.

Lyle flagged a cab and asked for the Higashi Shinjuku Hotel in Kabukicho. Kabukicho was in Tokyo's red-light district and a short ride from Marunouchi. Lyle had reserved his room under an alias.

Lyle had many names. Victor Kuyt would be checking in to the Higashi for $98 a night. And Victor would be taking Japanese Airlines flight 952 out tomorrow morning to Los Angeles. For Lyle, the legion provided everything.

Lyle dropped his bag onto the floor of room 329 and exited as quickly as he had entered, hardly noting the forgettable decor. He retired his Gilligan hat and disposed of the dress whites, never to don them again. Lyle could not wait to let his hair grow. He showered and slipped on a pair of black four-pleat Jesse slacks by Gino Sartore and buckled his Salvatore Ferragamo black belt. He buttoned the Replete dress shirt he'd found at Neiman Marcus and stretched his favorite black leather jacket. Lyle zipped up his John Varvatos boots. Dressed to kill.

The revolving door in the lobby spat him out into a sea of neon, an appropriate false light for the prostitutes and junkies and hypocrites that denied the colors by day. The doorman offered him a taxi, but Lyle preferred to walk.

Unfinished business led him into an alley where, behind the refuse, a teen shot China white.

Lyle stepped down a set of concrete stairs covered in restaurant grease. The cooks knew him from a previous visit but did not make eye contact. Lyle went farther down a flight of stairs to meet Junichi.

Junichi, the obedient one. Junichi showed little surprise at Lyle's visit. Junichi was fairly comatose most of the time, a condition essential to tolerate the squalor.

The needles lay carelessly on a table beside the inks. Lyle stripped his shirt and lay comfortably back into the seat. Junichi was to finish what he had started.

Lyle closed his eyes, and the pulsating pain soothed him. The scaled dragon swept from his right shoulder through his chest. The beast's eyes were now being colored with cadmium and mercury, bringing the serpent's eyes to life. The mouth roared, and the fangs of the lizard pierced Lyle's nipple.

Junichi was renaissance. Biblical with a needle. Detailed but emotive. He stepped back to admire his work but felt ill. The owner of the dragon stood and revealed the huge black wings that Junichi himself had cast. Edge to edge the wings stretched the expanse of

Lyle's broad shoulders. Shadows of gray and mist brought them alive, swirled masterfully into the black wings created from the death of thousands of souls. His work flowed elegantly across the shoulder, seamless in its transformation. Lyle turned to Junichi, eyes ablaze with what he was. Junichi was terrified of what he had helped create.

Junichi never asked Lyle for payment, mostly because he was afraid, but Lyle always left money on the table and vanished.

Lyle exited the same greasy alley into the action of Kabukicho. No one in this town cared that it was Christmas Eve. The very thought of Christmas made him nauseous and angry. He strolled up and down the avenue, peeking into the windows of bars. People were doing karaoke and drinking. Lyle paid the cover for a strip bar. He made a lap around the club, but nothing of interest sparked his attention. He headed back to the street. The neon was more inviting.

Lyle turned the corner and froze. Two women tussled with a bouncer at a bar. He handled the girls in a fairly rough manner. Lyle stepped in to intervene.

"Ladies, may I be of some assistance?" Lyle's disarmed them with his charming smile.

"You could get this thug off me to start," the spitfire railed against the bouncer.

Lyle spoke to the gentleman in perfect Japanese. "Sir, I would like to help these ladies. What can I do to solve this dispute?" Lyle stared into the ruffian's eyes, and the bouncer released his grip immediately.

The bouncer explained to Lyle that the girls had tried to leave without paying their bar tab. Lyle removed some money from his pocket, more than enough to cover the bill.

"What did you do that for? We paid the bill." Maroon-colored hair dropped to the middle of the little hellion's back.

"You are very welcome." Lyle grinned sarcastically, knowing he had spared the tourists quite a hassle. "What is your name?" He looked at the heavily decorated eyes of the redhead.

"Tiffany," she stated, reducing her defensiveness.

"My name is Brandon. Brandon Lyle. I am in the US Navy." That always helped relax the ladies. "And who is your friend, Tiffany?"

"My name is Mao," she spoke softly, in unsure English. Lyle extended his hand, and Mao grasped it out of thanks. Lyle held Mao's hand for a second longer. She smelled so good.

"What happened there, ladies, is one of the oldest tricks in the book," Lyle explained as he examined Mao's round face. "Did someone from the hotel recommend this bar?"

Mao nodded, and Tiffany said yes.

"Were they in the lobby?" continued Lyle.

The girls agreed.

"These are called touts. They seek out tourists who aren't exactly sure which club is the best, and they guide and encourage you to go to a specific club."

"So they don't work for the hotel?" Tiffany had started to figure it out.

"No. They work for the club," Lyle noted as they were walking. "Where are we headed?"

"Back to the hotel." Mao had had more than enough clubbing for the night. "And thank you for what you did back there. I was beginning to be scared." Mao giggled and showed Tiffany the open bag. "I took some bar nuts."

"Yes, thank you." Tiffany spoke to Lyle and snared a handful of Mao's pilfered nuts for good measure.

"Would you mind if I escorted you back to the hotel? I want to make sure you get home safely," Lyle suggested.

"That would be very nice of you," Tiffany accepted. Mao seemed relieved. "So why were the people inside the bar such dicks?" Tiffany was still hot at the bouncer.

"The tout takes you there and leaves. You have a couple of drinks, right?" Lyle knew the answer. "And then they gave you some outrageous bill, right?" The girls shook their heads. "They figure you can't count in yen, but one of you could and noticed the bill was far too large. Is that right?"

Mao spoke up. "Yes. Bill way too big." Tiffany laughed at Mao's comical English.

"If you figure the bill is too big, then they muscle up and put the fear factor in place," noted Lyle.

"Yeah! We threw more than enough money down and screwed out of there. They were trying to rip us off." Tiffany's face turned flush.

"That's why the bouncer had you outside. He was intimidating you to fork over more cash with the threat of hurting you. It happens all the time. Kabukicho has been a very dark place for hundreds of years." Lyle knew from experience. He wanted to change the topic. "Mao, what is your whole name? Where are you from?" He tried to make eye contact.

"I am Mao Iniesta. I am from Beijing." Lyle stopped and extended his hand again.

Lyle bowed. "I am Brandon Lyle. From Los Angeles, California. And you, young lady?"

Tiffany giggled as she bowed in mock reverence to a long-lost tradition. "Tiffany Kai. Seattle, Washington."

They all continued to walk, and Lyle extended the conversation. "What brings you ladies to Tokyo?"

"Mai is working here for six months, and we met here in Tokyo at the World Artistic Gymnastic Championships in 2011. So we kept in touch and decided to spend some time together." Tiffany stopped to tie her shoe.

"Almost did not happen," Mao spilled out.

"What do you mean it almost didn't happen?" Lyle's curiosity piqued. The pedestrians on the streets thinned as they neared the hotel.

"The Tōhoku earthquake happened. And then the tsunami. And then the nuclear power plants. The committee almost canceled the whole event." Lyle remembered all too well but liked hearing the story again. "But they figured it all out, and we came here in late October."

"Are you girls gymnasts?" Lyle continued. They came close to the Gokoku-ji Temple, and Mao drifted ahead.

"Oh no!" Tiffany laughed as Lyle reached his hands around her neck and pushed her up against the wall of a building. He held her forehead still and pointed his index finger toward her eye, and the finger extended and sharpened into a deadly stiletto. Lyle looked into her eyes and whispered, "It is not you I want," and then rammed his razor-sharp finger into Tiffany's eye and through her brain and out the back of her skull. He removed his finger from her head, and it regained its human form.

Mao turned to see Tiffany's body slide down the side of the building and slump into a quivering mess as the brain sent its last signals to the body. She was too petrified to scream, and Lyle had her in his vise grip, dragging her to the temple. Far too overmatched to fight, she tried to bite him, but she had no effect.

Within eyesight of the Gokoku-ji Temple was the cemetary of the meshimori onna and the unmarked graves of 2,200 prostitutes. The shamed, buried with no history or grace. An ideal place for Mao.

He laid Mao's head back and forced her to open her mouth. He bit into her tongue, chewed through it, and spit it onto the un-sacred ground. His finger extended for the second time in min-utes and sliced below Mao's belly. The incision opened wide, and Lyle reached in and pulled out her insides. Mao collapsed and died while Lyle dined. He left her there with the bones of a thousand gook tramps and prostitutes. Lyle threw Tiffany into a Dumpster and, through the shadows, found his hotel.

Kung Pao Mao. Nothing like Chinese food on Christmas Eve.

CHRISTMAS MORNING, TOKYO

Lyle felt stronger than ever. At half past ten, he checked out as Victor Kuyt, and the bellhop hailed a cab for Narita Airport. That evening at 2000 hours, he would board the red-eye Japanese Airlines flight 952 to LAX. He did not want to be caught up in security. Lyle did not want to see the sights and instructed the cab driver to take him to the airport.

CHRISTMAS MORNING, 2013
ARLINGTON, VIRGINIA

Madeline peeked from behind the shades at the white Christmas morning. Her brother, Oliver, and his Whoopi Goldberg dreads had woken everyone too early, but Daddy Raphael started rolling the cameras at half past eight, when they all came down the stairs.

The tree was resplendent, and gifts surfed to the carpet from under the tree. Oliver immediately started guessing at what hid inside his presents, but their mom, Sophia, put an immediate stop to that practice with a smile on her face.

Madeline had arisen early, even for Christmas, to apply a bounty of makeup. Her fair mother, Sophia, didn't mention the metal that still adorned her face: a bar in the eyebrow, a hoop in the lip, and of course, the treasure in her ears. Her fierce haircut, short and black in the back and the dyed flapping flip in the front, tapered over one half of her face, shadowing her beauty. Magenta was the hue for Christmas morning. Sophia knew Madeline hadn't been herself lately, but it was Christmas, and Raphael bellowed in harmony with Bing Crosby.

Both Oliver and Madeline got new Samsung phones, the newest 4G models. Google Play and Apple iTunes gift cards littered the stockings over the fireplace, bringing a smile their faces. Raphael got a new Adams fairway utility club for his golf bag and some expensive Titleist balls to hit into the woods. Not that he could hit them, but the fifty-something dad with the balding horseshoe George Jefferson hair dreamed of the links. Sophia wanted Raphael to shave the graying moustache he wore to compensate for what was absent from his head, but she loved him to death and it wasn't too bad when they kissed.

Madeline was far more reluctant to open presents than Oliver was. She thought it was all too much, but she accepted each gift and marveled at the treasures. One gift was a Bodycon lace back-fit flare dress by a. drea from Nordstrom that she would never wear. Another, a pair of TOMS desert wedge booties in taupe. She unwrapped the beautiful baby-doll dress embroidered with paper cranes from the juniors department. Madeline was appreciative; she just wouldn't wear these things. The Rip Curl "Jewel" open knit panel hoodie? It was not going to happen. Her mom so wanted her to be like other girls.

Oliver reveled like a pirate who'd found booty. A full set of Ralph Lauren T-shirts in a medley of colors. A Ralph Lauren baseball cap in blue and another in white. Then came the good ones! Oliver ripped open the box as Dad watched his son with an even smile. "Wow! A North Face Peril Glacier Track jacket in snorkel blue!" Oliver knew there was a follow-up to this present, and he couldn't wait.

Madeline feigned the same excitement as she opened the Osolita North Face jacket in parlour purple. All of this on top of the bonanza of gifts she had received last week on her eighteenth birthday.

Oliver went bananas when he shredded open the Nordica Fire Arrow F1 ski boots. He put them on and clunked around the living room, making an awful racket.

Madeline received a pair of Hell & Back H3 ski boots, thanked "Santa," and placed them gently on her pile. Sophia noticed Madeline's indifference.

Things became obscene when Madeline peeled back the wrapping paper to find a pair of bright mango, light magnet gray, volt, and space blue Nike KDs. Madeline had a closet full of shoes she already didn't wear. Oliver was stoked though to switch out of the ski boots and don the KDs he'd gotten, white and pure platinum lined with metallic gold.

A ski trip became the obvious theme. The new skis behind the tree weren't wrapped, far too cumbersome to drape the Elan Amphibio 88 XTi Fusion skis with ELX 12.0 Fusion bindings. Oliver got Volkl Code PSI skis with five motion 12.0 bindings.

Raphael opened a box with a pair of bedroom slippers shaped like green beans. He laughed, and Sophia and the children smiled. They were hilarious on him, and he roiled in the fun. The Deschampses were having a wonderful morning.

Madeline looked at the floor and stared.

"Thank you so much, Mom." She hugged her mom. "And Daddy." She hugged her dad. "I am going to take a shower."

"OK, baby." Daddy held his little girl. "Come down and have breakfast after that." He smiled and kissed Madeline on the cheek.

Madeline showered and put on pajamas and slippers and an oversize hoodie with no brand. She pulled the hoodie over her head and made an English muffin and, kind of brain-dead, watched the Macy's Christmas Day Parade. Sophia loved the parade.

Madeline slunk back into the kitchen, and Sophia trapped her into exactly the conversation she'd feared.

"Madeline."

Here it comes, thought Madeline.

"Is everything all right?"

Yep.

That was it. Things were not all right, but Madeline had no clue what was bothering her. It just was.

"I am fine, Mom." Madeline put her English muffin plate in the dishwasher.

"You know, moms know things. I can sense it." Sophia knew she walked a fine line. Madeline had always had a very even temperament. But lately, since before Thanksgiving, she had been out of sorts. "Is it a boy?" Sophia so hoped it was a boy.

Madeline stared at her blankly. "No, Mom. It is not a boy." She attempted to leave the kitchen.

"Madeline. Why don't you help me with the roast we're having for dinner?" Sophia didn't let Madeline off the hook.

"Sure, Mom." Madeline liked cooking. They just didn't do it a lot. She was surprised the family wasn't going out for Christmas dinner.

"Great!" Sophia smiled genuinely. "Grab the garlic. Do you know how to chop it up?"

"Yes, Mom. I know how to chop garlic." Madeline kept her head down and began peeling the skin from the bulbs. She loved her mother but knew the inquisition session would continue. She half imagined her mom was going to pull the hanging lamp over and shove it into her face.

"Are you on your period?"

Madeline threw up a little in the back of her mouth. "No, Mom. It is not my period. I don't know what's wrong." Madeline slipped.

Sophia pounced. "I knew it." Sophia swept her full mane back and pulled it tight with a scrunchie, ready to grill her daughter. "I wasn't going bring up your report card on Christmas, but your grades have slipped." Madeline rolled her eyes. "Something is distracting you."

Madeline tried to explain. "Mom. Something is bothering me, but I don't know what it is. I really don't, and I promise I will tell you when I figure it out." Madeline huffed, exasperated.

Sophia stared at Madeline with her discerning parental eyes. The glaze of tears came across Madeline's. Sophia glided over the kitchen and held her child from behind.

TOKYO, JAPAN

Lyle removed his sunglasses and cap and offered his Dutch passport, indicating he was Dirk Mandi. The travel photo featured Lyle with a well-kempt beard and considerably longer hair, as well as a distinctive mole under his left eye. Lyle added the small mole to his face to equal the image in the passport photo. The officer studied Lyle carefully, but there was no mistaking the pale blue eyes. The officer waved Lyle, or Mandi, through. The legion was everywhere. Lyle frittered away the afternoon in the massive Narita Airport. He purchased a new journal. The flight was ten hours and fifteen minutes; then Lyle would be home. Lyle heard the gentle tones of the Japan Airlines clerk, and the speakers sounded in the waiting area. Flight 952 to LAX began boarding promptly at 8:00 p.m. local time. Lyle stood to take his spot in the queue and caught a glimpse of the local news. A special report. Two tourists were murdered in Kabukicho. He remembered delicious Mao, her taste still fresh. They would be looking for him. Everyone would be. They would never find him. At least not until he had finished what he had come back to do.

ARLINGTON, VIRGINIA

Madeline rubbed the roast with garlic and salt when her body jerked violently. She held onto the oven door, trying to brace herself, but her eyes rolled into the back of her head and she turned ghostly white. She vomited on the roast and fell, listless, through her mother's arms and onto the floor.

Sophia collapsed onto the ground with her daughter, who quivered. Sophia shouted to Raphael, "Call 911!" and held Madeline's head close to her, not knowing what to do.

Raphael raced to the kitchen, confused. "What's going on?" He saw Madeline on the floor and gasped. "Christ!" He didn't have a phone.

A trickle of blood dripped from Madeline's nose.

Oliver came around the corner into the spacious kitchen. "Give me that." Raphael snatched the smartphone out of Oliver's hand and struggled with it. "How do you use this damn thing, Oliver?"

It was a new phone, and Oliver had already put a pattern lock on the screen. Oliver wiggled his finger in a zigzag pattern, hit the green telephone symbol, called 911, and handed his dad the phone.

"911. What is your emergency?" the placid operator asked.

"I don't know what the matter is. My daughter collapsed and is on the ground, shaking." Raphael tried to remain calm, still in his Christmas jammies and green bean slippers. Oliver, thinking quickly, turned the phone on speaker.

"Is your daughter breathing?" asked the operator.

Raphael looked at Sophia, and she nodded.

"Yes," Raphael confirmed.

"Is she conscious?" continued the tech.

"She is not conscious." Raphael's blood pressure rose.

"Lay her on her back and monitor her breathing. I will stay with you until the ambulance gets there."

"She did vomit. Is that a good idea?" Raphael stayed calm.

"No. Thank you. Roll her over on her side." Confirmed the tech.

Sophia rolled Madeline. "Get me a pillow, Oliver."

Oliver ran into the living room, grabbed a pillow from the couch, and rushed it back to Madeline. Sophia tucked it in gently under Madeline's head and brushed her magenta hair back from her eyes. Madeline groaned and moved her head.

"Ma'am, she is moving her head and making noises."

"That's good. Try to keep her still and continue to talk to her."

"Madeline, it's Mommy. Can you hear me?" Sophia said, kneeling beside Madeline.

Raphael dropped to one knee with the phone in his hand.

"Mom," Madeline spoke. "Why am I on the floor?" She tried to roll over to get up.

"Madeline, be still." She looked into Madeline's eyes. They looked so faraway. "You passed out. The ambulance is on the way."

"What do you mean I passed out?" Madeline did not like all this attention and sure didn't want an ambulance.

"You are going to be fine, but you gave us a horrible scare." Sophia didn't know exactly what to say.

"Sweetheart, the woman from 911 has been very helpful. She wants you to be still until the EMTs get here. Can you do that for me?" Madeline heard her daddy say.

Madeline choked back some tears. She wondered what was the matter with her.

Oliver patrolled between the kitchen and the dining room window. "The ambulance is here!" He stepped over to the front door and greeted the EMTs. "She's in here."

Along with the ambulance, an Arlington police officer arrived, joined by a hook and ladder, all with lights flashing, bringing the neighbors to their porches. Oliver thought it was cool. Madeline did not. Two lanky young men and a butch brunette entered the *Better Homes and Gardens* model home and followed Oliver to the kitchen. Sophia thanked them for arriving so quickly.

"How are you, young lady?" the handsome tech asked.

The mortified Madeline responded, "I am OK. I feel fine." She'd lied. She felt weak. And scared.

"Well, let's check you out and see what might be bothering you." He smiled at Madeline in a reassuring way. He activated the blood-pressure cuff, and Madeline's upper arm was crushed in the vise.

The handsome tech looked at his partner. "One eighty over one ten." The second tech prepared the gurney. "Pulse is one thirty five." The tech looked at Madeline. "You are pretty shook up, young lady. What happened?"

Madeline did not know. "Nothing happened. I was rubbing garlic on the roast and—"

"It doesn't smell like garlic anymore." The tech's joke made everyone laugh and eased the tension.

"And I do remember feeling sick to my stomach, but after that I don't remember anything."

Everyone in the room paused, and the butch EMT with broad shoulders and flabby gut asked to speak to Sophia for a moment.

They stepped into the living room, where wrapping paper was strewn from wall to wall.

"Hello, my name is Crystal Aerts, Arlington County Fire and Rescue." Sophia stood in front of the lighted tree. "Madeline's blood pressure is very high. She is hypertensive. Her blood pressure is one eighty over one ten, which qualifies as a hypertensive crisis."

"I am not sure what that means." Sophia's hands shook. She needed a smoke from the secret pack she hid in the garage on the shelf next to the extra freezer.

"It's a fairly serious episode. Does she usually have high blood pressure?" Crystal adjusted her utility belt around her portly waist.

"No, she doesn't." *What the hell?* thought Sophia.

Raphael spoke with the policeman on the front steps. "Has anyone in the family noticed a change in her behavior?" Raphael shook his head.

"Has anyone noticed a change in her behavior?" Crystal sought the same answer from Sophia.

"She has been a little moody lately." Sophia recalled the conversation from a half hour ago.

"Moody? In what way?"

"I don't know. The way teenage girls are m-moody," Sophia stammered. "What causes this?"

"Well, ma'am, a variety of things. We are going to take the young woman to the emergency room to run some tests." Crystal sucked snot back into her nose.

Now Sophia was queasy.

The techs strapped Madeline in and started to move her toward the door. Sophia worked her way to the gurney, and Raphael moved back inside to get his keys, change, and take off his green bean slippers. He saw Madeline on the way in as she was on the way out. "You're going to be all right, sweetheart."

"I know I will, Daddy." Madeline tried to smile as they wheeled her out of her own front door. She saw the official vehicles on the streets, lights ablaze, and the snoopy neighbors standing in the snow, freezing. What was everybody going to say at school? Madeline Deschamps did not need that attention. She felt scared.

"Oliver, get dressed," Raphael called to his son.

Sophia and Raphael scrambled through their dressers, looking for anything to wear. Sophia ran a brush through her dark locks, and Oliver ripped the tag off his new Ralph Lauren ball cap. They loaded into the charcoal gray Lincoln Navigator and headed to George Mason Drive, a few minutes away.

Parking was simple, and the filthy mounds of plowed snow peaked in no particular pattern. Virginia Hospital Center was very quiet and on a skeleton crew. After all, it was Christmas. The Deschampses went through the automatic doors into the uninviting sterile fluorescent light.

Raphael approached the nurses station. "We are here to see Madeline Deschamps." Raphael removed his Redskins ball cap, and his dome glowed. Oliver held his phone, and Sophia peered across the counter, wondering if they were going to get a slow moving nurse.

"Madeline is being assigned a room. It shouldn't be too long before you can go see her." The nurse smiled as politely as someone working Christmas Day could.

"How long is 'too long'?" Sophia wanted to be with her now.

"Sophia, I am sure Madeline is fine, and the nurse just said it wouldn't be that long." Raphael looked at the nurse, who appreciated the assist.

Each of them chose one of those chairs that are all connected and had two arms, forcing you to stay within your own confines. The corner table was littered with magazines that no one ever read, unless you were at the doctor's office. Oliver did notice that the chick on the *Women's Health* cover was pretty hot. He was getting to that age. CNN showed replays of the pope saying mass at the Vatican.

"What is the pope's name?" Oliver started a conversation.

"Benedict," Raphael said, educating his son.

Sophia shuffled through her purse, looking for a compact, and mentioned, "I think that pope quit. I am pretty sure it's another one now." She opened the compact and assured herself that she looked halfway decent.

"Mom's right," Oliver declared as the news program captioned Pope Francis's name.

A man in blue scrubs approached the Deschampses. "Are you Madeline's family?"

Sophia rocketed out of her seat. "Yes, we are. How is she?"

"She is doing fine. My name is Dr. Praveen Saito." Saito spoke in a squirrely voice. " I am the doctor on call. I would like you to come back and see her. And I have a few questions for all of you to maybe help find out what's going on here."

Raphael apologized for forgetting the formalities. "It is nice to meet you, Dr. Saito. This is my wife, Sophia, and our son, Oliver." They all shook hands. Oliver folded up the magazine with Jessica Alba on the cover. She was hot, even though he didn't know who she was. They headed down one of those never-ending hospital hallways to find Madeline.

For the time, Madeline had a room to herself, and the color in her face had returned. Her eyes were much more focused and clear. Raphael and Sophia breathed sighs of relief. Oliver played on his phone.

"How are you feeling, Madeline?" Raphael spoke as he and Sophia approached Madeline.

The tears came quickly. "I'm sorry I ruined Christmas, Mom." She hugged her mom. "Dad." She hugged her dad and wiped the tears from her cheek.

"Hi, Madeline." Oliver cared. He just didn't know what to say to Madeline. She was a girl. Even though she was his sister.

Raphael turned to Dr. Saito. "Doctor? What happened to Madeline?"

Dr. Saito put the pen in his pocket. "Madeline has a pretty bad case of hypertension. We have started her on a very low dose of Diamox, which is a diuretic, to help get the salt and extra fluids out of her system. We also started an oral dose of Lisinopril for the hypertension. As you can see, Madeline is feeling much better. Her color is back, and her blood pressure is down considerably. She is much more relaxed. What makes me curious is why this came about so suddenly." They all looked at Dr. Saito blankly. "Has this type of event ever occurred before?" He looked at Madeline's father.

"I am not aware of this ever happening before." Raphael looked the doctor in the eyes.

"Even as a child?" Dr. Saito pried. He held a clipboard and a pen in his hands.

"No." Sophia was certain.

"Madeline? Has this happened before and you have not told your parents?"

Her parents turned their attention to the bed.

Madeline skirted the answer. "I don't know what happened."

"Have you ever passed out before, suddenly?" the doctor pressed, needing information.

"No," Madeline responded truthfully.

"Has your nose ever started to bleed for no reason?"

"No." True again.

"Have you ever felt your blood pressure go up suddenly?" Madeline looked down, as if she didn't understand the question. "A feeling as if your brain is filling up with blood and your chest is expanding like a balloon?" Madeline knew the feeling.

Reluctantly, Madeline said yes. Both parents and even Oliver snapped their heads to attention.

"Can you describe when this happened?" proceeded Dr. Saito.

Madeline's face became flushed, but not because of the hypertension. She was just plain embarrassed. She might as well have taken off all her clothes. "I woke up a few weeks ago in the middle of the night and felt like this. I had a bad dream." Snippets of the dream splintered into Madeline's head as she spoke.

"Did you see blood come out of your nose?"

"No."

"How many times has this happened?" Dr. Saito went about the questioning clinically.

"That was the first time." Madeline did not look up.

Dr. Saito jotted a few notes on Madeline's chart. He turned his attention to Raphael. "Is there any history of hypertension in the family?"

Raphael didn't think it was a big deal. He needed to drop a couple of pounds. "My doctor said my cholesterol is high, but he hasn't mentioned anything about my blood pressure."

"How about your entire family history?" Saito explored.

"My aunt died of a heart attack."

"How old was she?" Saito questioned.

"Oh my," Raphael said. "She had to be in her midseventies."

"Anyone else with these types of symptoms?"

"Not that I recall."

"Diabetes?"

That was a direct hit. "I have type two."

"Have you noticed Madeline drinking a lot? Insatiably thirsty?"

"No." They both looked at Madeline.

Madeline responded, "No. Not more than usual."

Dr. Saito paused to ponder. "Thank you for answering my questions."

Raphael felt like he'd stepped down from the witness stand.

Sophia's testimony about family medical history and hypertension was benign.

Saito turned his attention to Madeline. "This dream you had. Would you categorize it as a nightmare?"

Madeline sure didn't want to talk about the dream. "Yes. It was a nightmare."

He refocused on the parents. "Did Madeline have night terrors as a child?"

Raphael and Sophia connected. Sophia spoke first. "She had some bad dreams and would come into our room and sleep."

"How often did they occur?" Saito asked, intrigued by the night terrors.

"I don't think they happened that often," Raphael chimed in unconfidently. "It was a long time ago."

"Twice a week?"

"No," both answered adamantly.

"Twice a month?" Saito narrowed it down.

"I would say when she was really little—two or three years old—they would happen once a month."

"And for how long did they continue?"

"I'm sorry; I don't understand. Like, how many hours?" Raphael dissected the question.

"My apologies." Saito looked up from the chart. "How many years did this go on for?"

"They went on until she was about five. I can't remember them going past that."

Madeline seemed shocked she didn't remember the childhood nightmares.

Saito turned his focus back to Madeline. "Do you feel anxious at times?" He flashed a light into her eyes.

"I don't know what I am feeling, Doctor. Sometime I am tense. Sometimes I can't stay focused. I know something has been bothering me. I just can't put my finger on it." She told him the same thing she'd told her mother—the truth.

"Madeline, do you use drugs?" Saito asked the hard question. Sophia felt her gut wrench. *Not drugs,* she thought to herself. *Please, not drugs.*

"No," Madeline answered truthfully.

"Marijuana?" Saito pursued the line.

"No."

"Hallucinogens?"

"No!" Madeline rolled her eyes.

Dr. Saito let it go for the time being. The nurse came in and checked Madeline's vitals. It was a good segue for the doctor to speak to the parents.

"Young man, would you stay with your sister while I speak with your parents?" Saito looked at the quiet boy with the phone.

"Sure," Oliver replied.

Their parents and Dr. Saito left the room and walked down the hall.

"Your daughter is here for a hypertension crisis," Dr. Saito said to Raphael and Sophia. "This is where the blood pressure rises very, very quickly, and it is quite dangerous." Raphael and Sophia said nothing. "I would like to keep her overnight to monitor her symptoms—"

Sophia cut in. "You said they were getting better."

"They are," Saito stated flatly. "I would like to see if this sudden hypertension reoccurs. It is important to watch for patterns."

"Why do you think this is happening, Doctor?" The parents still had no answers.

Neither did Dr. Saito. "That is what we are trying to find out. Hypertension is sometimes caused by severe anxiety." Saito looked for a reaction.

Severe. This was difficult for Raphael and Sophia to comprehend.

Sophia got defensive. "Doctor. My daughter is going through a spell like most teenagers. I don't think she has severe anything."

"Mrs. Deschamps." Sophia was impressed he remembered her name. "Your daughter is a senior in high school. There are tremendous forces swaying these kids. Something is bothering her. A boyfriend." Sophia wished but shook her head. "Grades, drugs, a teacher at school, a bully. I think we need to find the cause of her anxiety."

"What are you recommending, Dr. Saito?" Raphael took control from Sophia.

"Let me keep her overnight. I'll run some tests, and like I mentioned, we'll monitor the hypertension. I would like to have your permission to take some blood for a few tests, including a drug screening."

"She already told you she doesn't take drugs." Sophia was pissed now. Raphael pulled her close.

"No disrespect, Mrs. Deschamps, but your child would not be the first child to lie about drugs."

That's fair, thought Raphael. Sophia sobered up emotionally to acknowledge that it could be a possibility.

"And I think we should find the root of the anxiety," the doctor continued. "I believe Madeline should make an appointment with someone from mental health or your own psychologist if you have one."

CHRISTMAS DAY, LAX

The California sunshine blistered the sky, and Lyle applied the Oakley Whisker sunglasses to his face. He brushed his hands across his shadowy beard, a grooming chore he would never address again. He was greeted by no one. A dark magnet drew the hopeless to him. A porter. A passenger. A child sitting on luggage. A clerk at the magazine counter. Dead eyes locked onto his. The legion would arrive soon to retrieve its earthly master.

The candy-apple-red Lexus RX '15 pulled to the curb. A monkey-foreheaded behemoth drove the small car. Lyle got in and never said hello to the steroid-loaded Javad Nehwal. Javad didn't say hello to Lyle. "The valley," Lyle instructed.

Javad hated everything but his flex in the mirror, but he came in handy. For Javad, killing was a sport. They headed north on the 405.

CHRISTMAS DAY
NEW ORLEANS, LOUISIANA

Ke'Von Keshi walked into the Bayou Club in Lafourche Parish and put his money on the bar. "Wild Turkey." The bartender ponied up a shot glass and filled the whiskey to the top, making a dome just over the rim. Ke'Von slammed it back, and the wise bartender left the bottle on the bar. SportsCenter ran on the flat-screen, and some old gator hunter sat pie-eyed in the corner, holding himself upright.

Ke'Von drove a rig and had just pulled back into the parish, his home. But there wasn't anything waiting for him at home anymore. He filled his glass and popped it back. Ke'Von had buried his son, his only child, in September. DaMarcus had been blown up in Afghanistan by an IED, and they'd brought him home in a box.

There'd been a twenty-one-gun salute and majors and colonels in attendance on the rainy day they'd buried DaMarcus. They'd shaken his hand and told him stories of his son's bravery. How brave? *He was probably scared to death,* Ke'Von thought, *but he did what he was told to do and it got him blown up.* Killed. In a place Ke'Von had never heard about and never cared about. Why did they have to send him to Afghanistan? Why did he have to die?

He needed his wife now, but his woman had done run off with someone else. Ke'Von and DaMarcus had had plans. He loved that boy. They were going to open their own trucking business and change the world.

He loaded up the glass with no plans of going anywhere. The Bayou Club stayed open all night. Christmas would go away, but the ghosts never would.

There were no presents for Ke'Von this Christmas. Only debts to pay. *It is amazing how despair and anger shrinks the world in front of you,* Ke'Von thought. Somehow the only thing Ke'Von could think about was DaMarcus and how angry he himself had become at the world. Ke'Von stared at the tiny glass in front of him, longing for it to do its wicked magic and make him stop thinking for a moment. One small moment.

DECEMBER 26
TOKYO

The Tokyo Metropolitan Police combed the grounds of the ancient cemetery for evidence. The crime scene extended across the street into the alley where Tiffany's blood stained the concrete. Patrolmen blocked the streets, snarling traffic as the crime teams scoured the area for clues, the light drizzle hampering the process. The bodies of Mao and Tiffany had long been removed and taken to the morgue for examination. Both of the women's purses had been retrieved, robbery eliminated as a motive. It was murder, pure and simple.

The contents of the purses included the electronic key cards, the property of a hotel only a few blocks from the Gokokuji Temple. Were they on their way out to have fun? Were they on their way home for the night? Passports and the time-stamped dates defined them as tourists. Detective Masanori Tsukino had detectives at the hotel making inquiries about the girls, trying to create a timeline of the visitors' activities that evening.

Tsukino delegated instructions to the force. "Pull all the video from the local street cameras."

"Which street cameras, Masanori?" A young officer needed guidance.

"Work on a six-block perimeter in all directions. Time of death is between seven and ten in the evening, so expand the search from four until midnight." The officer hustled off. "I want the rest of you to comb through every bar, strip club, hotel lounge, and karaoke bar and show them the pictures of these girls." Tokyo Police had handed enhanced passport photos of Mao and Tiffany to each officer. "Every bartender, every doorman, every waiter, every DJ, all the touts and local cabbies. I want to know when they left the hotel. Follow each step. I want to know what they ate and drank, when they brushed their hair, who they flirted with, and what the bar tab was." Masanori's unit wafted off into the mist.

"Kyoto." Masanori accepted the cup of tea from his rising star. "You go have a friendly chat with our friends from the yakuza. See if they know anything about this. See if one of their own is this deviant. Remind them that this is not business and that we need their cooperation."

Kyoto left Masanori and closed the door of her squad car, off to pay a visit to the bosses of the Japanese underworld.

CHRISTMAS
NORTH HOLLYWOOD,
CALIFORNIA

Javad pulled up to the Puddy Tat adult club, and Lyle exited the vehicle, finding a demented Tweety Bird painted on the wall and pointing to the entrance. The scorching desert sun drew a bead of sweat to his brow even on the short walk to the door of the club. A bouncer checked his identification, and Lyle found a seat in a modest booth among the dozens of patrons gawking at the rancid dancers. Business was good for three in the afternoon.

Lyle made time to see Trixie Krull, an acquaintance he'd made before joining the navy. Trixie worked stage two, and the lonely parted ways with their Christmas cash. "Pour Some Sugar on Me" was almost done. That was Trixie's jam. And her closing song. Lyle declined a beverage from the naked cocktail waitress.

Trixie approached Lyle after partially cloaking herself in a less-than-modest sheer top. "Hello, Brandon." She knew what Lyle was.

"I need to get in touch with Sadie." There were no formalities. No European kisses on both cheeks.

"Always Sadie." Bemoaned Trixie the Bridesmaid. "She just got out a couple of weeks ago."

Sadie Davil was Lyle's confidant. Sexy in a fully bound, gag-ball-in-your-throat kind of way, Sadie ruled the night and the perverted, her hair as dark as her soul. What hospitalized most humans made Sadie hot. She reminded Lyle of the girls where he came from. He was putting the team back together, and Sadie was not afraid to die.

Trixie kicked Sadie's number and wondered why she wasn't enough for the "good" ones. Lyle wished her a sardonic Merry Christmas as she headed back onstage for another set.

ARLINGTON, VIRGINIA

Madeline rested comfortably at the Virginia Hospital Center, but Sophia did not in her king-size bathroom. They had long put Oliver to bed and had told him to put his phone on the charger.

"A psychologist, Raphael? A psychologist?" Sophia ranted and brushed her mane with frustrated vigor.

"Sophia, don't overreact."

"Don't tell me not to overreact!" Sophia drummed the brush on the bathroom counter. "This is Madeline we are talking about. She is the last person to need a psychiatrist." The brush gained momentum. "And all the questions about drugs. Ugh!"

"They were all legitimate questions, Sophia." Raphael peered over his glasses and rubbed some lotion onto his hairy arms.

"She doesn't go out to parties. She doesn't go out on dates, though I wish she would. She is here all the time, and she never looks 'high' or acts 'high.'" Sophia put down the brush.

"Baby, drugs are everywhere, and I don't think Madeline is using drugs. I really don't. But we did when we were her age,," Raphael acknowledged.

"That was pot, and that was a long time ago." It was a poor argument. Sophia and Raphael had already had the long parent-children conversation about alcohol, drugs, and sex. Flashbacks of her senior year in high school terrified Sophia for a seering second. The blitzkrieg image of the back of Graham Rodriguez's Ford Fairmont by the construction site sent a chill through her spine.

"That long time ago for us is the present for Madeline. She is exposed to a variety of different peer pressures. And I am pretty sure that you don't have to 'go out' to get pot."

"I suppose," conceded Sophia. "Hallucinogens?" The rant shifted gears. "What does that mean, exactly? What are hallucinogens?" Sophia knew but didn't know. "Is that LSD?"

Raphael bit his lip and remembered the Grateful Dead at the Cap Centre in '78. "Franklin's Tower." Jerry Garcia had been great. He'd written the whole set list on his jeans. He'd had lots of hair. "Well, I think they are referring to LSD or magic mushrooms."

"Didn't that go out in the sixties?" Sophia tucked herself under the comforter. Raphael felt a bit older than he should have. He wasn't that old.

"I suppose it's still around or it's something different. The bottom line is that something happened to Madeline today, and it is the doctor's job to figure that out." Sophia knew she was projecting. Facing fears was scary. "Madeline is going to be fine." Raphael was certain. "Let's just find out what is going on first."

Sophia rolled over and held Raphael close. "I love you."

"I love you too." He looked into her eyes. "Merry Christmas. Kind of."

They both smiled wryly, and Sophia turned off the light. "A psychologist? Really?"

"Good night, Sophia."

Sophia had a hard time letting things go and would not sleep well that night.

CHRISTMAS NIGHT
NORTH HOLLYWOOD,
CALIFORNIA

Lyle waited for hours in the dark, sitting alone among the filth. Bud Light bottles crashed around the floor, some broken. Partial and empty handles of Bacardi and cheap Aristocrat vodka decorated the floor and coffee table. Ashtrays that had been soaked in beer and not emptied for days dotted the living room. The toilet was draped with vomit, and the shower filled with soiled underwear and socks. The remnants of a line of some white powder lay sifted on a Christmas card ringed with beer stains.

The sink overflowed with dishes caked with tomato sauce, and the cockroaches danced festively through the pots and glassware. Lyle's shoes stuck to the linoleum, making the sound of tape pulling off a cardboard box each time he lifted a foot. The single bedroom was littered with clothing, and the stained mattress lay exposed as the sheets drooped lonely to the box spring. The nightstand was garnished with a lamp with no shade and a Tinkertoy-shaped glass pipe with milky-white residue at the base of the bulb.

Lyle heard the key scraping at the lock and the stumble that always followed.

"Hello, Raylene Stewart." Lyle stood quietly in the hallway with no bulb.

Raylene took a moment to focus, accustomed to the blur of unexpected visitors. "Stewart? It's Raylene De Vry now." Lyle noticed how deep her cheeks sank into her face.

"Raylene De Vry." Lyle added it to the list of names. "You have another man now?"

"I always have another man. I have a different man every day of the week if I want," she spoke in her charcoal voice. "What the hell are you doing here?"

"I just got out of the navy." He didn't lie. Raylene stripped out of her two-day-old outfit, struggling with her rail-thin arms and exposing her rack of ribs. She smelled ripe.

"Well, you can't stay here." Raylene moved by Lyle and headed for the nightstand. She opened a small plastic baggie and loaded the glass pipe with its dusty contents. Lyle hardly blinked, having seen it many times before. Raylene flicked the lighter and held it beneath the bulb. The white mist formed inside the circle. She sucked down any future she had left. Lyle waited to ask the next question while Raylene's eyes rolled into the back of her head. He averted his eyes as she lay back on the blank mattress, her bony legs and unshaved area woefully uncovered.

"Have you seen Bernard?" he asked in an obligatory fashion.

"Ha-ha." Raylene thought that was a knee-slapper. "I haven't seen that bastard for three years. He is doing fifteen at Pelican Bay for lighting some joint on fire. He's probably in solitary with his wise-ass mouth, or planning to kill the niggers with his skinhead pals."

"How's business?" Lyle changed the topic.

Raylene felt the full effect of the drug. She yanked at her scalp, slowly pulling threads of her hair and placing them gently on the bed, keepsakes. "Business is fine. My new husband"—Raylene laughed and coughed at the same time, taking several moments to compose herself as she prevented her lung from finding the cesspool masquerading as a floor—"has a place up in the Hills where he cooks the stuff. It's all about the meth. Meth this and meth that. But it's a good living." Raylene was living proof.

Lyle grabbed Raylene by what was left of her hair and slammed her into the wall. "You know what I need you to do?" Raylene shook her head, eyes peeled from the fear. "What do I need you to do, Raylene?"

Raylene whimpered. "I am doing it."

"Say it!" Lyle's voice barked.

"Make sure I keep giving it to the children. You kill the weeds by pulling them by the roots. If I do this for you, I shall have all that I desire." Raylene could not find a cell left that could fight Lyle's terror. Her addiction consumed her, and she vowed by oath to Lyle to take others with her.

"Kill them all, Mom. Kill them all." Raylene lay at the feet of her child. "I am going to spend some time downtown. I need to get out of here. You remind me of the girls at home."

Raylene watched as her son left her den on Christmas night.

DECEMBER 26, 2013

The Deschampses arrived at the Virginia Hospital Center early to get Madeline. She looked blah but had made it through the night with no episodes. As promised, the doctors were going to send her home. Sophia swaddled Madeline in her new Osolita jacket and brought the new KDs and some Elites to keep her feet warm.

"How is she doing, Dr. Saito?" Raphael inquired.

"Her hypertension seems to have completely subsided. I would still like her to take the prescribed medication for the next two days. It will help if she needs it but will not hurt if she is not having the hypertension." Dr. Saito seemed content.

"Are the results from the blood test in, Doctor?" Sophia pursued.

"The toxicology report was negative," Saito stated. "Madeline has no prescription or street drugs in her system."

Sophia nudged Raphael in a moment of victory.

"I would monitor her for shortness of breath or if she looks flush or faint. Keep your door open at night in case she has a dream, so you can go to her." Dr. Saito did not have enough information to truly diagnose. "And please make an appointment with a psychologist.

I believe that Madeline's condition is something more mental than physical at this point."

No one left the hospital feeling that this was over.

DECEMBER 26
TOKYO

Masanori Tsukino stood in front of one of the seedier bars in Kabukicho. His team found a bouncer who'd identified the girls and an unknown man who'd left with them.

"So, you are sure these are the girls?" Tsukino asked.

"Those are the girls," the bouncer confirmed.

"What happened two nights ago?"

"The girls tried to leave without paying their bar bill. They put some money down but were short, and they headed to the door. I stopped them."

"Did you handle them at all?"

"I grabbed one of their arms to prevent them from running."

Tsukino stared at the ruffian. "Then what?"

"A white guy walked up. He spoke to them in English. Then he started talking to me in perfect Japanese. He was very polite and offered to pay the remainder of the bar bill for the girls. He even left a little extra." The bouncer paused and finally broke his cool. "Man, I had nothing to do with those girls getting killed."

Tsukino paused. "Anything else?"

"He was in the military. Short military hair. White guy."

"Height?"

"I would guess five nine." The bouncer held his hand above Tsukino's head.

"Weight?"

"I don't know. Maybe one seventy. He was in shape. You know, like military people are."

"Do you remember his eye color?"

"Blue. Crystal blue. Like the water of the islands."

"What color was his hair?"

"It was so short it was hard to tell. Brown," the bouncer made his best guess.

Tsukino made sure this was all recorded. "What was he wearing?'

"He dressed well. Nice pants and boots. A really nice leather jacket. That's really all I could see."

Tsukino stared down the employee. He was a loser but not a killer. "This is my number if you remember anything else." Tsukino walked away and answered his cell phone. Street-camera video had been researched, and they had something he might be interested in seeing.

The technician cued up the video and cut through the hours that revealed nothing.

"You just said you talked to a bouncer outside a bar."

Tsukino nodded in the affirmative.

"At half past nine, this tape shows two girls having some type of altercation with someone outside a club."

"Pause." Tsukino pushed his hair back and looked closely at the screen. The video was scratchy, but fairly definitive. It was the bouncer he had just spoken too. He told the truth. Tsukino took a deep breath and continued to watch the last hour or so of Mao's and Tiffany's lives.

The bouncer grabbed Tiffany by the arm, and a dark figure walked up to the girls. At first it was tricky to see him as the group drifted to the edge of the sidewalk, away from the neon of the club. Then the stranger and the bouncer stepped aside, closer to the club, its lights illuminating the stranger's face. "Freeze!" Tsukino examined the frame closely. Well dressed. Military haircut. Five feet nine inches, give or take. "Get this picture to everyone on the streets and the train stations and the airports." Tsukino looked around to make sure everyone moved. "Run the tape." They observed an exchange of what was presumably the money. Mao, Tiffany, and the stranger said a few words to one another. The bouncer stepped back into the club, and Tiffany expressed herself adamantly while speaking to the stranger. They turned as a group and started walking in the direction of the Gokokuji Temple.

"This is the guy we are looking for!"

DECEMBER 27
USS *MUSTIN*, YOKOSUKA,
JAPAN

The seventy-two-hour leave ended, and roll call was presented to CDR Kexin. All sailors, some in better condition than others, were accounted for, minus one: Seaman Brandon Lyle.

Kexin authorized the report to be filed for unauthorized absence. Kexin was sure local authorities would pick Lyle up on some local charge of drunkenness, or maybe he would just sober up and check in. Lyle faced confinement in the brig for one month and reduction to the lowest enlisted grade, and he would lose two-thirds of his pay for one month. All for not being on time. *Stupid kids,* Kexin thought. He turned his attention to the exercises off Miura Peninsula starting at 0630 tomorrow morning.

DECEMBER 27
TOKYO

Tsukino sat at his desk, and the door opened. Summer Kagawa, the pathologist assigned to the murders of Mao Iniesta and Tiffany Kai, entered the room with an armful of reports. Tsukino enjoyed working with Summer, except for the morbid fact that they worked on homicides.

Summer had graduated from Osaka University, the daughter of American-born Japanese nationals who worked in America for Sony. Summer had gone to medical school at Stanford University School of Medicine and had graduated with honors. She'd leaped at the opportunity to move to Tokyo when her father had asked to be reassigned to Japan. She was a brilliant pathologist and quite a beautiful lady.

Tsukino and Kagawa exchanged pleasantries and settled in to review a somber session of police work. "What are your findings, Summer?"

"Which victim would you like to start with, Masanori?" Summer organized her envelopes.

"Let's start with Tiffany Kai."

"Tiffany Kai suffered massive trauma through the os frontis, or forehead. The protrusion entered the cortex and exited the occipital lobe."

Tsukino decided not to have lunch today. "What exactly does that mean?"

"Something entered her forehead, went in the front of her brain, and came out the back of her brain and skull." Summer placed a picture of the entrance wound on Tsukino's desk. "Tiffany died instantly."

"What was the murder weapon?"

"That," Summer said, looking flummoxed, "I have not been able to determine." She rotated the picture. "The entrance wound is two centimeters wide and almost perfectly circular. The diameter of the wound narrows through the frontal lobe and the parietal lobe before exiting the occipital lobe and the back of the victim's head, leaving an exit wound that shrinks to a miniscule two millimeters."

Tsukino paused to let his stomach settle. "What kind of weapon does that? Some kind of knife?"

"No. A knife would leave patterns and much more damage inside the brain. The funnel through the brain is very consistent in its measurements. We are looking for a weapon that is very, very sharp and narrow at the tip and expands to the handle or end. It is at least ten centimeters long."

Tsukino pondered.

"And, Masanori," Summer added, "the force of pressure required to enter the forehead is tremendous and precise. The entry wound is similar to a bullet. However, the exit wound is not consistent with any bullet I am aware of. The pattern through the brain I could explain, were the brain exposed and had the killer driven a narrow stake through it. But to enter the forehead and maintain an almost perfect ninety-degree angle is something I cannot explain. Look at the entry wound again." Summer slid her chair to Masanori's side of the desk. "A perfect circle bored right through her skull."

"Were there any materials found that could indicate the weapon?"

"No. There was no metal residue or shards on either the entry nor the exit wounds, and I followed the wound through the brain and found nothing there, either."

"Fingerprints were not found."

"The victim did have bruising around her neck, consistent with a grip. He held her against that wall and shoved something through her head. We just don't know what."

Tsukino sighed, deeply disturbed. "Let's move on to Mao."

Summer looked at Tsukino, a tad pale herself. "Mao had bruises on her triceps and the back of her neck, consistent with being forced or dragged to the temple." Tsukino thought of the terrified girl. "There was an incision, a transverse cut, made just above Mao's pubic line."

Tsukino interrupted. "What is a transverse cut?"

"A transverse cut is the technique obstetricians use when doing a lower uterine cesarean section. A C-section."

"Is this guy a doctor? The guy we are looking for is military?" Tsukino grappled his confusion.

"I don't know what he is, but the incision was precise and cut very quickly and deeply." Summer had more. "All of Mao's reproductive system was removed from her body through the incision."

"This is crazy."

"Her fallopian tubes are gone. Her ovaries are gone. Her uterus and cervix are gone."

"What do you mean gone? They are severely damaged?"

"No. They are gone." Summer had no other answer.

"What is the official cause of death?" Tsukino needed to make a report. How would anyone understand this?

"Official cause of death is exsanguination. She died from massive internal hemorrhaging." Summer bowed her head. "She suffered, Masanori." Summer's eyes filled with tears. "And there is something else." Summer paused. "Blood tests revealed that Mao was pregnant."

Tsukino stopped cold. "So is this some type of sick abortion? What do we have here? Some estranged boyfriend who didn't want to have the baby?"

"I don't know."

"How far along was she?"

"She was in the first trimester. About twelve weeks."

"Where is the baby?"

"I don't know. It's not there. None of it is there." Summer looked at the floor. "There are only minute traces of amniotic fluid, and the sac has completely vanished."

"Vanished?" Tsukino thought to himself. "So, he cuts into her like a surgeon, reaches into her, and removes all of her reproductive organs and an unborn child, and there is nothing left. Is that what you are saying?" Tsukino asked, incredulous.

"Those are my findings."

"How long would it take a doctor to perform this type of invasive surgery?"

"My understanding is that it would take one or two hours. But he took no care in doing this. He ripped her to shreds. From the inside out."

"This guy is carrying something very sharp to make this incision. Did you find any other blood types at the scene?"

"Nothing."

Tsukino paused. "What do you think he did with everything inside of her?" Tsukino looked out the window.

"I don't know. I don't think I want to know."

Tsukino agreed, but his job was to find the truth. "Tiffany Kai was murdered to get her out of the way. The killer wanted Mao and the baby. I believe this is a truth." There was a second truth, Tsukino kept to himself: a monster was on the loose.

DECEMBER 29
LOS ANGELES, CALIFORNIA

L yle hated his cumbersome, clunky human form. He yearned to shed his skin and open his wings. The downtown Los Angeles skyline came into view as he and Javad rounded a bend on the freeway. The law would be coming for him soon and much needed to be done.

Javad headed into the barrios of East LA, onto the turf of VNE, Varrio Nuevo Estrada. Lyle had an appointment with Kandy Asada. He wanted to have some work done on his body. Kandy belonged to the VNE and made it back and forth through the tunnels outside Tijuana and into the United States, smuggling heroin in her vagina. She learned her art and developed this incredible skill in the Mexican prisons.

Kandy opened the door. The long Carlos Santana T-shirt engulfed her track marks and hardly covered the G-string she wore. Other gang members counted money and drugs in preparation for the day's business. Lyle removed his shirt and lay patiently in the recliner as Kandy tuned her wares.

"Sadie, did you contact the politician?" Lyle spoke over the buzz of the drill. Sadie Davil sat opposite of Kandy. Javad watched the VNE members, cleaned his Glock, and shined his Mexican Mafia markings, making small talk with the dealers.

"The honorable congressman will be meeting us at Santa Monica's Windjammers Yacht Club in Marina del Rey on Saturday." Davil's patterned sundress concealed her deviance.

"Have you a place for us?" Lyle needed a secure base. They would be looking for him.

"I have," Sadie confirmed. "Rohit? Have you secured a vessel and made arrangements with Benayoun?" Lyle gazed into the night of Kandy's eyes.

"We have a vessel, and we are to rendezvous with Benayoun off the coast of Catalina. He is very intrigued by what we have to offer," Rohit Guzan spoke softly. Raised destitute and starving, he vowed to avenge the nightmares of this life. He was drawn to Lyle. He was drawn to destruction.

"He will be satisfied. Benayoun seeks power and control. And this he shall have. Is he bringing what I asked for?" Lyle negotiated.

"He will have what we asked for," Rohit answered.

"Where is Elroy?" Lyle wondered aloud.

"He is in county," Sadie offered. "He was pinched for possession of material to create an explosive."

"Imagine that," Lyle mused. That was the reason he wanted Elroy.

"The attorney is arranging bail. He should be out by Thursday or Friday and will meet us at the yacht club."

Elroy Floyd, the slimy white boy with the chin-strap beard and a penchant for blowing shit up. He loved to watch things burn.

Kandy unbuttoned Lyle's pants and relieved the tension on his zipper. She spread open his fly and worked the drill onto his lower abdomen. The zombies of the street shuffled in and out of the flat, delivering money. Exchanging drugs and weapons and ammunition. Accumulating cheap pot, expensive medical-grade marijuana, crack, heroin, inhalants, opium, benzos, speed, ecstasy, and cocaine. They distributed desired legal drugs—Ambien, Seroquel, Dilaudid, Xanax, Desoxyn, codeine, Adderall, OxyContin, and oxymorphone. All delivered across the southland by a diverse sales force to Bel Air, Santa Monica, Manhattan Beach, Rodeo Drive, Beverly Hills, Torrance, Gardena, Hawthorne. Huntington Park, Compton, Long Beach. Chatsworth, Canoga Park, Woodland Hills. They sold to the impoverished, the wealthy, the students, the street, the lawyers, the gangs, the Crips, the Bloods, the preppies, the jocks, the choir, the spics, the kikes, the towel heads, the dot heads, the jungle bunnies, the zipper heads, the nerds, mothers and fathers, aunts and uncles, children and adults, the stars and the hopeless. All generated by a continual cycle of greed and despair. Religion was no longer the opiate of the masses. *Opiates were the opiates of the masses*, thought Lyle.

One of the gang members took exception to Javad's Mexican Mafia presence. He felt it to be intrusive and drew his gun. Javad did not flinch. He pulled his weapon, and the two stared each other down with barrels pointed in the other's face. Business came to a halt, and the tension grew to DEFCON 4. Other gang members drew their guns in support of their member. Lyle stood from the chair, shirtless. The strong arms of the dragon reached around his rib cage. The scales stretched down across his stomach and emerged as great claws that spiked sharp deep into his loins. Lyle's eyes turned to flame, and the dragon appeared to come to life, the wings ruffling.

"Lay down your weapons." Each gun was withdrawn. Lyle placed his hand on Javad's massive forearm and pulled it down to his side.

"The time will come for you to use your weapons. Now is not that moment." He looked at Javad. "They have a job to do. They are doing it well."

Lyle and his crew left for a place Sadie had found. A place off the grid.

DECEMBER 31
ARLINGTON, VIRGINIA

Too early in the morning, Raphael struggled with the Raisin Bran. The new box and top of the bag should have been easier to open. He muscled up on the bag and pulled violently to separate the crease. The surge opened the bag, but the Raisin Bran flew all over the kitchen. "Damn it! Damn it! Goddamned bags!"

Madeline laughed out loud for the first time in many days. "It's going to be OK, Daddy."

"These bags. They are impossible. The glue or whatever they use is strong enough to hold a space shuttle together."

Raphael composed himself and grabbed a broom and dustpan. Madeline offered to take the latter. He swept while Madeline held the dustpan.

"Thank you, Madeline."

"What's going on?" Sophia appeared in the kitchen dressed and ready for the trip to Roundtop Mountain Resort.

"Daddy lost the battle with the Raisin Bran." Madeline smiled and looked at her pop.

"Well, you need to eat that, and we need to hit the road. I want to get some skiing in today, and the slopes are going to be packed." Sophia relished the upcoming adventure and family outing.

Oliver had never skied, and lessons started at ten in the morning. It had been a long time since Madeline had hit the slopes, and with an abundance of new gear, the Olympics, beware. The Navigator had been fueled and packed the night prior in anticipation of the spry commencement of the day. Oliver ran through his personal checklist of things necessary for the two-hour drive north to Pennsylvania. Phone, check. Earbuds, check. His iPad with Minecraft, Plants vs. Zombies, Clash of Clans, and Piano Tiles downloaded—check. Two stocking stuffers—the *World War Z* and *The Wolverine* DVDs for the Navigator television—check.

Raphael finished the labor-intensive cereal and dropped the bowl into the dishwasher. He locked the front door and armed the ADT home-security system.

Everyone nestled in his or her chosen spot in the car, and Raphael activated the seat warmers. "Does anyone have to go to the bathroom?" He looked at Sophia, who possessed a thimble-size bladder.

"Shut up and drive." Sophia smiled and buckled her seat belt.

Raphael hit 66 West and turned off the Dulles Access Road. Sophia worked on her cell phone, doing clandestine research on a psychologist. Hundreds popped up on the Internet. She wasn't ready to talk to friends about Madeline's issues. It could be much ado about nothing. She was wary about asking anyone about a psychologist—like anyone would want to admit they had one. Dr. Saito had recommended a couple, but none seemed to be a good fit. Dr. Ejike Hosseini. Dr. Nabil Yobo. *Hmmmm,* Sophia thought to herself. They were men. Madeline, Sophia felt, needed a woman.

The abundance of candidates staggered Sophia. They all seemed to want between $100 and $200 an hour, and all insurance plans were out of network. A few had degrees from schools she had never heard of before. Odessa Medical University in Ukraine. *No, Sophia.* She pictured a wrinkled Russian woman wrapped in blankets and eating borsch. Dayanand Medical School in Punjab, India. Sophia, sure they were all good people and nice doctors, weeded them out. There had to be some criteria. Some of the notations on the résumés seemed cheesy. She sought out the key word *anxiety* to narrow the search. Oliver was on the iPad being quiet for a change, and Madeline stared out the window. Sophia had a green light to pursue her secret research.

Sophia thumbed through pages and pages. She touched the screen for Dr. Sylvia Smalling. Dr. Smalling had graduated from Columbia University Medical Center. That was Ivy League. Quite a few of the key words Sophia had searched for were listed. *Failed relationships* (or *no relationships* in Madeline's case). *Anxiety. Poor performance at work* (or school) and *feelings of low self-esteem.* Her picture was a bit schoolmarmish, but Sophia pledged to make an appointment with Dr. Sylvia Smalling on Thursday.

Madeline looked outside at the rolling foothills of the Blue Ridge Mountains. The pines were covered in snow, and as they crossed the Potomac into Maryland, she noted that the river was frozen from the edges. The skies were overcast and gray. There was something calming about the mountains and the open sky. Being away from the city was a good thing for her right now. The world was a negative. She and everything around her were negatives. The traffic and the noise. The anonymous people and the bustle. Madeline felt like everyone stared at her. She was alone with her family. People she trusted.

"We could cancel the skiing and go to the battlefield at Gettysburg."

Madeline rolled her eyes at her father.

Then Raphael began to recite Lincoln's address. "Four score and—"

Oliver cut him off. "No, Dad. We will be late for the class." Oliver became responsible only to avoid the battlefield. Plus, he'd already been there with Mom and Dad on a class field trip.

"I know we are close." At least the GPS said so. Raphael followed the female's guiding voice. She sounded like a dominatrix hurling instructions. "Turn left, now!" And Raphael did what he was told.

There were miles between houses. Stoplights and turn lanes were nowhere to be found. There were no car dealerships or strip malls selling Peruvian chicken. No banks or Jiffy Lubes. No gated residential neighborhoods and no Section 8 housing. No metro buses and emergency sirens. The Deschampses were not that far from home, but they might as well have been on Mars.

They crossed through the serene valley, and Raphael eased into the parking lot of the resort. The slopes were already a hive of activity, and Madeline shrank a smidge. Oliver bounded out of the car and started unloading the gear. Team Deschamps hauled the equipment to the ticket booth, and Raphael paid the fees, all of them proud when they attached the sticky tickets to the zippers of their jackets.

Sophia found the lockers, stowed what they would not need, and walked the awkward walk in ski boots to the lesson area. The snowblowers worked overtime despite the ample base. Sophia and Raphael joined the lesson. Sophia pointed out to Raphael that it had been twenty-plus years since they had been to Saas-Fee in Switzerland.

A pair of instructors named Andy and Lisa addressed the group of fifteen as the blowers blasted the ice into the class. The slopes looked so glamorous, but the class was being conducted in what felt like Siberia. Andy and Lisa shouted over the garish blustering to the broad cross section of ages between six and sixty. They focused on the basics. How to step with skis. The snowplow positon.

Balance. Andy worked his way down one side of the class, checking each classmate's posture and balance. He grabbed Madeline by the shoulders to square her frame. Madeline winced. She felt uncomfortable when Andy touched her.

After a few more drills, Andy and Lisa worked the class over to the rope tow. The gaggle of beginners amused the instructors, but like salmon heading upstream, somehow they all made it. The slope eased down the hill, but gave each an opportunity for a test run. Oliver went wildly but managed a stop without disaster. Sophia fell on her butt, and Raphael helped her to her feet in a clumsy dance. Madeline stayed cautious. She tried to turn, then wiggled a bit but righted herself. Andy moved parallel to Madeline and bracketed her shoulders, helping maintain her balance. Madeline slung her left pole out and fumed, "Get your goddamned hands off me!" Andy pulled to a stop as Madeline hit the snow, her cheeks flush with anger.

Andy paused, confused at the reaction, as Raphael scooted down and slowed where Madeline tried to regroup and stand. "Can I give you a hand?" Raphael extended his glove, unaware of the drama.

"I'm fine. I can do it myself." Madeline just wanted that instructor away from her.

Andy looked at Raphael and shrugged. Raphael shrugged back, and Andy glided away, sure to keep his distance from "that" girl.

Madeline choked back the floodgates and, like a baby giraffe, stood onto her skis again and crawled her way back into the practice line. What just happened? Why did she freak out like that? What the fuck was happening to her?

The beginner class had ended, and Madeline made sure not to make eye contact with Andy. Raphael and Sophia were having a great time, and Oliver was a natural and fearless.

Sophia scooted next to Madeline. "Are you having a good time?"

Madeline manufactured a smile. "Sure. It's fun." Sophia wasn't convinced, but she was there to have a good time and did have an obligation to her husband and son. Madeline would just have to suck it up on the ski trip with the $1000 worth of new equipment.

Everyone tingled nervously as they approached the ski lift. No one wanted to be the boob that shut the system down. They all managed to take a seat, and Raphael and Sophia were eyeing each other in the chair ahead. Oliver rocked his feet and skis while staring at the moguls below. Madeline looked up at the sky. Bold and big. How big would the moon look from the top of the mountain? She breathed the icy air deeply to the exhilarating thought.

Jettisoning the chair felt like landing a plane. Except you were the pilot. Tips up. Feel the ground and gently let the plane slide down the runway. Some people don't like the takeoff. Others don't like the landing. Sophia squealed and slid upon touchdown. Raphael held her elbow the whole time. Oliver rifled off the chair, and Madeline closed her eyes, pulled her knees up, and hoped for the best. Still in one piece, she heard the sardonic applause from her family. They graded the level of their descent and chose an easier run that was not designated a black diamond. Madeline stood on the precipice, knowing she would not make it down the hill without falling on the steep slope. For a moment she did not care. On top of the mountain, she could see for miles in every direction. The air, thin and crisp, filled her lungs with innate joy. Her family disappeared down the side of the mountain while she soaked in the view of the valleys below and the other peaks reaching skyward. She was close to something. Something good. For the entirety of the day, Madeline would fall and pick herself up again, taking the lift to the top of the mountain and the majestic view.

The Deschampses regrouped at the base of the slopes. "How about some hot chocolate?" Raphael proclaimed.

"How about some lunch?" Sophia added. She was famished.

"Sounds good to me." Madeline preferred to be at the top of the mountain.

"Do you think they have sea bass?" Oliver salivated at the thought.

"Oliver. We are at the lodge of a ski resort in Pennsylvania. How about some nachos?" Raphael corralled his son by the back of the neck.

In the lodge a hostess with a unibrow seated them at a nice table in the center of the dining room. Oliver asked for a booth. The hostess obliged, though she furled the hairy caterpillar above her eyes. The family opened their menus.

"Dad? Do you like blue cheese?" Oliver asked as he removed his gloves.

"If you like a smelly sock in your mouth." Raphael looked over the top of his glasses.

Sophia looked at Oliver. "I like blue cheese. On a burger or a salad."

Oliver sneered. "I don't think I will like it."

"Madeline? Do you see anything you like?" Sophia wanted to see a smile somewhere along the way.

"I'll have a grilled cheese." Madeline numbly closed the menu and looked blankly at the wall on the other side of the lodge with the Holiday Inn artwork.

"Madeline." Madeline turned her head from her mother. "I know it has been a long week, but I would expect you to show a little gratitude and be just a little goddamned happy about something." There. She'd said it.

"Well, I am sorry to be such a disappointment to you, Mom. I am sorry I am such a pain in the ass. I am sorry I screwed up everyone's Christmas and now I am ruining everyone's New Year's fucking Eve."

"You watch your language, young lady," Raphael admonished her. The waitress had returned but quickly left, making the executive decision to come back in a few minutes. "Madeline," Raphael intervened, "it's been a long week, but you did not ruin Christmas. You haven't ruined anything. You are our beautiful daughter, and we love you."

"I don't feel beautiful. I feel like I am nothing but a burden." The tears dripped down her face as Oliver looked at her over his phone.

"Do we make you feel that way?" Sophia fumed. "Do we walk around the house bemoaning what a burden Madeline is?"

"No," Madeline conceded sheepishly.

"Then don't put this on us." Sophia excused herself to the lavatory but stayed standing by the table.

"That's enough. We are not going to do this here. We are a family, and we are going to stick together." Raphael paused to see if he had everyone's attention. "Madeline, we are going to do everything we can to find out what has been bothering you. I don't think it is anything more that you being a moody teenager." Madeline rolled her eyes. "You mother and I love you very much, but you have to smile once in a while. Things just aren't that bad." He got up and hugged Madeline.

"I have to pee." Sophia stomped away.

"Look, Dad. I got forty-seven on Piano Tiles." Oliver shoved the phone in his dad's face.

The waitress stopped by again.

"I will have the French dip and a hot chocolate," Raphael said. Then he ordered for Sophia. Then the kids chimed in.

No one uttered a word through lunch; it was the quietest meal they'd ever shared.

The Deschampses terminated the rest of the day's skiing activities and checked in to the hotel, the accommodations a far cry from the Mayflower on Connecticut Avenue, but they would suffice. Oliver took Raphael down to the indoor pool. The chlorine-filled water was steaming, and Raphael felt he was going to need a culture after swimming.

They found a local restaurant for dinner that had a salad bar and an original waitress from the opening in 1968. Madeline hardly ate. Sophia hated salad bars and didn't say a word. Oliver complained about the slow service. Raphael was stoked. His veal parmesan wasn't half bad, and the bill was only forty-three bucks, including a glass of red wine he was sure came from a jug. It was the second-quietest meal they had ever eaten together.

DECEMBER 31
TOKYO, JAPAN

A week had passed since the murders of Mao Iniesta and Tiffany Kai. Tsukino shared little hope that his suspect remained in Tokyo. He had a subpar street-camera picture of the side of his face and an artist's rendering based on the description given by the bouncer at the club.

Kyoto and her small army of police canvassed the streets. She believed the heads of the yakuza knew nothing of this murder. They had a vested interest in Kabukicho. An event like this would scare away business. Any "decisions" that needed to be made in the interest of the yakuza were strictly business. Tourists from all over the world came to Kabukicho to enjoy what the district offered. Why would they be involved in something that would frighten the customers?

They continued to search every rathole in the vicinity, and finally they went deep into the muck. Bleary from the constant use of opium, Junichi was pulled to his feet by the police and asked if he could identify the man in the photo. Junichi nodded and slumped back into the filth of the floor. The police righted him again, and Kyoto challenged him. "How do you know this man?"

Junichi slurred. "He came for a tattoo." The image of the dragon and the soot-black wings shot through his brain, and his focus came into view.

"When was this?" Kyoto interrogated.

This was a tricky one for Junichi, as time was an ethereal concept. "I don't remember. Maybe one week."

"What kind of tattoo does he have?" Kyoto asked about the identifying marks.

Junichi's eyes went hollow. He heard about the murders, and his soul knew that he was an accomplice in some inadvertent way. In a moment's time, he knew he had not been honorable. That he was a coward. Junichi looked down. "Terrible and evil wings on his shoulders and back and the dragon of death." Junichi barely make eye contact with Kyoto. Kyoto spoke to a frightened man.

"What is his name?"

"He never gave me his name. Only once did we speak, and that was about the tattoo. He would put down an obscene amount of money, and I would work."

Kyoto needed more. "Can you remember anything else? Did you see an ID card, a credit card, a key chain with something you might remember?"

Junichi thought as hard as he could, his mind a blender of drugs and madness. He shook his head. He mind was vacant. Kyoto gave him her card and told him to call if he remembered anything. She turned toward the stairs, thankful to get out of the living dungeon.

"He had a key card for the Higashi. One of those electronic keys." Junichi's knees wobbled as he whispered.

Kyoto had gotten a break. She headed for the Higashi, a place her team had canvassed before.

Kyoto entered the lobby and walked to the check-in desk. "I would like to speak to the manager." Kyoto showed her badge.

The clerk moved swiftly, and the manager came forth. "How may I help you, Officer Kyoto?" she asked.

"I need to see your registry of all guests that were in the hotel on the twenty-fourth of December." Kyoto pulled out the black-and-white photo of Lyle. "We came here last week and asked the staff if they could identify this man."

The manager acknowledged the picture. "Yes. We showed it to the staff, and they did not recognize this man."

"We have reason to believe he stayed here that night. I need to see the security tapes for the entire day of the twenty-fourth." The manager called the security director.

The security director escorted Kyoto to a private area with the console and videotape feeds of numerous cameras monitoring the hallways. The manager knocked on the door and presented Kyoto with the registered guests of December 24. She perused the extensive list of three hundred guests. She scanned for names in English. The security manager and her team eyed the feeds of the twenty-four cameras that surveyed the halls, fitness center, restaurant, lobby, and exits of the hotel. They accelerated the speed slightly to avoid having to watch it in real time.

The manager brought them tea and Pocky, biscuit sticks covered in chocolate. "There!" Kyoto stopped the tape. Through the lobby doors, a white man dressed in a US Navy uniform. The counter at the registration desk captured a complete image. The manager and Kyoto cross-referenced the time on the videotape and the computer-generated check-in time. This man had checked in as Victor Kuyt. Room 329.

"Is there anyone currently occupying room three twenty-nine?" Kyoto wanted into the room.

"I will have to check." The manager hustled back to the desk.

"Keep looking at the tape. I want to see when 'Kuyt' leaves the hotel. All of his movements," Kyoto instructed, and then followed the manager to the front desk.

The manager pulled up the screen on the computer. "No one currently occupies room three twenty-nine. Though we did have guests stay in that room for three nights from the twenty-eighth through the thirtieth. The room has been cleaned at least twice since this guest checked out on the morning of the twenty-fifth."

"May we visit the room anyway?" The manager had her master key ready, and the two headed to the elevator.

Kyoto entered the room as if walking into a temple. Quietly, she stepped past the bathroom, looking for something obvious, which she knew she would not find. Anything in this room would be forensic. "Have they given the carpet a shampoo since Kuyt checked in?"

"I do not believe so." The manager made a note on her list of things to do.

Kyoto dialed Tsukino on her cell. "Masanori, we have identified the man in the picture. He stayed at the Higashi on the twenty-fourth of December and checked out the morning of the twenty-fifth. My team is reviewing the rest of the tape. His name is Victor Kuyt." Kyoto spelled it out for Tsukino. Tsukino would run the name through the international crime databases. "When he arrived at the hotel, he was wearing a uniform. US Navy."

Tsukino needed to alert his commander. He would need some assistance. The US Navy had bases at Sasebo, Nagasaki, and Okinawa, offices in Tokyo, and the Seventh Fleet in Yokosuka.

"Masanori, I would like you to send a forensic unit. The room has been cleaned at least twice." Kyoto rued Japanese efficiency for the first time ever. "But I think they should inspect the carpet for any evidence." Tsukino agreed.

Kyoto's assistant entered the room and briefed her on the surveillance tapes. "We have the suspect entering the hotel at quarter to one in the afternoon and leaving again at half past one. He does not return until after eleven at night." That fit the time frame of the murders. "He is spotted again on tape with his luggage, and it is consistent with his checkout time of half past ten in the morning. The lobby camera shows the doorman helping him into a taxi."

"Find the doorman on duty. I need to find out where this man went."

Fortune joined Kyoto as the doorman was nabbed just before departing for the day. "Do you recognize this man?" She showed him the picture.

"An officer showed this picture to me last week. I do not recognize this person."

Kyoto took him by the arm and behind the scenes to the security cameras. She showed him the picture of Lyle checking in on the twenty-fourth and then a view of Lyle checking out on the twenty-fifth. Kyoto had the doorman watch the screen. The tape showed Lyle entering a cab and the doorman holding the door open and accepting a gratuity.

"I do remember this man." The doorman saw thousands of faces a day.

"Do you remember where this man went?"

"I do." His memory warmed. "He went to Narita."

Kyoto called Tsukino back. "He went to the airport."

Tsukino called airport security and started the hunt for Victor Kuyt.

JANUARY 1, 2014

C elia Nair heard the thumping bass vibrating through the ceiling. There were lots of people, and the smell of chemicals burned through and permeated the damp dark basement. Bound to the staircase, the chorus of "Happy New Year!" gave her a compass of time. Thirty-nine days had passed since she had been taken. She scratched at the post, marking another day. She balanced the days, her number accurate. Thirty-nine days since she had not seen her parents or fifteen-year-old sister, Jan. Thirty-nine days of living terrified of the next moment. She knew her parents were looking for her and were out of their minds worried. Why hadn't they found her? She asked the question every moment. She knew her sister was scared. But not as scared as she was. They did things to her. She feared they were going to kill her.

Celia wondered when they would come down to visit her next. They did almost every night. It usually happened when things got quieter and visitors left. Thirty-nine days of fighting the desire to die.

JANUARY 6
ARLINGTON, VIRGINIA

Madeline dressed to be as incognito as humanly possible. Despite not seeing anyone for more than two weeks, she felt someone at school would know about her "episode." This would be far too much attention. Madeline looked through her closet and found an innocuous pair of jeans, her new KDs to pacify her mom, and her Washington-Lee Generals hoodie.

"Madeline!" Sophia hollered from the bottom of the stairs. "Young lady, we are going to be late, and if you are late, I will be late!" Madeline had heard the same alarm a thousand times.

"I'm coming, Mom." Madeline threw herself together and faced her severe dread of the upcoming day.

Oliver bounced, ready to roll, spiffy in his new Christmas threads. His new Samsung in tow, the fifth grader prepared to rule the ten- and eleven-year-old minions. Oliver bounded into the front seat of the Navigator, and Madeline slunk behind him into the backseat.

Sophia spun the Lincoln out of the driveway and headed to Glebe Elementary School to disembark the king of the fifth graders.

Madeline said nothing, and her breathing accelerated. She took a deep breath and tried to control the growing anxiety. She would see Mackenzie Walters, her pseudo best friend, in first period. Mackenzie would give her the lay of the land in homeroom. She was hardwired to the school's gossip.

Traffic on Glebe Road flustered Sophia, and she cursed the red lights and poor drivers. She pulled into the kiss-and-ride and kissed Oliver, and he flew like from a slingshot out of the car. Madeline shifted in her seat as Sophia wheeled through the intersection toward Washington-Lee High School.

"Honey." Sophia looked through the rearview. "You are going to be just fine." Though Sophia wasn't so sure.

"I will be fine, Mom." Neither was Madeline.

Madeline kissed her mom through the driver's-side window and ventured off into the throngs of students gossiping and lying about their adventures with the opposite sex over the holidays. Madeline looked for Mackenzie, then peeked from underneath her hoodie. Adam Pooladi and Nick Harush turned their heads as she walked by, immediately talking and texting. The Kittens, a group of ultra-spoiled and ultrapretty girls, convened at the base of an oak and giggled as Madeline quickly passed, tucking deep back into her hoodie. She moved with impunity to her locker.

Sophia worked her way across the Roosevelt Bridge and glanced quickly at Watergate and the Kennedy Center. Traffic needed to pick up on this gloomy morning.

Raphael was already ensconced at his desk at the Department of State in Foggy Bottom. Raphael had made a fine career as a domestic civil servant. Sophia had to get to K Street and hit the ninth floor of Brewer and Smith. The environmental law firm had been good to her, and she to the firm. But today, when she got to work, her first phone call would be to Sylvia Smalling, the psychiatrist.

Madeline spun the face of her lock, and the bar popped open. She pulled out the notebooks and textbooks she needed for the first part of the day. Algebra II with Ms. Helen Mortimer, who had hatched out of the egg spouting equations. Earth Science with Mr. Avi Foster, the most uninteresting man in the world. Then Advanced Spanish with Mrs. Megan Jimenez. Mrs. Jimenez and Madeline got along, so Madeline enjoyed the class. Spanish came quickly to her, and she relished being Mrs. Jimenez's prize student.

"Hello, stranger!" Mackenzie arrived with the subtlety of a right hook. "You were off the planet over vacation. Everything OK?"

"Hi, Mackenzie." Madeline and Mackenzie gave each other a hug. "Everything is fine." Madeline felt that maybe Mackenzie hadn't heard.

"I heard you were in the hospital," Mackenzie whispered.

So much for the privacy. "Yes. I passed out on Christmas morning." Madeline didn't supply anything for Mackenzie to feed upon.

"That's intense! So what the hell happened?" Mackenzie drooled for the information that Madeline wasn't going to give.

"I don't know exactly what happened. I got real light-headed, and then I passed out. The doctor said it was something about my blood pressure." Madeline did not lie. "How did you find out?" Madeline researched the source of the spreading the news.

"My brother and his friend are friends with Oliver." Mackenzie applied a touch of eyeliner to her already colorful lids. "He texted them about Christmas Day and having to spend it in the hospital with you. He also said you were a bitch to your mom when you went skiing on New Year's."

Madeline tapped into the deepest part of her brain quickly to recall the vilest tortures of the medieval times. The brazen bull came to mind. A hollow replica of the animal made of brass, in which Oliver would be stuffed and have his tongue cut from his mouth. Then she would pile kindling all around the bull and light it on fire so the brass would ratchet up the heat, becoming an oven, and she and all of Arlington would gather to hear his screams. The iron maiden might be a better fate for the little blabbermouth. A coffin with spikes inside that when closed pierced the body, but only enough to let you bleed to death, not kill you immediately. Yes, she would make an iron maiden, just for Oliver. She and Mackenzie settled into homeroom.

Soon the bell rang, and students lurched out of their chairs and headed for their first class, all accounted for. Into the hallway, where it seemed every set of eyes stared at Madeline, she off to see Ms. Mortimer for Algebra II.

Sophia dialed Dr. Smalling's number. She did not reach her directly, but an appointment was available at half past three Thursday afternoon. She had Gail clear her calendar. Sophia checked her e-mails and called a few of the partners to update her calendar. Her secretary, Gail, neatly stacked her appointments and set a priority list on her desk.

JANUARY 7
TOKYO, JAPAN

The security tapes at Narita for December 26 gave them little. There were a few people who could have been Kuyt, but no one named Kuyt had checked in to the boarding area. Tsukino wondered if the doorman had been mistaken.

Tsukino fumed that, for once, technology had let him down. Facial-recognition technology had been placed in Narita and Haneda Airports in 2012, but it performed inconsistently. In fact, it was poor. The upgrade was approved as a plan to increase security for the Olympics in 2020, and the ministry set a target date of August 2014 to implement the new system and test it at the border gates.

Thousands and thousands of people flew through Narita Airport every day, and Tsukino seethed, frustrated that they had not been able to identify Victor Kuyt. Special agents from both the US and Japanese state departments checked for Kuyt and found no passport. What flight did he take? Tsukino had the passenger list for every flight leaving Narita on December 26 through December 30. His team looked at each individual picture of persons who flew on that day and the following days.

Kyoto knocked but walked right in with a portfolio of pictures the team had cross-referenced. Tsukino thumbed through the pages. He fumed that they had fallen so far behind. He drew his finger to one picture and then took it away. He dismissed several more. He sipped at some tea and looked into the blue eyes. "Blue. Crystal blue. Like the water of the islands." The doorman had said that. These were those eyes. These were Kuyt's eyes. These were the eyes of Dirk Mandi.

"Please, take this to the lab and remove the beard," Tsukino said to a technician standing nearby. "And take that mole off his face and give him a haircut. Then bring the image back to me." The technician moved quickly. "Kyoto. Add the alias Dirk Mandi to the report and issue it to the State Department in the United States and the FBI. Dirk Mandi took Japanese Airlines flight 952 to Los Angeles and landed on the twenty-fifth of December. He is wanted for a double homicide in Tokyo."

Tsukino didn't wait for the computer to reconfigure Kuyt or Mandi or whatever the name was. He had seen the eyes.

WEDNESDAY, JANUARY 8
SEA OF JAPAN

The USS *Mustin* steamed through the choppy surf in the Sea of Japan along with a strong contingent of the Seventh Fleet. CDR Matt Kexin stretched out onto his rack after being on deck for thirteen hours. Someone knocked on the door. "Come in," Kexin said, peeved.

Two seaman appeared behind the door as it was opened.

"Sorry to disturb you, sir." The seaman's red face matched his crimson hair. "Command sent out this likeness, sir." He handed the picture to Kexin. "This person is wanted for two murders in Tokyo." The passport photo was much more detailed than the gray images from the camera outside the bar or the grainy stills extracted from the hotel lobby camera. "They believe he is associated with the navy, sir!"

Kexin rolled out of bed and laced up his shoes. "That's because he is, son." He moved the seaman out of his way to grab a jacket. "That is Seaman Brandon Lyle, reported on unauthorized absence since just after Christmas." The two sailors stepped out of the commander's quarters to do their duty: report Seaman Brandon Lyle.

JANUARY 8
TOKYO, JAPAN

Tsukino read the report confirming the identity of the true killer, Seaman Brandon Lyle. He thought of Mao and Tiffany, their bodies long returned to their grieving families for the saddest of burials. Kyoto sent the information to the Naval Criminal Investigative Service Southwest Field Office in San Diego and the Federal Bureau of Investigation in Los Angeles, California.

Tsukino thanked Kyoto for her hard work on the case and asked her to pass down his appreciation to all of the officers who put in extra time to identify Lyle. They had forsaken their own families to help him hunt down this murderer. Tsukino couldn't help but feel he had not done enough to find Lyle more quickly. Almost two weeks had passed, and Lyle had a huge head start on the authorities in the United States. And he had escaped Japan. It was Tsukino's responsibility to find Lyle, and he had not done his job.

The light on the phone flickered, and Tsukino picked up the line.

"Tsukino."

"Masanori, it is Summer."

Tsukino was surprised to get a call from Summer but was delighted to hear her voice. "Hello, Summer. How may I help you?"

"I was contacted by a colleague in the Philippines. She received news of the murders of Mao and Tiffany and consulted me about a death near Tacloban in early December." Tsukino listened with curiosity. "The region is still in disarray after Typhoon Haiyan, and the medical services are still overmatched by the death and illness left by the storm. The body of a local woman was found eviscerated."

Tsukino felt a knot in his stomach. "Go ahead. I am listening."

Summer whispered into the phone for no good reason. "The locals blamed it on a black panther that had escaped from the local zoo during the storm. The panther became some type of urban myth, and when the girl's body was found in this condition, they blamed it on the cat."

"You don't think it was the cat, do you?"

"No. I don't. And neither do some of the local authorities. The locals hunted down the cat and killed it to collect the reward." Summer paused to gather herself. "They don't have any real clues as to who did this crime, but they are hesitant to announce to the public that there may be a killer among them. The streets are filled with fear as it stands."

"Why do you, or they, believe that it has anything to do with the deaths of Mao and Tiffany?" Tsukino was vetting Summer.

"Masanori, she was dissected completely at the waist." Tsukino's heart sank. "And, Masanori, she was pregnant."

Tsukino paused and gathered his wits. This Lyle person was going to do this again and again. "Summer."

"Yes." Summer waited for Tsukino's guidance.

"Have your friend in the Philippines send you the complete report of the autopsy."

"I will," Summer confirmed.

"And tell your friends that they do not have to fear a killer is among them. I know who he is." Tsukino took a short breath. "And he is no longer in the Philippines."

"Who is it, Masanori?"

"It is a US Navy seaman named Lyle. I will contact the base at Yokosuka and confirm he was in the Philippines in early December." Tsukino already knew the answer. "Thank you, Summer, for the information."

Summer softly said good-bye, and Tsukino hung up the phone. *Victim number three,* he thought to himself.

JANUARY 9
FEDERAL BUILDING,
LOS ANGELES, CALIFORNIA

Los Angeles was a world away from the FBI Academy in Quantico, Virginia. Agent Jeremy Alcott loved his Maui Jim shades and new Jeep Wrangler, a treat for himself after he'd finished his grueling tenure at the academy. The sun was out, and the top was down. His Jeep was a far cry from the Ford Crown Victoria they forced him to drive on the job.

Alcott stepped off the elevator and glided to his desk. His prescription transition lenses lightened only slightly, but hid his heterochromia iridium; his multi-colored eyes. Alcott liked his eyes. They were unique and different, but clerks and baristas would delay his day asking questions about his eyes. His opthamologist said his eyes folded all the colors of the universe into one. Alexander Khan, Alcott's boss, stood behind Alcott's desk. "Good morning, Alcott." Khan looked out the window toward Santa Monica and the Pacific.

"Good morning, sir." Alcott extended his hand and wondered why Khan was in his office.

"Japanese police in Tokyo and their customs department have identified a sailor with the Seventh Fleet as the main suspect of a double homicide in the Kabukicho district." Alcott's head spun around. "NCIS in San Diego has been notified, and one of their agents, Bruno Sommer, should be contacting you very shortly." Alcott looked at Khan, needing a little help, not quite awake at half past seven in the morning.

"There is a complete file on this sailor, Brandon Lyle, on your desk." Alcott opened the file and started to read. "I need you to find him, Alcott."

"Yes, sir." Alcott hesitated to ask the stupid question. "Do we know where he is?"

"Read the file, Alcott." Khan stepped away from the window and toward the door. "He got off a flight at LAX on Christmas Day. That's the last we know of his whereabouts."

Christmas Day, thought Alcott, *an eternity of time for a fugitive.* Khan left the office, and Alcott raced through the files. He read Tsukino's report about Mao Iniesta and Tiffany Kai. The dossier detailed their gruesome deaths.

He turned the page and saw Lyle's pale, deadly blue eyes. Something primal triggered in Alcott's brain. The honest eyes of an assassin. Alcott had only ever hoped for a case like this. He had trained for this.

Alcott continued to look at Lyle's files.

"Jeremy, can you pick up line two?" Chardonnay Rahmani, Alcott's secretary, appeared in the doorway and stepped into the room with the inter-office mail. Chardonnay smiled and smacked the gum she was chewing, and Alcott responded with a polite "Good morning, Chardonnay." Jeremy didn't want to encourage her. Chardonnay flirted with him, but he had been taught not to get mail and tail in the same place. Despite her rocking body,

Chardonnay's squeaky voice and material-girl mantra were simply not his thing. Thank goodness for her efficiency.

"Alcott," he answered line two while Chardonnay continued to smile at him.

"Jeremy Alcott?" The voice on the other end broke up.

"Yeah. This is Jeremy Alcott."

"Bruno Sommer, NCIS."

"Uh, hello, Agent Sommer. I was expecting your call." Alcott reached for a pen or pencil. Chardonnay got up and handed him one of each as well as a pad. She looked down at him over the desk and smiled, her sweater pulled tight. Jeremy blinked his appreciation.

"Looks like we have some work to do, young man." Alcott listened to Sommer through the static.

"Where are you? You sound like you're on Mars." Alcott really needed to talk to this guy.

"I am on the 405. I will be at your office in about forty-five minutes." This guy worked fast.

"OK, I will see you when you get here." Alcott had woken up feeling great, and now he felt like he had missed a week. He scrambled to finish reading the report.

"Chardonnay?" She turned from her desk and winked at Jeremy. "Can you get forensics to pull the videotape from LAX on Christmas Day?"

"Mr. Khan already got a team on that, Jeremy." Chardonnay blew a bubble and looked back at her computer, her giant gold hoop earrings tangled in her hair. Jeremy hustled to catch up to Khan.

Jeremy thumbed through the file and tracked Lyle's basic history from childhood and his arrest record through NCIN, a criminal database. Lyle had been arrested twice, once for assault and once for possession. Lyle was a suspect in the cold case of Sienna Fucile, a sixteen-year-old found murdered on the beach near Venice, California. Lyle had been scrutinized, but authorities could not find DNA or fingerprints to link him to the crime, though witnesses had placed him with the girl earlier that evening.

"Chardonnay, see if you can contact a Detective Jorge Rimando." Alcott wanted to speak to the detective who'd been on the Sienna Fucile case.

Alcott continued to look at Lyle's file. Born January 17, 1994. Five feet nine inches and 155 pounds. Hair, blond. Eyes, blue. Wiry build and the beginning of a tattoo on his back shoulder. Alcott couldn't help but look into those eyes. Lyle had not finished high school, but he'd taken his GED and suddenly joined the US Navy in 2012 just after his eighteenth birthday, shortly after the Fucile case went cold.

Lyle's parents were of note as well. Raylene Lyle. Thirty-eight. A real piece of work. Alias Raylene Stewart and now Raylene De Vry. It seemed she went through husbands as easily as the Jack in the Box drive-through. Multiple counts of class-one narcotics. Multiple court-mandated appearances at rehab. A regular at the Los Angeles County jail. A true junkie. The arrest photos created a time lapse of Raylene's physical deterioration, showing each tooth that seemed to fall out of her head every time she'd gotten a mug shot.

Lyle's father was no prince. Bernard "Bernie" Lyle. Forty. Arsonist and thief. Drug addict and fighter. But Bernie wasn't going to be causing the public any problems in the near future: he was locked up in Pelican Bay for burning down a Mattress Heaven in Torrance in an insurance scam, and for throwing a Molotov cocktail into a Vons grocery store in West Covina after the clerk wouldn't sell him beer for not having an ID. Three people were burned seriously, and the store was almost completely destroyed. Along with being a firebug, Bernie was a dyed-in-the-wool drug addict, a racist, and a known member of the Aryan Brotherhood. *Sweet parents,* Alcott surmised on Lyle's behalf. But it didn't look like the apple fell too far from the tree.

Alcott studied Lyle's known associates.

Elroy Floyd. Nineteen. Caucasian. Five feet five inches and 145 pounds. Eyes, green. Hair, light brown or shaved. Gauge-style earrings. Floyd had the numbers 14 and 88 tattooed to his left forearm. The 14 represented the number of words in a quotation of former Nazi leader David Lane: "We must secure the existence of our people and a future for white children." The 88 stood for the eighth letter of the alphabet, which was *H*. Two *H*s were *HH*, or *Heil Hitler*. Suspended from Northeast High School near Glendale for blowing up a series of urinals in the men's bathroom with M-80s. Never finished high school and joined the white supremacist gang the Nazi Lowriders. Subsequently arrested several times for possession of blasting caps, dynamite, and material to make explosives. Just released on bail from county for possession of explosives.

Sadie Davil. Twenty. Caucasian. Five feet seven inches and 115 pounds. Eyes, brown. Hair, black. Tattoo of a boa constrictor wrapped completely around her waist and shoulders and eventually around her neck. Lyle's high school girl. A known madam and prostitute, she had developed an eclectic clientele that enjoyed her especially painful idea of sexuality. Davil's record listed distribution, pandering, obscenity, and prostitution. She was acquitted of a charge of pimping her sister to do lewd acts for a USC professor. Her sister would not testify.

Rohit Guzan. Twenty. Indian. Five feet eight inches and 165 pounds. Eyes, brown. Hair, black. No distinguishing marks. Met Lyle at Northeast High School with Davil and Floyd. Computer wizard suspected in several identity thefts and the complete shutdown of the Northeast High School computer system, which was brought down by a virus known as "the Beetle." Prosecutors could never peg Guzan for the crimes, though he remained the main suspect. Guzan was a known collector of guns large and small.

Javad Nehwal. Twenty-one. Classified as an African American, but no one was sure of his race. Six feet eight inches and 275 pounds. Eyes, brown. Hair, black but balding. Mexican Mafia tattoos on various sections of his body. Known steroid abuser. Violent and angry. Javad was thrown out of Northeast as a sophomore for pummeling another student for "looking at him the wrong way." Nehwal spent time in the California juvenile system and was released as an adult. Nehwal took the unpredictable turn of joining the Mexican Mafia; though he was not Latino by birth, they welcomed him with open arms, as legend has it, "because they were too frightened not to" and certainly did not want this angry behemoth to join a rival gang. Convicted for possession of anabolic steroids. Out on probation.

"Jeremy," Chardonnay buzzed on the intercom. Alcott could see Chardonnay's desk through the glass partition. "Line three." It was probably the navy stiff caught in traffic.

"Alcott." Jeremy kept one eye on Lyle's file.

"Mr. Alcott?" It wasn't Sommer.

"This is Agent Alcott. Who is this?"

"My name is Detective Masanori Tsukino. I have been handling the case of Seaman Brandon Lyle here in Tokyo."

Alcott sat straight up in his chair. He tried Tsukino's name but struggled with the pronunciation, and Tsukino struggled with his English. "It is good to hear from you, Detective Tsukino," Alcott finally managed. "Thank you for all of your efforts."

"I am afraid I have not done enough. Lyle is still, how do you say, 'on the run.'"

Jeremy paused. "Yes, sir, he is still on the run, but you have given us a terrific start."

Suddenly an older gentleman with a touch of gray in his sideburns and around his ears stepped through the doorjamb. Chardonnay turned and looked through the glass and mouthed the name *Bruno Sommer.* Alcott had figured that out. Jeremy shook Sommer's hand while clenching the phone between his shoulder and chin. "Detective Tsukino, I am putting you on speaker. Agent

Sommer from NCIS has joined me. We will be working together on this case."

"Agents Sommer and Alcott, as you know, we have been working on this case since the twenty-fifth of December and have been slow to find out the true identity of this Seaman Lyle." Alcott let Tsukino proceed. "Commander Kexin of the USS *Mustin* called Yokosuka and allowed us access to Lyle's belongings. I believe there is something you need to see."

"Tsukino? Did you find the murder weapon?" Alcott guessed at this while he watched Chardonnay listen through the glass.

"Agent Alcott, maybe I misspoke. It is something you need to read. We found a journal with Lyle's belongings."

"Can you make a copy and send it to us by e-mail?" Bruno chimed in.

"I anticipated this and just want to confirm your e-mail."

Alcott confirmed the secure e-mail address and thanked Detective Tsukino, informing him they would call back if needed. They waited for the little sound that would indicate a new e-mail.

"Agent Alcott."

"Agent Sommer." Bruno sat and opened his files. "Have you caught up on your morning reading?"

"I have. There is a nasty little bug running around the southland. Looks like he is back on his home turf."

"Yes, sir. And my money is on him wanting to go see his momma after arriving on Christmas Day." Alcott detected a small twang in Sommer's accent.

"South Carolina?"

"North Carolina. But that's a damn good guess." The ding of a new e-mail sounded, and Alcott opened the attachment sent by Tsukino. Sommer read over Alcott's shoulder, Alcott thankful Sommer chewed gum to mask his atrocious breath.

I am a constant. I come to the surface to serve you and you alone. It pleases me to do your wish. I yearn to sit at your feet.

I have ridden with armies before, intent on the slaughter of a race. With glee I watched as humankind turned on itself for wealth and power at the expense of life. I return as the general of my own army, intent on igniting the world into a furnace of hatred and self-destruction. My reward is to please him *by destroying his enemies. Thou hast gifted to me the taste of human flesh, and savor it I shall. It is my indulgence.*

An abomination of an animal. A race that hides behind its own God to justify its fear. How weak a creation he hath made. I am here to fan the flames of hatred and destruction that have persisted for eons. To help put them out of their misery and watch them scorch the earth and create a lifeless, desolate planet. I am here to show them that there is more peace in death and flame than in the false hope of life and God's dishonest promise. To feast on a carcass in hell is far better than to slave at the feet of an impotent ruler.

Alcott and Sommer stared at the diatribe, mouths agape. Jeremy buzzed Chardonnay. "Can you ask Mr. Khan to join us?" Chardonnay put down the Crystal Light mixture she was drinking and contacted the boss.

Alcott and Sommer reviewed their notes together. "We have Lyle in the Philippines on the nineteenth of December, and the slaying of Esther Perez is consistent with the death of Mao Iniesta in Tokyo on the twenty-fourth."

"The killing of Tiffany Kai is not consistent with the other two," Sommer noted.

"I think Tiffany was just in the way."

"I agree. Lyle wanted Mao for a reason. A specific reason."

Alcott adjusted his glasses and lightly massaged the chronic ache in his front left shoulder. "But why?"

"I don't know," Sommer conceded.

Sommer poured some coffee with a touch of cream and a Sweet'n Low. "Tsukino did good work."

"The bouncer and the street camera." Alcott turned the page.

"The tattoo artist and the videotape from the hotel."

"The passport bothers me." Alcott felt there was something more sinister going on. "This is post-9/11, and we have an American sailor who has at least three aliases that we know of. He has a California driver's license with the name Victor Kuyt. He has a Dutch passport with the name Dirk Mandi that was approved at Narita. I don't feel that safe right now." An image of the World Trade Center collapsing ran through his mind.

"He has some help." Sommer rued the reality of an unsafe world.

"That help doesn't come from these clowns who he pals around with." Alcott rubbed his eyes.

"I don't know if that's true." Sommer's experience had proven different. "Davil, Guzan, Nehwal, and Floyd. One-on-one, each of them is bad enough, but their tentacles and influence could easily drape into subcultures and dark corners."

Alcott knew Sommer was right. "We will look into that later."

Khan entered the room. Sommer and Khan had worked together before on a drug smuggling case with the USS *Jefferson City* submarine in Port Loma.

"It's good to see you, Alexander." On a first-name basis with the boss. Alcott rolled his eyes behind his darkened transition lenses.

"Bruno!" Khan extended both arms for a bear hug. "How are Linda and the kids?"

"They are terrific." Sommer exhaled after being released from the bear hug. "Linda and the kids send their love. Well, the kids aren't really kids anymore. Stan is thirteen, and Abby is ten."

"Has it been that long?" Khan looked hard at his old friend. "You look good."

"You too, Alexander."

Jeremy broke up the reunion. "Mr. Khan. We received some disturbing papers from Lyle's journal. Detective Tsukino e-mailed them over, and I would like them to be analyzed by a forensic psychiatrist."

"I will give them to Dr. Ariel Senderos." Chardonnay handed an eyes-only copy of Lyle's journal to Khan.

"What's next?"

"We are going to review the videotape at LAX and see if we can get anything from that."

JANUARY 9
ARLINGTON, VIRGINIA

Sophia called the front office of Washington-Lee High School, and Madeline waited for her mother in the office. Madeline did not utter a word on the drive to the doctor.

Soft blue shades decorated Dr. Smalling's office, and the receptionist smiled brightly as the two entered the room. Madeline remained tucked deep inside her hoodie and found a corner portion of the couch. Sophia exchanged her insurance card for a clipboard and joined Madeline.

"I am not crazy." The voice came from inside the hoodie.

"No one said you were, Madeline." Sophia clicked the pen. "Dr. Saito recommended you see a psychologist."

"Because he thinks I am crazy."

"No!" Sophia tried to focus on the medical sheet. "It's because he isn't sure why you fainted, and he believes it could be stress related."

"I am stressed because Oliver told everybody that I was in the hospital and that I ruined Christmas."

Sophia turned to her not-so-sweet child. "Madeline. I will speak with Oliver. In the meantime you need to be honest with this Dr. Smalling, and maybe we can find out what is bothering you and this will all be over."

Sophia could see Madeline's pupils inside the shadows of the hood, her eyes dark and lifeless.

The door opened, and a chipper short-haired blond woman with a suit the shade of soft pink approached the Deschampses.

"Hello. My name is Dr. Smalling."

"It is nice to meet you, Dr. Smalling." Sophia smiled, looked down at the doctor, and removed her Prada eyeglasses. "My name is Sophia. This is my daughter, Madeline."

Madeline slowly unraveled from the couch and offered Dr. Smalling her dead fish handshake.

"It's nice to meet you, Madeline."

"It is nice to meet you too," Madeline lied. She tried to sit back down but was immediately reeled upward by Sophia's grasp.

"May I call you Sophia?" inquired Smalling.

"Of course."

They settled on the couch. "Since Madeline is eighteen, she does not need a parent present in the room. In fact, I think we would achieve better results if we were able to spend time alone."

"I agree."

"Madeline." Smalling noted that Madeline paid no attention to her. "I do need to let you know that while we are working with you and your anxiety, it is important that your parents are completely in the loop." Finally Madeline nodded. "There may be times when it is beneficial for all of us be in the room to talk about any issues we discover."

"OK," Madeline agreed.

Madeline and Dr. Smalling retreated to her office. Madeline sat pensively in the armchair in front of Smalling's desk.

"Where do you go to school, Madeline?" Smalling settled into her chair.

"Washington-Lee High School."

"Not too far from here."

"No."

"How are you doing in school?"

Madeline thought of her mother's request to be honest. "I could be doing better. My last report card was not that great."

"Do you want to go to college?" Smalling relaxed in her chair, holding a pad and pencil.

"I have applications out."

"To which schools?"

"James Madison. Radford. VCU and I sent an application to UVA, late."

"Which school do you think you have the best chance of getting into?"

"Probably none of them." Madeline shrugged.

"You applied to each for a reason, correct?" Smalling jotted something on the pad, catching Madeline's attention.

"I suppose. Probably because my parents wanted me to."

"Why VCU?"

"VCU has a good art school." Madeline fiddled with her hoodie.

"Are you good at art?" The winter sun silhouetted Smalling's hair.

"I don't know. I used to think I was good, but there are so many people who are better."

"Madeline. Would you mind taking off your hoodie? I would like to see your face."

Madeline slid the garment back off her head. Smalling noticed the plethora of studs and earrings in both ears, and the floppy mess that covered a beautiful face with high cheekbones and deep dark eyes. Smalling noticed that Madeline was not wearing makeup. The choice of the baggy loose-fitting clothes told a story.

"What is the thing that you are best at?" Smalling continued.

Madeline looked straight down. "Nothing, really."

Dr. Smalling made a note. "Why James Madison University?"

"That's where a lot of my friends applied, so I figured I would apply too."

"Is there a specific curriculum JMU has that interests you?"

"No. Not really." Madeline worked her hands in a slight wringing motion.

"Why did you list the University of Virginia last?" Smalling was curious.

"Oh. There is no way I could get into UVA. I'm not smart enough for that. I did it for my dad."

"Does your dad put a lot of pressure on you to go to UVA? Or a really good school?"

Madeline's voice chirped for the first time in the session. "No. Daddy is very supportive. That is where he went to college, and he took me there to visit last spring."

"Does your mother drive you to go to a good school?"

"No. Mom cares a lot, but she is very busy with work."

"Your mom works a lot?"

"Yeah. She is an attorney with Brewer and Smith."

Dr. Smalling continued to make notes. "Why Radford?"

"Everybody gets into Radford. Hopefully I can get in there. They say it is a party school."

Smalling went with the flow. "Do you like to party, Madeline?"

"Not really."

"Have you ever been to a party?"

"Sure. Mackenzie has lots of parties. I've been to those. Nick Harush had a party at his house once." Smalling noticed that Madeline's eyes did not spark when she mentioned the parties.

"What did you do at these parties?"

"Not much."

"Were people drinking beer?"

"Sure."

"Were they smoking pot?"

"Some do."

"Did you drink beer or alcohol?"

"I have," Madeline stated frankly.

"Did you get drunk?" Smalling wanted to see how far Madeline had gone.

"I got a bit tingly at Nick Harush's house. But I wouldn't say I got drunk."

"Did you smoke pot?"

"I tried it once. It didn't do anything for me. It made me sleepy." Smalling looked at Madeline's passive reaction to the questions.

"How about boys?"

"Do you mean to ask if I have a boyfriend?" Madeline responded stoically.

"Yes. Do you have a boyfriend?"

"No. I do not have a boyfriend," Madeline stated flatly.

"Do you hook up with boys?" Madeline was kind of surprised Dr. Smalling knew what *hook up* meant.

"No."

"No? As in 'I don't hook up with boys' or 'I have never hooked up with boys'?"

"I don't hook up with boys. I don't care if other girls do it. I don't think they are sluts or anything. I just haven't found the right boy. I guess I'm picky." Madeline adjusted herself in the chair.

"Have you ever been on a date?"

Madeline cocked her head. "Yes. I went on a date with Austin Lee."

"How do you know Austin?"

"We've known each other since middle school."

"Were you interested in going on a date with him?"

"Not really. He asked me if I would like to see a movie with him, and I said yes." Madeline rubbed her knees.

"How did that go?" Smalling turned the light down a shade.

"He took me to see *The Hunger Games: Catching Fire* at Ballston Common."

"Did you enjoy *The Hunger Games?*"

"It was all right. It's not real. It's just a movie."

"Do you identify with Katniss?"

"No. She is the hero."

"Which character do you identify with?"

"I suppose Rue. The little girl who dies."

Dr. Smalling got back on track with the date. "Where did Austin take you after the movie?"

"We stayed in the mall and got milk shakes."

"Did he drive you home?"

"Yes, although I could have walked."

"Did Austin try to kiss you?" Smalling looked for a reaction and got a small blush.

"He did." Madeline pulled her hands inside her sleeves.

"Did you like it?"

"I wouldn't let him. I was going to, but it didn't feel right." Madeline paused. "I pulled away."

Smalling waited for Madeline to expound, but nothing ever came. "Did this upset him?"

Madeline recounted how disappointed Austin had been. He had been a perfect gentleman all evening, and they'd truly enjoyed the movie and the milk shakes. She'd had a good time, but when it had come to kissing him or any other boy, she just wasn't that interested. She didn't know why; it was just that way.

"Are there any boys in school you would want to kiss you?"

"No," Madeline responded quickly.

Smalling took a chance. "Are there any girls you would want to kiss you?"

Madeline's face remained placid. "No."

Smalling decided to change course. "What do you want to be when you grow up, Madeline?"

"I don't know. I just want to get out of high school at this point."

"Do you play sports?"

"I run cross-country."

"Do you enjoy that?"

"I used to." Madeline looked out the window.

"You don't anymore?" Smalling closed the curtain.

"I always feel like I am running in mud. Not going anywhere."

"Are there any other sports you've enjoyed?"

"We went skiing over the break. That was a disaster. I sucked. And of course, Oliver was a whiz. Flying down the hill like he was born on skis."

"Oliver is your brother?" Smalling knew this answer.

"Yes. Oliver is my annoying brother."

"Why is Oliver annoying?"

"Because he is Oliver. He is always in my business." Madeline's face remained still. "He texted everyone that I was in the hospital over the holidays."

"Is that so terrible?" Smalling asked. "Maybe some of your friends were concerned about you."

"In our school no one is really worried about anyone else. Everyone just wants to be the one with the scoop on someone else's problems. Then they can talk about you behind your back. It's a mean world." Madeline curled up in the chair.

Dr. Smalling stared at the girl with the chocolate eyes who struggled to enjoy life.

A small chime sounded, and the initial visit of Madeline and Dr. Smalling ended. Smalling asked if Sophia could come into her office. Madeline retreated to the waiting room.

"How did the visit go, Dr. Smalling?"

"It was very productive. As I mentioned in the waiting room, I would expect to have several visits before I can properly diagnose Madeline, but I believe she is suffering from a bit of depression and anxiety. During the process it is essential to find the source of this anxiety."

"Of course."

"Madeline displayed negative feelings about herself. She doesn't feel she is college worthy. Her general appearance suggests that she thinks she is not worth looking at. The hoodie. The hair falling in her face. She has strong negative feelings about herself and at least some of her classmates."

"Isn't this fairly normal for teenagers and high school in general?"

"Some of it is very normal. But when a lot of these feelings exist together, it is a sign of a deeper problem. During the session Madeline was very passive. She expressed her negativity with certain aspects of her world, but she was emotionally numb overall. She was not positive about any topic we touched upon."

"That hasn't always been the case, Doctor." Sophia removed her blazer.

"That's a good sign, Sophia. We need to find out when these changes began. You could be helpful with that. Maybe you could find some time to jot down some notes about when her behavior began to shift."

Sophia became flushed and struggled to determine when Madeline's mood really started to change. Between work and more work. *How could she have let this happen?* "I will do that for you, Dr. Smalling." Sophia opened her purse and looked for her phone. "What do we do next?"

"I would like to see Madeline again in two weeks."

"What do we do in the meantime?"

"Your daughter has anxiety, not malaria. All of this came to light in the last few weeks. Monitor Madeline for the hypertension. The sudden anxiety is what we should worry about most, but she never had an episode before Christmas and hasn't had one since. What we should do is continue therapy and find the root of the anxiety."

Sophia scheduled the meeting in her phone and thanked the doctor. "One last question, Dr. Smalling."

"Yes?" Smalling looked up from her desk.

"Did you discuss her dreams?"

"Not yet. I believe our session went well today, and we established some trust. Dreams are complicated and often misleading. It doesn't mean they are not real for the person having them, but it will take more confidence for Madeline to express her feelings about her dreams."

LOS ANGELES, CALIFORNIA

Images of Seaman Brandon Lyle and all known associates flashed through the Internet at the speed of light, posted on every law-enforcement site in the world. The search for the candy-apple-red Lexus and Lyle had begun.

Alcott and Sommer entered the Coffee Roaster in Sherman Oaks. Detective Rimando waited for them and for his nuclear-hot black coffee to cool at a table in the corner. Sommer got a round of java and joined Alcott and Rimando.

"Detective, we are following up on a case from 2009. Sienna Fucile."

Rimando poked a hole in the paper napkin. "That brings up a lot of bad memories, gentlemen. It has taken a long time to get that out of my head," Rimando reflected on the grisly murder.

"Can you give us some details?" asked Sommer.

Rimando composed himself. "She was just a kid. Some stoners said they heard screams coming from down the beach. They found her on the sand just south of Venice." Rimando started to unravel. "Her sundress was pulled over her head, and…" Snot started to pour from the deputy's nose. "And there was blood everywhere on the sand. She looked perfect from the waist up, but he destroyed her down there." Rimando sobbed. "Like he went in there with a shovel."

"Was she pregnant?" Alcott pursued the issue as gently as he could.

Rimando seemed surprised by the question. "The autopsy did not reveal that she was pregnant." Rimando took a moment. "What is this all about? Is there new evidence? Did that creep Lyle do something else?"

Alcott and Sommer looked at each other. "Maybe. There were three murders overseas, and Lyle is a suspect. These have similar causes of death to that of Sienna Fucile. And Lyle is back in the United States."

Rimando pored through his mental notes. "We knew it was him, but there was no physical evidence. Nothing. No saliva. No semen. No DNA. Not even a fingerprint."

"That was a pretty messy crime scene. Was there blood on Lyle?"

"Not a drop."

"What was his alibi?"

"He admitted to being with the girl on the walk. She was with some friends. He was with some friends. They were drinking near their cars and hanging out. Lyle went for a walk on the beach with Sienna. Nine people confirmed this. They walked about a mile down the beach. About an hour later these junkies heard some screams. They ran down the beach to find out what was going on, and they found Sienna."

"Where was Lyle?"

"Lyle was sitting in the sand about a hundred yards farther down the beach. No one knew he was there. He just sat in the shadows. Even when the first officers arrived, they secured the scene, and a deputy walked down the beach looking for clues. That's when they found Lyle. The deputy said it looked like Lyle was in a trance."

"How did he explain what happened to Sienna?"

"He said he had no idea." Rimando wiped his face. "He said that she was feeling dizzy and wanted to sit for a moment. Lyle said he walked farther down the beach to think."

"That's a pretty lame excuse." Sommer finished his coffee.

"Yep. Very lame. I took him in with me for more questioning, and he never varied from his story." Rimando looked at Alcott and Sommer. "He even passed a lie detector test. He gave us samples of hair and saliva." Rimando paused. "That kid never cried. Never blinked. Never asked for a lawyer. Never called his mom or dad. There was no sadness or remorse over Sienna's death. He just stared at us with those cold blue eyes. I felt like he was laughing at us."

"How long did you hold him?"

"For a few days. Eventually a public defender came, and we all knew we had no evidence. No weapon and no blood. Not even an eyelash. The district attorney was as frustrated as we were. We didn't even file the complaint. It was like a ghost came out of the ocean and bored that girl to death."

Alcott and Sommer found Raylene's house somewhere between the base of the Verdugo Mountains and hopelessness. They knocked on the slightly opened door.

"Raylene?" No one responded, but the cloud of acrid smoke indicated she was there.

"Raylene?" Sommer edged the door open. "This is NCIS agent Sommer and FBI agent Alcott. We are not here to see you. We want to know about your son, Lyle."

Raylene cackled and spat. "What do you want with him?"

Alcott and Sommer eased into the living room. Raylene lay in the fetal position, naked, the glass pipe still hot from the hit she'd just taken. Raylene's lithe and corroded body jerked like a snake that had just been killed. They stepped over debris and found a sweater to cover Raylene's exposed body. She threw it off herself.

"Raylene!" Alcott called.

She rolled over, her mad eyes focused on the young agent.

"Have you seen your son?"

She laughed again, sending herself into a coughing convulsion. Gray sputum oozed out of the corners of her mouth and dripped onto the floor; some of it lay like cursed Jell-O on her skeletal cheeks. "I saw him."

"Do you know where he is?"

"He is everywhere."

"Do you know where he is staying? Or who he is staying with?"

"He goes wherever he wants." Raylene reached feebly for the couch, trying to pull herself off the floor.

"Do you know if he is still in Los Angeles?"

"How the hell should I know?" Raylene slunk to the couch, showing the agents even more than they'd bargained for. Alcott almost lost the sausage and egg McMuffin he had had for breakfast.

"Your son is in a lot of trouble." Sommer eased closer to Raylene.

"You're in a lot of trouble." Raylene smiled wryly, offering her cracked smile.

"If you love him, you will help him." Alcott pleaded with Lyle's mother.

"Love!" Raylene harangued the agents with mocking laughter. "There is no love in that child's heart. There is only death. It is his birthright."

Raylene curled up on the couch, happy to be properly medicated for the time being. She closed her eyes and slipped away from the harsh light of day.

JANUARY 11
LOS ANGELES, CALIFORNIA

Lyle's beard prickled on his face, and his hair had grown enough that he had to groom it. The heat seared the sidewalk near the Windjammers Yacht Club in Marina del Rey. Just the way he liked it. Sadie Davil spotted Lyle on the sidewalk and removed herself from her cocktail at the bar. They headed to the dock and boarded the ninety-seven-foot state-of-the-art vessel *Trigger*, the private vessel of Congressman Danny Motta.

"I thought you said you would be coming alone, Sadie." The congressman spun his portly frame around in the chair.

"I planned to, but I had a friend who very much wanted to meet you." Davil introduced Lyle.

Guzan, Floyd, and the muscular Nehwal boarded the boat.

"And who are these"—Motta hesitated—"other people?"

"Let's get going." Lyle put the cruise in motion.

"This is my boat, and I tell people when we are going or not going," Motta protested, and reached for his phone. Nehwal pinned his arm against the wall. Motta whimpered. "Sadie, what's going on?"

"Congressman." Sadie tapped him on the nose. "You and I agreed to talk business. Since you are such a good client of mine, I thought you might want to meet some of my friends. I think you will find what they have to say very interesting."

Guzan navigated the boat out of the harbor and headed south toward Catalina Island. Lyle stood next to him, looking out to the endless Pacific. "The feds are looking for us. We are all over the scanners and the Internet." Guzan noted.

"I am surprised that it took them this long," Lyle said. "We will be leaving very soon. Arrange for transportation and identification." Guzan nodded. "And new phones," Lyle added. He sat with the petrified congressman in the stateroom of the craft.

"Danny 'Trigger' Motta," Lyle mused. "'Vote for Danny Motta—he's not afraid to pull the trigger on what's right for California.' Isn't that right, Danny?"

"Yes. That's right. What is this all a-about?" stammered the five-term congressman.

"This is about you and your political future." Lyle took an apple from the fruit basket and polished it on his shirt. "This is about how I own you, Congressman."

"Own me! What the hell are you talking about?"

Davil pressed play on the DVD player.

The congressman protested for naught. "You bitch. You set me up." He glared at Davil. Davil gleamed.

"No one set you up, Congressman. That's all you on that screen. You and the boy." Nehwal forced Motta's head up and made him look at the video. "Little Gregory Jefferies. How you sodomized him in the lavatory while your wife entertained 'your friend' Congressman

Jefferies and the lot of rotten politicians. I am sure the nation would love to see that on YouTube." Lyle crunched. "This is a good apple."

Motta pleaded inside the cabin as the yacht moved down the sunny Pacific coast. "What do you want from me? Money? I can get you money."

Lyle was amused. "For these sins you cannot repent. You shall spend eternity as a servant of Satan."

Lyle left Javad with Motta and stepped out onto the deck. Catalina loomed in the horizon, and Guzan slowed the ship. From the portside, another grand yacht slowed, meaning to join them. Floyd helped the lengthy beauty *Sonrisa de la Madre* join the *Trigger*, his attention broken by the stunning teenage girl that stretched gloriously on the bow. Misty Vika, a world-class piece of ass.

Javad moved the congressman aboard the waiting ship. Abel Sakai peered through his binoculars, looking for any law-enforcement ships or aircraft that might be lurking in the distance. "Misty," Sakai commanded the beauty, "would you bring me some Macallan?" The skies were clear, and the sea was calm. He looked at Lyle. "Why do bring a stranger on my ship?"

Sakai headed the powerful European ORBIS Cartel. The legion had arranged the clandestine business meeting for Lyle.

ORBIS was a network that supplied weapons to organizations and governments in every continent. Funded through heroin smuggling across all borders throughout the twentieth century, ORBIS had become a global player after World War II.

"Did you bring what I asked for?" Lyle requested of Sakai.

"Did you bring me what I asked for?" parried Sakai.

"I brought you something far greater." Lyle treated Sakai with respect. He did a good job for the legion. Lyle looked at the politician. "This is Congressman Danny Motta, from the state of California."

Sakai looked bemused. "For what reason do I need a hostage?"

"He is no hostage. He is yours. A slave on market. Sold for the price of his lust."

Lyle handed Sakai the DVD. "You own him. You own his considerable influence. You own his vote. It is worth far more than the codes you seek."

Sakai looked at the pitiful congressman kneeling before him like a trained dog. "I need real-time information from the FBI and Interpol on ORBIS and all the cartels operating in the Western Hemisphere." Sakai sipped on the scotch. "I need you to broker a deal that releases a few of my friends from your heinous prison system." He stepped gently on Motta's hands.

"Anything is possible," Motta reassured.

Sakai handed Motta a list of international criminals working for ORBIS. Lucia Cassano, a prisoner at the Central California Women's Facility and Sakai's granddaughter. Peter Benayoun, his longtime associate and an ORBIS leader convicted on weapons charges. Guatram Blind, the ORBIS accountant in a federal prison in Kentucky.

Lyle handed Sakai an envelope with pictures of Motta's wife and children. "If the tape fails, then kill his family."

Javad and Floyd moved the crates from the *Sonrisa de la Madre* to the *Trigger* as the boats wafted gently in the tide. Guzan started the engines and released the lines. Sakai watched his investment float away and pondered how much interest his congressman would pay.

Lyle inspected each crate. Three Uzi Action Arms IMI carbine nine-millimeter rifles. Twelve Mossberg 500 A Pistol Grip Persuaders twelve-gauge shotguns. Twelve SIG Sauer M11-A1 pistols. Twelve Mexican FX-05 assault rifles. Twelve German Heckler & Koch G41 assault rifles. Twelve Israeli IMI Tavor TAR-21 assault rifles.

Ammunition and guns galore. The gifts from Sakai pleased his crew.

"Equal opportunity killers. What else?" Floyd fondled the abundance of toys.

"This should make you very happy." Guzan showed Floyd the twenty-five pounds of Semtex and two hundred sticks of good old-fashioned dynamite.

Javad sifted through the wrapped stacks of one-hundred-dollar bills. The last crate contained two million in cash. They would need the spending money.

The last rays of daylight fell on Marina del Rey. Lyle had what he needed. They left the congressman on the *Trigger.*

JANUARY 13
ATLANTA, GEORGIA
FORD DENIED BAIL

The Atlanta Journal-Constitution—Bayleigh Debuchy

Massive crowds flooded the lawn at the Fulton County Courthouse for the preliminary hearing of defendant Horace Ford in the murder case of Georgia State freshman Savannah Green.

Ford, accompanied by his attorney, Eva Jo Diamond, appeared before the bench of Charlotte Wilshire. Prosecuting attorney Leo Gargano presented evidence against Ford, and Judge Wilshire confirmed that there was sufficient evidence to support the charges against Ford.

Diamond argued that Ford should be granted the right to have bail, but Wilshire declined the request.

"The case against Horace Ford is a strong case, and we are on the right path. Judge Wilshire has made accurate decisions through the whole court process, and now we will work on setting a trial date with the superior court," noted prosecuting attorney Leo Gargano.

JANUARY 16
ARLINGTON VIRGINIA

Dr. Smalling sat with Madeline for another hour. Madeline had taken the time to dye the front of her hair blond and shave the back tight to the neck. The makeup shadowed her face, heavy and deep around her eyes and cheeks. Smalling asked Madeline several times to remove the hood. Madeline shoved the hood behind her head and shifted in the chair.

Smalling prodded with gentle questions in an effort to continue to lay a foundation of trust. Madeline's responses continued to be flat and self-derogatory. Madeline exhibited some guilt. Or at least some shame at the events of Christmas. Dr. Smalling reassured her that she should bear no such guilt.

"How have you been sleeping?"

"All right." Madeline rolled her eyes.

"'All right'? Do you wake up chipper? Rested and ready for the day?" Smalling smiled with the enthusiasm of a first-year camp counselor.

Madeline moved the hood back over her head and slipped it off again. "Some mornings I feel rested." Her hands fidgeted inside the pouch of the sweatshirt.

"Madeline, have you had any other dreams since Thanksgiving?"

"No." Madeline put the hood back on. Her eyes met the killer' in a measure of the dream.

Dr. Smalling silently glared at the garment. The tell revealed the lie.

"What happens in this dream?" Smalling sat upright.

"It's nothing I can really explain. It's just a bunch of shadows."

Dr. Smalling knew Madeline was lying. She would get to the dream eventually. Inside the dream lay a key. Smalling was sure she could unlock the dream.

When the session was over, Dr. Smalling excused Madeline and asked if Sophia could stay for a few minutes.

"Thank you for making the time." Dr. Smalling sat down behind her desk.

"It is my pleasure." Sophia turned off her phone, sat down, and gave the doctor her undivided attention.

"Madeline is scared. This is creating her anxiety."

"Scared of what?"

"I don't know, but I feel the dream she had just before Thanksgiving will provide us some clues."

"Did she talk about the dream today?" Sophia hoped for a small breakthrough.

"No. She doesn't trust me enough to talk about something that personal. Not yet. In fact, Madeline is frank about a few things and very private about others." Dr. Smalling noted Sophia's tension. "And Madeline is not averse to lying about something when she doesn't want to talk about it."

Sophia shrank in the chair. "What did she lie about?"

"The dream," Smalling stated. "She made up some cockamamie story." Sophia got smaller. "Don't fret, Sophia. This is a normal part of therapy. I did want to ask you a few questions about your daughter. I think it will help me find my way in more quickly."

"Sure. What do you want to know?"

"How have your daughter's grades been? Not just recently but historically."

Sophia straightened up. "She is actually a fantastic student. Honor roll and straight As."

"And only recently have you seen her grades slide."

"Yes, only on the last report card."

"Are you aware of her college applications?" Smalling reviewed her notes.

"Yes. Of course. She applied to James Madison, University of Virginia, Radford, and the one in Richmond…VCU."

"With her outstanding grades, are you surprised that she didn't shoot a little higher in her choices for college?" Smalling tapped the pencil on the notepad. Sophia did not have a good answer. "Madeline has low self-esteem." Sophia opened her mouth to speak, but Smalling cut her off. "Other than the nightmares that Madeline had as a child, did she have others in her early grades or adolescence?"

"No. We told Dr. Saito that."

"What are some of the things that Madeline absolutely loves?"

Sophia remembered Madeline's childhood. She craved a cigarette. "Madeline always wanted to touch the moon. Ever since she was a little baby. She would crawl on the couch and scratch at the window…reaching for the moon. She used to find the highest places in the city to have that same sensation. The Washington Monument. Iwo Jima. Rooftops. Yellow moons. Blue moons. She learned to read a calendar at such a young age and would find when the moon would be full and beg us to take her someplace she could look at it. It was never high enough."

"When was the last time you looked at the moon together?"

Sophia couldn't remember. She put her chin on her chest. "I don't know."

"When did she start wearing her hair like that?"

"I don't recall exactly. Maybe at the beginning of the year."

"How did she wear it before? Do you have a picture in your phone?"

Sophia pulled her phone out of her purse, and scrolled through her photos. She showed one to Dr. Smalling.

Madeline was all smiles, her long dark brown hair pulled back or on top of her head. She wore little to no makeup, and her choice of clothing was much more stylish.

"Sophia." Smalling stood and pointed at the phone. "Six months ago that was your daughter, Madeline. The young woman who sits in my office is not the same person." Smalling paused. "At least not outwardly.

"What do you think changed?" Sophias focused on the photo, stunned at the difference.

"I was hoping you could help provide some clues. Something has changed since the beginning of the school year, and it has had a dramatic effect on Madeline. Can you recall any specific incident in which she came home out of sorts?"

Sophia struggled to recall any such incident.

"Does she talk about boys?" Dr. Smalling pressed.

"I wish."

"Has she ever expressed anger over being part of an interracial family?"

"No. Not that I am aware of."

Smalling took a breath. "Her appearance could be a way to draw attention to herself. A sign she is not getting what she needs from her peers, the opposite sex...or the same sex." Dr. Smalling read her notes as she looked over her glasses.

"You are suggesting my daughter is a lesbian." Sophia looked at her lap, mortified by the doctor's suggestion and wrestling with the craziness that had become Madeline.

"I do not know your daughter's sexual preferences. It would not be abnormal for girls of her age to experiment sexually."

"Madeline hardly leaves the house, much less dates." Sophia was flustered.

"Sophia. That doesn't mean she doesn't have those thoughts, but that is not really the point."

"Well, what is the point, Dr. Smalling?" Sophia wanted answers. Real answers.

"She may not be getting the attention she needs from her family."

"So now it's our fault." Sophia stood and paced the room, crossing her arms.

"It is a theory, Sophia." Smalling stayed calm. "However, my intuition is that her outward appearance is more of a mask. Camouflage." Dr. Smalling looked straight at the prowling Sophia.

"A mask? Camouflage? What does that mean?" Sophia started to cry. "First you said she needed attention. Now it is a mask. You can't have it both ways, Doctor."

"I said it was a theory." Smalling spoke very calmly. "She seems to be disguising her true self. She is hiding. I believe she is afraid. Afraid of something. Or someone?"

"That's absurd. Who is she afraid of? *Who?*" Sophia sobbed.

"I don't know, but it is an avenue that I want to pursue in our next session." Dr. Smalling paused. "Sophia…do you know of anyone in your family who may have abused Madeline in the past?"

Sophia exploded. "I have had enough of this, Dr. Smalling! First there is your theory that Madeline may be a lesbian. Then it's that the family doesn't give her enough attention. Now you think we are abusing her. What? Do you think Raphael is sneaking into her room in the middle of the night? Maybe you think it's me. Maybe I sneak into her room in the middle of the night and abuse my own daughter to make her a lesbian? Is that what you think, Dr. Smalling?"

Smalling knew better than to take the bait. Sophia paced the room. Smalling extended the tissue box to Sophia. Sophia snatched a Kleenex and paced. She brushed it across her face, leaving it soiled with rouge, snot, and tears.

Dr. Smalling stood and walked toward Sophia. "I am not saying any of those things happened." Smalling put her arm around Sophia. "This is where the sessions are leading. I need to follow the signs." She righted Sophia and placed her squarely in front of her. "I need you to be strong. We don't want you in here." They both laughed and gave each other a hug. "The good news is that Madeline has not had any additional episodes. Let's stay the course, and we will find the answer."

It all seemed so simple to the psychologist.

JANUARY 18
LOS ANGELES, CALIFORNIA

Sadie Davil sipped the chamomile as she hunted on the Internet. Easy prey posted for the world to see. Davil remained patient, searching for the flawed creature Lyle sought. The lonely existed among the preening and the vain in the advertised world of men seeking women. Men seeking men. Woman seeking both. Everyone seeking everything. Thousands and thousands of posts. Davil frolicked in her natural habitat, lathering herself in the slime.

The Century luxury apartments afforded Lyle a dazzling sunset. An incredible view of the city he would burn. He stepped in from the balcony and stood behind Davil.

"I have someone for you." Davil clicked the post. She shuddered when he leaned over her shoulder.

Sweetevelyn34
WF looking for WM. Tired of all the phonies and liars. Not swim-
suit material, but round and warm. Looking for something real. No
bars or clubs. If right, I will give you everything.

"Her zip code is 30312. Atlanta. Five feet three inches tall, and she weighs one hundred forty-five pounds. She lists herself as full figured. She's a nasty, pudgy thing." Davil grimaced. "Red hair. Blue eyes. She lists herself as politically conservative and a Christian. She finished high school and makes under thirty thousand a year. No kids, and she smokes. And she's a Sagittarius."

"That's her."

Davil wrote back to sweetevelyn34 from Atlanta. She created and online alias for Lyle. A sailor would be moving to Atlanta: *Looking for a serious relationship and tired of all the games. Hopefully, Sweetevelyn34 could be that girl, but he didn't want to get hurt again. Oceanlove12.*

Davil, satisfied, shut down the laptop. That would be enough to pique Evelyn's interest.

Davil and Lyle left the Century. A pair of newly acquired Dodge Grand Caravans waited for them outside the lobby, one green and one black. "Kind of slumming it, Javad." Davil sneered.

"I was told to lay low." Javad wanted to choke the skinny bitch. "Where is Guzan?" He was ready to leave town.

"I sent him ahead. We will meet him in Atlanta." Lyle shut the door. Nehwal turned the car north into the Hollywood Hills. Floyd captained the following van.

Lyle and his team were leaving Los Angeles. The FBI, NCIS, and LAPD were stalking them. Nehwal navigated the distorted canyon roads to the crest. Elroy Floyd removed a canister from the back of the green van. He sprinkled the gasoline over the edge of the canyon like a grandmother waters her garden.

Davil sidled next to Lyle. "We could stay. You could rule this city."

"This city already belongs to me. It has fallen. A city that breathes its idols and worships the human sins its God forbids. It would take but a small fart to burn this city to the ground. We have an entire world to destroy."

The flaming desert sun turned the underbrush into tinder. Floyd struck the match and dropped it into the brittle brush. The flames reached skyward and raced along the ridge of the mountain. Lyle stretched his arms outward and stepped closer to the inferno. The heat seared his face while he prayed to his master in hell.

ARLINGTON, VIRGINIA

Madeline curled up in the corner of her bed against the wall. She held her knees to her chest. She pounded at the keyboard on her phone, hoping Mackenzie was awake and would text her back. She was petrified. Every time she laid her head on the pillow, she could see the blue eyes that haunted her. The eyes always seemed to be looking into her soul, pulling it out of her. She was tired and needed some sleep. Her phone registered quarter to three in the morning. Mackenzie wasn't going to answer.

Madeline knew her phone alarm would be going off at half past six. She had been getting up early to apply makeup to her swollen, baggy eyes. She was becoming an old woman at eighteen. She got out of the bed and went to the bathroom. Madeline pulled up her shirt. She had become so thin. She knew she needed to eat more, but nothing appealed to her. Cross-country and lack of sleep depleted her energy and reserves. She yearned to sleep but feared the dream. She reached under the sink and grabbed the basket. Under the extra tube of toothpaste and cotton balls were the remains of the bottle of Ketel One vodka she had pinched from her parents' liquor stash. There was about a third left. She tilted the bottle over her head, the sleep pouring into her throat. It didn't take long. She would sleep, but she would not dream.

JANUARY 19
LOS ANGELES

Violet and royal colors of sunrise cast a soothing backdrop to the fiery crimson teeth of the inferno that swallowed the spine of the Santa Monica Mountains.

"Where are you?" Alcott screamed into the phone at Sommer.

"Almost to Torrance," Bruno replied on his cell.

"Don't bother. Westwood is evacuating. I am heading toward UCLA Medical Center. We are moving patients to Cedars-Sinai and Saint Vincent. They are not safe here. This fire is out of control." Alcott felt the heat in the wind feeding the flames.

"My God."

"There are helicopters dumping water everywhere!" Alcott yelled over the vibrations of a fixed-wing firefighting plane swooping onto the scene. "The 405 is blocked north and south. The fire has made it all the way to the Palisades."

"Are you safe?"

"Nobody here is safe. Reports are that some twenty-five hundred homes have been destroyed. Cedars is full of burn victims. Some really badly burned. The fire marshal fears the death toll is in the hundreds. They died trying to protect their homes." Alcott ducked as another tanker buzzed overhead. "One fire chief says it's the worst he has ever seen."

"Are they getting help?"

"There are volunteers coming from all over the country. They just can't get here fast enough. I don't know how long these guys can last." Jeremy passed a fireman sucking on oxygen. "Turn around, Bruno."

"I am. Any news about Lyle on your end?" Sommer found an exit to head back to San Diego.

"Nothing." Alcottwatched as the tanker cascaded its payload of foam over the houses of Brentwood. "It's like he just disappeared."

PHOENIX, ARIZONA

L yle drew the curtains and gazed out at the crystal-blue waters of the mountain lake swimming pool in the backyard. He opened the door, and the furnace of desert air leaked into the living room. He stretched his legs on the ottoman and watched his hometown burn on the Channel 5 news.

Sadie Davil sauntered through the spacious living room wearing only her phone. She handed it to Lyle. "A young woman named Evelyn Cahill is interested in meeting a certain naval officer when he comes to Atlanta."

"Get her phone number and send her a text or two," Lyle instructed. "Be sweet." He winked at Davil.

"Already have." Sadie added a smiley Emoji and pressed send.

FEBRUARY 3
FRANKFURT, KENTUCKY

PARENTS WORRY FOR MISSING DAUGHTER
State Journal

The Frankfurt Police Department is posting a missing-persons report for Lila Chait, seventeen years of age. Lila has been missing since Friday, January 31. Lila was last seen attending the Western High School–Frankfurt High School varsity basketball game. She was last spotted around eight in the evening, when she left the gym to go to the refreshment stand.

Lila is a junior at Western Hills High School. Lila was last seen wearing a Western Hills sweatshirt; blue, black, and green plaid slacks; and black flats. Lila has several earrings in both ears and bright red hair. Lila has blue eyes. She has freckles on her face and wears glasses. Lila is five feet three inches tall and weighs ninety-eight pounds.

If you have seen or know the whereabouts of Lila Chait, please call the Frankfurt Police Department at 502-555-6777.

SATURDAY, FEBRUARY 8
PHOENIX, ARIZONA

Lyle's sandy beard filled his face. His frame and face had thinned, no longer force-fed the navy chow. He ventured into a CVS drugstore to purchase a brush. A wonderful smell enveloped his senses. He stepped into the maze of Crest, deodorants, and Kleenex. He followed his nose. It deposited him at the prescription counter of the pharmacy, next to the OneTouch glucose meters.

Three young children, one still in Pampers, sat playfully on the chairs next to the coin-operated blood pressure cuff. The toddlers took turns sliding their slender arms into the device. They giggled and wrestled for another turn.

"Amber, play nicely with Alexis and Stuart." The mother sat with her brood, her open purse on her lap.

Lyle sampled the new *Cosmopolitan* from the rack and sat quietly next to the mother and joyful children. Lyle opened the magazine but focused on the mother. One of the sweet children shrieked and lashed out. The mother swiveled. Her purse fell from her lap while she wrangled with the threesome, spilling the majority of the contents to the floor.

"I am so sorry," the mother apologized to Lyle, and juggled the kids.

"For what?" Lyle smiled and reached down to help the mother gather the splayed items from her purse.

"They are just being devils today. Stuart!"

Lyle raised an eyebrow, amused by the irony.

The mother stared at the two-year-old as he tried to free himself from her bear hug. "Please behave. We will be leaving soon." She craned to retrieve her belongings. "They are so loud."

"They are just being kids." Lyle laughed. He continued to help gather the items on the floor. "This is for Sanctuary at Camelback Mountain?" Lyle handed the brochure to the mother. "It is a lovely place."

"Have you been there?"

The kid Alexis ran from the seats only to be snared by her mother's arm.

"Yes," he lied. Lyle noticed the name on her prescription bottle: *Meadow Chandler.*

"I am meeting my husband there on Friday. We are so excited." Meadow tucked her hair behind her ear and smelled Alexis's diaper.

"I though you said Daddy doesn't come home until Saturday." From the mouth of one of the babes.

"That is very smart of you, Stuart. You are right. Mommy is going a day early and will meet Daddy on Saturday." She wiped Stuart's mouth after Alexis smeared his face with Mommy's lipstick. "Alexis! Give me that!" Beads of perspiration formed on the mother's forehead.

"Mrs. Chandler?" the clerk called.

"Yes." Meadow balanced her disarrayed purse on the chair. "If you all sit still for just one moment," Meadow said, shifting them each into a seat, "Mommy will get you each a lollipop." Cheers echoed through the neighborhood CVS.

Lyle noted the address of Sanctuary Camelback Mountain Spa and Resort on the brochure where Mr. and Mrs. Chandler would rendezvous.

FEBRUARY 11
FORT WAYNE, INDIANA

POLICE SEARCH FOR COLLEGE GIRL
Journal Gazette

The Fort Wayne Police Department is posting a missing-persons report for Huang Lodygin, sixteen years of age. Huang is a math prodigy at Ivy Tech Community College and was last seen on Tuesday, February 9, leaving the Regal Coldwater Crossing movie theater. Huang was there with friends but had driven her own car. Her car remained in the parking lot after friends called the police when Huang would not return their phone calls.

Huang is of Korean descent and has black hair and dark brown eyes. She is five feet four inches tall and weighs 106 pounds. Huang was last seen wearing a bright red winter ski jacket, jeans, and brown lace-up shoes.

If you have any information regarding the disappearance of Huang Lodygin, please call 260-555-2954.

FEBRUARY 14
ARLINGTON, VIRGINIA

The big red hearts on the beige flats made Sophia drop her fork into the chicken curry. "Madeline! You look fantastic!" Sophia would have chosen something other than the jeans ripped at the kneecaps, but Madeline wasn't wearing sweatpants or a hoodie.

Raphael gave his daughter a big hug. "You look sensational!" He slipped a fifty into her hand. "Have a great time tonight. Call me if you need a ride." Madeline rolled her eyes but appreciated the gesture.

"Where are you going?" Oliver wanted to go.

"Mackenzie is having a Valentine's Day party for all the people who don't have valentines." Madeline picked some lint off the Tucker + Tate cashmere sweater.

"So it is a party for losers." Oliver poked at his sister, an earbud dangling from his side.

Madeline punched him in the arm. "You're a loser."

"What are we going to do if Madeline gets to go to a party?" Oliver moped, not willing to be cheated.

"We will have some quality boy time," assured Raphael.

Sophia hoped Madeline would have some quality boy time.

"Should I take the Navigator or the BMW?" Madeline toyed with both sets of keys.

"Take the Beemer," Sophia offered over her dinner. She hoped they had reached a turning point. Dr. Smalling said Madeline's mood had lightened, and early tests at school showed reinvigorated grades. And now a party.

Madeline slipped into the garage. She put her phone in the driver's seat of the silver BMW 3 Series Wagon. She headed north on Glebe Road into North Arlington. Parking near Mackenzie's house was formidable any afternoon, and now her driveway was jammed with vehicles borrowed from wealthy parents. She squeezed into a spot a block away and heard the bass thumping Iggy Azalea from Mackenzie's back deck.

Sidewalks and driveways were cleared from the heavy snow that had fallen the day before. A few of Mackenzie's rambunctious guests mounted charges up the face of the highest snow pile, an effort to be king of the hill as the effects of a beer set in. An impromptu and anatomically correct snowman graced the front lawn.

Mackenzie entered the vestibule and waded through a throng of high school students. She only recognized a few. Madeline had intended to be fashionably late, but the party seemed to have been going on for quite a while. One boy was passed out on the Steinway piano stool next to a couple making out on a bag of Doritos. Beer cans were stuffed into the soil of the potted areca palm. A snowball fight blossomed between the rulers of the kitchen and the lords of the den. Madeline passed through the war zone and found Mackenzie on the back deck, passing a joint with a few dudes she did not know.

"Hey, girl." Mackenzie pulled Madeline into the circle. "This is Damon and Brian and…" Mackenzie fumbled the last name.

"Joe," Joe added, disappointed Mackenzie didn't remember his name.

"This is my friend Madeline." Madeline smiled halfheartedly and declined the joint. Joe shifted his gaze to Madeline. Madeline felt a strange feeling in her stomach. She despised being looked at, but something far more sinister than Joe worried her. The horrible tension she had come to know all too well. A fear she needed to stop. She reversed course on the blunt, took a drag, and gagged profusely.

FEBRUARY 14
SCOTTSDALE, ARIZONA

S anctuary at Camelback Mountain spoiled the senses. Lyle extended his legs on the king-size bed with crisp, tight sheets and
fluffy down pillows. The duvet, splashed with soft lime green hues,
paired with the muted lavender curtains. The balcony overlooked a
private pool warmed by a fire pit at night.

A small nook on the balcony was properly set for breakfast in
the waking desert sun. Lyle moved to the expansive living room of
hardwood floors, warmed with handmade persian rugs. A print of
a happy, loving couple garnished the mantel.

Lyle lavished himself in the stern stream of the shower in the
spacious bathroom. The edges of the toilet paper folded like origami, the towels rolled tight and smelling of spring.

The winter sun faded behind the crags and carrot-hued desert
coral speckled the landscape at the Sanctuary. Lyle turned on the
fireplace. He adjusted the Moët in the ice and fluffed the pillow on

the couch. He drew the plunger and filled the syringe with liquid Valium.

The handle turned on the door of the residence, and Meadow Chandler dragged her rolling luggage into the vacation house, the wheels bumping over the doorjamb. She shed the purse from her shoulder and set it on the floor. Lyle waited until the front door latched before stepping out from the bedroom.

"Hello, Mrs. Chandler." Lyle prowled into the living quarters.

Meadow stopped cold and trembled. She fumbled with her glasses and scrambled to put them back on her face. She stepped back, tripping over her suitcase, falling on her ass. Lyle hovered over her.

"I know you." Meadow couldn't release the scream inside her. Lyle grabbed a full fist of Meadow's long blond locks and heaved her across the living room onto the glass coffee table, smashing it to pieces. A gash opened on her forehead.

"You have no idea who I am." He pulled her close and stuck the syringe into her neck.

Lyle enjoyed the silence. He hauled Meadow by her feet to the bedroom and hoisted her onto the soft duvet splashed with lime green. Lyle tucked a fluffy down pillow under her head. He checked the temperature on the champagne and polished a flute. Lyle started with the buckles of the Chaos Metallic gold ankle-wrap sandals from Manolo Blahnik. He placed them side by side in the closet. Button by button he removed Meadow's blouse, sliding it over her shoulders. He shook out the wrinkles and hung it in the closet over her sandals. Lyle rolled her over and gently unlatched her mulberry-tinted Victoria's Secret bra. He placed the garment lightly in the dresser drawer. Lyle slipped the leather belt through the loop and tugged it politely. The latch separated, and he fingered the button of her slacks. Gradually, the zipper released, and he removed her slacks with compassion. He folded the pants and placed them in the drawer below the bra. He ran his razor-sharp nail on the hip string of her panties and snapped the threads. Lyle pushed the panties in his pocket and removed the hand-cut rope. With precision and care, he tied her appendages to each post of the bed.

Delicately, he removed the thin gold chain with Jesus on the cross from around her neck. He slid the cross off the chain, turned it upside down, and placed the chain back from where it came. He stretched the electrical tape across her mouth and waited for Meadow to awake.

Lyle removed his clothing and placed it gingerly on the chair near the fireplace.

Lyle dimmed the lights in the bedroom and lay fully clothed on the bed next to Meadow, brushing his fingers across her forehead. Her eyes began to open. She tried to speak but could only make garbled noises.

"You look delectable lying in this light, Meadow." Meadow's eyes howled what her voice could not. "I have had thousands like you. A creator of little angels." Lyle took a deep breath through his nose, savoring her aroma. "While you are not the banquet I seek, you are a very special lady." Lyle sat on the edge of the bed. "You are a feast. You are my caviar." Lyle opened the French champagne; the bubbles flowed over his fist. "I search for the one. I seek to gorge myself on her perfection. Then I will claim victory again. They will toast me at his table, and we shall share our tales of victory against humanity and reminisce of conquests long ago. We will have celebrations at the great table and dine on souls. Souls whose lives were so promising and turned rancid. Those who fed on the seeds of temptation we laid before them."

Lyle enjoyed his Valentine's dinner at the five-star Sanctuary at Camelback Mountain Resort. He left a Valentine's heart candy on Meadow's forehead that said *Love Bug*.

ARLINGTON, VIRGINIA

Arlington County police officers knocked at the front door of Mackenzie's house. Kids scurried from the residence like roaches from the light. Mackenzie sheepishly opened the door.

"Ma'am. We are going to have to ask you to break up this party and tell everyone able to drive home." The officer nosed into the doorway. "Is there an adult present?"

"No. Officer? We have a big problem."

"I'd say, ma'am." The officer motioned to his partner. "Round these kids up. Don't arrest them, but I am sure they are all under-age, and I don't want anyone driving." He looked back at Mackenzie. "Let's see if their parents will come and get them."

"Officer," Mackenzie pleaded. "My friend is locked in the bathroom and is freaking the eff out. Can you help me?" Mackenzie stepped out of the way, and the invited officer entered. "She's this way." Mackenzie walked up the stairs with the officer and knocked on the bathroom door. Two boys and a girl scrambled to put their clothes on, and sneaked down the stairs into the waiting net of assisting officers.

"What's going on in the bathroom?" asked the officer.

"It's my friend Madeline. She just started going crazy." Mackenzie tried to stay composed.

"Has your friend had anything to drink?" The officer looked Mackenzie in the eye.

"No, but she did smoke some pot." Things were getting worse for Mackenzie, and the officer spoke into his Velcro-attached communicator, asking his team to search for drugs.

"Does she have any weapons?"

"She has a knife."

"A knife. What kind of knife?" The officer seemed surprised.

"A kitchen knife. A chef's knife. One of the big ones with the sharp tip at the end." The officer asked Mackenzie to go downstairs and wait near the front door with the other officer.

"What is her name again?"

"Madeline."

The officer knocked on the door. "Madeline, this is Officer Velozo, Arlington County Police." A female officer joined Velozo. "I am with Officer De Jong."

Officer Vanessa De Jong spoke through the door, hoping her female voice would reassure Madeline. "Hi, Madeline. My name is Officer De Jong, but I want you to call me Vanessa." There was no response. "Madeline, we are not here to hurt you. We are here to help. What's going on in there?"

Both officers looked at each other, wondering what to do next. Then they heard a voice. "He is after me. I can't come out. He is after me."

"Who is after you, Madeline?"

"The man with blue eyes," Madeline growled in an unfamiliar voice.

"Why is he after you?"

They could hear the sobbing through the door. "I don't know," Madeline bellowed through the tears.

"Madeline, do you have a knife?"

"I need it."

"Why do you need the knife?" De Jong tried to disarm the youth.

"Because he is trying to kill me!" Madeline screamed in a dark guttural voice.

De Jong backed off, worried that Madeline might try to harm herself, but she did not want to exacerbate the situation. She asked Velozo to bring Mackenzie back upstairs.

De Jong stepped into a bedroom with the high schooler. "Where does this girl live?"

"Over near Route Fifty off Glebe."

"Do you have a number for her parents?"

"Yes." Mackenzie pulled out her cell. She froze when Mr. Deschamps actually answered and then handed the phone to the police.

"Mackenzie?" Raphael was confused.

"This is Arlington County Police. Do you have a daughter named Madeline?" De Jong spoke calmly.

"Yes. Is Madeline all right?" Raphael asked.

"We have a situation. Madeline is locked in a bathroom with a kitchen knife. She sounds very frightened. I would like you to see if you can't help. Can you come to…" She looked at the girl.

"Mackenzie."

"Mackenzie's house?"

"I will be there right away." Raphael hung up.

De Jong questioned Mackenzie. "How much pot did Madeline smoke?"

Mackenzie knew she was in deep but told the truth. "I only saw her take a drag."

"But you haven't been with her all night, right?"

Mackenzie had been with Yossi Beckerman in the basement for about an hour. "No."

"Did you see her have anything to drink? Alcohol?"

"No."

"Has Madeline ever had any issues like this before?"

Mackenzie didn't want to be a snitch, but this seemed important. "She had something weird happen over Christmas break."

"What do you mean 'weird'?" De Jong needed more.

"I don't know. She has to go to a psychologist now." Mackenzie commenced bawling.

De Jong asked Velozo to call in a police psychologist to be safe. She knocked on the bathroom door. "Madeline, its Vanessa De Jong with Arlington Police. Why don't you put the knife down and open the door? There is no one here who can hurt you. I won't let them."

"You can't stop him. He is out there." Madeline did not open the door. "He wants me."

"Madeline, I called your father." De Jong listened to the heaving despair from inside the bathroom. She received no response but monitored the crying.

Mackenzie cried in the bedroom while Madeline cried in the bathroom and a host of teens cried in the foyer, knowing their parents were on the way.

Suddenly Raphael bound up the stairs. "I am Madeline's father, Raphael Deschamps. Where is Madeline?" De Jong nodded at the closed door. "Madeline, it's Daddy. Honey, everything is going to be OK. Please open the door."

"It's not going to be OK, Daddy. I'm scared."

"I know you are. I know you are. I won't let anything happen to you." Raphael pressed his hands against the locked door.

"I am afraid he is going to hurt you. And Mommy. And Oliver."

"I won't let that happen."

"You can't stop him." Madeline opened the door, gripping the knife in her right hand and holding it by her side. Blood leaked from her nose, covering her face and soiling her sweater. She was ashen and drenched with sweat and tears. Raphael rushed in and knelt to hold his daughter. She stared at De Jong with her black, soulless eyes, maintaining the grip on the knife.

SCOTTSDALE, ARIZONA

Lyle curled up in the bed next to Meadow stroking her forehead, her lifeless eyes fixed on the ceiling fan. The blood from her forehead coagulated and pooled near her eyes. "Meadow. Meadow." Lyle sighed, fingering the upside-down cross around her neck. "Good things don't always happen to good people. Your soul will clamor for heaven, the loneliest place. You should join the party in hell."

Lyle stretched, crossed his legs, and folded his hands behind his head. "When we first saw each other today, you said you knew who I was." He matched her gaze at the ceiling fan. "We should get to know each other. Let me tell you a little about myself." Lyle spooned onto her hip. "We are always in the shadows. We have been since the beginning," Lyle whispered softly in her ear. "We are a virus. Corrupting the chances for humanity to succeed since its inception. We weren't good enough for your so-called God, and he cast us out. We infected his creation with chemicals, weakness, and pain. We changed the game before it began. Humanity was doomed to fail. We changed people's nature so that they cannibalize themselves.

We delight as they plunder their world of resources. So many indulging in the spoils while others starve beside them. Despising the differences among themselves, manifesting in murder and genocide. I don't think that is what your God had in mind when he shaped humanity in his image." Lyle raged. "But your God is flawed. He has failed you, and he has betrayed me. He abandoned and exiled us for being what he fashioned. For this he will pay. For this I serve a true master. One sincere in purpose. Helping God's faulty humanity destroy itself."

Lyle raised himself to the edge of the bed, holding Meadow's hand in his. "Sometimes humanity needs a little push. That is why I am here from time to time. To help the infection fester. To defile. To kill. To foster a polluted species." Lyle propped Meadow on the pillows and took a selfie with the departed. "I am a specialist. Assigned by my lord to seek the one. The one who carries the light inside of her. The only light that can destroy us. There are many resembling you, but you are a glow. The one I seek is blinding. Your smell brings me to nourish and savor. She brings me to victories through time. I only come to this wretched earth to destroy her. I prefer to not wait for the birth. I kill the carrier of the germ. The flavor is much sweeter. They are simple to find. I can smell them. And others can smell them too. I am a rapist at heart."

Lyle stood and pranced slowly around the room. "Everyone thinks the apocalypse is going to happen one day. Boom! Everything goes black. That's not how it works." Lyle moved Meadow's head so her dead eyes recalibrated to gaze at Lyle, her skin fading to gray. "The apocalypse is like cancer. Sometimes it goes into remission, but you know it is going to come back. And it is eventually going to kill you. It's just a matter of time." Lyle stoked the logs in the fireplace. "I was there when the powers of Rome salivated at the domination of the known world, mauling any civilization in its path. Souls fighting war in the name of freedom became slaves to death. When they ravaged Palestine, we gorged ourselves on the women and children. We rejoiced at the plagues of Europe in the year five hundred as the dead littered the streets. We sustained the practice of trading humans as slaves and opened trade in Africa, an enterprise that from the beginning of time has proven humanity's disregard for its own flesh and blood. Where was your God when the Mongols slaughtered China or the Spanish destroyed the Aztec civilizations? He is but a coward and will betray you again. Where was he tonight when you needed him most?" Lyle shifted to Meadow, moved her face to his, and licked the blood from her eye.

ARLINGTON, VIRGINIA

They said nothing as Raphael held Madeline close in Mackenzie's bedroom. Her nails pierced into his shoulders as she shook. He could feel her tears on his neck. Raphael wanted everyone to leave so her peers wouldn't see her like this, though he could hear the gossip from the foyer, along with irate parents called to pick up their wayward children.

Officer De Jong expedited the line of students and their parents, handing out citations for underage drinking. An officer found stashes of marijuana tucked behind books, in the kitchen cabinet with the pasta strainers, and clogging the toilet. Fathers and mothers collared their kids and shoved them into the backs of their vehicles.

"Most likely your son will lose his driver's license for thirty days," De Jong explained to one mother.

The mother glared at her son. "Looks like you are taking the bus," she sneered. "Maybe it will be that little yellow bus."

"There will also be a fine. You can call the court to verify the fee, or you can appear in court to fight the ticket." Velozo handed the yellow copy to the father. The father guided his son to the car, looking a bit tanked himself.

"Depending on what the court says, you daughter may have to enroll in an alcohol-education program," De Jong advised another mom.

"But she has dance and French club after school," protested the mother.

"That is for the court to decide, ma'am." Velozo smelled pot on the next kid's clothes. "It is possible they may have to do community service."

"I should let him spend the night in jail." The mortified mother needed help with her child.

De Jong marched up the stairs and gently knocked on the bedroom door, where Raphael and Madeline were regrouping.

"Mr. Deschamps." De Jong eased open the door. "This is Michael Osaka, Arlington County Police psychiatrist."

"Tell him to go away!" Madeline shouted into her father's neck.

"It's OK, Madeline." Raphael stroked Madeline's hair. "Let me speak with him." De Jong and Madeline switched spots, and Raphael joined the shrink in the hallway.

"Mr. Deschamps, how is your daughter doing in there?"

"She's calming down." Osaka could see the worry in the father's eyes.

"The officer briefed me on a few things before I came upstairs. I was hoping you could verify a few things." Osaka removed his notepad from his pocket. "This is a fairly serious situation."

Raphael acknowledged the gravity of Madeline's behavior. "Whatever you need."

"Is your daughter currently visiting with a psychologist?"

"Yes."

"For what?"

"Anxiety. Stress."

"Which psychologist?"

"Dr. Sylvia Smalling."

"I know her. She is very good." Osaka looked over Raphael's shoulder at Madeline. "Has Dr. Smalling made a diagnosis of what is creating your daughter's stress and anxiety?"

"No. My wife tells me that it could be a myriad of things, but the doctor hasn't pinpointed exactly what is driving this." His voice tapered.

"Officer De Jong said that Madeline said 'he' is after her. Do you know who 'he' is?"

Raphael shook his head. "I don't."

"Madeline first started seeing Dr. Smalling after Christmas?"

Raphael confirmed this. "Madeline had what they described as a hypertensive episode or something like that." Osaka listened. "We took her to the emergency room, and the doctor reduced her blood pressure but recommended she see a psychologist."

"How often does Madeline smoke pot?"

"Never as far as I am aware."

Osaka raised his skeptical eyebrows and inched away from the bedroom. "Mr. Deschamps, has Madeline ever grabbed a knife or other type of weapon before?"

"No!" Raphael exclaimed at the absurdity of the question.

Osaka gathered his thoughts. "Mr. Deschamps, has Madeline expressed any thoughts about suicide?"

"Suicide? No! Absolutely not." Raphael went on the defensive. "My daughter has been a model student until a few months ago. She is going through a tough time, and she will come out of it fine. I think she just had an adverse reaction to the marijuana."

"That is possible. Most kids just eat a bag of Cheetos or listen to Pink Floyd, not grab a knife and tell the police that someone is out to get them. That is textbook paranoia."

"Madeline has never spoken of someone 'out to get her.' Who would be out to get her? She's a nice kid. She doesn't have any enemies."

"It doesn't have to be an enemy. This isn't a world where unicorns shit glitter, Mr. Deschamps. There are a lot of wicked people. Even in Arlington. Your daughter is scared of someone. It is an educated guess, but whatever triggered these episodes started just before Christmas, right?"

Raphael conceded. "Yes."

"I believe your daughter is suffering from PTSD." Raphael couldn't remember what the acronym stood for. "Posttraumatic stress disorder," Osaka clarified.

Osaka let Madeline go home with her father but warned that the night could still sour. Raphael promised to take Madeline to Dr. Smalling as soon as possible.

Madeline would not leave her room the entire weekend and barely slept. Sophia found the bottle of vodka under the bathroom sink, and the Deschamps household disintegrated into a conflagration of words and despair as Madeline's world unraveled.

FEBRUARY 15, 2014
SCOTTSDALE, ARIZONA

The flight on the Gulfstream 6381 TT from Santa Monica Municipal Airport took off, touched the clouds, and ping-ponged back down to Scottsdale Municipal Airport. Alcott asked the pilot for a bird's-eye view of the scorched landscape as they left Los Angeles. The frames of a thousand destroyed homes looked like so many scattered charcoal briquettes on the side of the hills. Soot smeared the mountains. Mother Nature was an impossible beast to tame, and having an arsonist as an accomplice left a depraved disaster.

The tarmac at Scottsdale seared through Alcott's shoes, and the sweat evaporated as quickly as it left his pores. Bruno Sommer removed his blazer instantly, and both slipped into the waiting FBI car with air conditioning, a short nine-mile drive to Camelback Resort.

Blake Chandler sat in shock on the curb outside the rental home that his wife, Meadow, had selected for their rendezvous. A blanket shrouded his shoulders, despite the unearthly heat. Sommer and Alcott entered the residence. Arizona crime-scene investigators fingerprinted and photographed each room with precision. Alcott craned his neck into the bedroom and saw the stiff and mutilated corpse of Meadow Chandler.

"Are you Alcott?" The CSI tech extended her smile as her hands worked inside plastic gloves.

"I'm Alcott, and this is my partner on the case. NCIS agent Bruno Sommer."

"I am Livia Gobin, CSI. Sorry to meet you under the circumstances." Gobin flashed her stunning hazel eyes behind plastic goggles.

"Hello, Livia. What do you have for us?" Sommer unbuttoned the top of his shirt.

"The victim suffered a contusion to the head. As you can see by the mess in the living room, we feel the perp tossed her around. There is a tinge of blood on her neck. We haven't gotten toxicology, but he drugged her. That allowed the perp to move her to the bedroom, where he tied her to the bedposts." Alcott and Sommer examined the scene. "The perp was relaxed and confident. He took his time. It was like he knew he was going to be alone. He even took the time to fold her clothes and put them in the dresser."

"Where is she from?" Sommer asked.

"Phoenix. Her purse is in the other room. The husband confirmed they were on a special weekend."

"Anniversary?" Jeremy surmised.

"No. The husband said they were trying to have a baby."

Alcott's neck snapped.

"Do you think he met her here?" Sommer inquired.

"I don't think so. Hotel clerk has her checking in at roughly seven in the evening. Time of death is eight thirty, give or take. She didn't go to the bar. Her suitcase wasn't open. All her toiletries are there. A girl doesn't go out unless she's primped." Gobin shifted to the end of the bed.

"My God!" Alcott winced as he saw Meadow's remains up close.

"The victim died of internal trauma and exsanguination." Sommer and Alcott were familiar with both terms.

"A precise incision was made at the base of the vagina. On a perfect ninety-degree angle, the incision opens to the anus from the vulva." Alcott hoped the husband didn't walk in. "This allowed an abundance of access. The vulva and urethra are damaged but present. The vagina has been ruptured, but her fallopian tubes and uterus are completely gone." Gobin sounded dazed.

Alcott and Sommer donned gloves and opened Meadow's suitcase. Lingerie mingled with activewear and a few stylish blouses. Shorts. Tennis shoes. Typical for a resort. Toiletries. K-Y Warming Liquid. A pair of Clearblue pregnancy tests. The two agents presented themselves to the husband.

"Mr. Chandler, we are so sorry for your loss." Alcott wasn't good at this part. Blake Chandler never looked up from the blanket. "Sir, we just have two questions for you."

Chandler shrugged. "What part of Phoenix do you live in?"

"Gilbert."

"I understand you and your wife were trying to have another child. How did you know this was the best weekend?"

Blake and Sommer both scrutinized Alcott. "You're not married, are you? We knew she was ovulating."

Sommer and Alcott asked the driver to take them to Phoenix. Alcott put men on the ground in Gilbert and surrounding areas immediately. Forensics caught Lyle on a security camera. The desert sun was aflame. They were sure Lyle would be feeling the heat.

On the fleeting drive to Phoenix, Alcott and Sommer reviewed the psychological profile for Brandon Lyle. Sommer drove, and Jeremy opened the folder that forensic psychiatrist Ariel Senderos had given him during their briefing in Los Angeles. Senderos had handwritten in the margin:

Hell is empty. And all the devils are here.
—William Shakespeare
Agent Alcott: You have a true sociopath on your hands. This is a very dangerous, sick mind you seek. Be careful. AS
Lyle seems to have an Old Testament pathology. B. Lyle, or Belial, is a demon from hell charged with leading eighty infernal legions. The Dead Sea Scrolls refer to him as a key player in the "War of the Sons of Light and Sons of Darkness."
"But for corruption thou hast made Belial, an angel of hostility. All his dominion is in darkness, and his purpose is to bring about wickedness and guilt."
He believes in what he is doing and comes straight from the Revelations playbook.
Lyle believes he has an army helping him.
Lyle believes he is part of the apocalypse.
Lyle may truly believe he was sent by Satan. The Old Testament regards Belial as being an equal to Satan in evil.
He believes he is more than he is and has developed this persona from being insignificant.
This does not preclude his being a very dangerous enemy.
He is violent and has no remorse. This will get worse before it gets better.

Alcott read selected excerpts from Revelations chosen by Senderos. "'And there appeared a great wonder in heaven; a woman clothed with the sun, and the moon under her feet, and upon her head a crown of twelve stars.'" Alcott ran his finger under the small print. "'And she being with child cried, travailing in birth, and pained to be delivered. And there appeared another wonder in heaven; and behold a great red dragon, having seven heads and ten horns, and seven crowns upon his heads.'"

"Sounds like we should get some chain mail." Sommer looked at Alcott. "Maybe you should bone up on your jousting skills."

"'And his tail drew the third part of the stars of heaven, and did cast them to the earth: and the dragon stood before the woman which was ready to be delivered, for to devour her child as soon as it was born.' There it is, Sommer. He is devouring the child. It's not about the females as much as the children inside them."

"Or about to be inside her like Meadow. So the mother has some special part in this," Sommer concluded.

"'And she brought forth a man child, who was to rule all nations with a rod of iron: and her child was caught up unto God, and to his throne.'" Jeremy closed the folder and adjusted his shades. "That is one special child."

FEBRUARY 17
ARLINGTON, VIRGINIA

"Madeline. I spoke with Dr. Osaka this morning. I am sure you are aware of this." Madeline's eyes said yes. Dr. Smalling was sincere but firm. "He saw a very scared girl on Friday night. When anyone takes possession of a weapon, it is a sign she needs to defend herself against something. I need you to share with me. I need to know what is happening to make you react with such fear." She paused and squatted before Madeline in the chair. "Tell me about the dreams. It will help you."

Madeline's hands trembled. She attempted to utter something, but nothing came out. Smalling slid another chair close.

"It is a man in my dreams. He has evil blue eyes. He does horrible things to these girls. Women." Madeline choked it out.

"How do you see him?"

"What do you mean?"

"Do you see him outside? Does he appear in a room?"

"I never saw him until around Thanksgiving. He just popped into my head. There was a field. It was dark—well, almost dark, like sunset. He was hiding. He was hiding in some type of weeds. A girl was running through the field. He reached out and grabbed her and threw her to the ground. Then I saw her face looking up. She was so scared, and she screamed. She tried to fight, but he was too strong and he held her down with his hand over her face. He put his knee on her chest and reached under her dress. I could tell she was in so much pain." Madeline's chest started heaving.

"Breathe, Madeline." Smalling spoke gently.

"There was so much blood." Madeline curled her knees into her chest and rocked back and forth. Smalling was ready to quit the session. "Then she died. I could see the blood everywhere. And the flies. Flies swarmed everywhere."

Dr. Smalling offered Madeline a drink. Dr. Smalling concluded she needed one of a different kind, but she wouldn't reach for the special drawer. "Do you have the same dream over and over?"

"No." Madeline sipped on the water. "I don't always see that dream, but I know it is there. It started to go away after a few days. I guess I was blocking it out, but..." Madeline's voice trailed off.

"But what, Madeline?"

"On Christmas I saw his face again. It was different. In a different place. It started when I was helping my mom make dinner. I tried to make it go away." She curled into the fetal position. "But it stayed in my head." Madeline grabbed her hair and sobbed. "And he was talking to these girls. Everything was very dark in my dream, but I remember the two girls were Asian." Smalling offered Madeline a tissue. "And then he pushed the taller one against the wall and shoved something into her head. It looked like his finger, but it wasn't a finger. She fell dead against the wall." Madeline, barely coherent, continued. "He dragged the other girl. There was a graveyard. It was so dark, I couldn't see what was happening, but I heard her plead. She begged for the life of her unborn child. Then I saw the blood. And that's the last I remember before the ambulance arrived."

"Did he come back to you on Friday night?"

Sheepishly Madeline responded, "Yes."

"Was it a reoccurrence of the previous dreams or a new event?"

"A new dream." Madeline looked pale, but Smalling felt it was important to continue. "I could see everything. His face was clear. His hair had gotten longer, and he had a short beard. But it was him. It was those eyes."

"What color is his hair?"

"Sandy blond. It was the first time I noticed. The other dreams were so dark."

"Where was he?"

"I don't know. It was inside. A house or apartment. He attacked her as she walked in. She had a suitcase, and he threw her. Then he hit her on the head."

"All of this came to you while you were at the party?"

"Yes. I was on the deck outside at Mackenzie's house. I got really scared."

"I can imagine."

"His eyes seemed to be looking straight into mine." Smalling stared straight into hers.

"Is this after you smoked pot?"

Madeline rolled her eyes. "After."

"Did you feel high?"

"I felt scared. I felt he was coming for me. I grabbed a knife in Mackenzie's kitchen and ran upstairs. I locked the door, and then it happened."

"What happened?"

"He killed the girl. I could see everything." Madeline glowered at the floor in shock. "He was naked. He had a dragon tattooed across his chest. Giant talons wrapped around his hips. Then the skin around his face peeled away. Three red eyes bulged through his forehead, and his skin slid oozing to his side. He had shining wings on his back and they fluttered crazily behind him. It was like he disappeared."

Smalling slid to the edge of her chair.

"He was gone and some type of fucked up fly was there in his place," Madeline went on. "Tiny hairs grew on the body and these tentacle things waved from its head. The arms and legs changed into little black sticks that stuck out from the belly. It crawled onto the bed, little claws and suction cups poked the woman's skin. The red eyes stared right at her as two antennae things stretched from the face and nudged her hips, moving closer to her." Madeline gagged as she told the story. Smalling place her hand on Madeline's wrist. "A large tube came out and pushed in to her." Madeline pointed at her vagina. "Sharp teeth went inside her and began chewing her insides. It made this horrible slurping noise in its mouth. Its stomach started to swell as it ate the poor woman."

Dr. Smalling moved to Madeline's chair and rocked with her. She felt the sweat on Madeline's neck as she stroked her hair. The bell sounded for the session, but Smalling stayed with Madeline. The next patient would have to wait. Smalling felt clammy, and her stomach roiled in knots after sharing Madeline's nightmare.

Dr. Smalling regrouped and sat with Sophia and Raphael, who had both taken personal days. "Madeline shared her dreams with me today. They are extremely violent and sexual in nature. I have not concluded if these dreams stem from an occurrence in her life, but I surmise that they do." Raphael and Sophia sat, incredulous. "You daughter has endured a trauma. This trauma is creating this anxiety. This anxiety is severe. This caused the fight-or-flight scenario on Friday night."

"What is she running from?" Raphael asked.

"She is running from a man in her dreams who is harming other women and she believes he wants to harm her." Smalling paused. "I believe he already has."

Sophia started to cry as Raphael held her close. "Who? Who did this to our daughter?"

"It is imperative we find that out."

"Did she tell you?" Sophia blurted.

"No. I don't believe Madeline knows this person."

"So she was raped by a stranger?" Sophia became hysterical.

"We don't know what is causing the trauma, though today's session was very intense. We made a huge breakthrough. She told me about the dreams. It is vital to understand that these are not just dreams. These manifestations come at any time. And they are not the same reoccurring nightmare. Each one has its own specificity."

"What do we do next, Doctor?" Raphael consoled his wife.

"I believe your daughter has posttraumatic stress disorder. She may even be bipolar."

Sophia cried out, "You are talking of someone else, Doctor!"

"I am afraid I am not. An event, I believe in the fall, activated this change in your daughter's psyche."

"How do we treat this? Make her better?" Raphael asked.

"Continued psychotherapy. I want to put her on Klonopin." The parents were ignorant of the drug. "It is a sedative. This will help her relax and sleep. She is exhausted and needs to build up her strength. She is fighting this battle in her head. We will see how she reacts."

"What are the side effects?" continued Raphael.

"Some users report being drowsy. Motor functions may be impaired. Others say they wake up feeling like they have a hangover. Madeline should not use alcohol or any street drugs while taking Klonopin."

The Deschampses took the prescription, gathered a shaken Madeline, and headed off into uncertainty.

FEBRUARY 21
PHOENIX, ARIZONA

Agents from the FBI scoured the streets, showing pictures of Lyle, Javad, Elroy, Rohit, Davil and Guzan to customers in grocery stores, banks, shopping centers, and movie theaters. They were now privy to the security tape from the CVS pharmacy where Lyle encountered Meadow Chandler. Lyle's appearance had become more bohemian since he'd left the navy. His beard had grown, and his hair was longer. It looked like he had lost some weight. Alcott made certain that all the bulletins were updated.

"Any leads at all?" Alcott asked Bruno.

"Yes." Bruno put the file on the desk.

"Awesome! What did you find?" Jeremy jumped at the potential new leads.

"I showed a picture of Sadie Davil to one gentleman, and he identified her as the actress in the porn movie *Cara Loft: Womb Raider*. Another woman was certain Javad Nehwal played for the Arizona Cardinals. Another blessed me because she believed Rohit

Guzan was the leader of a Mexican cartel, and then she ran with her hair on fire away from me." Jeremy rolled his eyes in frustration. "It's like playing pin the tail on the wind." Bruno slumped into the couch.

"Do you think they left town?"

"Probably, but the only reason we even know they were here is because of Meadow. For all we know they could have been in the region for a couple of nights at a fleabag motel. It's been a week, Jeremy. They could be in Maine. Or even out of the country."

"They are not leaving the country," Jeremy stated flatly.

"How can you be so sure? They have resources. And someone is funding them. Lyle doesn't make those passports in his rack at sea. We know Floyd and Nehwal are armed and dangerous. Guzan and Davil are the contacts Lyle needs. They could be anywhere. Stowed away on a private plane."

"He is here for a reason."

"What reason?" Bruno played devil's advocate.

"I don't know." Alcott slapped his hands on the desk. "He has a plan. A target. A goal."

"Then why Meadow? She didn't seem to be a target."

"Meadow. Mao. The girl in the Philippines. They were all pregnant or trying to get pregnant. Tiffany Kai was not, and he was not interested in her."

"In the Philippines, Lyle had no previous contact with Esther Danilo…"

"Esther—that's her name…"

Bruno continued, "By all accounts he had no prior meeting with Mao or Tiffany. These women do have pregnancy in common but little else. I don't see a connection or pattern."

Alcottlet Bruno's comments sink in. "I think you're right. I think he has a larger, more destructive goal. I think these women are his weakness."

"But how could he know they were all pregnant? How could he just know? Maybe Meadow. We saw on the tape that her purse spilled on the floor. He could have known she was trying to get pregnant. Mao? In the fifteen minutes he knew her, he found out she was pregnant? I don't buy it. She wasn't far along and wasn't showing. And Esther. Naval investigators put her on the ground in Lyle's proximity near a helicopter handing out emergency supplies. He is going to notice her and then find her and murder her? A lot of coincidence here, Jeremy."

"I don't know how he picks his victims. The forensics don't lie. They were all maimed in the same way with the same results." The partners went back to work searching for Brandon Lyle.

FEBRUARY 28
PHOENIX, ARIZONA

Lyle and Sadie sat comfortably on the couch playing on their cell phones while the Phoenix police, FBI, NCIS, and US marshals scoured the region. Floyd worked with the C-4 in the garage, and Javad prepared the vehicles for their departure. They needed to lie low for a while.

Lyle sent a text, under his Victor Kuyt alias, to his new catch, Evelyn Cahill, in Atlanta. She seemed smitten and messaged him several times a day. Davil responded for Lyle, mostly. Lyle added a personal touch: *Can't wait till July. Seeing you in person for the first time will be a dream. Really enjoy having you in my life. I am so lonely. Can't wait to be with you. Send me more pics!*

Lyle thumbed through the gallery and viewed the growing library of nude and seminude pictures this flabby glutton Evelyn had texted.

MARCH 1
ARLINGTON, VIRGINIA

"Madeline." Sophia knocked on the door. "It's time to get up. You have cross-country today." There was no response. "It's nice out, and we are supposed to get snow on Monday. It would be a really good day to go to practice." Sophia tried to turn the knob. "Madeline! We talked about locking this door!"

The door creaked open, and Madeline stood before her mother, eyes swollen from sleep, and hair displaying a wicked case of bed head. Madeline said nothing and shuffled back toward her bed.

"Madeline! You have to come out of your room. You can't keep hiding in here."

"I don't have to do anything, Mom." Madeline got back under the covers and pulled them over her head.

"Yes, you do!" Sophia yanked the blanket off Madeline's body and sat on the edge of the bed. "You don't do anything anymore. You go to school like a robot and come home like a zombie. Your report card was terrible. You are not running with your team. You love running. You love being outdoors. Look! It's a great day!" Sophia pulled up the blinds, allowing the sunlight to flood the room. Madeline winced.

"Mom!" Madeline turned over, putting her back to the wave of light. "I don't want to go anywhere. They are always staring at me." Madeline put a pillow over her head.

"Who is always looking at you, baby?" Sophia rubbed Madeline's back.

"Everyone. Everyone at school. The students. The teachers. My so-called friends. I hear the whispers after I walk by. 'There's the girl who freaked out at the party.' 'There's the knife-wielding killer.' 'Don't go near her. She's crazy.'"

Sophia heard the sniffling start. She stretched out on the bed lengthwise with her daughter and put her arm around her.

"Kids can be mean," she said. "I'm sorry for that. It's been two weeks, and this will all go away." Sophia could only pray. "It's been a long two weeks since that night. You haven't had anything else happen since then. Maybe the Klonopin is helping."

"The drugs make me feel like a zombie." Madeline stayed under the pillow.

"They help you sleep," Sophia offered.

"I don't sleep well. I don't dream."

"But you don't have bad dreams. And that's the point, I suppose. At least until we find out what is bothering you."

"True." Madeline decided to make a point of her own. "But no dreams are unnatural."

Sophia decided to lay off the cross-country. "Have you given any more thought to which college you are going to attend?"

Madeline groaned. "No."

"You are going to have to make a decision very soon. Your father and I are very proud you were accepted to all of the universities that you applied to."

"I am really not thinking about college right now, Mom."

Sophia lost her composure for a moment. "Well, what are you thinking about?"

"Not much," Madeline sassed back.

Raphael stepped in from the hallway. "Madeline. Come down for breakfast when you are ready. No later than ten o'clock. Can we agree on that?" Madeline nodded in agreement from under the pillow.

She continued to hide under the pillow. She had told her mom about the kids at school. What she didn't tell her about were the contorted and grotesque faces of the people on the street. Their red, bloodshot eyes. The skin melting from their fingers and elbows. The dripping discharge that leaked from their mouths, noses, and ears. Not everyone. Every now and then. Walking through the mall. At the drugstore. On the street corner. These creatures never seemed to notice her, but Madeline would file between the crowds and witness the manifestation of unnatural souls.

MARCH 3
ARLINGTON, VIRGINIA

The most uninteresting man in the word drew an equation on the blackboard. "The point-slope formula," he said, the chalk squeaking, drawing the equation $y-y1 = m(x-x1)$. Madeline scratched it into her notebook, but it made no sense. She couldn't imagine a scenario in her entire life in which she would implement the point-slope formula. Unless it involved something rolling down onto Oliver's head.

Madeline stretched her legs and yawned in class. She had not slept well the night before. She pondered whether taking the medicine was worth it. Even when she slept, she never felt rested. Now she felt dizzy. Sophia had told her to eat breakfast, but she didn't listen. The class room started to spin, and the last thing Madeline remembered was her classmate Nick Harush yelling, "Madeline!"

MARCH 3
PHOENIX, ARIZONA

"Boss, you might want to see this." The tech guide cued up the video. "This just came in from the Arizona Highway Patrol. Interstate Ten traveling east. Approximately ten in the morning." Sommer and Alcott waited. "This is Arizona state trooper Florence Hugo. As you can see, she has pulled over a late-model Ford F-150 with a cover over its bed. Hugo called in the stop for speeding, but she is clearly intrigued by the bed. She waits for the license and registration, and as the driver hands it to Officer Hugo, you can see"—the tech enhanced the in-car video—"the numbers 14 and 88 tattooed on the driver's forearm." The tech paused the video.

"Elroy Floyd. I'll be damned." Alcott pumped his fist.

Bruno jumped at the opportunity. "Where is he being held?"

"There's more." The tech grew somber. "Officer Hugo seems to be engaged in a verbal altercation with the driver." They watched as the highway patrolman pointed to the bed of the pickup. "The driver starts to exit the vehicle, and Hugo steps back to draw her weapon."

As Officer Florence Hugo stepped backward onto Interstate 10 East, another massive Ford F-150 traveling at obscene speed plowed through the patrolwoman, launching her over one hundred feet into the sandy desert and cacti of eastern Arizona. Sommer, Alcott, and the tech rewound the video solemnly, trying to isolate the license plate of the second truck to no avail.

The truck driven by Floyd peeled off out of the picture. "Exactly how long ago did this occur?" Jeremy inquired of the tech.

"Ten in the morning."

"It's eleven now. They have an hour head start."

"The Arizona Highway Patrol is working with the New Mexico State Highway Patrol to capture both vehicles. There are eyes in the air already."

"I need to be patched in to the helicopters. I want to see what they see." Alcott was getting closer.

ARLINGTON, VIRGINIA

"I am fine," Madeline lied to the school nurse.

"Your father is on the way." The nurse made Madeline lie back down.

"I just forgot to eat breakfast." Madeline pleaded her case as she sipped the orange juice provided by the school.

"That may be, but I think it's better to be safe than sorry."

Madeline didn't want any more attention. She didn't want to be perceived as a freak. She just wanted her life to go back to normal, but she couldn't get the image of the pulverized state trooper lying dead in the desert with scorpions crawling in her mouth and out of her head.

THE NEW MEXICO DESERT

J avad Nehwal ripped down a desert road, heading south toward Mexico, followed by Elroy Floyd. Lyle worried about the lack of vehicles on the road. The helicopters were sure to be out, and the two Ford F-150s would look like lonely tanks in the desert. "Turn left," Lyle commanded. The convoy moved east into the Peloncillo Mountains.

By one in the afternoon, Lyle had found a ravine covered by a rock formation deep in the New Mexico desert. They'd eluded the authorities for the day, aided by a furious sandstorm that had blanketed the desert for hours. They would have to travel carefully at night. They needed new vehicles, but everyone in New Mexico drove a pickup truck. He would make somebody a very good trade.

MARCH
SOMEWHERE

L ila flinched when the handle turned on the bedroom door. The old man with the craggy face walked into the room. "Come with me."

"No." Lila curled up defiantly.

"Don't make me beat you." The old man's mouth curled downward, his eyes becoming dark.

"I won't go anywhere with you, you freak!" Lila scurried to the other side of the room. The old man, hobbled by age, tried to trap the child. His legs were weak, but his hands were strong. He snatched Lila by the hair and slammed her into the wall. Lila kicked at the man and tried to wriggle free, but his grip maintained the tight snare. He held her against the wall and backhanded Lila across the face. Blood trickled from her mouth. He gave her another slap for good measure and dragged her out of the small bedroom.

Lila kicked and screamed as the man dragged her across the short shag rug. Her foot snagged the tripod, toppling the camera.

"Looks like we have a feisty one." The elderly woman went to the closet and grabbed a shotgun. She pointed the barrel at Lila's face. Lila made the choice to live.

"She's a hellcat." The old man smarted from the kick to the groin. "She had better straighten up. I know a place where no one will find her." He returned the tripod to its original positon. "Where is the other one?"

The grandmother handed the rifle to the man with the craggy face. The den reeked of his cigar. "Take off your clothes," he instructed Lila. Lila refused. He cocked the shotgun without a blink, his dead eyes fixed on her chest. Lila removed her shirt. "All of them." Lila removed her bra, her brain disengaging from reality, avoiding the repugnant deed she was being forced to engage in. She slipped the sweatpants over her hips, leaving on her underwear. The old man savored every step. "The underwear." Lila's eyes pleaded for the old man's mercy, but it had vanished decades before.

The woman reappeared with a pale and petrified girl with long brown hair. Her innocent brown eyes were surrounded by dark circles of fear. Lila covered herself with her arms. "Now take off your clothes and sit next to the other girl," encouraged the matriarch. The youngster made no protest and removed her nightgown as told. She sat on the other side of the couch with Lila Chait.

The old man with the craggy face poked a couple of buttons on the video camera at the top of the tripod, and the picture appeared on the flatscreen. "You two are going to be Internet stars." The camera's stark light shone on the girls. "You just do what I tell you to do." Lila felt vile. The other girl sat silently stunned and afraid. "Mother? Are you ready?"

"I am."

The obese gray-haired woman sat between the two naked high school students wearing a cardinal-hued button-down cardigan and elastic-waistband comfort pants. She put her arms around the trembling adolescents. She pulled them into her chubby bosom and rubbed the girls' bare skin with her wrinkled hands. She leaned over to the brunette and pressed her lips against her mouth, sliding her tongue around her lips. "Kiss her," the old man commanded. The brunette opened her mouth, and the old woman thrust her tongue inside.

At gunpoint, Lila unbuttoned the hag's sweater and removed her blouse. The brunette unhooked her bra, and the mammoth breast fell low to her midsection. The woman brought the two girls' mouths to her nipples, her veiny hands searching the young children's bodies to reciprocate.

MARCH 4
NEW ORLEANS, LOUISIANA

Ke'Von had just made a short run from New Orleans to Hattiesburg, Mississippi, and back. Not a long day in the trucking business. He eyed the liqour store, but that meant he would have to drink at home. Too many lonely ghosts at home. Ke'Von wanted his stool at the Bayou Club.

Parking was a bitch. The celebrations had gone completely mad. Grown men dressed like fairies. A five-foot Frankenstein. A group of dancing Zulu warriors. Girls flashing their breasts to anyone with a string of beads. Marie Antoinette. Drunken hicks wearing T-shirts. A fifty-year-old with a beard to his chest wearing a T-shirt that said 50,000 BATTERED WOMEN AND I STILL EAT MINE PLAIN. A skinny queen with NEW KIDS ON MY COCK emblazoned on his garb. The haggard middle-aged woman represented her shirt that said I AM NOT AN ALCOHOLIC. I AM A DRUNK. ALCOHOLICS GO TO MEETINGS. Throngs of people hiding behind masks. Ke'Von just wanted to see DaMarcus's face. Mardi Gras induced the frenzy, but Ke'Von was never in a mood to celebrate. He waded his way through the crowd and into his neighborhood bar. There were no stools.

Ke'Von stretched through the patrons and shouted over the bar, "Shot of Wild Turkey!"

"Don't need no trouble tonight, Ke'Von." Bartender Emilia Seferovice's voice offered reason in Ke'Von's troubled world. Busy mixing hurricanes and pouring shots of Fireball for the twenty-something crowd, she made time to provide Ke'Von his whiskey.

"Won't make any trouble if no one gives me no trouble." Ke'Von placed his back against the wall and watched the costumed crowd.

Six shots in, Ke'Von's mind wandered to the dusty mountains of Afghanistan.

DaMarcus lay in the camouflaged tent with the other privates, breaking balls with his mates. A banner stretched across the wide wall: THIS WE'LL DEFEND. The US Army motto. The second lieutenant poked his head into the tent and called them to order.

DaMarcus inserted the pads into the knee sections of his flame-retardant army combat uniform trousers. He fastened the two-inch nylon belt, checked his supplies in the two calf storage pockets, and secured the Velcro. He pulled the tan laced combat boots over his dreary olive socks.

DaMarcus secured the mandarin collar over his tan government-issued T-shirt and commenced donning the improved outer tactical vest with enhanced small-arms protective inserts and side ballistic inserts.

His Kevlar advanced combat helmet employed a double-thick bill with an internal pocket. They called it a "boonie hat." DaMarcus's friend PFC Sebastian Endo referred to it as "the boon for the coon." DaMarcus fortified the night-vision goggles. He stepped out of the tent onto the sandy, mountainous region in the Ghazni Province of Afghanistan, certain he could not be detected with the Universal Camouflage Pattern of slate gray and desert sand with foliage-green pixel.

"Today we are going to take a trip down the Kabul-Kandahar Highway to a small city called Qarabagh. Intelligence says elite members of a Taliban unit have come down from the mountain. We believe they are still infiltrating the good folks of Qarabagh. This platoon will be equipped with a M1126 Stryker ICV, an M1117 Armored Security Vehicle with forty-millimeter Mark 19 Grenade Launcher, an MRAP, and an L-ATV. We leave at 0930. Full gear and ready to rock out with your cock out."

DaMarcus tried to catch some extra shut-eye in the MRAP, but the Kabul-Kandahar Highway was a bumpy ride. The convoy pulled into Qarabagh, and few eyebrows were raised. The US Army had visited before in 2007 when Taliban militia had kidnapped twenty-three Korean aid workers. The platoon disembarked the safety of the armored transports, and the second lieutenant fanned the troops out among the poor transient cities at the base of the Seya Mountains.

Sebastian Endo and DaMarcus Keshi moved south along the highway, scouting the area. DaMarcus took a wrong step, and the IED produced a tremendous blast the knocked Endo into the ditch and severed both of DaMarcus's legs at the waist. Flesh splattered on Endo as he tried to regain his bearings. Several team members rushed to DaMarcus's aid, but all the armored trucks and Kevlar gear and night-vision goggles and foliage-green pixel camouflage couldn't prevent DaMarcus from being blown up in the mountains of Afghanistan by a group of backwoods terrorists.

Ke'Von threw back his ninth portion of Wild Turkey. "They are going to send all of you!" he screamed to the celebrating crowd. The five-foot Frankenstein started recording the tirade on his iPhone.

"You are all going to die! Your government is going to send you all to your death!" Ke'Von's legs wobbled, but his voice resonated over "Pompeii" by Bastille blasting on the jukebox. Emilia escorted Ke'Von out of the Bayou Club for the night.

MARCH 14
DEMING, NEW MEXICO

Lyle and company sought refuge with a devout member of the legion in Deming, New Mexico, a spit across the Mexican line. Ruben van Gaal was their host, a wolf in sheep's clothing who exploited immigrants illegally crossing the border into the United States, bilking them of their last dollars as they burned in the Mexican desert waiting for final instructions from their devious guide. He was equally adept at bartering for sexual favors from desperate husbands willing to make trades with their wives for safe passage. Guns, drugs, and child trafficking fell under his corporate umbrella.

Lyle utilized van Gaal to obtain new vehicles. It was an ideal place to hide for a while. They were climbing the most wanted list, but days had passed. The FBI did not know where they were. Van Gaal asked for little in return. The only thing that bothered Lyle was the Catholic church across the street. Iglesia de la Almas Pura. The Church of the Pure Souls.

MARCH 17
DURANGO, COLORADO

POLICE SEEK INFORMATION ON MISSING MIDDLE-SCHOOL GIRL
Durango Herald

The Durango Police Department is posting a missing-persons report for Ilana Landreau, fourteen years of age. Ilana is a student at Escalante Middle School and was last seen on Friday, March 15, getting into a late-model, lime-green El Camino with a suspect between forty and fifty years old with brown skin and light graying hair.

Ilana is five feet one inch and weighs 125 pounds. She has brown eyes and brown hair, and her hair was last known to be dyed light blue or purple on the left side. Ilana was wearing a pair of dark-colored sweat pants with the brand PINK identified on the back. She was wearing a dark purple or dark blue hoodie sweatshirt and Nike tennis shoes. She had a purple-and-gold backpack. Ilana has a noticeable scar on the upper-right section of her forehead.

If you know anything of the disappearance of Ilana Landreau or her current location, please call the Durango Police Department at 970-555-5598.

MARCH 18, JEFFERSON CITY, MISSOURI

Almost four months had passed since the disappearance of their daughter, Celia Nair. No smiles graced the Nair residence. Claire Nair prayed with the pastor of the church for Celia's return. Grim-faced law-enforcement officials culled statistics that indicated she would not. Claire and Robert Nair refused to believe in the stats. Robert called the sheriff's office at nine every morning to see if there was any new information on Celia's disappearance. Every day Robert received no new information.

Robert and Celia went to the Walmart in Jefferson City each weekend hoping for magic. The drive took them past the fields in which more than a thousand volunteers marched in subzero temperatures looking for Celia's body. Masked Samaritans cloaked in doubt and fear.

Cindy Nair, Celia's sister, hid from the world in her bedroom, lost without her mentor and companion.

MARCH 19
ATLANTA, GEORGIA

FORD PLEADS NOT GUILTY—GARGANO SEEKS DEATH PENALTY

Atlanta Journal-Constitution—Bayleigh Debuchy

The Fulton County Courthouse was packed with reporters and protesters for the arraignment in the superior court of suspect Horace Ford. District Attorney Leo Gargano filed the official information document, and Judge Charlotte Wilshire determined there was probable cause to support the charges of the rape and first-degree murder of Savannah Gabriel in September of 2013. Ford entered a not guilty plea through his attorney, Eva Jo Diamond.

Horace Ford appeared in court in the familiar orange jumpsuit, leg-irons, and handcuffs worn by prisoners. Despite the gravity of Mr. Ford's legal issues, he was caught grinning during the hearing and seemed to be in generally good spirits.

DA Gargano spoke to the droves of local and national press after the hearing. "The judicial process is taking its course, and we are right on track to convict Mr. Ford of this terrible crime. I ask that the people of Atlanta be patient as we go through the process. Every defendant has legal rights."

"Absolutely" was Mr. Gargano's response when asked if the DA's office would seek the death penalty. "This is a prime example of why we have such a punishment." Mr. Gargano also noted his office would not accept a plea for a lesser penalty in this case.

Defense Attorney Diamond was asked how Ford could plead not guilty with such overwhelming evidence. "Mr. Ford pleaded not guilty because he is not guilty. Mr. Ford has become a scapegoat for the district attorney's office. The trial will show that the evidence that led to Mr. Ford's arrest was fabricated and that other evidence was tampered with in an effort to point the finger at my client."

Ms. Diamond's statements inflamed the protesters who were present to remember Savannah Gabriel and Breanna Green. Civil rights activist Leroi Stocker made this statement to the media: "We will not forget Savannah or Breanna. We will stand by them until the needle enters Horace Ford's arm. There can be nothing less in this case. The African American people of this community and the world will never be at peace while racists like Horace Ford walk the earth."

MARCH 21
ATLANTA, GEORGIA

The voice echoed in her headset. "I want one chicken breakfast burrito." Evelyn tapped on the computer while the driver made up her mind. "Give me one of them sausage-egg-and-cheese biscuits, and could you two shut up?" Evelyn listened to the mother scream at her kids. "Give me a plain biscuit. No, no, you'd better make it two. I'll take one Chick-fil-A chicken biscuit. Now, I told you two to shut up or you ain't going to get nothing to eat. I might put you on the side of the road." Evelyn waited for the rest of the order. "Give me another one of them breakfast burritos. And some chicken minis."

"Will that be all, ma'am?" You had to be superpolite at Chick-fil-A.

"You know what?" the woman asked. Evelyn didn't. "And give me one of those Chick-fil-A Asian salads."

"I am sorry. Those are only available at lunchtime." Evelyn was sugary sweet on the mic.

"Are you telling me you don't have the ingredients in there?" Evelyn could almost hear the mother sour in her driver's seat on such a sweltering morning.

"I am sure we have the ingredients, but it is not available until eleven."

"Put your manager on. And what is your name? This is not the customer service I have come to expect from Chick-fil-A."

"My name is Evelyn." Evelyn shrank at the register.

"What is your last name?" The guest became more agitated and much louder.

"Evelyn Cahill. Here is my manager, ma'am." Evelyn handed over her headset to the manager. Evelyn rushed to the back near the storage room and tried to hold back the tears.

"That woman was a bitch, Evelyn." Her friend Radiance put her arm around Evelyn. "You can't let those people get to you."

"I don't know what I did." Evelyn was pleading her case.

"You didn't do anything. She probably just wants something for free."

One of the cooks scrambled into the walk-in refrigerator and found the ingredients for the Asian salad. Evelyn and Radiance both rolled their eyes as the manager offered the woman a cinnamon cluster for her "inconvenience." Evelyn listened to the woman bellow at the manager at the drive-through window. He promised it would never happen again.

The manager came around the corner and handed the headset to Radiance. Evelyn started to speak, but the manager cut her off. "I heard most of the transaction. You kept your cool very nicely." Evelyn cracked a wry smile. "However, if a customer has a special request, take a moment and ask me."

"But we don't serve that item until lunch," Evelyn protested.

"I know. But it doesn't happen often, and if we can make a certain dish, let me help decide if we can make it happen." The manager stood up and hoisted Evelyn back to her feet. "Take a smoke break and get yourself together. It's almost lunch, and we are going to be serving a lot of those Asian salads." He winked and sent Evelyn out through the back door. She slipped behind the Dumpster and lit up a menthol. She pulled her phone out and checked to see if Victor had sent her a text. Probably not, as it was still early out West. She found his avatar. He had sent her a picture of him. She loved his crystal-blue eyes and had to crop the picture to fit it in the space allowed for the avatar. There was something so loving in them. She shot off a text: *Having a hard morning. Work sucks. I miss you and wish you were here. It would be better if I were holding you.*

Evelyn took a long drag and let the minty smoke fill her lungs. Her phone buzzed. She got a text back from Victor. It was a symbol of a big red heart. Evelyn Cahill was falling in love with a man she had never met.

MARCH 30
SALEM, OREGON

Mehrad Musa parked his Volvo at the entrance of Willamette Mission State Park north of Salem, Oregon. Mehrad had finally coaxed his coworker Naomi Ki to go hiking with him on the picturesque trails. Naomi was not as thrilled, but long hours as a certified public accountant left her short on exercise. She kicked herself, knowing that she had fed the cat, and soon Mehrad would be back at her desk asking for another date.

"Did you know this park is the proud home of the world's largest cottonwood tree?" Mehrad brushed his comb-over with his fingers to keep it in place.

Naomi tried not to roll her eyes. "I did not know that," she replied as she placed her foot on the trunk of the Volvo and tied her shoes very tight.

"Thank goodness, the rains gave way to the sun. I was very much looking forward to today." Mehrad looked at Naomi's formfitting pants rather than at the sky.

Naomi stretched and secretly prayed for a tornado. The drive had been awkward enough. Mehrad waved his arms around in a circle as if he wanted to take flight. Naomi stretched her hamstrings and lower back.

"Shall we begin?" Mehrad gazed at Naomi.

"Absolutely," stated Naomi, knowing that if it began, it would end.

"Let's head toward the wildlife overlook first and then head down toward Mission Lake." Mehrad had thought through this trail since Wednesday, when Naomi had agreed to the date.

The hike to the wildlife overlook was brisk and the conversation thin as the pace took their breaths. The strained pair opened their packs and refreshed with water, and Mehrad provided a Bear Naked Layered Fruit & Nutty granola bar.

Mehrad unwrapped his snack. "Why are you still single, Naomi? You are so beautiful."

Naomi choked on the water and the question. "I don't know." *Probably because of guys like you,* she thought.

"I used to do this walk often. It is a good to stay fit. I need to lose a couple of pounds." Mehrad pinched an inch. "How much do you weigh?"

Naomi wrapped up the rest of her granola bar and put it in her pack. "I think I could lose a couple of pounds too." Naomi zipped the pack. "Let's roll. I don't want to stiffen up." Naomi hit the trail with Mehrad bumbling behind her.

The trail brought them through the forest and to Mission Lake. Mehrad slowed the pace, his special day winding to a close. He stopped to catch his breath, his hands on his knees. Naomi stayed active, reaching her hands to the sky and back down to her toes.

"What do you think that is?" Mehrad focused on the lake.

Naomi had stopped paying attention to the world's largest cottonwood tree. "I don't know."

"It looks like an Oregon sweatshirt." Mehrad snapped a branch and reached for the floating garment. He stretched the crooked stick out over the water like an old finger. The stick snagged on the sweatshirt, and Mehrad pulled. The slimy decomposing face of a young woman rolled toward them. The girl did not look at the hikers from the grave. Her eyeballs had been nibbled away by the fish in Mission Lake. Mehrad and Naomi had discovered the body of Aditi Buffon.

MARCH 31
ATLANTA, GEORGIA

Evelyn grimaced inside when Radiance showed up with her next new girlfriend. It was supposed to be girls' night out. Evelyn supposed it still was girls' night out, but not exactly the way she'd envisioned it. "Hi, Radiance!" Evelyn feigned excitement.

"Hey, girl." Radiance approached arm in arm with Erika Veltman. "You remember Erika." The tiny but busty Erika extended her hand, and Evelyn grabbed it loosely and then pulled it away.

"I do." Evelyn knew she should mention now that it was supposed to be a night for her and Radiance, but she couldn't find the will. She decided to let it roll.

"Hey, Ev?" Radiance only used that nickname when she wanted something. "Erika would rather see *Better Living Through Chemistry*." Evelyn's heart sank. "She thinks Olivia Wilde is hot." Radiance and Erika squirmed together.

"OK." Evelyn's shoulders curled inward unnoticeably. She followed the smitten couple into the multiplex and quietly ripped up the two tickets to *Divergent* she had already purchased. Radiance got Erika's ticket, and Evelyn was fast to avoid the clerk she had purchased the other tickets from. That would be humiliating.

"Are you going to get something to eat?" Erika inquired of Evelyn.

She noted to herself that she was already out thirty bucks, but she said screw it.

Radiance and Erika stayed attached at the hip as they perused the candy case.

"Nerds?" Radiance wanted to choose the right thing for Erika.

"How about Sour Patch Kids?" Erika's eyes exploded in joy when Radiance agreed. They got the big box to share.

"I will have a medium popcorn and nachos. And a large Coke, the one in the refillable cup with Captain America on it." She so wanted Victor to be at the movies. The high school idiot behind the counter shuffled, spilling the Coke and giving her lukewarm cheese for her nachos. She paid the $25 extra and balanced her feature-film buffet, deftly using fingers, palms, and the crooks of her elbow. She followed Radiance and Erika to theater twelve.

The theater was fairly empty, which did not surprise Evelyn, because she was certain the movie would suck. Erika chose three seats that were far too high. They settled in, and Evelyn sorted out her snacks. She put the soda to her left so it wouldn't bother Erika's elbow. The popcorn went on the floor so she could devour the nachos while the cheese was still edible.

"That's a lot of food, Evelyn," Erika noted as Radiance turned her head and tried to hold back a snicker.

"I didn't have lunch. I'm starving," Evelyn lied.

"Can I have some popcorn?" Erika reached into the bucket and grabbed a handful.

"Sure."

"That's really salty." Erika winced as she crunched on a kernel.

"I like salty things in my mouth." Evelyn felt strongly that that would shut Erika up for a while.

The lights dimmed, and the odd threesome suffered through the previews, including one for *Divergent*. Erika and Radiance sighed when Olivia Wilde came onscreen. Radiance reached into Erika's lap and took a Sour Patch Kid from between her knees, where Erika was holding the box. Erika put her arm around Radiance, and Radiance put her left hand on Erika's thigh. Evelyn squirmed to indicate that she felt unnerved, but it had no effect as Erika reached over and slipped her tongue into Radiance's open mouth. Radiance's hand slipped past the box of candy and onto Erika's crotch, lightly rubbing the outside of her jeans. Erika obliged and moved the sweets next to her hip, allowing Radiance to roam free. Erika's left hand left the armrest, reached over, and fondled Radiance's breast, palming it freely and firmly as Radiance's fingers moved firmly between Erika's open legs.

Evelyn tried to stare straight ahead and focus on her Captain America cup. It reminded her of Victor Kuyt. Her sailor who would be coming to see her soon.

APRIL 1
ARLINGTON, VIRGINIA

The annoying alarm went off at 6:50 a.m. Madeline smacked the clock radio, and the squawking ceased. She grabbed her phone and saw there was a text. Half asleep, she rolled to the side of her bed and zigzagged her password across the screen.

I am coming to get you. An emoji of a creepy orange-faced devil with long teeth and black hair was attached to the text. It came from a number she did not recognize. Madeline dropped the phone and locked the door. She burrowed deep into her closet and covered herself with sweat pants and a winter coat.

Raphael looped the knot on his tie and pulled it tight. He squared his briefcase, double-checking that his final report was present and ready for the day's vital meeting.

"Good morning, Oliver." He rubbed his hand on the young man's head as Oliver enjoyed some Cinnamon Toast Crunch.

"Good morning, Dad." Oliver slurped the cereal milk.

"You shouldn't watch *SpongeBob* in the morning. We talked about that." Oliver lowered his eyes like a puppy and turned off the cartoon. "Is Madeline up?"

"Nope. Haven't seen her." Oliver got up and dropped his bowl into the sink. "When are we going to leave?"

"Give me a minute. I want to make sure Madeline is awake and dressed." Raphael snared him and gave him a kiss.

"I'll wait in the living room." Oliver threw his backpack onto the couch.

Raphael climbed the stairs and knocked on Madeline's door. "Madeline. Time to get up." There was no response. The door was locked. "Madeline. It's time to get up. We've talked about this door being locked." The house was still. Raphael pulled at the knob. He knew the door wasn't going to budge. He felt his blood pressure rise. He retreated a couple of steps and slammed his shoulder into the door. Oliver peeked around the banister. The door nudged but didn't open. He rammed into it again. The door creaked. On the third try, the doorjamb split, and Raphael entered the room. "Madeline!" he shouted. There was no response, and Madeline was not in her bed. Raphael noted that the window was not open. He took a deep breath and heard a scratching sound. He opened the closet and saw Madeline's toe sticking out from under some clothes. He threw them off her. Madeline hadn't turned to the safety of her father since the night at Mackenzie's. She continued to etch into the wall with her fingernail. "He's coming."

Raphael talked to his daughter with little response. He managed to get her out of the closet, but she stayed close to the wall and would not get dressed, despite his requests. He took out his phone and dialed Dr. Smalling on her cell. He was comforted when she answered. "Dr. Smalling. I am so sorry to call you at such an early hour."

"That is fine. I was getting ready to go to work. Who is this?" Dr. Smalling sounded flustered.

"This is Raphael Deschamps. Madeline is having some type of episode."

"Is Madeline breathing regularly?"

"Yes. But she seems very distant. He eyes are dark, and she doesn't seem to acknowledge anything I say."

"Is she showing any signs that she may hurt you or herself?"

"No. She has just pinned herself against the wall and won't move."

"Mr. Deschamps, I am going to come to your house right now. What is your address?"

Raphael gave the doctor the address to the house and followed her instructions to call her immediately if Madeline became a threat to herself or violent toward him. Raphael called work and informed his boss that he would not be at the meeting. Then he called Sophia, who postponed everything on her calendar and headed home. Raphael sat on the edge of Madeline's bed and called both children's schools. Madeline gripped the wall and stared vacantly.

Raphael and Sophia stood in the broken doorjamb of Madeline's room. Dr. Smalling took Raphael's place on the bed and coaxed Madeline off the wall and into her arms. Madeline showed Dr. Smalling the text. Raphael showed Dr. Smalling the scratching of the closet wall. Dr. Smalling left the room and brought the parents together in the kitchen, feeling Madeline was OK to be in her room by herself. Sophia put a teapot filled with water onto the stove.

"The text is disturbing," Dr. Smalling said. "I would advise you to contact the authorities and see if they can identify the number."

The kettle screeched, and Sophia poured Dr. Smalling a cup of chamomile tea. Meanwhile, Oliver listened from around the corner.

"This could be the first tangible evidence that Madeline has someone in her life who is a legitimate threat." Smalling sipped the hot chamomile tea. "The scratch she made into the wall concerns me. I believe Madeline is suffering from schizophrenia."

The Deschampses gasped. Raphael consoled Sophia. "What does that mean, Doctor?" Raphael asked.

"It means she has multiple personalities!" Sophia cried out. "She has 'someone' inside her!"

"That is a common misconception," Dr. Smalling said. "I don't believe she has multiple personality disorder. Schizophrenia is a mental disorder and very treatable. Over the past few months Madeline has exhibited telltale traits. These dreams, I believe, are hallucinations. At times she has shown unclear and confused thinking. False beliefs."

"That text is very real," Sophia noted.

"As I mentioned, the text is disturbing, and we need to find the source."

Oliver appeared from around the corner, his face flush, his eyes brimming with tears. "I sent the text." The horrified adults glared. "It's April Fools' Day."

"Have you lost your goddamn mind, Oliver?"

Oliver winced; Raphael rarely raised his voice. "I'm sorry," he mumbled through his shaking lips.

"Apologize to Madeline!" Sophia raged at her son.

Oliver snuck away toward Madeline's room, and Raphael followed him. Oliver hugged Madeline, who hugged back. As he tried to sneak out of the room, Raphael grabbed Oliver by the shoulder and hauled him to his room.

In the kitchen, the remaining adults heard the consequences of Oliver's poorly timed prank.

Dr. Smalling took Sophia's hand, drawing her attention away from Raphael and Oliver. "Sophia, the simple fact remains. Madeline is terrified. Whether real or imagined, this period of stress and anxiety has taken a toll on her psyche. We need to calm her down. We need to relieve this stress."

"It sounds like you want to give her more dope. She already confided in me that she feels like a zombie."

"That is normal when taking some of these medications. With continued psychotherapy and medication, we can get to the root of Madeline's issues. We need to find the source of the trauma."

"And in the meantime she is zonked out of her mind."

"Sophia. Two hundred years ago, they would have burned Madeline at the stake for her behavior. This is modern science. We know so much more about the human brain and how to treat this."

"What do you want to put her on now?"

"A low dose of Seroquel along with the Klonopin she is taking already." Smalling rose from the chair and set the teacup in the sink.

"What is that going to do to her?"

"Seroquel is a short-acting antipsychotic. It's a tranquilizer. First-generation tranquilizers often impair motor abilities. This doesn't. The drug suppresses dopamine activity receptors."

Raphael returned to the kitchen to rejoin the discussion. "What are its side effects?"

"She will be sleepy. I am prescribing a low dosage, but we will have to monitor somnolence. Dry mouth, dizziness, and headaches. If these occur with frequency, I would need to know. We know that Madeline has had hypertension, so you would need to monitor her stress. In rare cases, diabetic ketoacidosis, jaundice, restless legs syndrome, pancreatitis, tardive dyskinesia, and suicidal thoughts."

"That's just great. You want me to put my daughter on something that will make her yellow and shaky, blow up her organs, and leave her trying to kill herself when we are trying to make her not depressed." Sophia crossed her legs and tossed her hair, looking away from Dr. Smalling.

"These happen in less than one percent of cases. The benefits outweigh the risks. There is also the chance of weight gain." Sophia smiled. Even in this trying moment, Dr. Smalling had gotten Sophia to smile.

APRIL

SOMEWHERE

L ila Chait hoisted up the oversize sweat pants they made her wear. Having no string made it difficult. She tapped on the wall and received a coded tap back. It was the safe code. Sometimes he would leave in the morning and not come back for a couple of hours. Lila went to the window and saw the buds on the trees from the second-floor glass. *It must be spring,* she thought. Lila tapped again on the wall, securing the safe sign. It came back again: *OK.*

Lila pulled the string from her Western Hills sweatshirt and painstakingly threaded it into the sweatpants. She cursed herself for not doing that task last night, but she would have gotten a beating if he had caught her. *Such a waste of time,* she thought to herself. She pressed with all of her might on the window lock. It would not budge. She removed her sock, wrapped it around her knuckles, and blasted at the lower left pane. It shattered, and she picked at the remaining teeth that clung to the wood. She pounded at the remaining frames, and the glass fought back, ripping the tendon in her thumb. Blood pressed into the sock and began to leak onto the floor. Lila tightened the sock around her hand and folded another around her wrist. She clawed at the wooden frame, wrestling it out of the groove. She checked for any lingering shards and lifted her foot into the opening. Lila leaped out of the window and into a bush, which abetted her fall. She looked up to the window next to hers and saw the fearful face of the poor girl who had knocked on the wall. She waved for her to join her. The girl moved the curtain over her face, and Lila started running.

There were no houses to be seen. The road was narrow and damp from rain. The sky was still gray, the freedom much colder than she had anticipated. She couldn't decide if she should go left or right. She saw the number on the mailbox: 9387. She repeated the number over and over in her head so that when she found some-one, they could help the other girl. Lila decided to go right. She ran in bare feet, her hand drenching the sock with blood.

There was no traffic on the road. No gas stations. No 7-Elevens. No intersections or red lights. Lila was not sure how far she had gone, but she had expected to see some sign. In the very far dis-tance, she saw a single flashing yellow light. It was her next goal. She kept running.

Lila panted for breath, and the yellow light beckoned her to come closer. She thought of her parents and of taking a bath. Her body was weak, but she kept moving. Her thoughts had become a trance, and she did not hear the truck behind her until it was too late.

"Where do you think you are going, sweetheart?" The timeworn man with the craggy face rolled down the window and pointed a dou-ble-barreled shotgun at her face. Lila kept running, and the barrels exploded, sending fragments into her thigh. Lila fell to the ground. The man stopped the truck and walked slowly around the front. He threw his cigar to the ground and rolled Lila over with his foot. He knocked Lila in the head with the barrel of the gun. She lay uncon-scious. He picked her up like a deer and threw her into the cab.

APRIL 14
ARLINGTON, VIRGINIA

The butter seared the pan. The last time Sophia had seen Madeline at the stove was on Christmas. She smiled as Madeline flipped a grilled cheese, the bread perfectly griddled.

"Hi, honey. Do you need some help?" Sophia put her keys into her purse.

"I'm fine." Sophia hadn't heard that in a long time. Madeline turned and gave her mother a big hug. Sophia pulled her daughter close.

"Your grilled cheese smells yummy."

"I am hungry." Madeline reached inside the refrigerator and pulled out the ketchup and a pickle. "I got asked to the prom today."

"Madeline! That's awesome! Who is the lucky guy?" Sophia blurted.

"It's Austin Lee. The boy I went on the date with." Madeline slid the spatula under the sandwich and slipped it onto her plate.

"Did you say yes?" Sophia asked tentatively.

"I did," Madeline responded, also tentatively.

"You don't sound sure about this, Madeline. Do you feel comfortable going with Austin?" Sophia's real question was, *Was Austin the root of all of Madeline's issues?*

"He's a nice boy. I don't know if I like him in that way, but it's my senior year, and I would like to go to the prom. And he asked." Madeline squirted ketchup onto her plate and dipped the corner of the sandwich in the Heinz. She chomped on the gooey cheese and bread.

It was music to Sophia's ears. "We'd better find a dress for you, young lady."

"I was hoping you would say that, Mom." Madeline smiled.

"When is the prom?" Sophia loved to shop.

"Saturday, April twenty-sixth. It's at the Key Bridge Marriott."

"Then we had better get to work. Better clear your calendar on Saturday."

Madeline smiled again. "We will have to go later in the day. I have cross-country in the morning."

Madeline was cooking and hungry. Madeline gave her a hug. Madeline was going to the prom. Madeline was running. Madeline smiled. Maybe things were looking up.

APRIL 16
ATLANTA, GEORGIA

Evelyn's shirt was untucked in the back, and her Chick-fil-A pants were sagging. She was exhausted and knew there was cold beer in the fridge. She stopped to get her mail from the box: 2B. She pulled out the papers, relocked the box, and groaned as she could not find the energy to walk the one flight up the stairs.

Evelyn held on to the railing and forged ahead. The apartment was steaming. Her fan didn't cut the mustard in this heat. She plopped down onto the couch and tossed the mail onto the coffee table. Among the power and cable bill and the junk mail was a letter. In the upper lefthand corner was a colorful stamp in the shape of a heart. The pastel colors formed a bouquet of spring flowers, and threaded through the heart were the words *Yes, I do.*

There was no return address, and Evelyn found the handwriting on the outside of the envelope a little girly. She slid her nail through the crease and removed the note inside. Her eye was drawn immediately to the signature at the bottom of the personal note. It was from Victor. She felt the air leave her lungs.

Dear Evelyn,

As each day passes, I feel closer to you. I long for the day we will meet, and your face is in my mind every minute. One thing you don't know about me and that I kept to myself while I was in the navy is that I like to write poetry. I hope you don't find this weird. I wrote this poem for you. I hope you like it.

In the desert I long for your sweet kiss
In the mirage I see your face in the mist
The sun beats strong on me from above
Into the eastern morning I march to your love
There is no mercy in the desert skies
No tenderness like the refuge of your eyes
No comfort in the night sand to rest
No place of solace as is your breast
I walk along the rivers dry with fire
Only seeking my heart's true desire
Warding off the circle of the scavenger
Until I step into the fields of lavender
I smell the fragrance of your nape
And into your arms I will escape

—Victor

Evelyn read the letter until she had memorized the verse. Kuyt had pierced her with Cupid's arrow. Her need to be with him consumed her. Her desire piqued and pounding, Evelyn removed her clothes, stretched out on the couch, and thought of Victor. She would satiate his thirst from the desert when he arrived in Atlanta, but she needed to satisfy herself right away.

Somewhere Sadie Davil was laughing her ass off.

APRIL 20
DEMING, NEW MEXICO

Lyle took a moment and remembered Adolf Hitler in the most reverent way. The 200,000 dead in Warsaw. The 870,000 executed in Treblinka. The 35,000 lives lost in the ghetto of Theresienstadt in the Czech Republic. The 278,000 who perished in the Polish labor and extermination camps of Stutthof, Soldau, and Sobibor. The women's camp at Ravensbrück took 90,000 racially polluted lives of Gypsies, Poles, and Jewish hags. Lyle saluted the tremendous victories at Auschwitz, Buchenwald, and Dachau, the systematic slaughter of humanity in the factories of death. Today was Hitler's birthday, and the despot's heroics were rewarded with a seat by his master's side in hell. Lyle watched across the street as the children frolicked at the playground of the Church of the Pure Souls under the supervision of nuns wearing the black habits of the Sisters of the Annunciation of the Blessed Virgin Mary.

APRIL 22
SARASOTA, FLORIDA

HIGH SCHOOL FRESHMAN MISSING

Sarasota Herald-Tribune

The Sarasota Police Department is posting a missing persons report for Yael Almeida, fifteen years of age. Yael is a freshman at Riverview High School and was last seen sunbathing on Sunday, April 20, on a stretch of beach near the Gulf Beach Resort Motel on Benjamin Franklin Drive. Yael was with her brother, David, and when he came back from a walk on the beach, she was not there.

Yael is five feet seven inches tall and weighs 112 pounds. She has sandy-blond hair and hazel eyes. She wears a ring in her belly button and an ankle bracelet. She was last seen wearing a dark green bikini.

If you know anything about the disappearance of Yael Almeida or her current whereabouts, please call the Sarasota Police Department at 941-555-2038.

APRIL 26
WASHINGTON, DC

Adapper Austin Lee sat across from the elegant Madeline Deschamps at the dazzling restaurant the Hamilton in Washington, DC. Austin had avoided the pratfall of renting a cream-colored tuxedo and went with a sleek black look with a white bow tie twist and matching cummerbund. Madeline had pinned Austin with a boutonniere of buttonholes with feathers and berries.

Madeline was careful getting into the booth wearing a short, strapless, sequined, black-and-turquoise dress. The octopus necklace made Austin focus his eyes in an appropriate place. Madeline kicked off the uncomfortable but stunning four-and-a-half-inch Ivanka Trump pointy-toed pumps she and her mom had found at Nordstrom. Madeline hoped the white whisper wristlet corsage wouldn't interfere with eating.

The waiter approached. Austin lost his nerve and abandoned any thoughts of trying to order a glass of wine. He opted for a Sprite, and Madeline stuck with water.

"Do you like sushi?" Austin perused the menu.

"My brother loves it." Madeline worried that the wasabi would make her nose run. It always did. "You kind of have to be in the mood."

"I agree. I don't know if I am ready for a fire dragon roll." Madeline giggled. She was having fun.

The waiter returned promptly with their beverages, and Austin ordered the fried calamari with pickled fresno chilis, garlic aioli, and lemon. The server recommended the dynamite rolls, and Austin and Madeline shared a laugh.

"Madeline, what would you like for dinner?" Austin folded the menu and looked at his date.

"I will have the pork sausage ragù with ziti." She handed the menu over.

"Would you like the entrée?" the waiter asked.

"I would like the appetizer. I need to save room for dancing tonight." And it was only $12 dollars. Austin had been so sweet.

"I take it you are going to your prom?" the waiter said.

Both exclaimed yes.

"Well, you will need to save room for chocolate gooey cake."

"Oh my God. That sounds delicious!" Madeline focused on Austin. "I have a serious weakness for chocolate."

The waiter turned his attention to Austin. "I'll have the dry-aged ribeye frites." Austin was glad he had his dad's credit card.

"And how would you like that cooked?"

"Medium is fine."

Madeline stretched her hands across the table. She made up her mind to kiss Austin tonight.

ARLINGTON, VIRGINIA

"Officer Velozo?" The captain of the Arlington County Police called for Paolo. "I want you to meet Father Salvatore Moutinho. He is a priest at the National Cathedral in Washington, DC."

"It's nice to meet you, Father," said Paolo.

"It is very nice to meet you, Officer." The priest held Paolo's hand warmly in his.

"Father Moutinho is going to join you as part of the ride-along program this evening."

Paolo hated ride alongs. Especially at night. But he didn't have much of a choice. "I hope you brought your rosary. Saturday nights can be adventurous," Paolo joshed with the holy man.

"I said my prayers this afternoon." The Episcopalian priest closed his eyes as he spoke. "I am sure the children of God will be well behaved."

"The children of God will. I don't know about everyone else," Paolo remarked as the captain rolled his eyes.

The priest opened his eyes again. "You seem to be very well prepared for this evening's shift, Officer Velozo." He watched as Velozo took inventory of his police belt. "What all do you carry there?"

"Well, Father." Velozo didn't want to go through the whole belt, but the captain would kill him if he was impolite. "Starting on my left, I carry a regular set of handcuffs. As I move around my waist to my left," Paolo said, shifting his hand, "there's my Taser."

"What does a 'Taser' do?"

"You've never seen a Taser?"

"No, my son. This is why I so wanted to join a policeman and observe him do his job. I want to be more helpful to the troubled children in our society. Of these things I am not informed." The priest bowed slightly, asking for the officer's patience.

"A Taser looks like a gun, but instead of bullets, it carries a large electrical surge that shocks the perpetrator. It is also known as a stun gun."

"Does it hurt the person?"

"Hell yes!" Paolo exclaimed. "I am sorry. I did not mean to swear."

"It is all right, my son. Of this language, I have heard much worse. Continue. I apologize for having so many questions."

"You can ask all the questions you like, Father. The next thing on my belt is my radio holster, which I use to communicate with the rest of the force. This little holster is for my keys. Then this is my PolyTac LED 220–lumen flashlight." Paolo shone the light in the father's face for effect.

The priest winced. "That is very bright."

"Then I have a second pair of handcuffs in case I have to arrest more than one person. These are PPE gloves."

"PPE?" questioned Moutinho.

"Personal protective equipment. Sometimes we have to work with some pretty nasty people. You never know what kinds of diseases they might be carrying."

"Yes. Some of God's sheep are very sick."

"This is my twenty-six-inch ASP expandable baton. It is a very dangerous and painful device. It can be a deadly weapon if used in the wrong way. And this is my Glock 17, and this is pepper spray. Finally there are the magazines that hold the extra hollow-point bullets for the Glock."

"It seems I will be in good hands with Officer Velozo, Captain."

"You certainly will. He is one of our best." The captain gave them a thumbs-up as they headed out to the streets of Arlington.

WASHINGTON, DC

Austin navigated through Georgetown with Madeline's help on the phone.

"Take this left onto the Francis Scott Key Bridge," Madeline instructed.

"Isn't that the guy who wrote 'The Star-Spangled Banner'?" Austin looked over the Potomac River and the illuminated Kennedy Center in the foreground.

"I think so. Stay in the right lane. I see the hotel." Austin fixed his eyes on the turn lane.

Austin wheeled the Mercedes-Benz S-class sedan to the front door of the Key Bridge Marriot. The valet opened the door for Madeline and hustled to give the ticket to Austin. Austin slipped the guy a ten-spot. The couple entered and felt the floor reverberating from the DJ in the Potomac Ballroom.

The ballroom exploded with the color of spring dresses long and short. Earth science teacher Mr. Foster and Ms. Jimenez greeted Madeline and Austin at the door.

"You both look great tonight," Mr. Foster said.

Madeline had never seen Mr. Foster look so relaxed.

"Madeline, you look so beautiful!" Ms. Jimenez reached in and gave Madeline a rich hug. "I love your hair! You should wear it down more often. And let me see that beautiful face. It's always hiding in that hoodie." They enjoyed the laugh. Everyone was so nice.

Then Mr. Foster gathered their tickets and told them to have a great, great night.

Mackenzie bounded up to Madeline with Yossi Beckerman in tow. It was the first time they had been out since the fateful Valentine's night. Yossi flashed a flask in his jacket pocket, having not learned his lesson. Madeline and Austin declined the drink but joined them both on the dance floor. Nick Harush, the coolest kid in school, looked like a dork cutting the rug, and Adam Pooladi fought with his date, Dawn, because he thought she was flirting with Ron. Riley was in a corner with Ashley ragging on Morgan's dress, and Shelbi was shooting lovey looks at the DJ so he would play all her favorite songs.

Mackenzie dragged Madeline off to the ladies' room. "Where did Austin take you for dinner?"

Madeline took the time to check her makeup while Mackenzie used the toilet. "We went to the Hamilton in DC. It was very nice."

"Yossi took me to Tallula," Mackenzie bellowed from the stall.

"I heard that's awesome." Madeline touched up her lipstick.

"It was all right. My parents take us there all the time. I'm just bored of it." Mackenzie flushed, swung the door open, and joined Madeline at the mirror. She started to wash her hands. "Yossi has been uptight all night."

"Why do think that?" Madeline straightened her skirt.

"Because he wants to get laid tonight, and I told him I'm not ready for that." Mackenzie fluffed up her hair. "And if he keeps acting like a douche, he might not get anything." The seniors exited refreshed and up-to-date and returned to mingling with the students at the Washington-Lee High School prom.

ARLINGTON

Officer Velozo moved west in the squad car on Washington Boulevard and turned south onto North Taylor Street. They cruised past 11th Street and North Fairfax Drive through the quiet neighborhoods of North Arlington.

"What kind of calls do you get on a Saturday night, Officer Velozo?" Father Salvatore Moutinho sat belted into the passenger's seat.

"The fun doesn't start until after midnight. That's when the drunks rear their ugly heads. Bar fights. We will get domestic violence calls. We watch for drunk drivers. We look for indigent people causing trouble with pedestrians." Velozo turned east, passing the Ballston metro.

Moutinho gave notice to the shotgun clipped to the dashboard. The constant radio chatter directed units throughout the county. "Are there an abundance of violent crimes in Arlington?"

"Fortunately, tonight's ride is one of the calmer beats. Not that violent crimes don't happen around here. South Arlington has a tendency to be more violent."

"Why South Arlington?"

"Father, I guess it boils down to socioeconomics. The people there aren't as well-off as they are in North Arlington."

"So crime is directly related to money?" Moutinho wanted to engage the officer in a friendly debate.

"I didn't say that, Father. But there are the haves and the have-nots. The have-nots want what the others have." Velozo passed the Virginia Square metro station and followed a car with a bunch of kids joyriding.

"Is it the same with domestic violence or violent crimes?"

"Statistics show that more violent crimes happen in South Arlington. The presence of gangs influences those numbers. Drug dealers. Drug dealers have guns. These crimes are usually the result of drugs, money, or a woman."

"So in North Arlington they don't have drugs, money, or women?" Moutinho clutched the dashboard as the car with the kids swerved across the double yellow line.

"I didn't say that, either, Father." Velozo was happy to turn on the lights and pull the kids over. He felt like he was being painted into a corner by the Episcopalian priest.

DEMING, NEW MEXICO

The historic adobe-style Church of the Pure Souls was surrounded by a coyote fence. The original settlers had protected the church by digging deep holes and filling them with the trunks of slender timber that had been whittled to a razor point. Each piece connected with the others, preventing hungry scavengers from slipping through any cracks. The fence stood six feet high, and the deadly tips provided strong encouragement to the desert coyotes not to become creative and attempt to crawl over for a feast.

Sadie Davil entered through the gates of the church. Lyle waited in the shadows until Sadie waved Lyle and the others forward. Entering the house of God made Lyle's skin crawl. Five nuns were cleaning the church after the Saturday mass. Sadie sealed the door after they entered.

"Welcome to the Church of the Pure Souls." The benevolent woman approached Lyle. "How may we help you?"

Lyle crossed the woman's face with the back of his hand. She collapsed into the pew. "Tonight you will surrender your souls to the true and rightful master. Tonight you will sacrifice your virtue on the altar of your lying, putrid God, and in his unholy house you will bleed and suffer as he has made the souls in hell endure. You worship a wretched God who hides behind a mask of love and kindness, but his soul is dark, like the soul of the humans he has created. My Lord hides from no one! Tonight you will accept the true joy of pain."

Sadie bound one nun and burned her flesh with the flames of the votive candles, dripping the scalding wax into her eyeballs. Lyle ripped the tunic from other and pressed her face against the floor, sodomizing her with the still hot candle.

Elroy Floyd danced in delight as he chased another sister through the pews, pinning her to the wall next to the station of Saint Veronica wiping the face of Jesus. Elroy shoved his hand between the virgin's legs and raped her with his hand and then forced her to pleasure him with her mouth, gagging her with his penis and violently jerking her hair.

The massive Javad relished in the carnage, dragging two holy sisters and alternately penetrating them with a thurible, the cone-shaped metal container that burns incense during solemn occasions. He forced the eldest nun to shove her rosary into the younger sister's anus.

Lyle laid the trembling youth on top of the altar, stripped naked and bare. He emptied the paten and filled her mouth with the blessed Communion hosts, ramming them into her throat and choking her. He stood on the altar over her, raised high with Christ on the cross. He mocked Jesus as he spread his arms open. He forced the girl to rub him until he ejaculated into the chalice and then forced her to drink his semen from the cup. Sadie handed Lyle the monstrance. At the top of the vessel was the host, exposed for the congregation to witness. The host was circled by the sun's rays, sculpted of gold and piercing at the tip. Lyle inserted the edge into the young nun's throat and ripped her down through the abdomen, her intestines dripping over the side of the altar. The remaining sisters wept.

They corralled the survivors and led them to the courtyard. One by one Javad lifted them over his head and dropped them onto the sharp spears of the coyote fence, impaled and suspended in the moonlight. Lyle spat on the ground, walked across the street, and opened the garage. They left New Mexico, the bodies of the raped and murdered innocent silhouetted in the desert night sky.

ARLINGTON

Madeline made it to the lobby but vomited before the exit. The doorman asked if she was OK, but she kicked off her Ivanka heels and ran. Madeline avoided the roadways and hid behind parked cars and trees. She ducked into ravines and shuffled through storm drains. She blindly crossed the busy Route 29 in Cherrydale on the receiving end of angry horn blasts from the drivers who almost plowed her into the asphalt.

She hid in the gloom of an embankment and vomited again. Madeline weaved her way to nowhere, stripped of her awareness and saddled with fear. She slunk along fences and avoided the melting faces and angry eyes of the pedestrians in the crosswalks. The evil was everywhere, staring as she walked past their shops and restaurants. They glared at her from the windows of the cars. The red beaming eyes implanted in the skull of the clerk. The renegade youths on skateboards drooling phlegm from their mouths. The jagged teeth of the homeless man. The rotting flesh falling from the cheek of the man in the window drinking his beer. The bloodstained claws of the college student with her bookbag. They were all watching for her. They were watching for him. He was coming to kill her. Like he'd killed all those others.

Mr. Foster was on the phone with the Arlington County Police. Austin Lee was on the phone with Raphael Deschamps. "I am so sorry, Mr. Deschamps. I am so sorry." Madeline was his date, and he was responsible.

"Austin, it is not your fault. Has someone called the police?" Raphael stayed cool on the outside.

"Mr. Foster. He's on the phone with them now."

"What happened?"

"I went to the bathroom, and when I came back, I couldn't find her. I looked everywhere, and I saw the doorman talking to Mr. Foster. I went to find out if he knew anything, and I heard the doorman say this girl vomited in the lobby and then just took off running like a bat out of hell. I knew it was Madeline."

"Do they know which way she went?"

"She turned right as best as the doorman could see. She was headed into Arlington." Austin began to hyperventilate.

"Thank you, Austin." Raphael ran to the garage. He was going to look for his daughter.

The alley was dark and lonely. There was a Dumpster behind a restaurant with dozens of cardboard boxes. Madeline tucked herself behind the Dumpster, shielded from the street. She covered herself with one of the grease-soaked boxes. Madeline was cold. Her sequined dress wasn't helping. She knew she was close to home, but the street was filled with demons. She would never make it. Madeline thought maybe it was better to die. She was tired but too scared to sleep. Madeline hid wide-eyed at three in the morning as the rats rustled through the Dumpster.

Officer Velozo trolled down Washington Boulevard. A group of guys stumbled home, plastered from a night of drinking.

"You hanging in there, Father?" Velozo knew the priest was exhausted. Few stay up until four in the morning.

"The coffee has surely helped." The priest warmed his hands on the cup. "You are driving very slowly. Why?"

"I like to move slowly past the alley, Father. It is in the dark where things happen." Velozo shone the spotlight into the void. "A boy might take an inebriated girl in the alley and force himself upon her. The drunk boys we just passed are targets for a robbery. A drug deal." Velozo moved to the next alley. "Everything has been pretty quiet tonight. All we had were our regular stops at the local bars and that one traffic violation early in the evening. That's about it." Paolo was ready to call it a night.

"Stop!" The priest almost spilled his coffee.

Velozo stopped the vehicle. "What is it, Father?"

"I am not sure, but I thought I saw a foot."

Velozo turned the lights on and exited. He removed the PolyTac flashlight from his belt and approached the alley. "I'll be damned," he muttered to himself. "Father, stay a few steps behind me."

Velozo steadied the flashlight on the tiny foot sticking out from behind the Dumpster. He prayed that no one had been murdered. He placed his right hand on his Glock but did not remove the weapon from the holster. Paolo stepped around the Dumpster and heard a tiny muttering voice coming from under a cardboard box. "Arlington County Police. Please remove the box slowly from over your head." There was no response to his command, but the muttering continued. Father Moutinho blessed himself and folded his hands in prayer. "Arlington County Police! Remove the box from over your head and put your hands where I can see them." Velozo gently reached down with gun drawn and flicked the box to the side. The young girl made no sudden moves. Her eyes remained focused straight ahead, and she continued to speak softly in a language neither had ever heard.

Velozo spoke into his radio. "I need an ambulance at North Irving and Washington Boulevard."

He retreated to the squad car and returned with a blanket. He placed the blanket around the girl's shoulders as she shivered in the dewy morning air. "Are you hurt?" The girl did not make eye contact. Velozo and Father Moutinho raised the young woman to her feet, swaddled her in the blanket, and walked her to the warmth of the squad car. The siren of the approaching ambulance echoed in the distance.

"She doesn't look like a homeless person," Moutinho said, analyzing the swanky dress.

"No, Father. She isn't a homeless person. I have met this girl before. She is a very troubled young woman. Her name is Madeline Deschamps."

APRIL 27
ARLINGTON, VIRGINIA

Raphael and Sophia clamored outside of Madeline's hospital room, Oliver in tow. Raphael recognized Dr. Michael Osaka, but the priest sitting in the chair outside the room sent them into a panic.

"Dr. Osaka, how is Madeline?"

"Madeline is resting. She has experienced another traumatic episode."

"Can we see her?" Sophia pressed her shoulder to the door to peer in at her daughter.

"You can, but she is going to be very groggy if she is awake at all. Madeline was in a severe state of shock, and I gave her secobarbital, a sedative, to calm her down."

"Is Madeline going to die?" Sophia glowered at the priest.

"No, Mrs. Deschamps. This is Father Salvatore Moutinho. He was with the officer when they found Madeline in the alley."

Moutinho stood and held Mrs. Deschamps's hand in both of his. "I am concerned for your daughter. I stayed at the hospital to pray for her."

Sophia sighed, relieved. "Thank you, Father. Thank you for helping Madeline, and thank you for your prayers."

"I would like to see her. May I come in?" Moutinho asked politely.

"Yes, of course." Sophia offered.

Dr. Osaka opened the door, and the family and Moutinho entered Madeline's room. The oxygen-saturation monitor was clipped to Madeline's finger. Wires ran under the warming blanket, and Sophia held her hand to her mouth as she noticed the sticky pads attached to Madeline's chest, monitoring her heart rhythm. The blood pressure cuff on her arm inflated periodically. Little beeps and flashes indicated Madeline was being kept stable.

Sophia ran her fingers through her daughter's hair and stroked her cheek. "You are going to be all right, baby. We are going to get through this."

Raphael whispered in Sophia's ear and kissed her lightly on her forehead. He squeezed Oliver's shoulder.

"May I speak to all of you for a moment?" Dr. Osaka waved them out of the room. Oliver stayed with Madeline. "Does Madeline speak another language?"

Sophia hesitated. "She takes Spanish in school. It's one of her favorite classes."

"Does she speak any other language?" Osaka pressed.

"Other than English, no," Raphael interjected. "Why?"

"Officer Velozo and Father Moutinho have informed me that when they found Madeline, she was mumbling in a language neither of them could understand."

"Do either of them speak Spanish?" Sophia questioned.

"They both do. For both of them, it is their native language."

Sophia's shoulders slumped.

"So what does that mean, Doctor?" Raphael braced Sophia.

"I am not sure. Research and studies have found that the brain and body can perform in amazing ways in times of extreme stress. You've heard the stories of people lifting cars or heavy objects to free a trapped person after an accident." The Deschampses nodded. "Other energies are released in a myriad of ways."

"Maybe she was speaking complete gibberish," Raphael commented.

"That is a possibility, but I would have to hear what the officer and Father Moutinho heard."

"How are you going to do that, Dr. Osaka? I am not going to let you scare my daughter into some unreality. She has already been through enough." Sophia warned.

"I am going to consult Dr. Smalling," Dr. Osaka said, dithering. "I am going to suggest that we try to hypnotize Madeline."

Sophia threw her hands in the air, exasperated. "You are acting like she is possessed. This is crazy."

"Are you and your family religious, Sophia?" Moutinho asked.

"We don't have time for religion, Father."

Moutinho bowed his head.

"Will hypnosis help Madeline?" Raphael asked Dr. Osaka.

"I think it will help. I believe there are many layers to Madeline's problem. We need to peel some of those layers away to reveal what's inside." Dr. Osaka squared his jaw. "Madeline is getting worse, not better. We need to try every avenue available. I want her to have an MRI and drug tests, and I would like to try the hypnosis. I have worked with an excellent hypnotist. His name is Diego Zahavi."

The Deschampses conceded that Madeline was not getting better.

Father Moutinho caught Madeline's parents and her brother before they left the hospital. He met them outside Madeline's room. "With your permission I would like to visit Madeline. Either here at the hospital or possibly after she returns home. I have worked with troubled children before in my parish."

"What church do you serve, Father?" asked Raphael.

"I work at the National Cathedral in Washington, DC."

Raphael appreciated the Father's help and concern. "Of course, Father. We thank you for your help." Sophia gave the priest her number.

Dr. Osaka exited Madeline's room. "We are going to keep her overnight for observation, and I am going to schedule the MRI for tomorrow. I should be able to give you an update by early afternoon." Dr. Osaka scribbled on his pad. "Will you be returning today?"

"Yes, Doctor," Raphael said. "It's been a long night." He put his hands around Oliver's neck. "We are going to run home and shower. We'll be back to talk to Madeline."

APRIL 28
ARLINGTON, VIRGINIA

Balloons and flowers filled the hospital room. There was a giant card from Austin Lee signed by many of Madeline's classmates and teachers. She didn't know how she would say thank you.

Madeline felt safe in the hospital. She really enjoyed Vaselyne Ambrose, her nurse.

"How are you feeling today, Madeline?" Vaselyne secured the tabs on her chest.

"I feel OK." Madeline watched as the green line bounced up and down on the EKG monitor.

"Just OK? You look a thousand percent better. The color is back in your face," Vaselyne said, recording the data from the machine. "And your heart is very strong. You must exercise a lot."

"I'm on the cross-country team, though I haven't done as much this year as I have in the past."

Vaselyne removed the tabs. "I'm going to draw a little blood. Are you afraid of needles?"

"Not really. I just don't look."

Just then Madeline's parents stepped into the room. Madeline looked away, ashamed she had made both of them miss work.

"Good morning, Madeline," Sophia and Raphael said in unison, coming to the other side of the bed as Vaselyne gently inserted the needle into Madeline's vein, drawing blood out into little tubes. Then she labeled them one by one.

Madeline gave her parents a one-armed hug. "I am so sorry."

"I don't want to hear all that crying." Vaselyne snapped a look at Madeline that made her grin. "We are going to find out what's wrong, and we are going to fix it and get you back to school!" Vaselyne's confidence rubbed off, and Sophia and Raphael smiled too. "Now, parents. Madeline had a very good morning. She ate like a horse. Her blood pressure is back to normal. Her EKG was tip-top."

Dr. Smalling and Dr. Osaka entered the room.

"But she has a very busy day," Vaselyne went on. "We are going to get these blood samples to the lab, and then tech Harris Ramirez will be by to take her for her MRI. So no playing Twister."

"Will do." Madeline saluted Vaselyne as she left the room. "What is an MRI?" she asked the remaining doctors.

Dr. Osaka tried to simplify the process for the teen. "MRI means 'magnetic resonance imaging.' We are going to take some pictures of your brain and central nervous system and make a map out of them."

"Why do you need to do this?" Madeline asked.

Then Dr. Smalling complicated things. "We will be looking for small tumors in the posterior fossa. An MRI is better than a CT. The contrast provided between gray and white matter is essential in helping diagnose epilepsy, dementia, cerebrovascular disease, or any number of infections that could be causing your behavior."

Madeline furrowed her brow, confused. She didn't know what a CT was.

"I think it is best to wait until the images come back," noted Dr. Osaka.

"Of course," concurred Smalling. "Madeline, later this afternoon I want you to take a nap. Tonight Dr. Osaka and I are going to introduce you to a hypnotist."

Madeline looked for approval from her parents. They both nodded.

"Hypnosis doesn't work on everyone, but we feel it is worth a try," Dr. Smalling went on. "A lot of this will depend on the results of the MRI."

"You're not going to make me do anything stupid, are you?"

Everyone chuckled. "No. It's just another state of awareness that can help us find out what may be in your dreams."

Madeline woke suddenly from her nap. She felt trapped. She was relieved to be in her hospital bed and not inside the narrow MRI contraption. She was relieved to see her mother talking to Dr. Osaka. They shifted their chairs toward her. "Madeline, I was just explaining to your mom that the MRI was clean. Your brain and central nervous system show no imperfections or tumors. That is really terrific news."

There was a quiet rap on the door, and Father Salvatore Moutinho appeared, holding a bouquet of flowers. Madeline looked confused. "Madeline. This is Father Moutinho. He was with the police when they found you the other night. He stayed with you in the hospital yesterday for hours. He was very concerned."

"Hello, Madeline. It is nice to finally meet you." Moutinho handed her the flowers.

"Thank you, Father. The flowers are beautiful."

Moutinho smiled solemnly at the child.

Vaselyne came in with a wheelchair and helped Madeline out of bed.

"Where are they taking Madeline?" Moutinho inquired.

"They are taking her to a private office. They are going to try to hypnotize her," Sophia shared.

After Madeline had been wheeled out, Raphael arrived with coffee. "Hello, Father. I would have brought you a coffee had I known you were here."

"I couldn't stop thinking about Madeline. I felt compelled to visit."

"MRIs were completely negative," Sophia informed her husband.

"That's awesome." Raphael sounded comforted. "Where's Madeline?"

"They are taking her for the hypnosis." Sophia followed Madeline. "Father. Would you like to join us? The more good karma, the better."

"It would be my pleasure."

The executive's office was plush and comfortable. Osaka introduced Madeline, her parents and Father Moutinho to Diego Zahavi, the towering hypnotist. Zahavi's soft brown eyes were camouflaged by bushy brows that belied his bald head. Any additional hair was tied into a ponytail that draped over his purple paisley dress shirt. Madeline's hand disappeared into his when introduced.

"I would ask that everyone become comfortable and please," Diego said, politely, "be very quiet." He switched on the video camera.

He spoke to Madeline quietly, and she gently closed her eyes. Her body slumped into a relaxed state, and Diego kept talking to her softly. Madeline had scored very high on the Stanford susceptibility scale for hypnosis. She was going to go deep into her subconscious.

"Madeline," Diego began, "do you understand that you are going to be hypnotized?" Madeline nodded. "Have you ever been hypnotized before?" She shook her head. "I am going to be with you the entire way. We are a team. I want you to understand that you will not do anything under hypnosis that your mind doesn't want you to do. You should feel completely relaxed and free. You will not remember everything that happens during your relaxation, but we can discuss it later. I want you to close your eyes and relax your shoulders." Madeline exhaled. Diego measured his voice to the meter of her breathing. "Imagine it is a soft spring day. The creek is babbling along, and the petals from the flowers are wafting on the breeze. Relax your feet. All the energy and stress is leaving your feet and ankles. Let your feet float to the sky. Relax your knees and thighs. Let them melt around you. Feel the gravity leave your legs and your hips. You are starting to float above the creek. Your body is free, and your mind is calm. Relax your shoulders and arms. Feel the wind start to carry you."

Sophia snapped herself awake and nudged Raphael to do the same.

"You are rising into the sky, taken by the breeze," Diego continued. "It feels amazing. All of your concerns and fears have left your body and gone into the sky. Feel yourself flying. High above the world. All your worries are gone. You are very relaxed. You are going to become more relaxed. There is a heavy burden lifting from you. It is leaving, and you are becoming more relaxed. You are falling into a very peaceful and deep state." Diego's words repeated like a chant, and Madeline released her consciousness. Madeline had completely shut down, but Diego noticed that her frame had become rigid and defensive. Her brow was stern, and her eyeballs flickered under her lids. He proceeded.

"Now you are resting in a deep comfortable peace. You will follow my suggestions." Diego shifted to the edge of his chair across from Madeline and asked Madeline to wake by putting his middle finger on her forehead. "Madeline, when you open your eyes, you will be with your family, Dr. Osaka, and Dr. Smalling."

Madeline looked from the comfortable chair, and her eyes opened wide with fear. She leaped over the back of the chair and searched for an escape. Raphael approached his daughter, and she kicked the lampstand toward him. She picked up odd objects and hurled them at those present. Her posture and demeanor were combative, trained, and defiant. Madeline cried out in a twisted tongue. Sophia wailed as she watched Madeline's contorted face writhe in confusion.

Dr. Osaka ran from the room to find a sedative. He returned, and Raphael and Diego rushed Madeline and overpowered her, each taking a punch to the temple in the process. Madeline's gown flailed around her neck, exposed and raw. Dr. Osaka shoved the Valium into her arm. The spirited Madeline retreated into an unconscious lump on the executive's floor.

Under the capable care of Nurse Vaselyne Ambrose, Madeline was taken back to her room on a gurney. Her parents followed, unnerved and dejected. Dr. Osaka and Dr. Smalling remained in the executive room to review the videotape with Diego.

"I am sure the doctors will have an explanation for what happened," Father Salvatore Moutinho reassured the Deschampses when they'd returned to Madeline's room. They waited.

Soon Dr. Smalling asked the parents to reenter the executive's suite.

When Sophia approached the room, she charged in. "What the hell happened to my daughter? This nut rolls in here and turns Madeline into some kind of crazy person." She trembled and pointed at Diego.

Dr. Smalling took the lead. "Sophia, the hypnosis worked perfectly. After reviewing the videotape, we are of the belief that Madeline is suffering from dissociative identity disorder."

Sophia's face filled with blood, about to erupt. "What is dissociative identity disorder, Doctor?"

Raphael stepped in front of Sophia.

"Many know it as multiple personality disorder," Dr. Smalling replied.

"This is some bullshit," Sophia spit. "Five months ago you said Madeline had hypertension from anxiety. Then she had anxiety and depression. Then it was posttraumatic stress disorder. Less than a month ago you said she had schizophrenia and assured me that schizophrenia had nothing to do with split personalities. Now you say she has multiple personalities. You're all a bunch of quacks. I am getting my child and finding another group of doctors who don't subscribe to hypnosis and voodoo. You're all a bunch of charlatans."

"Mrs. Deschamps, please." Osaka spoke calmly. "Your daughter is very sick. Multiple personality disorder is a very rare malady. Posttraumatic stress disorder and schizophrenia are quite often diagnosed prior to ascertaining that the symptoms truly indicate multiple personality disorder."

"This is insane." Sophia turned to Raphael and Father Moutinho. They consoled the frantic mother.

"How did this happen, Doctor?" Raphael kneaded information from the psychiatrists. "Madeline has been a very kind and loving child. She has never exhibited any signs of having multiple personalities."

Dr. Smalling sat at the edge of the executive's desk. "Many who experience MPD are aware that they have such a condition. At the very least, they know something is 'wrong' with them. They often suffer from periods of amnesia or confusion. Blackouts. For others it manifests in different ways."

"Madeline told you of her nightmares." Sophia was seething.

"That is true. As I mentioned, some are aware, while some are not."

"And?" Raphael pursued answers.

"Statistics have revealed that almost ninety-seven percent of cases involved severe childhood physical trauma or sexual abuse."

"Back to the parents. You really want to pin this on us. My husband and I never hurt our child!" Sophia seethed. "No one said you have, Sophia," said Dr. Osaka.

"Then why?" Raphael began to show frustration.

"That's why we did the hypnosis," Zahavi interjected. "So we could attempt to get Madeline to speak about her dreams and anxiety in a subconscious state. We think the hypnosis brought a different personality to the surface."

"When you say 'multiple personality,' what do you mean?" asked Raphael. "How many personalities do you think Madeline has?"

"We don't know," said Dr. Osaka.

"Most patients with multiple personalities have been known to have several." Dr. Smalling gave them the facts.

"Oh my God! You people are off your rockers. My daughter doesn't have thirteen people inside her." Sophia balked, disgusted with the psycho mumbo jumbo.

"The multiples are part of what we call fragmentation. The trauma experienced is so tremendous that one single personality can't bear the weight. Multiple personalities are created to bear the pain. The more suffering, the more personalities," Dr. Osaka explained.

"When will we know about these personalities?" Raphael was skeptical.

"We don't know, Raphael. This process could take quite some time," Dr. Smalling conceded.

"What is the process, Doctor? More psychotherapy?" inquired Raphael.

"Hypnosis is the best avenue," explained Dr. Smalling. Sophia rolled her eyes. "We have seen at least one of Madeline's personalities reveal itself."

"And we saw how that went. She went berserk. How do you consider that productive?" blasted Sophia.

"It begins with being able to communicate. No one here could identify the language Madeline was speaking. We need to be able to speak to"—Dr. Osaka hesitated—"that specific personality. I know a translator. Salome Mohammed. I will take the tape to him, and I believe he will be able to discern the language."

"Do you believe there are any religious implications?" Moutinho spoke for the first time.

Sophia gave the priest an incredulous look. The psychiatrists paused.

Dr. Smalling glanced at Osaka. "I don't believe that we have any evidence needed for an exorcism."

"You thing my daughter needs an exorcism?" Sophia gawked at the priest.

"I don't think she needs an exorcism, Mrs. Deschamps. I think she needs an angel." Father Salvatore Moutinho thumbed his rosary solemnly.

APRIL 30
ATLANTA, GEORGIA

E velyn wrapped her Chick-fil-A number one combo into the cute little Chick-fil-A bag and scooped a large order of waffle fries into the container. She topped off her large Coke and schlepped to her Honda Civic, whose lime-green paint had long since faded. She plopped into the driver's seat and swiped yesterday's wrappers off the passenger's seat and onto the floor, where they joined the cemetery of dead, green Marlboro Menthol boxes. Tomorrow, she thought, would be the day she grabbed a Hefty bag and disposed of a week's worth of Styrofoam cups, fry boxes, and sandwich wrappers that had piled in the front of her car. She threw the stick into reverse, and the fan belt groaned as she activated the air conditioner. She knew she had to get that fixed. Summer was coming, and it was already boiling in Atlanta.

Evelyn shoved a waffle fry in her mouth and turned up Imagine Dragons's song "Demons," kicking herself for forgetting to get ketchup. Evelyn chomped the next waffled treat and sang at the top of her lungs, little pieces of potato flying onto her greased, soiled Chick-fil-A uniform shirt. She remembered to take off her uniform hat, tossing it onto the backseat and shaking loose her shoulder-length flaming red hair. Her hand reached into the bag like the claw at the movie-theater concession games and lowered and resurfaced with a handful of waffle fries. Winner! She shoved them all into her mouth and soaked them with a giant suck of Coke.

Evelyn turned sharply into Tower East Beer, Wine & Spirits. She was off on Thursday and had a plan to party by herself and text Victor. She took a sharkbite-size hunk out of her sandwich and lurched forward into the store. Evelyn's shirttails fell over her high-water work pants. The liquor store was cool and provided relief from the humidity. Evelyn scoured the store for a new beer that would dazzle her, but she settled with old reliable Miller Lite in a bottle. She grabbed a twelve-pack. Calories counted. Her eye caught the vodka row. Her mind said no, but her body turned down the aisle. All of the good ones were so expensive. Victor wanted to watch her do a little performance on Skype. She had never done that before. She was a little nervous. Evelyn decided to treat herself. It was a special night for her and Victor. She grabbed a pint of SKYY.

"Will that be all for you, young lady?" The middle-aged African American clerk smiled and maintained eye contact.

"Can you add two packs of green Marlboro Menthols in a box please?" Evelyn smiled back politely.

"Looks like you are going to have a little fun tonight!" the clerk noted. Evelyn thought it sounded as if he were hoping to be invited.

Evelyn had been there and done that. Not the type of guy she could take home to Daddy. No way. Her eyes twinkled. "I am going to have fun tonight." Evelyn shot the clerk a shit-eating grin. "With my boyfriend." Evelyn walked proudly out of the Tower East, loaded for bear. A twelve-pack, a pint, a pack of cigarettes, and her Magic Wand at home. Evelyn was ready to get naked on the Internet with Victor.

THE MADELINE SESSIONS:
MAY 2
ARLINGTON, VIRGINIA

Sophia finished making pancakes for Madeline and the translator Salome Mohammed. Mohammed applied a generous helping of syrup and passed the bottle to Madeline. Raphael walked in through the garage after taking Oliver to a friend's house for the night. The doorbell rang, and Dr. Smalling and Dr. Osaka arrived with Diego, who dipped his head to avoid the chandelier in the lobby. He headed toward the kitchen, where he assumed Madeline was.

"Which room do you think would be the best place for this?" Sophia nervously asked the doctors.

Dr. Osaka surveyed the beautiful home. "The living room looks like a place where you have shared many wonderful moments. There is ample room for everyone. Let's have the session there."

Sophia ducked in to pick up a few of Oliver's toys and strewn clothes. Madeline watched and listened from the kitchen as the adults shook hands and acquainted themselves. She had no memory of what had happened on Monday, but she had heard the whispers from the doctors and her parents. Everyone was tense. She was just thankful to be home.

Then the doorbell rang again. Raphael answered it. "Welcome, Father Moutinho."

"I apologize for my tardiness," the priest said. "I went too far on Route Fifty and ended up near the Home Depot at Bailey's Crossroads."

"Yes, that's quite a bit out of the way." Raphael took the priest's hat but had no place to hang it. He walked into the hall to put the hat on the top shelf of the closet. He returned to the living room, where Moutinho, Sophia, Dr. Osaka, and Dr. Smalling were sitting.

Diego sat down at the kitchen table and sipped on a glass of water Sophia had brought him, and Madeline and the translator pushed the pancakes away, stuffed. Diego reviewed the hypnosis process with Madeline.

In the living room, Dr. Osaka took a deep breath. Then he called to everyone in the kitchen and invited them in. Raphael turned off the Brooklyn Nets–Toronto Raptors playoff game. Zahavi dimmed the lights and spoke in steady, lilting song.

Madeline closed her eyes and was soon flying again, high above the stream, in perfect harmony with the sky and the world.

The doctors observed her unique posture adjustment. Madeline's shoulders rose and pushed back against the chair. Her jaw jutted, and the muscles in her cheeks became taut. She pushed her chest outward and tightened her belly.

Diego, more prepared this time, slowly brought the person inside Madeline to light. The transformation entranced her parents. Madeline's eyes opened, but they were clearly not associated with the daughter they had raised. The girl in the chair focused on Diego. This time she did not panic.

"My name is Diego Zahavi." His eyes held fast to the girl's gaze. "Are you the person inside Madeline?"

Salome Mohammed listened intently. The girl said nothing.

Zahavi approached with a different question. "What is your name?"

In broken English the girl answered, "Wanikiya." Her eyes roamed around the room of strangers. She searched to find the words. "Where is Samuel?"

Zahavi spoke clearly and evenly. "Who is Samuel?"

The girl tapped her foot incessantly.

Mohammed gently entered the conversation. "Do you speak English?"

She shook her head. "Only some. I learn from Samuel."

"My name is Salome. What is your language?" Mohammed asked.

The girl tensed. Her physical body became defensive. "I am Lakota."

Zahavi looked at Mohammed and passed the torch of questioning. "Lakota is an Native American tribe." He turned to Zahavi. "I do not speak Lakota. It is a very rare Native American language." He paused. "I have an idea." He turned back to Wanikiya. "Parlez-vous français?"

Wanikiya's eyes expanded. "Oui."

Salome breathed a sigh of relief. He spoke French fluently. In French he asked, "Wanikiya? Who is Samuel?"

Wanikiya responded confidently. The words rolled off her tongue. "Samuel is my fiancé. Is he still alive?"

Mohammed struggled to respond. "I do not know Samuel. Where do you think he is?"

Wanikiya's face burned with anger. "I believe the soldiers have taken him to the stockades. If so, I wish to be hanged with Samuel."

"There will be no hanging today."

"Then I request to speak to Red Cloud, leader of the Oglala Sioux," Wanikiya spoke sternly.

Salome paused and turned to Dr. Smalling and Dr. Osaka. He whispered, "I am a just a translator. I am in uncharted territory. I need some help."

"Don't look at me." Diego shrugged.

"What's happening?" Sophia asked. She and Raphael were shocked.

Dr. Osaka huddled with the group. "The regression has brought forth an incarnation." He looked at the blank faces of the parents. "Trapped inside Madeline is the soul of another person. She may be the key to Madeline's anxiety."

"Another soul?" Sophia asked, incredulous.

"Many psychiatrists believe that the person inside Madeline could be a confabulation," Dr. Smalling pointed out. "It's a lie but not a lie. A story is created but not one meant intentionally to deceive. Often the stories or characters are fabricated to alleviate the psychological reality that haunts a person in his or her current life. It's a coping mechanism."

"What if it is not a lie?" Diego was spooked.

"That's what we are trying to find out." Dr. Smalling turned toward Dr. Osaka. "Dr. Osaka, please work with Salome. Let's find out where Wanikiya thinks she is. She seems to want to talk about Samuel. Let's get her heading down that road." She looked at Sophia and Raphael. "I'll find out about some information about the Oglala Sioux. It might be helpful to verify some of these statements." She asked permission to use Oliver's tablet, which was sitting on an end table.

Dr. Osaka asked questions, and Salome directed them at Madeline. "Wanikiya. Where do you think you are?"

"Captured by the US Army. Taken to Fort Laramie."

"What year is it?" asked the translator.

"In the year of the white man, it is their centennial," Wanikiya announced.

Osaka changed directions. "How did you meet Samuel?"

Wanikiya's eyes warmed. "I saw Samuel for the first time in Minnesota. He was playing the piano in a saloon. The notes were heaven to my ears. He spotted me in the doorway. I startled him. He stopped playing. I think I frightened him, but he looked back at me. He had the most amazing eyes. So many colors folded together. His eyes captured the universe."

"Why were you in Minnesota?"

"I traveled in the spring with Red Cloud to Washington, DC, to visit with President Grant. We were joined by Spotted Tail and Lone Horn. The United States reneged on its treaty with the Lakota. We went to defend our rights and our land." Wanikiya lowered her eyes. "We left empty-handed, faced with more war."

Sophia approached slowly with a glass of water. Wanikiya accepted it suspiciously.

"What do you mean the United States reneged?" Salome asked.

"The white man began to come to our lands for gold before the year I was born. Settlers pillaged our hunting grounds. And then the soldiers tried to drive us from our land. I remember the meetings of the elders throughout my childhood. The young braves fought with Red Cloud. They met the armies of the United States in the battlefields. They came to steal our land. The villages celebrated at the victories of Red Cloud, Crazy Horse, and Sitting Bull. But Red Cloud wanted no part of a long war with the armies. He wanted peace, so he negotiated treaties, giving the Lakota, the Cheyenne, and the Arapaho their land and sovereignty. It restricted the rights of miners and railroads to pass through our lands, but the greed of the white man continued. The government made promises it did not keep. We were to receive money and supplies from the white man. Sometimes they would come. Most of the time they did not. Red Cloud went to Washington to defend our treaty with the president, and they offered to move us to Nebraska. Spotted Tail left the president with these words: 'When I was here before, the president gave me my country, and I put my stake down in a good place, and there I want to stay. You speak of another country, but it is not my country; it does not concern me, and I want nothing to do with it. I was not born there. If it is such a good country, you ought to send the white men now in our country there and let us alone.' With these words we left on the long journey home."

"And that journey took you through Minnesota?"

"Yes. We visited with the leaders of many tribes on our passage. Red Cloud warned the tribal leaders that their existence was in jeopardy. That the guns and cannons would soon be upon them."

Osaka continued to direct the questioning, with Salome. "How did Samuel become part of your life?" he asked.

"The leaves were beginning to turn the colors of gold and maroon. We gathered supplies and began the last leg of our expedition across Dakota. We traveled slowly, only making ten to fifteen miles a day. The rains made the earth soft, and the western winds began to chill. Our wagons churned in the mud. For ten nights we slogged through the plains, and the skies grew dark. It was early in the season to see the snow, but it came in a bounty. The winds slashed and whipped the snow high above the wheels of the wagon. The horses were freezing and hungry. We hid inside the wagon and tried to stay warm. Our supplies dwindled, and Chapawee and Pretty Owl became very ill."

"Who is Pretty Owl?"

"Pretty Owl is Red Cloud's wife. Chapawee is an old woman. Her husband, Enapay, was killed during Red Cloud's War. She traveled with us to speak to the president of her loss and plead for harmony among the races. He would not receive her."

"Chapawee is a Lakota name?"

"Yes."

"Why do you refer to some of your people by their Lakota names and not others?"

"The officials in Washington often became confused when I spoke of my people with their Lakota names. For the white people, I have become accustomed to calling them by their translated names." Wanikiya had slipped in a dig.

"What does *Chapawee* mean?"

"It means 'industrious.'"

"And *Wanikiya*?" Salome asked.

"*Wanikiya* means 'savior.'"

Sophia felt like she couldn't breathe. She stepped out to the garage and found the pack of cigarettes in the Playmate cooler. She pulled on the smoke with conviction while her daughter sat in a trance speaking through the voice of a Lakota girl from the nineteenth century.

"Dawn brought the sun, but the wind seared into our skin," Wanikiya continued. "The horses survived the night but were weak from the fight and struggled to pull the wagons. On the horizon we spotted another wagon and set that as our goal. We trudged through the snow and made up time between the waist-high drifts. As we approached the wagon, White Eagle saw a white boy with a rifle. Red Cloud told us to approach with caution but felt that the wagon had been encumbered by the blizzard and that we should offer our help. We watched through the front of the wagon over the horses' heads, their manes frozen. A familiar face appeared from the stranger's wagon. A tribal acquaintance, Remy Zusi, waved and smiled. Remy was a French trapper, the man who taught our village their language.

"'Bonjour!' Remy always had a smile. 'I am glad to see you made it through the night.'

"Red Cloud welcomed the sight of his old friend. 'I would not have expected you, Remy.'

"'We have some additional travelers who were ensnared by the sudden weather.'

"The young man with the rifle was terrified. Others in the wagon dared to leave. Remy opened the canvas. They were so afraid of us. There was murder in their eyes. My feeling is that they believed the tales of crazed Indians who would scalp them and leave their flesh to the wolves. White Eagle was wearing the head of a buffalo. It was intimidating to the white travelers." Wanikiya cracked a small smile. "And then I saw the boy with the many-colored eyes. The eyes that captured the universe. He would not stop looking at me, and I would not stop looking at him." Wanikiya stared off, seemingly into the distant memory. "Remy and Red Cloud made introductions with the eldest traveler of their fold. He introduced himself as Thomas Knapp. He labored from sickness, but he spoke French as well, making things easier. White Eagle and Shadow both held their knives as a giant of a man came from the front of the wagon, his burly beard iced. They calmed when he smiled. His name was John. Big John Miles."

Salome let Wanikiya continue. Sophia returned and Wanikiya continued her tale. "One by one they exited the wagon. A strong-faced woman, Harriet, was Thomas's wife. Another meek female, Emmy Lou, was Big John's wife. She was frail, and you could tell she carried a burden in her soul. The young man with the rifle was the youngest child, Angus. The boy with the many-colored eyes—his name was Samuel. Samuel Knapp. Remy spearheaded the plan of surviving the blizzard. One of the wheels of the Knapps' wagon cracked in the storm. White Eagle and Big John unhooked the horses and hitched them to the front of our wagon. The extra horses proved invaluable in dragging the added weight. Harriet assisted with the ailing Pretty Owl and Walks as She Thinks, Red Cloud's mother. They swaddled the infirmed, including Thomas, with beaver pelts Remy had trapped along the Missouri River. Fever drained their strength. The men joined whatever food supplies remained. Smoked trout, chokecherries, potatoes, turtle meat, peas, dried berries, hominy, and buffalo jerky would have to be rationed to finish the journey."

Dr. Osaka wanted to test Wanikiya. "What was your destination?" he asked in English.

Salome translated into French.

"Mathos Paha. The white man calls it 'Bear Mountain.' To the Lakota it is a very religious place. A place of meditation, peace, and prayer."

"How much farther did you have to travel in the blizzard?" Dr. Osaka continued, and Salome translated.

"We struggled for four more days. We could see Paha Sapa."

"Paha Sapa?"

"Literally translated it means 'Black Hills.' For our tribe, it was home. The trip left us all exhausted and starving. The white visitors were greeted with scorn and fear. Red Cloud spoke to the elders. Thomas Knapp was very ill, but Red Cloud brought Thomas to speak with the elders in the tent. It was the warmest fire I can remember. Our faces glowed as Red Cloud informed the tribe of our visit to Washington. The braves called for war. Red Cloud could not deny there would be more bloodshed. He would seek the company of many chiefs to rally the Sioux nation to be one against the US Army. Red Cloud took the pipe and handed it to Thomas, who accepted the peace offering. He choked on the spirits of the pipe." Wanikiya closed her eyes in amusement. "I remember his Mr. Knapp's voice, grave from sickness but poignant and persuasive. 'I come from a place across a great sea. I have seen the powers of the armies of the French and English. It was my life's work as a diplomat to negotiate for England with both her allies and enemies. I have traveled to Portugal and Spain. Poland and Prussia. The Ottoman Empire and Persia on behalf of Britain. I have told the lies that have led to war. I have seen the armies of these nations destroy entire cultures for the gain of land, gold, and pleasure. The world is at war with death and greed is at the helm. I relieved myself to seek the New World and the hope it offers but found America to be grasping a familiar sword. My intent was to lead my family to the lands of the West. To settle and farm in the new fields of Oregon, far away from the violence and genocide that permeates our continents. But death follows me. As a diplomat of some renown, I was invited to sit with the generals of the US Army while in Minnesota. Great leader, Red Cloud, make no mistake that the goal of the United States is to obtain the Black Hills, a decision cemented in policy long before you signed the treaty at Fort Laramie. They will not come just for the gold. They will seek to mine the timber of your lands and float them down the Missouri. They will settle and build more forts on your land. They will drive the great railroads through the mountains, and thousands will arrive to push you away. The army knows you will not cede these lands peacefully. They are planning to annihilate the Sioux and Cheyenne and Arapaho. I retired from the meeting understanding that I would change the path of my travels to warn the Sioux. Fate would have it that I met the very man I sought, Red Cloud, en route.' The response from the braves was virulent. They raised their bows and voices. Red Cloud, his eyes beleaguered, could not make such a promise. His duty was the survival of his people." Wanikiya stopped. She gripped the side of the chair. "My people stood on the brink of their greatest fight against the white man. Yet it was a white man who came to warn us of danger. At that point I saw the white man in a different light. I also knew it would be possible to love Samuel. It would be many nights before I would sleep, as my thoughts were always on the boy with the eyes with many colors folded together."

Diego Zahavi signaled to Salome that it was time to end the session. He brought Madeline out of the deep sleep that had introduced their world to Wanikiya. Madeline appeared groggy and asked to be excused, unaware of the dramatic revelation.

"Sophia and Raphael," Dr. Osaka said.

Then he and Dr. Smalling thanked both parents for the use of the living room.

"Today was a tremendous breakthrough," Dr. Smalling said.

The parents looked as groggy as Madeline. Then Sophia spoke. "Dr. Osaka." She cleared her throat. "What I saw today was impossible to believe. What happened here?"

"I am glad you asked." Dr. Smalling, interjected while straightening her skirt. "Has Madeline ever shown an interest in Native Americans?"

"No," the parents answered in unison.

"The stories we heard from her, or Wanikiya, were quite detailed. I haven't had a chance to review the videotape, but I plan to bring it to a friend of mine who works at the National Museum of the American Indian. His name is Yoshito Park. He can verify parts of the story for authenticity."

"How could she make that up?" Raphael asked.

"We spoke of fragmentation," Dr. Smalling answered. "That doesn't mean that the psyche blows up into a million pieces. Often it divides into different personalities that share similar traits. They are not carbon copies of one another but overlap, in a sense."

"Is this a 'fragmentation' because of multiple personality disorder or an incarnation?" Sophia needed another smoke.

"It is going to take many sessions to bring all of this to the surface." Dr. Smalling gauged the Deschampses' response.

"Reincarnation is historically well documented." Dr. Osaka said. He had the Deschampses' full attention. "Barbro Karlen comes to mind."

"Who?" Sophia asked.

"Barbro Karlen was born in Sweden in 1954. At the age of three, she told her parents to stop calling her Barbro. She told her parents that her name was Anne Frank."

Sophia gasped.

"Anne Frank died in the Bergen-Belsen concentration camp in 1945. The notion that a three-year-old would be aware of the plight of Anne Frank is astonishing. She wouldn't call her parents Ma or Pa. She told them that they were not her real parents. Barbro told them stories of her childhood, believing she was Anne Frank. The parents felt that she had a tremendous imagination. She also detailed nightmares of men climbing the stairs to where she hid and kicking in the door to the attic. A clear representation of the Gestapo searching for Jews who had created spaces in the walls to hide. The parents took her to see a psychiatrist. It seems Barbro had gotten wise about discussing her past with, well, anyone. She noticed they got 'tense,' so she clammed up. The psychiatrist dismissed her as completely normal. It came to a head in grade school, as her teacher began the lesson on the real Anne Frank. Barbro became disoriented and confused. She could not rectify how they were talking about her in the past tense."

Sophia was white as a sheet.

"When Barbro was ten, her parents toured the great cities of Europe, including Amsterdam, where Anne Frank lived in hiding for two years. Barbro's father rang for a taxi to take them to the Anne Frank Museum when, as testimony reflects, Barbro insisted on walking, saying, 'It is not too far from here.' I was in Amsterdam once, and the streets are a constant maze. Barbro walked the parents to the doorstep. Let me remind you that the office of Otto Frank, Anne's father, had been reconstructed into a museum. Barbro became discombobulated as she stood outside the old office. It didn't look familiar to her. Her confidence waned. But when she walked in and up a long winding flight of stairs, her mother observed Barbro's mood had become one of terror. She held Barbro's hand, which had become icy cold. Barbro stood before a bare wall and smiled. Her color came back to her cheeks. She commented to her parents how delighted she was that they had left the pictures of the 'film stars.' Her mother grew concerned as no pictures graced the walls. Barbro was forced to acknowledge that the wall was barren, yet her mother confirmed that the pictures did exist but had been removed to be placed in a glass casing that would prevent vandalism and theft. Barbro had described each picture to perfection and identified exactly where its place was on the wall. Barbro's mother, as they say, 'freaked out.' She challenged Barbro, wondering how she could possibly know this information. Barbro became weak and hysterical. She cried as they left the museum, eventually falling to the sidewalk, traumatized by the experience."

The Deschampses sat, dumbfounded.

"This episode caused a rift in Barbro's household. Her mother became a true believer in reincarnation, while her father, a devout Christian, accepted that something amazing had happened to Barbro but could not reconcile them with his firm Christian beliefs. Barbro struggled with much of her phobias into adulthood. Barbro felt the need to flee when near a police officer or someone in uniform. Barbro never ate beans, as that was the staple diet of the Franks while in hiding. Barbro would only bathe, never shower, a testament to the deadly showers of Bergen-Belsen."

Dr. Osaka pulled out his phone and searched the web. He found corresponding pictures of Anne Frank and Barbro Karlen. "Side by side, at roughly the same age, they carried very similar traits in look and posture."

"Do you think Madeline is Wanikiya?" Raphael sat stunned on the couch.

"That's what we are trying to find out," Dr. Osaka confirmed.

Miles away, the buttons on a cell phone dialed Brandon Lyle. "I have found the one you seek. She is in Arlington, Virginia."

"Keep her close. I will be there." Lyle knew the legion was everywhere.

MAY 5
ATLANTA, GEORGIA

Evelyn bent down to get her Nikes, and the crack of her ass fell out of her high school sweatpants. She hiked them back up her ample junk in the trunk and squeezed into an Atlanta Falcons hoodie. She didn't have to fawn over Matt Ryan anymore. She had Victor Kuyt, and Evelyn was determined to drive the sailor wild.

She stepped out of the apartment building and into the blinding sun. The humidity was already starting to build, and Evelyn could feel the sweat beading on her fleshy back. She put the hoodie over her head and threaded the earbuds into place. Evelyn pressed shuffle on her iPod and began her first workout since her senior year at Henry W. Grady High School.

Evelyn had no route, so she turned left and started a dawdling jog to the rhythm of Pharrell Williams's "Happy." Her brain forced her trunk-sizd legs forward, but they protested. It was like she was dragging a sled in the snow. Evelyn slogged around the corner, her breasts and flab bouncing under her red-and-black sweatshirt.

Evelyn made the better of the four blocks, and her lungs started to wheeze. The menthols reared their ugly head, and the phlegm surged up her windpipe into the back of her throat. Her legs deadened, and she slowed her pace to a walk. The bass in her ears pounded Robin Thicke and Pharrell singing the catchy "Blurred Lines." The vision of that naked white girl in the video frustrated Evelyn. She wished she had won the genetic lottery. Evelyn put her hands on her knees and huffed the lyrics: "You the hottest bitch in this place." She knew she wasn't. The naked white girl was. Evelyn turned, aborted her workout, and walked slowly home, her body rejecting the physical exercise she had rejected for years.

The single flight of stairs took the last of Evelyn's strength. She opened the apartment door and removed her hoodie. She groaned as she removed her perspiration-drenched T-shirt and bra. Her sweatpants stuck to her legs, and she peeled them off, tripping as she yanked them off her heel. She kicked them aside and found herself standing in front of the full-length mirror behind the closet door. Evelyn started to look away but decided to take inventory. Her high-standing breasts, her pride and joy and the talk of junior high, had become obese and cumbersome. Her panties dug into the flesh on her hips, and the fat fell draped over the bands of her underwear. The flaccid white belly bulged as if in a circus mirror. She could pinch way more than an inch. She needed a ruler. The bottoms of her arms sagged. Her inner thighs were billowy and pocked. Evelyn noticed the immediate need for some spring-cleaning, as her winter bush had run amok.

Evelyn decided to take a shower. Victor was just going to have to love her for who she was, fat and all. She filled her Double Gulp cup from 7-Eleven with ice and smothered it with Coke from one of the two liters in the pantry. The oven went on to four hundred degrees, and she peeled the plastic off the DiGiorno four-meat pizza and placed it on the rack. Her shower wouldn't last more than fifteen minutes, and she needed something to eat before going to work.

THE MADELINE SESSIONS: MAY 11 ARLINGTON, VIRGINIA

Diego Zahavi loosened his tie on the unseasonably warm spring evening. Recently, spring seemed to be a thing of the past in Washington, DC. Winter turned to summer as spring winked and ran away to hide. Diego knocked on the door.

In the Deschampses' kitchen, Dr. Smalling and Dr. Osaka approached American history expert Yoshito Park. She turned her head to see if Madeline was in the vicinity. "Were you able to view the entire videotape?" she asked Yoshito.

"I was, Doctor. Historically, Wanikiya was accurate about the political climate of the period. Her geographic analysis is spot-on as well. I did some research. The *Lincoln County Advocate* of the Dakota territories reported a sudden blizzard in late September of 1875. There was an article about the snowstorm next to a paragraph offering his Negro wench for services."

"Unbelievable." Dr. Smalling escorted the historian to the living room, where Madeline and her parents were sitting. Dr. Osaka followed. Once again Oliver had been sent to a friend's.

"One thing, Doctor," Yoshito said. "Wanikiya is a true Lakota name. But it is a boy's name." He raised one eyebrow.

"Interesting. Yoshito, please ask Dr. Osaka to ask any questions you might have to impeach Madeline's story. Reincarnation is very rare, if not impossible. It is more likely that Madeline has created a separate personality to mask her trauma. Any inconsistencies could be vital in verifying a diagnosis."

"Will do, Doctor."

The doctors gathered along with Salome. The Deschampses and their newfound friend, Father Salvatore Moutinho, settled into the comfortable living room. The expanding group made small talk in Madeline's presence so as not to spook the young woman. Sophia lowered the lights, Diego induced Madeline into a trance, and Wanikiya came to life again.

"Good evening." Salome cleared his throat and began to formulate his thoughts in French.

"Nacece," replied Wanikiya.

"What does that mean?" whispered Sophia to the historian.

"'I suppose,'" commented Park.

"Do you speak this Native American language?" Raphael asked.

"A few words and phrases." Salome shot them both a stern look, and they shut up.

"A reminder that we are speaking in French." Salome smiled, directing his comments to Wanikiya. "The last time we spoke, Wanikiya, you had arrived at your village near Bear Mountain with Samuel's family. Thomas Knapp warned Red Cloud of the US Army's impending expansion and willingness to annihilate your race." Wanikiya did not respond.

Osaka whispered in Salome's ear and Salome translated. "Tell me more about Samuel."

"Thomas Knapp remained very ill. The elders spoke with the family, Big John and his wife, Harriet. The elders were thankful for Thomas and his warning. They felt the need to reciprocate the kind act. They asked the family to stay, at least until Thomas recovered, despite the protests of the braves. The family gathered in a separate tent. The snow still lay on the ground, and the air was very cold. The fear in Emmy Lou's face was apparent. Big John spoke for the group, and they decided to stay with the tribe. Thomas was too weak to travel. They were very gracious. My heart secretly smiled. I would have the opportunity to speak to Samuel." Wanikiya's eyes saddened "My heart desired Samuel, but I was promised to Chayton."

"Chayton?"

"Falcon." Wanikiya's lips pressed together. "He is a strong brave. Son of Blue Earth and Singing Voice. But I knew my life changed when I saw Samuel's eyes. I knew that the elders would not allow such a thing. It is not the way of the Lakota. Being promised to someone is not the same as love."

"How did you know you loved Samuel so quickly?"

"I am speaking to one who has never known that feeling in his heart." Salome admitted to himself that Wanikiya was right.

"How did the village react to the family and their decision to stay?" Salome pressed on.

"At first there were many protests. Industrious made the first helpful gesture. Industrious can be a hard woman. She chased the braves with a switch, chiding them to help build the Knapps a tepee. Thomas suffered in the tepee of Red Cloud, but the entire Knapp family proved themselves to the tribe. Big John went with Angus and White Bear to chop the poles. Samuel worked with Harriet and Industrious on tanning the buffalo hide to cover the tents. Emmy Lou fashioned rope. Soon the community worked together to build the Knapps their home. Bird helped them make mattresses, and Mina, Bird's eldest daughter, gathered firewood. That evening we savored a stew of porcupine and potatoes Star had made for our visitors. It was the first time I spoke with Samuel." Wanikiya reminisced. "He asked if I spoke French, and I said yes. He asked me what was in the stew and mentioned that it was very good. Then I told him it was porcupine, and he dropped the bowl." A huge smile stretched across Wanikiya's face. "I tried not to laugh. I could feel the eyes of Chayton bearing upon me. I could tell he was very jealous, and he left the tent in a rage."

"What is your name?" Samuel asked.

"Wanikiya," I told him.

"That is a very beautiful name."

I couldn't stop looking into his eyes. "I saw you playing the piano in Minnesota. Do you remember?" I asked.

"I do. You surprised me."

"Did I scare you?"

"You didn't scare me. I had never seen..." Samuel's voice trailed off.

"An Indian?"

"No. Not in person." Samuel paused. "All of the tales I had heard were of a violent, ruthless subspecies. Then you stood before me. Beautiful and curious. My father spent his life trying to convince cultures around the globe that despite differences in culture and color we are all beautiful in our own way. That we need to open our hearts and accept people for who they are."

"So you do not fear me?"

"I do not. I want to know more about you."

"I have a fear of your people." My heart pounded as I spoke.

"You have a right to. What the army is doing to the Lakota is a travesty." Samuel spoke like his father.

"You have traveled the world?"

"Yes. I have been many places."

"Tell me where you have been. I want to see the world. Where are you from?"

Samuel scratched his thin beard. His long curls fell over his forehead, and he pushed them back, revealing his thin face to the fire. "My family is from England. I was born in a town called Derby. Derby is the home of the first water-powered silk mill in England."

"I have heard of silk."

"Silk is a very soft fabric. Soft as your cheek." I blushed when he spoke those words. "My father was a diplomat for England. When I was a small boy, we moved to London for his job. And we often traveled with him throughout Europe."

"Have you traveled to France?" Remy the trapper had given us accounts of France.

"Yes. Paris is an incredible city. The architecture is spectacular. The Cathedral of Notre Dame. The Arc de Triomphe. The Fontaine Saint-Michel. The Louvre."

"Did you enter the Louvre?" I dreamed of seeing the art.

"Yes. My father insisted we go. There were many great paintings by the masters of the Renaissance. The *Mona Lisa* by Leonardo da Vinci. The sculpture of Venus de Milo is sensational."

"The *Venus de Milo*." I was unfamiliar with this piece.

Samuel explained, "It is a Greek statue of a woman holding an apple. Experts believe it is Aphrodite, the Greek goddess of love and beauty. When it was discovered from the ruins, both of Aphrodite's arms had broken off."

I waited on every word that left his lips. He brought me through time to places of which I could only dream. He took me inside the Louvre and back to the streets of Paris.

"I loved the classics, but I found the street artists to be doing some exceptional new work. They call it impressionist painting. Claude Monet, Renoir, Cézanne, Manet, and a woman named Mary Cassat. Simply stunning. I encouraged my father to purchase one from the street fair, but he thought they were rubbish."

"Tomorrow we will create Lakota art on your tepee. It is tradition."

"I would like that very much," Samuel said.

"Where else have you been?" I wanted to listen to him talk more.

"Our travels were not always museums and street fairs. We traveled with a tutor. Miss Agnes Valentine. We often mocked her with a poem Emmy Lou had jotted down: 'Agnes Valentine, she doth do her part. Agnes Valentine, the tutor that has no heart.'" We giggled together. "She is a demanding woman, and she had a job to do. My father worked tirelessly with the governments and ambassadors. My mother would often join him in the evening for social events. Agnes kept the three of us properly in-line. Agnes had courage as well. We often voyaged to dangerous parts of the world. We were in Vienna when Prussian armies invaded Austria. We could hear the cannons fire from the fields inside the Carltheater while trying to enjoy Franz Von Suppé's operetta *Die schöne Galathée*. It was a very difficult time for my father. He was negotiating with Prussia and Austria along with the Italians, who were embroiled in their own war for Italian unification. My father insisted we leave Vienna. As we left the great city, we saw the dead in the fields of battle, slashed by bayonets, limbs lying next to bodies, and we heard the cries of children not much older than Angus."

"How did you come to America?"

"My father grew weary of the politics. He wanted a simpler life for himself and his children. He labored over his decision for years. His loyalty is to Queen Victoria and the Union Jack, but he could not reconcile Britain's policies in India, especially after the rebellion of 1857 and a century of war with the French in India's backyard, using them as pawns in a global struggle for land, resources, and wealth. Slavery was being abolished throughout Europe, but my father felt that Great Britain viewed India as a slave force for its own profits. It was counter to everything my father was trying to achieve. Peace. Europe was undergoing a crisis in every nation. England was right in the mix. We would have departed for America sooner had it not been for the civil war. My father said it would be 'like leaving the frying pan and going into the fire.'"

"What was the ship like?" I had never seen the great ocean liners.

"We boarded the SS *City of Washington* on the fifth of May in 1873, in the harbor of Liverpool. The great ship inched into the gloom of the Atlantic with five hundred seventy-six souls aboard. Twenty-eight hundred tons of wood and iron crashed into the choppy seas, the sails reached toward the heavens, and the boiler churned in the ship's belly. Emmy Lou, Angus, and I hung on to the rails and waved good-bye to our home, yet we were excited to see the new world. It was an emotional farewell for Emmy Lou. She said good-bye not only to England but also to her husband of only three months, who had passed from meningitis." Samuel could see my confusion. "Emmy Lou met Big John in New York."

"You sister seems to carry a weight."

"She does. She and John have tried to conceive. We are all concerned that Emmy Lou may be barren."

"For her I will pray."

"Thank you for your prayers." Samuel paused. "Our journey to New York would take us first to Queenstown, Nova Scotia. Captain William Robert Phillips asked our family to join him at the captain's table, where we dined on halibut and drank wine. The journey was far from peaceful. The waves thrashed the ship, and lookouts scouted the horizon for icebergs. We watched from the deck as great whales leaped skyward, breathed the sea into the air, and flowed by the frolicking dolphins, playful and kind. My mother suffered from seasickness and spent most of her time in the cabin. Seeing the gulls was a welcome sight, and we were allowed to disembark in Queensland for the afternoon."

"Tell me of New York," I said.

"The jubilance of sailing into New York was a moment I shall never forget. The city was alive and vibrant. My father accepted a position from an old friend at Jay Cooke & Company in the banking industry. We moved into a small townhouse on Second Avenue, a far cry from the residence in London. Emmy Lou became a nanny. Austin began attending Collegiate School. I tried to enroll at Columbia University but was delayed until the winter semester. My father obtained a job, sweeping and cleaning, for me at the bank. We seemed to be settling in for the life my father wanted for us, but then the banks collapsed in September of that year. The great Panic of 1873. The wars in Europe had taken their toll. The banks in Vienna crashed, and poor investments across the globe depleted the cash supplies of banks and countries around the world. My father was released from his job. Events moved so quickly when we moved to New York. Every day something happened. That was the first time I had read about the Sioux. A General Custer was celebrated for protecting the railroads from Sioux warriors."

"Is that how they tell the story?" I could not contain my anger. Samuel inched away from me, and the woman in the tent heard the discontent in my voice. "The US Army enabled the railroad and miners to violate the treaty Red Cloud signed with President Grant in 1868. They had invaded our sacred grounds." Samuel touched my hand lightly, and my anger disappeared. He seemed to be able to make me calm and peaceful. I apologized and asked him to finish his story. He told me never to apologize for something I felt strongly. I never forgot that.

"My family and I stayed in New York for two years. My father had seen that New York was as corrupt as all the others cities he had visited professionally and personally. The politics, the gangs, the violence and brutality, and the crime led him to seek the West and its promise."

"How did Emmy Lou meet John?"

"John was a relative of the family in which Emmy Lou was a nanny. I had never seen her as happy as when she cared for that child. Meeting John renewed her. She felt happiness and hope. He had survived the war but suffered the malady of many soldiers who had seen too much death. Emmy Lou helped John from the whiskey. He needed her, and she needed him. It was a glorious spring day that they were wed."

"Laughing Maid is watching me," I told Samuel.

"Who is Laughing Maid?" he asked.

"My mother." I explained that the evening had ended and that I hoped to hear many of his stories in the coming days. He tried to hold my hand as I left, but Laughing Maid would have no such thing. She is a meddlesome one.

Dr. Osaka's phone buzzed in his pocket. He read the text and gently removed himself from the session to be with his family for dinner on Mother's Day.

The animated Wanikiya shared her story, and the tape ran on for hours.

MAY 15
EL PASO, TEXAS

"What the hell is going on out there? We have given you an army to find one guy, and he is running rampant across the desert, murdering women, killing cops, and slaughtering nuns. What is it going to take to catch this guy?" Alexander Khan verbally bludgeoned the beleaguered duo.

Jeremy Alcott and Bruno Sommer huddled in the El Paso, Texas, office of the FBI and took their medicine. "We always seem to be one step behind him, Mr. Khan."

"No kidding." Khan snorted.

"He has no pattern. None that we can discern," Bruno asserted.

"Other than killing everything in his path," Khan persisted.

"The killing of the cop was a necessity for Lyle. The murders of the nuns were strictly religious. Lyle believes he is the devil. The ritual-style slaying of the women..." Jeremy took a breath. "I believe that Lyle feels these particular women are a danger to him."

"Why?"

"I don't know."

"Well, that's not good enough. He's creating chaos, and I want him stopped before others are killed," Khan fumed.

"I think chaos is what Lyle is looking for," Bruno added. "I think he has the connections and the means to do something catastrophic."

"That's just fucking great. Where do you think he is now?"

Jeremy and Bruno stared at each other, knowing they had no good answer. "We are not sure. Our guess is that he and his crew are still heading east."

"Your 'guess,'" Khan popped off. "I have two of the best on this case, backed by the entire FBI and Homeland Security, and I get a guess. Gentlemen, that's just not good enough. I've got people up my ass to find this guy. No one sleeps until he is dead or behind bars."

MAY 12
HOT SPRINGS, ARKANSAS

THIRTEEN-YEAR-OLD MISSING, POLICE SEEKING HELP
Hot Springs Daily

The Hot Springs County Sheriff's Office is posting a missing persons report for Maryna Bichman, thirteen years of age. Maryna is a seventh grader at Lakeside Junior High School and was last known to have been walking to the Walgreens around noon to get her mother a Mother's Day card.

Maryna was wearing a light blue tank top, dark blue Lakeside Junior High School athletic pants, and a pair of white Reebok tennis shoes. Maryna has dark skin, brown eyes, and black hair. She is five feet four inches tall and weighs one hundred pounds. She had her hair in two pigtails with blue ties.

Please contact the Hot Springs County Sheriff's Office if you know anything of Maryna's disappearance or know her whereabouts. Call 501-555-3320.

MAY 13
HOT SPRINGS, ARKANSAS

"I am telling you, if you find Luther Bichman, you will find my daughter. He is a drunken scoundrel of a man." Latrice would have no other explanation for the disappearance of her daughter Maryna.

"I understand, Mrs. Bichman." The detective stayed cool.

"Don't you call me 'Mrs. Bichman.' I divorced that man after he left me alone with Maryna. And Alevonta. And Yonette. And Raynell. My name is Mrs. Sanderson now. That's my husband." She pointed to the gentleman drinking a can of beer in his wife-beater with his jeans halfway down his ass.

"I apologize, Mrs. Sanderson. When is the last time you saw Mr. Bichman?"

"Ha! 'Mr.' That will be the day." Latrice stood with her hands on her hips. "The last time I saw that bastard was in the county jail."

The gentleman drinking the beer started laughing.

"Why was he in jail, Mrs. Sanderson?"

"He was drunk! He was always drunk."

The detective looked at the gentleman drinking a can of beer.

"He never had a job. Never had any money."

"Why do you think he took Maryna?"

"Are you stupid?" Latrice sprayed it. "The other children are all grown. Maryna came along later. Like, too late. I should have left him long before we had Maryna."

"Do you know where he might have taken her?"

"How the hell should I know? He ain't got no place to stay."

"Does he have any relatives in the area?"

"No relatives here. Hell, he ain't got no friends. The closest relative he had was his fat aunt Jozell up in Fayetteville."

"Do you know if he has a vehicle?"

Latrice and the gentleman drinking a can of beer fell over laughing. "Pat and Charlie. That's the only way that man gets around, unless some fool gives him a ride." Latrice patted both of her legs.

"If he was such a poor father, why do you think he would have taken Maryna?"

Latrice mellowed for a moment. "He did love that baby girl. She was always his favorite."

MAY 13
ARLINGTON, VIRGINIA

D r. Osaka sat in his office and reviewed the videotape made on Sunday, still smarting from the tongue-lashing administered by his wife and mother of his two children for being late to Mother's Day dinner. He started from the point at which he had departed, listenening to Wanikiya's story.

The winter of 1875 was one of the most difficult I had experienced. The women worked hard to forage for roots. None worked with more fervor than Harriet and Emmy Lou. The men endured the cold to hunt for prairie dogs, deer, and the elusive buffalo, often hiking high onto the slippery stones of the mountains. We prayed to the creator to bring the buffalo to the plains. Many a night we went hungry. The Knapps reduced their portions and offered more to the children. Every day was a grind for survival.

Harriet cared for Thomas daily. After many months, Harriet allowed the shaman to visit the tepee. He burned black cohosh to relieve the pain and soreness in his muscles. Spiritual drums pounded, and the tribal women chanted on Thomas's behalf. Great bonfires burned away the evil spirits that haunted Thomas's body. Harriet promised the shaman their horse as payment.

Emmy Lou gathered firewood and helped the women cook. She found comfort with Star, who was with child, fathered by Lootah. She spent countless hours with the lonely wife as Lootah sought the company of warriors in the north, waiting to war with the white man. Emmy Lou tried so very hard to conceive with Big John. We could hear their attempts in the night, but she remained alone in her womb.

Samuel tended the horses. He loved the animals. He kept them warm and clean. He made sure they were fed and exercised, even when the snow was deep. Samuel and I would steal away whenever possible, away from the eyes of Laughing Maid and her prattling old women, whispering behind our backs of the half-breeds that would arrive if we were to marry. We were extraordinarily cautious when Chayton returned from the hunt. Samuel would teach me English, and I would teach him Lakota.

Red Cloud invited the Knapps to his tent and shared the pipe with the family. We prayed to the White Buffalo Calf Woman, who brought our people the pipe and the art. Samuel and I began a Dakota weave, creating a diary of the winter on an extended quilt. We shared the dream that one day the quilt would be a thousand miles long.

We walked to the river with pails to fetch water for the village and the horses.

"Do you see the Canoti?" I asked Samuel. Samuel looked to the sky, as if seeking a bird. "No. In the woods."

Samuel could see the little ones hiding, following us like the braves follow the army. "Why do you call them 'Canoti'?"

"Canoti are little ones. Like fairies of the woods. They are of the stories we share by the fires at night. Part of our history."

"They certainly seem real to me."

We laughed. When we got to the river, it was frozen. Samuel smashed the ice with his foot, and we dipped our buckets into the icy river. We made this trip several times a day.

I asked him to tell me of Rome.

"Rome is a magical place in stories and pictures, but in reality it is dusty and dirty. Unless you like stepping in the droppings of pigeons." Samuel smirked, and I playfully punched him in the arm. *"Though the majesty of the Colosseum captures the imagination. It's when you explore the hearts of the churches that you find the true treasures of the city. Of course there is the Vatican and the wonder of the Sistine Chapel."*

"I have never heard of these places."

"Well, I shall take you there someday." My heart skipped. To see Rome with Samuel would fulfill a dream. *"Michelangelo was a sculpture in the early sixteenth century. The head of the Catholic Church resides in the Vatican. At the time, the pope, as they call him, was named Julius II. He was known as the warrior pope. It's odd that the person who represents peace and love is known for war and death. He commissioned Michelangelo to paint the Sistine Chapel. There were so many beautiful works of art. God creating Adam and humanity.* The Last Judgment *graced the wall behind the altar."* Samuel touched his finger to mine and explained that that was how God had touched Adam's finger. The boys in the woods giggled. Samuel turned to them, and they ran away.

That night Laughing Maid brought me to the shaman and the elders. My legs trembled, but I knew they were to discuss Samuel.

"You have been promised to Chayton," Red Leaf spoke. *"You are to be his wife."*

"I don't love him. I love Samuel."

"We have accepted the white family, but we will not accept them into the tribe as family."

"Your words are crooked, Red Leaf. Samuel is a man, just as you. Just as my father. Just as Chayton." The elders gasped. *"Why should I not be allowed to marry the man I love and be happy? Let Chayton choose a woman who will make him feel the same way."* I stood my ground.

"You are passionate, Wanikiya, but naive. This is best for the Lakota. Our tribe."

"Would you not love the son of the white man in my belly? Do you hate the white man so much that you would deny my child's blood?"

"Silence. We will not discuss this further. When Chayton returns from the hunt, we will discuss plans for your wedding."

I left the elders and could not bear the light of day for several weeks. Only secret messages passed to me by little Butterfly from Samuel saved my heart.

Winter waned, and the ground became soft. The trees had not yet shown their leaves, but the ice had left the river, and the creatures had begun to roam the earth once again. On a sunny day the hunters returned with a bounty of food. Chayton celebrated the kills of young Angus, and the village rejoiced and planned a feast for all to enjoy. They told the children that Angus had seen Chiye-tanka, the woodland spirit that stood eight feet tall and was covered in fur. The soul that taught the warriors to hunt.

I could not bear to face the elders and Chayton. A shriek from the Knapps' tent disturbed the joy. Harriet cried into the air that her husband, Thomas Knapp, had died. The mood of the village changed from elation to sorrow. I felt something much worse. I felt that Samuel would be leaving the village.

That evening the moon stood bright and full against the night sky. A ring of light circled the moon. The shaman gathered the village in prayer for the soul of Thomas Knapp. I mourned for the soul of Samuel's father. We found each other's eyes, and I could feel his sorrow. And he could sense my fear. I saw his finger move, a signal that he wanted to touch my finger, the way he'd touched my finger on the way home from the river. The way God had touched Adam in the Creation painting on the ceiling of the Sistine Chapel. That simple movement gave me hope. The shaman called upon the great spirit of Wakan Tanka to guide Thomas Knapp's soul through the cosmos. The drums of the braves beat strong; Big John introduced the tribe to a new instrument, the weeping wind of the bagpipes; and the sorrowful voices of the Knapp family sang "Amazing Grace."

A warm wind blew through the branches on the day we laid Thomas Knapp to rest. I still had limited contact with Samuel and yearned to hear his voice and dream to his stories.

Harriet chose a spot on the bluff that overlooked the valley. Harriet spoke for the family. "Last night Thomas whispered in my ear that he had never loved as he has loved me and that the proudest moments of his life were watching his children strive to be the men and women who they would become. He felt that he had fallen short of his life's work but had taken personal strives to complete his dream of true freedom. The freedom from the fear and persecution that oppresses the world. He wished to thank Red Cloud and all of the members of the village for bringing them into a place where they were cared for and loved. In those thoughts he expressed his hope that his boys would marry their hearts' desires, as only true love can bring happiness to the heart." Harriet looked directly at Laughing Maid. "He asked me to share these wishes with the family and convey how much he loves all of you and that he would be watching from heaven down upon us all."

We said good-bye to Samuel's father. Red Cloud sent the scout Mahkah to Fort Laramie to inform the army of the distinguished man's passing, in hopes that the news would be reported to his home in England.

As we returned from the bluff, a child scurried to the gathering. Panting, he informed us that Star was having the child of Lootah. On the day we buried one, another arrived. The mood of the village lightened, and the tribe moved quickly home. Lootah stood nervously outside the tepee. The agony of Star echoed through the valley. The woman known as Hair Storm assisted in the birth, but sadly, she reported that the baby was breech and would soon suffocate inside the womb.

Harriet grabbed my arm and pulled me into the tent. "I can help this woman keep her child. You must tell her to do exactly as I say. We have little time." Harriet's voice boomed instructions to me in French. I translated the commands to Star. Harriet twisted Star's hips and massaged her stomach as she tried to shift the child into position inside her stomach. The arms and legs pressed against her belly as Star screamed in suffering, trying to save her child. Hair Storm massaged the belly from the opposite side. The two women puffed and groaned. Harriet stretched two fingers inside Star and gently moved the infant's arm away from the side of its head to the front of the chest. Harriet extended the other tiny arm through the pelvis, and the head slowly exited Star's body. Harriet pulled the baby into her arms as Hair Storm swaddled the child in a blanket. On that day we welcomed Michante, My Heart, to the village.

The men and women of the village swarmed Harriet with appreciation for saving the life of the unborn boy. Harriet held each of them close and reminded them that this was what all of humankind should share with one another. Harriet, for the second time that day, spoke for her family, announcing, "If it is amenable to Red Cloud, the Knapps would like to stay with our Lakota family."

The village roared in approval. I cheered inside my skin. Samuel was going to stay.

WEDNESDAY, MAY 14
DURANGO, COLORADO

"It's too hot!"

Andres forced Ilana to sit in the tub. "Sit down. The hot water will make you look like you have color." He grabbed the bar of soap and lathered the fourteen-year-old, making sure to clean every orifice.

Ilana held her hands over her eyes. "I can do this," Ilana begged Andres to leave.

"No, sugar. I like helping." Andres turned on the showerhead and grabbed the shampoo. The stream burned Ilana's skin. Andres ran his soapy hands through her thick hair. His hands were covered in foam, roaming over her skin. He spun her blossoming body around and rinsed the soap from her hair. "OK. You're done." He helped Ilana to her feet and watched her stand naked in the shower. He wrapped her in a towel and rubbed her dry. Andres led her out of the bathroom and passed her off to Vincente.

Vincente sat her in the towel on the kitchen chair and combed Ilana's hair. He put it in tight pigtails, wrapped with fresh robin's-egg-blue ribbons. Vincente labored to ensure every hair was perfectly in place. He guided her into the bedroom and made her sit on the rocking horse. He removed her towel. Ilana's skin was still flush from the searing shower.

The flash of the camera reflected off Ilana's eyes. Her forced smile captivated Andres. He moved her from the rocking horse to the Barbie house, making her sit with her legs open. He made her pick up the toys. And read a book. And pretend like she was taking a nap. Ilana did what she was told, or Andres would hit her with his belt buckle.

MAY 16
NEW ORLEANS, LOUISIANA

"I am angry." Ke'Von sat at the mosque Masjid Al-Islam with Cleric Rahman Mesbah.

"Why are you angry, my friend?" Mesbah guided Ke'Von to a more private place.

"Your people killed my son." Ke'Von glared at the holy man. "America killed my son."

"For your loss I am very sorry. I see that you still grieve for your son. What was his name?"

"DaMarcus. He lost his life in Afghanistan."

"Was he a soldier?" the cleric asked.

"He was in the US Army. He was blown up by an IED." Mesbah remained silent. "I don't understand why the United States is fighting a war halfway around the world with our children. What purpose will it serve? How many lives will be lost?"

"John F. Kennedy once said, 'Mankind must put an end to war before war puts an end to mankind.'"

"There are others who should pay for the death of my child." Vengeance filled Ke'Von's eyes.

"On whom should you exact your revenge?"

Ke'Von struggled to answer.

Rahman Mesbah continued, "Governments have sent children to fight their wars since the beginning of time."

"I miss him so much." Ke'Von choked back the tears.

"As do the parents of the fallen around the world. They are all the victims of Satan's plan to exploit the weakness of humanity and destroy the world through them. Unfortunately, we are making it all too simple for Iblis."

"Iblis?" Ke'Von did not understand the reference.

"That is what the Koran calls Satan." Mesbah tapped the holy book. "So why are you really here, Mr. Keshi?"

Ke'Von summoned the courage to face his fears. "I want to stop the hate in my heart. I want peace."

"You have chosen the righteous path." Mesbah rejoiced. "Do you have a Bible?"

"I destroyed my Bible," Ke'Von admitted shamefully.

"Take this copy of the Koran." Ke'Von hedged. "You will find that the lessons are the same. The Bible. The Torah. The Bhagavad Gita. We all worship a good God, no matter what the name." Ke'Von took the holy book and placed it on his lap. "You yearn for peace in your heart. That peace will come through forgiveness. Only through love of one another will humankind find peace and harmony. I admire the path you have chosen. It shall not be easy. The demons will arise. It is how we handle that temptation and what we do in the future that Allah, or God, will respect."

Ke'Von thanked the cleric. His heart accepted a ray of light.

FBI agents monitoring the activities of the mosque made a note in their log about the unusual visit to the Masjid Al-Islam mosque by a character they had never witnessed before.

MAY 22
ARLINGTON, VIRGINIA

"I don't want to do it today, Mom! I'm tired. I just want to take a nap." Madeline heaved her backpack across the kitchen and it smashed into the legs of the chairs. Dr. Smalling and Dr. Osaka slipped into the living room, waiting for Sophia to resolve the family matter.

"Madeline," Sophia began, "these people are trying to help you. They have given countless hours of their own time working to solve this problem." Sophia saw that the guilt was not working. "I know this has been a nightmare, but the doctors think we are getting somewhere. Just stick with it. How about an orange Push Up?" It was hard for Madeline to resist the cool sherbet treat, given that it felt like the earth had been jolted by a solar flare.

Madeline closed her eyes, took the pop, and followed her mother into the living room, where Diego activated the video camera.

The men came early from their tents wearing no shirts—just the leggings that tied to their belts. I was able to hang my buffalo-skin robe and tuck away my mittens. The smell of spring danced on every leaf. The sky above was a bold blue, stretching for an eternity into the eastward sun. The sparrows, ducks, and geese were returning. As were the soldiers of the Union army.

We'd gathered with Red Cloud the previous night, and Keyan had told us of the battle with soldiers of Colonel Joseph J. Reynolds at Powder River. The army had burned the village. They'd killed women and children. They'd taken the horses. The warriors had pushed the army back into the snow, and they'd run like cowards. They'd left their soldiers in the snow and had not returned. In a dark raid on the enemy camp, the warriors had retaken their horses.

"In the winter they asked us to send for all of our people. They asked us to stop hunting. Return to the reservation, they said, or we would be subjected to military action." Okatay seethed. "Now we hear of more attacks on our villages as the snow melts. As the waters of the mountains run toward the Sioux, so the Union army shall die at the tips of our spears!"

The young warriors let loose a battle cry.

Red Cloud, the elder, tried to think it through for the young and brave. "Our horses are tired from the fight of winter."

"They will become strong," debated Okatay.

"Who will hunt? Who will farm while the men are at war with the white man?" Okatay did not answer the wise leader. "Our men are brave, and they will fight with their hearts, but we do not carry the guns of the white man. We have but few. They have many. How do we battle against the guns and the cannon?"

Big John provided news from Fort Laramie. Big John had traveled with Okatay to the fort on the Nebraska border to examine the newest proposal offered by Major General Philip Sheridan, commander of the Department of Missouri, and President Ulysses S. Grant.

"The government had no interest in stopping the miners or the railroads, Red Cloud. They will continue to come. Indian Inspector Erwin Watkins has said that the Sioux needed to be 'whipped into subjection.' More soldiers will come from Fort Laramie, Fort Lincoln, and Fort Ellis in the summer. You must prepare for war." Big John had served with Sherman when he'd burned Atlanta. He knew what these men were capable of. "They plan to destroy you. And the Cheyenne, the Crow, the Shoshoni, and anyone else who stands in the way of their gold."

I had never seen Red Cloud so troubled. He passed the pipe and watched the fire. Then he spoke. "The time for war is gone. I cannot send my people to their death."

"You will not send us, but you will not prevent us from fighting with Crazy Horse or Sitting Bull."

"No." Red Cloud wept in his heart for the lives that would be lost in the coming months.

The hunters saddled the horses in search of deer, ram, and buffalo. Chayton led the brigade, again taking young Angus on the journey. Big John worked the horses with Samuel. Chayton whispered words of anger to Samuel at every opportunity.

Emmy Lou came from the tent, wearing a smile as wide as a sunset. She gave a warm welcome to the morning, passing by the women. She made a special stop to visit Star and the new child, My Heart, having knitted the infant a warm cover. The children of the village surrounded Hair Storm as she taught them about the medicine wheel and its power to heal and understand the universe. Emmy Lou sat with the fascinated children and watched them learn of the circle, which represented the outer boundary of the earth and a continuous flow of life and death. Two lines pass through the circle, and in the center humanity stands to pray to Wakan Tanka, the Great Spirit. Four sections of the circle bore four different colors. These were the directions. To the east, the color yellow. And from the east comes the brown eagle. The world adapted to the consistent pattern of the sun traveling east to west. Emmy Lou and the children followed Hair Storm's finger and gazed upon the morning star of wisdom and new beginnings.

Hair Storm looked north to the last breaths of winter, the color of red on the medicine wheel. Time would tell that she had but a few winters left in her life, so she shared her wisdom with the little ones. From the north come the crane, the buffalo people, and the Calf Pipe Woman. She warned the children that those who misbehaved looked there for guidance to the straight path.

Good Road, the son of White and Raccoon, asked of the black portion of the wheel. Hair Storm screwed up her eyes and opened her mouth wide, allowing the children to see the few teeth she had left. She spread her arms like wings and shouted, "Thunderer!" The children roared with approval, and some of the smallest ones' eyes filled with tears and fear. Emmy Lou brought them into her arms as Hair Storm explained the legend of the sky spirit that patrolled above in the form of a giant bird that shot lightning from its eyes and flapped thunder from its wings, forever protecting the Lakota from the mortal enemy Unktehi, the horned serpent. Hair Storm kneeled down with the children and taught them that from the west came not just Thunderer but the rain. The rains and the purity of water. And from water came growth, not just of the plants and flowers but of the mind and body.

"Which color is left?" The children pointed at white. "Have any of you seen the eagle with a white head?" In unison they chanted yes. "From the south, my special students, come warmth and happiness and"—Hair Storm looked at Emmy Lou, thinking of her mother—"generosity."

Emmy Lou looked at Hair Storm and thought of how grateful she was that they had found a place on earth where they could be part of a unique and wonderful world.

I followed Emmy Lou to the river as she carried the clothes to be washed. Her radiance belied her.

"May I help you?" I took some of her load.

"Thank you." Her cheeks were flush with work and excitement.

"You seem to be in a jovial mood today." I didn't know how to start; what I said next just came out of my mouth. "Are you pregnant?"

Emmy Lou was shocked that I was so brazen, but then the smile returned, and she began to tear up. "Yes!"

I had never been hugged so hard in my few years. Emmy Lou spoke more to me in the one hour that we spent by the river than she had in the eight months she had been part of the village. We took a long walk beside the river, climbing higher, and we sat on the ledge that overlooked the bend. A place of quiet and reflection. A place to look to the south and be grateful. A place where the water raced around the giant rocks and beat and pulsed downstream. The flute-like chirping of the birds and the haunting howls of the owl filled the clear and warming skies, the symphony of nature playing just for us.

"Have you shared the news with Big John?" I inquired.

"Yes. He knows. He is so happy. We have been trying for such a long time."

"We know. Some in the camp have given John a nickname. They call him Wahkan. Has Much Practice."

Emmy Lou turned the color of a tomato, but we laughed until our ribs hurt.

"Do you love my brother?" Emmy Lou returned the brazen favor.

I almost slipped from the edge to the river down below. "I guess it is not nearly the secret I thought it was."

"Hardly." We laughed from deep in our bellies.

"It makes no difference how I feel. I am promised to another."

"Samuel loves you, too. And where there is love, anything is possible." Emmy Lou rubbed her tummy. "Look at me!" She was right. Love would find a way. I had to continue to believe that.

We shirked our chores for much of the morning. Below we saw the deer creep to the water to drink. A beaver scurried across the rocks. Two eagles soared high into the clouds. And two men with rifles, dirty beards, and pans sifted through the river rocks for gold.

In the weeks that followed, the village foraged turnips and potatoes of the summer in order to survive the next winter. Samuel was sent to collect the dung of the buffalo that we used as fuel to send smoke signals. Others resented this chore, but Samuel remained humble and accepted each chore for its importance. The hunters found the herd grazing at the edges of the forest. Chayton took Angus, Samuel, and Big John into the trees. Chayton instructed them to ignite the forest. The fire drove the herd through the hollow into the waiting hunter's spears or to their death over the cliffs.

To the village they brought a hundred head to the cheers of the tribe. The men, women, and children went to work on Wakan Tanka's great gift. Hotah skinned the giant beasts and gave them to Chapawee, who removed the hair and stuffed small pockets of skin to make balls for the children or to line a crib. Angus learned how to make a paintbrush and a rope. A shield and part of a saddle. Samuel stretched the skins with Hanska to form new tepees and to make saddlebags and rattles for the babies. Emmy Lou took hide with the hair and sat with Tahcawin, fashioning warm winter clothing, moccasins, blankets, and covers for the tepee floors. Emmy Lou laughed at Big John when he was asked to take the buffalo's brains and prepare the hides. Big John chased Emmy Lou around the village, bringing glee to the day's hard work. Bird and Mina cut off the hooves to make glue. The young men worked with the older warriors, taking the face muscle and crafting it into string for their bows and with which to sew. Macha and Chumani took the horns and carved headdresses, cups, and spoons. The teeth became necklaces, the beard decorations for weapons and clothing. Laughing Maid and Hair Storm boiled, roasted, and dried the meat. The bladders became waterproof bags, and the stomach became a cooking pot. The warriors gathered the rib bones and created arrow shafts and runners for sleds.

When the day's work was done, the men would train for war with the young braves, teaching them to defend and attack. They measured their bows to fit each child's reach and sharpened the stone, bone, and sinew to deadly points. The same spears used to kill deer and rabbits had the same effect on people. The youngsters were trained in how to hold and handle the tomahawk, slay with both a short and long knife, and bludgeon with a club.

One week, Big John took the wagon to Fort Laramie to garner supplies. When he returned, he opened two large wooden cases filled with guns. Starr revolvers, Colt Army Models, Springfield 1870 rifles, Smith & Wesson Model 1s, Burnside carbines, and many more. I asked Big John how he was able to obtain all of these weapons. He reminded me that "with money, you can get anything you want." I asked Big John where he got the money. He told me, "Wanikiya, in the world we came from, money was everything. Here, we don't use money. I have no need for money. Whatever I had, I spent to protect the tribe."

Big John taught the warriors to shoot. Shoot from their bellies and from their knees. From a horse and from a tree. Samuel was terrible with a rifle. His brother, Angus, was a crack shot. They were so different, but they loved each other so much.

In the evenings Samuel would strum his guitar, and Big John would sing and blow his harmonica. Kangee blew into the instrument and made the sound of a crow, alarming the children. Emmy Lou would sing with John and Samuel if encouraged, and the three taught us many new songs.

We lost many of the men as they migrated north to join the forces of Sitting Bull and Crazy Horse in preparation for the battles that were anticipated, making the work in the village doubly hard. On a particularly hot late afternoon, the women gathered near the pond and bathed in the cool waters. Industrious helped Walks as She Thinks into the water, her bones creaky and skin worn from the cold winter winds, tattered by time. Emmy Lou removed the string from her bright red hair and sank her freckled, pale skin into the pond, lightly massaging the growing bulge in her belly. Hair Storm taught the girls to swim, and Star dipped her newborn, My Heart, lightly in the water like a leaf that floated.

I dipped my head deep into the water, soaking my hair. I ran my fingers through my locks to remove the tangles, and I kicked with my legs, stretching the tired muscles. The pond removed my pain and eased my mind, the waters soothing my skin. I thought of the warriors, the crops, the hunters, and the children. I thought of my vision quest and the meaning of my life. I mostly thought of Samuel—his eyes that folded the colors of the universe and his long brown hair. I worried that he would remain so thin yet work so hard. I dreamed of when and how we could be together. My arms stretched and pulled me to the farthest edge of the pond. I heard Samuel's whistle, a sound I had grown familiar with and fond of. At first, I believed his song was in my head. I walked from the pond and through the reeds, wondering if I had tricked myself. Samuel was walking the horses to the pond to drink. I did not think to move as he looked up. My eyes met his, and he stopped. I stood tall in the weeds, letting him see me as I was, as Wakan Tanka had created me. We were together as I had dreamed of being only for a moment. The children called my name and wondered where I was.

In the late spring in the year of the centennial, the skies of the west turned black, and the rains fell with fervor. In the beginning we were joyous, for the gardens needed the water, but they continued for many days. The banks of the river began to swell, and the veins of the water flooded the gardens and drowned the crops. On the last day of the rains, I left the tepee and walked through the mud to see Emmy Lou and bring her a bowl of dried turnips and fruit. I called from outside, wishing for a response so I could come in from the rain.

As I shivered in the rain, a huge hand wrapped its fingers around my wrist and pulled me inside. Big John looked of the bear that had slept all winter, his hair tousled and fur covering his chest and back.

"Where is Emmy Lou?" It was odd that she would have left the tepee in such dreadful conditions.

"I don't know. It is awfully early." Big John stretched and growled. "Maybe she went to Harriet's tepee." Big John lay back down for an early morning nap.

I set the bowl of dried turnips and berries next to where Emmy Lou usually sat, and I saw blood. My heart froze, and I poked Big John and showed him.

He leaped to his feet and jumped out into the rain. "Emmy Lou!" His shouts awakened the whole camp. "Emmy Lou!"

"John, I will walk to the river to look for her."

"I will go to the pond."

Samuel and Angus appeared from their tent with Harriet. Star and Lootah appeared holding My Heart close to them in a blanket, protected from the rain. Butterfly and Laughing Maid gathered in the village, confused and disoriented from the sudden awakening. Shadow and White Eagle moved swiftly to their horses and began to search, the community alerted.

I found the edges of the river. The tide had risen beyond the banks. The current ripped around the rocks, churning mud, broken trees racing like mad rafts and smashing into splinters on the backs of the boulders that knifed the rapids. The rain created a sheet before my eyes, and I could not look far into the distance. I started to travel up the hill, to the place where Emmy Lou and I had shared our hearts. The ground was wet and slippery. I could see a path where someone had fallen, the grass matted to the ground. I held the branches of the trees, attempting to hoist myself to the top of the ridge. My feet fell beneath me as I held the branch. I pulled, and the weight released as Samuel pushed me from behind. He grasped my hand and the branch and yanked his way to me. I put my arms around him, and he pulled me close to him.

"Where are you going?" he asked, speaking loudly between the falling rains.

"A place that Emmy Lou and I have been. A wonderful place where she shared that she was with child. It is just around that bend, overlooking the river."

Samuel and I slogged through the mud and wet grass. We came around the bend, and Emmy Lou stood on the edge of the cliffs, drenched in the mist, her wet clothes clinging to her breast and her skirt soaked in the blood of her lost child.

"Emmy Lou!" Samuel screamed into the gray.

I could see behind the tears and into the lost and hopeless soul. We ran to her, but she slipped into the spray. "No!" Samuel ran to the edge and fell to his knees. I collapsed beside him and held him, preventing him from chasing after his sister. We watched as Emmy Lou's body bobbed down the enraged gorge, careening into the boulders.

The villagers walked the banks of the river in the deluge, searching for Emmy Lou's body. At sundown the rains ceased after five days. The clouds broke, and orange and red streams of light warmed us from the west. Shadow rode into camp, he and his horse covered in mud, exhausted. He'd pulled the body of Emmy Lou Miles off the back of his horse, and he held her in his arms. He walked through the village to the bowed heads of all who had come to love the shy, sad woman who'd idled on the verge of being a mother. On the verge of being happy. He passed her lifeless body into the strong arms of Big John Miles, her husband and survivor of the Civil War, a war that would have slayed him long after the battle if not for the love of Emmy Lou Knapp. Big John fell to his knees and wept.

MAY 23
ATLANTA, GEORGIA

"Evelyn, you have to come!" Radiance was persistent. "It's Memorial Day weekend, and we never have off on a holiday."

"I am not off the whole weekend. The drive to Panama City takes almost six hours. I have to work Saturday night." The trip sounded fun, but Erika would be tagging along. Sharing a hotel room would be icky. Plus, there was the money.

"Chick-fil-A is closed on Sunday. We will pick you up early. Like, five in the morning. You can sleep in the car on the way down, and we will come home Monday night." Radiance heard nothing on the other end of the line and decided to play her ace. "Victor is coming in just over a month. Don't you want to get a tan?" Radiance held her breath.

Evelyn pondered the risk versus reward. She did need some sun. Sun was hard to come by in the drive-through. Evelyn checked her bank app on her phone. She had $102, but the rent for June was paid. There was a paycheck coming on Friday. "OK. I will go." Radiance gave a woo-hoo, but Evelyn had a bad feeling in the pit of her stomach.

Evelyn heard the knock on her door and looked at the digital clock. "Who in God's name is at the door at five in the morning?" Evelyn couldn't fathom the idea. "Oh! Shit!" It was Sunday morning. They were going to Panama City. Evelyn bounded out of bed and opened the door, her hair matted on the side of her head. Radiance and Erika stepped into her apartment, both with hair still wet from their morning shower.

"It will only take me a second to get ready," Evelyn said.

Radiance and Erika treaded lightly in the shadowy apartment. The smell of menthols permeated the carpet, and cigarette ashes powdered the simple coffee table. A few empty bottles of Miller Lite decorated the kitchen counters. They were able to make out the shapes of Chinese to-go containers in the morning gray. The odorous remnants of beer, smokes, and moo shu pork were the antithesis of bacon and eggs.

They listened to the suitcase as it bounced onto Evelyn's bed, to the dresser drawers opening and shutting repeatedly. The water in the sink began to run, and Evelyn gagged as she polished her teeth.

Finally Evelyn presented herself. "Sorry. But that didn't take too long." It certainly didn't look like it had taken too long. Evelyn was a morning disaster.

Erika was driving. Radiance bubbled. Evelyn squeezed herself into the backseat and went back to sleep.

The three amigas underestimated the need for reservations on Memorial Day weekend. They cruised up Highway 30A, stopping at the desks of the Top of the Gulf and the Emerald Beach Resort all the way down to the pricey Landmark Holiday Beach Resort, which had a vacancy but was $229 a night and had a three night minimum.

They doubled back, crossed the bridge over St. Andrew's Bay, and zeroed in on the lovely Buccaneer Motel.

Evelyn squeezed her way out of the backseat, and they walked into the lobby.

"Hi!" Radiance was very chipper for eleven in the morning. "We were hoping you had a vacancy for the night."

The clerk noticed the three of them. "How many rooms will you need?"

"Two." Erika planned on moving Evelyn out.

The clerk tapped on the keyboard and raised his eyes. "I am sorry, ma'am. We do not have two rooms available. We do have a double with two queen-size beds."

Erika's face soured as she pouted to Radiance. "Maybe we should try one more place." Erika didn't want Evelyn around with what she planned to do with Radiance.

Radiance pulled Erika aside. "We've wasted more than an hour. It has a pool and a little beach on the bay."

"And it has Wi-Fi," Evelyn chimed in. "I could Skype with Victor."

Erika stomped but conceded. "We'll take it."

ATLANTA

Rohit Guzan knew Evelyn was at the beach with her girlfriends. Brandon Lyle had told him. He moved unobtrusivley up the stairs to her apartment door and slid the credit card into the lock. The door opened quietly.

The apartment was abhorrent. It was stale and smoky. Underwear was strewn across the bedroom floor, and bras hung on the bedroom door. The bathroom sink was covered in toothpaste film, and the shower had a historic ring of mildew. There was a Tampax floating in the toilet bowl. Rohit went to the kitchen and found what he was looking for on top of the microwave. He thumbed through the bills—the cable bill, the power bill—and some leftover pay stubs from Chick-fil-A with Evelyn Cahill's social security number. That would make his job a little bit easier.

PANAMA CITY

E velyn ordered a vodka and cranberry to kill the pain. Erika and Radiance both sported pastel-colored sundresses that accentuated their bronze tans and stunning legs and shoulders. Erika's hair seemed to have gotten blonder throughout the sun-filled day. They grabbed frozen margaritas with salt and hit the dance floor. They teased the bartender by making out.

Evelyn glowed like Chernobyl. She had fallen asleep on her stomach at the pool. Little bubbles filled with puss from sun poisoning had erupted on her back. Evelyn sat at the bar trying to remain very still and nurse the pain. And not ooze. She was tired of being the third wheel and needed Victor. Despite this disastrous Memorial Day weekend, Evelyn was determined to have the summer of her life.

MAY 30
NEW ORLEANS, LOUISIANA

In the bowels of an industrial warehouse, the excited crowd milled, high on alcohol, coke, meth, pot, bath salts, and death. The chain-smoking clerk with the black eyes, pouring sweat, took the cash for the bets being placed on the two combatants who would fight until one of them surrendered his life.

The tournament bracketed sixteen fighters; the survivor would win one million and his freedom. Seaman Brandon Lyle found this far more entertaining than the movies. He escorted Sadie Davil to the cage and handed her a hundred grand to place his bet on the wiry Vasily Mahini, who was smuggled out of Iran, where he faced certain death by hanging for being a homosexual. The rugged Mahini had cultivated the burgeoning gay underground in Tehran but was arrested and sentenced to death, only to be bartered into the human death match with a small bribe of cash and weapons. Davil doubled the wager.

Elroy and Javad hated going against their boss and wagered $100,000 on Ahmed Mata, the former heroin addict busted in Indonesia for trafficking and sentenced to die by firing squad.

The jeers and cheers erupted as the two men entered the makeshift ring surrounded by barbed wire. The heat in the depths moved the mercury to the top, and the smell of smoke, booze, drugs, and body odor lingered in the air. There were no seats, and the bodies of the bloodthirsty fans pressed against the razors of the wire, which sliced into the skin and dripped blood onto the floor and into the water.

Mata was bruised, scars on his face and lacerations scabbed on his arms and torso from his first-round success. Mahini removed the cast off his hand.

"No one told me his hand was broken." Sadie wanted her bet back.

"And he's a fag," noted Elroy Floyd.

The two men stepped into the center, wearing nothing but tight-fitting shorts. No gloves. No shoes. There were no rounds. There was no clock. There was no referee. There were no rules. The invisible faces of their managers watched from the catwalk above the stage.

Mahini drove into Mata with his shoulder and took him to the floor. Lyle was close enough to hear the breath leave Mata's lungs. Mahini pummeled him with fists to the face, Mata covering his torso with his elbows and knees. Mata tried to roll, but Mahini forced him back and stretched his hand around Mata's throat and began to squeeze. Mata's face bloated purple, and the veins in his neck filled with blood that had nowhere to flow to.

Mata tried to stop Mahini's choke. He removed his right hand and poked Mahini's eye, blood spurting to the concrete floor. Mata stood, dragged the suffering Mahini, and slammed his head into the barbed wire, his face now crimson. He raked his face sideways, opening gashes on the corners of his mouth and nostrils. Mahini held his broken hand over his eyes. He threw a wild elbow that caught Mata in the groin, sending him to the floor.

Javad screamed at Mata to get off the floor. Floyd held the behemoth back, worried he might go to the ring and take matters into his own hands. Javad shook the barbed wire, his hands bleeding as he compelled his fighter to rise and finish the queer.

Mahini, his vision blurred by the blood dripping into his eyes, pounced onto Mata, pulled him by the back of his hair, and pounded his skull into the cement. The crowd silenced as Mata's forehead splintered before them, his cheekbones cracking and the dust seeping into his skull as his brains leaked out. Mahini crushed Mata's head long after the addict had stopped breathing. A man wearing a black mask entered and pronounced Mata dead. Half the crowd erupted as Javad ripped his ticket.

"You're an idiot to have taken Mata. The guy's a pussy," a heckler chided Javad.

"Did you just call me an idiot?" Javad fumed, lifting the man by his collar and heaving him into the barbed wire.

Lyle and Sadie ducked as Javad's prey landed at their feet. Javad threw punches at anything that got close. Elroy Floyd tried to weasel his way out of the combat zone but found himself embroiled in the melee. Sadie was downed by a rolling body, and Lyle helped her back up but took a punch to the mouth that removed an upper front tooth. Lyle connected with a punch, but the crowd started yelling, "Cops!"

Lyle slipped into the darkness with Sadie, and the rest of the roaches scattered into the halls and into the night.

MONDAY, JUNE 2, SOMEWHERE

The dog mat provided little insulation from the concrete floor. The knit blanket allowed the dank to seep into her bones. They wouldn't let her sleep on the makeshift mattress against the wall. That was saved for the other things. They had partied all night, not that Celia was going to sleep well tied up to the post next to the dryer.

Celia had stopped scratching the days into the post. The sliver of light that sliced through the basement window made her wince and reminded her of hope. They mostly left her alone in the daytime. It was when the light slipped away that she wanted to die. So many times she had tried to remove the tie that held her captive. So many times she yearned just to look out the window. The dreams of crawling through and running away consumed her thoughts.

Harlow brought her water and leftover macaroni and cheese. She sensed that Harlow had a heart, but when he smelled like beer, he was just like all the rest. Celia prayed for herself. She prayed for her mom and her dad and her sister.

Celia wanted to shower and brush her hair. To smell a fresh towel and to brush her teeth for hours. The one they called Colt said she was nasty when he was on top of her. The only time they had let her shower was when she was bleeding or they'd made her bleed. Harlow always sat on the toilet taking a dump when she showered. He called it multitasking. Watching her and doing his business. Harlow wouldn't let Celia close the shower curtain.

JUNE 4
MODESTO, CALIFORNIA

POLICE SEEK MODESTO TEENAGER
Modesto Bee

The Modesto Police Department office is posting a missing persons report for Shay Bertrup, fifteen years of age. Shay is a freshman at Peter Johansen High School and was last seen at a party late Saturday night, June 2, around two in the morning on Dillingham Avenue.

She was last seen wearing high-waisted Levi's shorts, a beige camisole, platform sandals, and turquoise beads around her neck. Shay is Caucasian, five feet ten inches tall, and 120 pounds. She has long blond hair and blue eyes.

Please contact the Modesto Police Department if you have any information on Shay's disappearance or if you know her whereabouts. Please call 209-555-3932.

JUNE 5
SEATTLE, WASHINGTON

The rain did not come down in buckets; it just came all the time. Bethany hobbled on her crutches down the stairs of the apartment building with the ugly yellow walls. Too much roughhousing and copious amounts of vodka with the cute boy in 5C had resulted in a cracked ankle. Huang opened the door and helped Bethany into the passenger seat of the gray Toyota Camry.

"Where is the doctor's office?" Huang adjusted the seat to suit her smaller frame.

"It's on East Madison Street." Bethany pointed to take a right, knowing that Huang wasn't Seattle savvy.

"I haven't driven in a while." Huang checked the steering column for the turn signal and wipers.

Bethany scratched underneath her cast as Huang eased out of the spot and headed toward the stop sign. She took the prerequisite right turn, and the blue lights of the Seattle Police Department flashed in the rearview with that whoop sound that made you freeze up. Huang pulled to the curb.

"License, registration, and proof of insurance, ma'am." The officer stood in the rain at the driver's-side window.

"Officer, this is my car," Bethany explained to the young man. "This is my friend, and she is driving me to the doctor." Everyone acknowledged Bethany's cast and the bounty of colorful symbols, pictures, and autographs.

He looked at Huang. "Then I will need your license." Then he looked at Bethany. "And your registration and insurance."

Bethany handed them over, and the officer disappeared. Huang gave the officer her Indiana driver's license.

Huang sat nervously, her fingers shaking.

"Calm down," Bethany said. "I'm sure we'll just get a warning."

Huang turned to her friend. Bethany had found Huang at a local coffee shop; she'd been like a lost puppy. "I haven't been exactly honest with you, Bethany," Huang confessed. Bethany looked confused. "I didn't move here from Indiana." Huang stared somberly at the wheel. "I ran away from home."

"Are you in some sort of trouble?"

It would be the first time Huang had ever discussed her life with anyone. "My father abused me."

"He hit you?" Bethany was aghast.

"No. He had sex with me." Huang began to cry.

"Oh my God!" Bethany reached over to hug Huang. "Why doesn't your mother divorce him?"

"She knows about it."

"Oh my God!" Bethany digested all of this new information and then puffed out her ample chest. "Well, that's all over now. You're an adult, and you don't have to go back to Indiana," Bethany reassured her.

"That's the other lie," Huang said, mustering the truth. "I am not eighteen. I am only sixteen."

"Christ," Bethany uttered under her breath.

The officer knocked on the window. Huang knew what was coming.

"Ma'am. I have to take you into custody."

"What did I do wrong, Officer?" Huang tried to bullshit one last time.

"I don't know if you did anything wrong, miss, but you are on a nationwide list of missing children. It's my job to return you to your parents." Huang leaned away from the window. "Don't make me cuff you, miss."

"I can't go back there. My father makes me have sex with him," Huang pleaded.

This stopped the officer cold. "Young lady, I will do everything I can to help you. But right now you have to come with me." He placed Huang in the back of the squad car. Bethany missed her appointment and the officer dropped her off at her house. She fretted about Huang all day and coaxed the despair with copious amounts of vodka.

THE MADELINE SESSIONS:
JUNE 12
ARLINGTON, VIRGINIA

Big John hadn't said a word in weeks. On a crisp morning, the dew still on the grass, John hitched the horses to the wagon and headed to Fort Laramie. He told Samuel that he would return in a few days' time. The mood in the village had been somber since we'd lost Emmy Lou, yet we went about our daily chores in the growing summer heat.

The night remained warm. Harriet crafted a dress by the light of the fire until the embers turned to a glow. The sliver moon hid behind the clouds, casting only the faintest light. We did not see the return of the hunting party until they were inside the village. Their faces were tired and bore no celebration of victory in the mountains. Chayton rode behind Angus on the back of his horse, his body limp and in pain. Samuel had been coaxed into the hunt by Chayton. I had thought of Samuel for the two days, knowing that he was not skilled with a bow and was unsteady with his father's rifle. He looked haggard and drained.

Wapasha dismounted his horse as Talutah, the young maiden, ran to comfort Chayton. Wapasha asked to speak to Red Cloud, who had left the village to convene with Sitting Bull and Crazy Horse to the north in the unceded Montana territory.

"I shall speak to Appanoose," Wapasha asked, seeking the elder who'd been given the name Chief When a Child.

Wapasha entered the tepee with Angus, Samuel, Chayton, and several others from the hunting party.

"What story does Wapasha wish to tell me?" The wise Appanoose smoked a pipe.

Wapasha deferred to Chayton, who spoke softly. "Two mornings past I corralled a group of hunters, ready to climb into the mountains to hunt bear. Angus grabbed his bow, thrilled at the opportunity to slay the giant. I encouraged Samuel to join with the hunters, wishing him to learn the ways of the hunt. We started our journey early and traversed the canyons of the Badlands on our way into the high country. We paused to let the horses drink from the stream and ate jerky. Angus told tales of the fair women in Europe, and we listened with open ears. Late in the afternoon, as we climbed into the Black Hills, we heard the clashing of the bighorns. We scaled the narrow paths to where the air is thin. We quietly assembled on a landing to view the great sheep and position ourselves for the kill. Two great, tremendous rams faced off for the affections of the ewe. The older ram squared with the young contender, raising high and slamming its horns into the oncoming force. The echo stretched across the valleys, as the rams recovered from the blows. They stared each other down for a second time, the youthful ram delivering a massive strike, staggering the proud ram. We viewed the fight with awe and respect until the sun began to fall behind the trees. After a brilliant fight, the elderly ram moved away in defeat." Chayton lowered his head. "We made camp for the night, and my thoughts turned dark. For this I am ashamed and have come to ask the forgiveness of the elders. I have disgraced the tribe."

"What actions do you speak of, Chayton? Tell me of these dark thoughts."

"As the sun rose in the morning, Samuel prepared a meal for the hunters. We had camped high in the mountains, hoping to meet the ram with our bow. I instructed the group to split and cover the mountain in small groups. I used my leadership for my own intentions, specifically choosing to partner with Samuel. I purposely led Samuel on slender mountain paths that look far down over the cliffs to the trees below. I secretly wished he would slip and fall. At times I felt the need to push him and watch him cascade to his death."

"Why do you wish to harm Samuel, Chayton?" Appanoose passed the pipe to Industrious.

"I am promised to Wanikiya, yet I know her affections lie with Samuel. The white man has taken our land, our buffalo, and our pride. I swore not to let another white man take anything from me. Samuel was not going to take Wanikiya."

"Yet you did not throw him down the mountain. I am curious." Hair Storm packed her own bowl neatly.

"I could not find the courage. I decided to wait and find a place in which I would prove who was the stronger man, as the bighorns had in their battle the night before. We would use our skill to decide who more was worthy."

"Yet you are all standing before me."

"It would not be that way if it were not for Samuel." Chayton looked to the ground. "The path took us to a landing below a great face of the mountain and another trail descending to the river. In the shadows of the cliffs I drew my knife and challenged Samuel. He pleaded that he wanted no part of a fight with the people he had grown to call family. I called him a coward and slashed at his belly. He refused to draw his blade yet stood his ground and did not run. I swiped at his face, drawing the blood from his cheek, yet he remained still. I asked if he loved Wanikiya, and he said yes. I cried a battle cry as my blood boiled inside me. I wanted to see his blood stain the white face of the peak. From the shadows the bear rose to its feet, as high as the branches of the trees and pushing me to the edge of the cliff. Samuel screamed at the bear, which pushed forward and reached for me with its great claws. I leaned away from the beast and fell from the landing so that I hung over the edge, my fingers sliding. Samuel charged the bear with his knife, plunging it into its neck. He pushed the blade in deep, the animal's blood like a waterfall flowing over the cliff. The bear fell, and I saw its claws scratching the edge, pushing back for its life. I could hear Samuel's blade slashing into the face and eyes of the bear until it plunged over the side, tumbling down the rocks to its death. Samuel's arms and chest bore the mark of the bear's teeth and claws, yet he reached his hand over the side and took mine. He pulled me to the landing, and we fell to the earth. Samuel lay bleeding, and I took his rifle and fired a shot into the sky. I reflected on my vision quest as I looked into the sun. It was foretold that I would be granted forgiveness for a great sin and that I would share my stories so that others would learn from my mistake. My prophecy told that I would be a valiant warrior and a great man. I have told my story to the village, and I am ashamed. I do not ask for your mercy, for Samuel has already forgiven my actions."

"It is a humble lesson for you, Chayton. The prophecy has said you will be a valiant warrior and great man. I hope you prove the prophecy to be true, for that is your quest. I think we also have among us a great and wise man in Samuel. Youth is slow to see and forgive, yet you have wisdom that comes from many seasons. These lessons will be told by the campfire to generations of children, teaching the ways of compassion and love." Appanoose crossed his legs.

"I have more to tell." Chayton steadied his chest. "It is the way of the Lakota to have promised me to Wanikiya, but I do not love her, nor she me, in the way that spouses should love each other. I know that she yearns to be with Samuel and he with her. I ask that Wanikiya be allowed to be with Samuel. I also ask that I may seek the hand of Talutah, for she is the one I see when she walks in the flowers."

Hair Storm dropped the pipe, and Appanoose stood to speak. "It is by the grace of the creator that the bear did not strip you of your lives. The destiny of the day is that you each will be a great leader," Appanoose said, sighing, "with the woman you love by your side."

Samuel came to my tent and told me the story as Harriet and I tended to the deep gashes caused by the bear. Harriet agreed that I could stay with her and Samuel through the night to tend to his wounds. Never in the history of injury have so many bandages been changed in one night.

JUNE 13
SALEM, OREGON

The detective stood outside of the room. He looked through the window at high school senior Eytan Chiellini. He loosened his tie and waited for the young man to consult with his attorney. The somber-faced lawyer went through pages of notes with the frightened student. The attorney stepped out of the confinement.

"Does you client wish to make a statement?" The detective asked.

"He does. He wants to cooperate," offered the attorney.

"He didn't cooperate until he got caught," remarked the detective.

The attorney tested the waters. "He's a scared kid. I was hoping we could get this down to manslaughter."

"That's up to the DA," the detective said upon entering the room. "Mr. Chiellini, I hear you might have something to say to me." Eytan remained silent. "Look at me, kid." The trembling kid raised his eyes from the floor. "Did you kill Aditi Buffon?" He eyeballed the boy.

Eytan's mouth quivered. Snot ran out of his nose, and he rubbed his eyes, trying to dam the tears. He nodded.

"I need to hear it," pressed the detective.

"I did it. I killed her. It wasn't supposed to happen." Eytan stood and smashed his forearms into the wall.

"What was not supposed to happen?"

Eytan cried into his arms in the corner of the room. "We had been going out for four months. And then I heard rumors that she had started seeing some asshole from another high school." The detective and attorney let him talk. "She wouldn't return my calls or texts." Eytan slumped into the corner. "I followed her one Friday night, and she was with him. I saw them kissing."

"How did you get her out of the mall?" the detective wondered aloud.

"I was shopping and saw her and her friends. I followed them for a while, but I needed to talk to her. I saw her go to the bathroom, and I followed her there."

"What happened next?"

"She came out, and I was waiting for her. She was surprised, and I just asked her if we could talk." Eytan became red in the face. "She said she didn't want to, and I flipped." His chest heaved, and he screamed with all his might.

"Tell him the story, Eytan," implored the lawyer.

"I grabbed her arm and told her I needed to talk to her. She seemed scared but said she would talk to me. We went out the back door, and we were cool. She was listening to me, and I was with her, and we were talking about us. Us. I wanted to know why she hadn't returned my texts or calls."

"What did Aditi say?"

"She said she didn't know what to say. She just hadn't." Eytan took a deep breath.

The detective scribbled on his pad. "What happened next, Eytan?"

"We got in the truck. It was cold, and Aditi was shivering." There was a prolonged pause.

"You have to tell him everything," the attorney informed him.

"We got in the car, and I brought up this other guy." The attorney and detective sharpened their focus. "She told me she had been with him, and I freaked out."

"What does 'freak out' mean, exactly?" asked the detective.

"I punched her in the face." The room hushed. "And then I grabbed her around the throat and just started choking her. I couldn't let go. I just held her neck and squeezed as hard as I could, screaming at her." Eytan glared at the floor. "Then she stopped moving."

"Did you know she was dead?"

"Not at first. Then her lips turned blue. That's when things went crazy. I was out of my mind. I just started to drive."

"Why Mission Lake?"

Eytan scratched at the floor, never moving his gaze. "I just wanted to be far away. I started driving. My family had been there before. I didn't know what to do. I should have killed myself."

"How did you weigh her down?"

There was a long pause. "I tied her hands and feet to cinder blocks that were in my father's truck. And I rolled her into the water."

JUNE 18
NEW ORLEANS, LOUISIANA

The secretary found an empty conference room on the eighth floor of the New Orleans FBI for Jeremy Alcott and Bruno Sommer. They were thankful it had a window. A junior agent brought in the witness.

Islam Azeen smelled of the streets, his jeans tattered, his T-shirt covered in dirt and grime. His nails were black, and his hands seemed like they had been dipped in soot. "Why are you bringing me here? I haven't done anything."

"You are not being charged with a crime, Mr. Azeen," Jeremy assured the man, who he believed was an urchin. "On the thirtieth of May, you were picked up and questioned by the police about an incident at a warehouse."

"Yeah. I told them all about that night. They didn't charge me with anything."

"Why were you there that night?" Bruno inquired.

"I was there to see the fight," Azeen complied.

"What kinds of fights were these?" Bruno pressed.

"You know, the real kind."

"A man was found dead," Bruno reminded Azeen.

"Yeah. He lost." Azeen grinned at the detectives.

"Will there be more of these fights?" Jeremy cut in.

"Sure. They happen all the time," Azeen added nonchalantly.

"Here in New Orleans?"

"I don't know. They happen all over the world. This one was here. It's like the Super Bowl. It comes to New Orleans once in a while."

"I would hardly consider it the Super Bowl, Mr. Azeen." Bruno straightened the witness's chair.

"I am interested to see if you can identify any of these people." Jeremy spread the photographs of Brandon Lyle, Sadie Davil, Javad Nehwal, Rohit Guzan, and Elroy Floyd onto the conference room's oval oak table.

Azeen decided to try to play the detectives. "What's in it for me?"

Bruno laid it down. "You can avoid five to ten for obstruction and accessory to murder."

"You can't pin that shit on me." Azeen pushed the pictures to the middle of the table.

Jeremy tried a softer approach. "How about I make those possession charges disappear?"

"That's a little more like it," Azeen sneered at Sommer. "I saw this guy. He started the fight." Azeen identified Javad Nehwal.

"Any others?" Jeremy said, hopeful.

"I saw this bitch. She was about the only female in the house. A fine-looking ho."

"So you can positively identify these two?"

"I saw them," Azeen confirmed.

"Thank you, Mr. Azeen. I will speak to the district attorney about those charges."

Jeremy and Bruno spared the high five after Azeen had been escorted out of the room. They were still way behind, but they felt like they were back on the trail.

"That's one mean-ass white boy." Sommer loathed men like Azeen. He thought they were scum.

"Why does it have to be about black and white? Because you are black?" Jeremy challenged his partner.

"No one ever says 'mean-ass black boy,'" Sommer said, trying to lighten the mood.

"I wouldn't. I don't see color."

"You don't see much behind those glasses," Sommer said, referring to Jeremy's light-adjusting frames.

"I am going to the hotel."

"Jeremy. I was just busting your balls." Sommer had never seen Jeremy be so sensitive.

"I'm just tired."

Alcott checked into his room and opened his laptop. If chasing Lyle weren't enough, the whole world seemed to have gone mad. Death matches in the United States. He read an article about a child with Down syndrome in Pakistan who had been stoned and burned to death for blasphemy. The poor kid was living outside and burning pages of the Koran to stay warm. So they killed him. It was the going rate for his crime. Alcott thumbed through the pages of missing girls, pondering their fate, searching for the one that carries the light inside her, trying to save her. He stood before the bureau and removed his shirt. He stared at the scars that decorated his torso since birth. The doctors had told him they looked like claw scratches and bites. They acknowledged they were the most peculiar birthmarks they had ever seen. He rubbed his finger across the raised welt on his chest and remembered the dreams of death from another life and that he was tracking down his killer, Brandon Lyle.

JUNE 19
DURANGO, COLORADO

Ilana Landreau sat quietly on the couch. If she made noise, she would get a beating. She monitored the welts on her upper arms and legs where Andres had hit her with his belt buckle. Many of the old ones had started to disappear but had been replaced by fresh bright purple ones. She did notice that her eyes weren't as swollen as they had been. Ilana was learning.

Ilana flinched when she heard the knock on the door. She saw *gordo* Vincente, grinning his gold-toothed smile, open the door. She heard the people at the door talking about her. They had been there before. The police had too. Each time it was the same.

"Hello, we are here to ask if anyone in this household knows the whereabouts of Ilana Landreau." The woman at the door handed Vincente a flyer with Ilana's school picture on it.

Vincente fake lamented, "I heard about this girl. That is so sad." He paused to study the flyer. "I am sorry I don't have any information that would help."

"Please, if you see her or hear anything, call the number on the flyer."

Vincente closed the door, but Andres kept the pistol shoved into Ilana's temple.

Vincente spoke mostly in Spanish to Andres, though he knew English very well. "You can put the gun away, Andres."

"Not yet. She can still scream, and then they would come back. We need to get out of here—soon!" Andres fiddled with the cock on the gun.

"Put the damn thing away. You are making me nervous." Vincente cracked open a beer.

"When do we leave? When do we get our money?" Andres peeked through the blinds.

"I am sure we will get the call soon. Be patient. It will all be worth it."

"There are cops all over the place. They haven't given up on this girl." Andres ran his short fingers through Ilana's hair.

"Leave her alone, you pervert. There are others for your needs. She will bring a high price. She is young, and she is a virgin." Vincente peered out the window as well. "They have no idea where she is. They are grasping at straws. For all they know she is in Mexico…or dead."

Ilana had looked out the same windows as Vincente and Andres when they weren't looking. She knew exactly where she was. She had walked her dog around this street before. Her house and her mother were about three blocks away.

JUNE 20
ARLINGTON, VIRGINIA

Sophia glued the baby picture of Madeline to the board, completing the shrine of embarrassment that would show a history of bad hairdos, zits, poor wardrobe choices, and uncomfortable smiles. Sophia made sure to include the photo of Madeline raising her hand in victory after a cross-country race, her armpits unshorn. Sophia placed the photo on the easel she had borrowed from the law firm and called the caterer for the fifth time to confirm the arrival time and quadruple-check the details for the menu. Forty guests would be gathering to celebrate Madeline's high school graduation.

Oliver yanked at the knot around his neck. He despised the tie, but Raphael insisted he keep it snug to his neck. Sophia pinned the black graduation cap to Madeline's coif, fearing it would blow off in the light breeze. Sophia gave her senior a giant hug.

Later, at graduation, Sophia settled onto the bleachers with the boys.

The commencement speech dragged on, and Sophia scrambled for a tissue when Oliver pulled a giant greeny from his nose and attempted to wipe it under his seat. The speaker spoke of a troubled world and the challenges the seniors would face as "leaders of society." Sophia's mind drifted to the previous six months and the long, strange journey they had taken. She tried to reconcile the insanity of the past six months and the uncertainty of Madeline's future. Ten months prior, the excitement of this day and the dream of unloading Madeline's belongings into a dormitory room at a fine university were a fingertip away. Now they were here, and there was no sure path.

The night before, Raphael and Sophia had stayed awake far too late, coming to the conclusion that there was no recourse but to postpone Madeline's entrance into college until her "matters" were resolved. The medicine, hypnosis, and therapy had exposed them to a different world—literally. Dr. Smalling and Dr. Osaka were convinced that continued hypnotherapy with Madeline and Wanikiya would lead to the true source of Madeline's trauma. It had been almost two months since Madeline had had a major episode. Maybe all of this was working. They hoped, at least.

The speaker saluted the graduates and wished them well on their new journeys. The students reciprocated with applause, half for his words and half for him being done. The student body, a sea of black gowns and caps, roiled in the stands like a wave in the night, anxious to rid themselves of the bonds of high school and to enjoy the freedom of adulthood.

Principal Shola Welbeck stepped to the microphone to a deafening roar. Madeline's Spanish teacher, Ms. Jimenez, was acknowledged as teacher of the year. Raphael spotted Mr. Foster and recalled Madeline's fateful prom night. Principal Welbeck honored Austin Lee for not ever having missed a day of high school. Sophia thought that such an honor, while admirable, was kind of dorky.

The principal called Yossi Beckerman. They were in the *B*s. The *D*s would be soon. The names were clamored, and Raphael positioned himself at the end of the stage to snap the eternal shot of Madeline receiving her diploma. He elbowed the throng of other parents, feeling like paparazzi trying to photograph Kate Middleton. Sophia surveyed the crowd. There were so many people she knew and recognized. She saw Madeline step out of the bleachers. She saw Madeline's friend Nick Harush, and in the back, she heard the unmistakable voice of Mackenzie Walters. Father Salvatore Moutinho had made a promise to attend, and he stood at the base of the stands.

Principle Welbeck called the name Madeline Deschamps. She received no more or less applause than the others had. Sophia shouted her name, and Oliver actually looked up from his phone to watch his sister graduate from Washington-Lee High School. A General forever. She had promised to be proud and not cry, but Sophia could not control her tears or her smile.

Raphael joined them back in the bleachers, and Sophia watched the crowd, noting the faces of other parents, work associates, members of the club, and families in the neighborhood. The one face she would not have recognized was that of Rohit Guzan, who taped the entire ceremony.

JUNE 27,
ATLANTA, GEORGIA

"I want you to take the death penalty off the table." Eva Jo Diamond rolled her pen on the thick file.

"Not a chance, Eva Jo," protested Leo Gargano. Judge Charlotte Wilshire was monitoring the pretrial conference. "Horace Ford gets the needle this time."

"You may want to make the deal, Counselor."

Gargano and Wilshire wondered what cards Diamond was holding.

"If I do my job and Ford is acquitted, the streets will run wild. Do you want that on your conscience?"

"Eva Jo, don't play politics with me. Or extort a plea with the threat of violence. You know your client is guilty and deserves to die."

"Counselor." Judge Wilshire gave the district attorney a stern look.

"Detective Lake Busquets." Diamond opened the folder.

"What about her?" Gargano fumed.

"I have depositions from other detectives in the sheriff's office that say Busquets had an ax to grind and that she would 'get that son of a bitch any way she could.'"

"A lot of people were upset when Ford was released. Of course she had an ax to grind. So did I."

"But you didn't botch the evidence. Detective Busquets's evidence failed to follow the chain. For two days the evidence was unaccounted for. Nor did the lab follow procedure on the blood and hair samples taken from Mr. Ford's truck. Three DNA samples are corrupted and inadmissible. I have national experts who will testify."

"I have experts too, Eva Jo. We have a rock-solid case, and it is my duty to the people to see this through."

"It only takes one, Leo. It only takes one."

Leo left the pretrial conference unimpeded by Eva Jo Diamond's bluff. Surely, when the jurors saw the dismembered body parts of Savannah Gabriel, hacked and piled on top of one another in a black plastic leaf bag, it wouldn't take long for them to convict.

JUNE 30
DECATUR, ILLINOIS

I t was already half past six in the evening, and Ke'Von had a long haul back to Louisiana. His cargo was due today, but postponements during loading had pushed delivery back to first thing tomorrow morning. Ke'Von was exhausted. He understood the life of a trucker. He shifted the smooth gears of the 2012 Peterbilt 579 and began hauling the massive tank of ethanol from the Archer Daniels Midland refinery in Decatur, Illinois, overdue on his route.

Ethanol was mostly delivered by train, but the trucking industry was making inroads on the growing market. He turned onto the exit ramp of Highway 51 South, and a lone young man stuck out his thumb, looking for a ride. Ke'Von hadn't picked up a hitchhiker in a long, long time. He was tired and could use the company. He slowed the truck and pulled to the shoulder. The young man scrambled to the side of the cab. Ke'Von opened the door.

"Where are you headed, young man?" Ke'Von inquired before allowing the man on board.

"South. New Orleans."

"Well, you are in luck. That is my final destination." Ke'Von got a good vibe from this youngster. "My name is Ke'Von."

"Brandon. Brandon Lyle." The two settled in for the long trip down the Mississippi, followed in the distance by two cars driven by Elroy Floyd and Javad Nehwal.

"Do you like Chuck Berry?" Ke'Von slid the CD into the player.

"I don't know who he is," Lyle stated flatly.

"He is the grandfather of rock and roll. We are getting near Saint Louis. He is from Missouri. I think about these things while I am on the road," Ke'Von commented, trying to make conversation.

Lyle shuffled through his backpack, exposing a bottle of Wild Turkey. "He's pretty good," Lyle noted as Chuck stomped through "Maybellene." Ke'Von eyed the Wild Turkey, desiring a nip. It had been forty-five days.

"Why are you heading to New Orleans?" Ke'Von said, distracting himself.

"I have to meet a girl down there." Lyle meant Sadie Davil.

"Oh! A girl!" Ke'Von dwelled on DaMarcus and wished he were having this conversation with his son. "You must be pretty tight if you're willing to hitchhike to New Orleans."

"She's a very special lady." Lyle texted Floyd, making sure they were on the trail.

"Get comfortable. We have eleven and a half hours ahead of us, but old Ke'Von might make it in ten and a half. Might even have some breakfast before unloading. There are some chips and soda behind you if you feel a bit hungry. But I hope you can hold your pee." Ke'Von winked. "I don't like to stop."

"I'm fine. Thank you for giving me a ride." Lyle grinned at Ke'Von.

Ke'Von shifted the rig to speed and found the fast lane.

The midnight hour passed, and Ke'Von left Memphis, Tennessee, in his rearview mirror. They were on schedule. Ke'Von tapped on the steering wheel to the beat of more Chuck Berry, glancing at the bottle of Wild Turkey that Brandon had between his feet. Even though his lips hadn't touched the bottle, its powers had turned his concentration to DaMarcus. "What do you do, Brandon?" Ke'Von tried to preoccupy his thoughts with conversation.

"I just got out of the navy." Lyle told him the truth.

"My son was in the army." Ke'Von knew he was opening a dangerous door.

"Where was he stationed?" Lyle sounded interested.

"He died. He was killed in action in Afghanistan." Ke'Von shifted gears and passed a slow mover.

"I am sorry to hear that." Lyle feigned sadness. "When?"

"Last September. It's been almost a year."

"Did you have any other children?" Lyle said, knowing he was opening a wound.

"No." Ke'Von grimaced at the red taillights ahead.

"Are you married?" Lyle noticed Ke'Von did not wear a wedding band.

"No. She left me for another man. How did you like the navy?" Ke'Von said, changing the subject.

"It was awful. Floating in the ocean aboard a war machine. America has serious issues." Lyle opened the bottle of Wild Turkey and took a swig.

"Shouldn't America have the right to defend itself?"

"Against whom? We should just leave those people alone. I fear our government more than the Taliban." Ke'Von understood the sailor. "If we weren't always at war, maybe your son would still be alive." Lyle took another swig and offered a tasted to Ke'Von. He thought once about saying no but succumbed. Ke'Von took a nip from the bottle. "You gonna be OK to drive?" asked Lyle.

"I can drive this rig in my sleep." Ke'Von stole one more quick sip. "How do we stop the government from sending our children to war?"

"'The tree of liberty must be refreshed from time to time with the blood of patriots and tyrants,'" Lyle quoted Thomas Jefferson.

"I like that." Ke'Von felt the whiskey surging. "Do you have a pen? Can you write that down?"

"I don't have a pen. Would you mind if I left you a note in your phone?" Lyle spotted the Droid charging in the console.

"That's a good idea," Ke'Von said. "I would lose a piece of paper."

Lyle snatched the phone and entered the quote. "There is a lot of soul-searching to be done at the bottom of a bottle of Wild Turkey. How long to New Orleans?" Lyle put the phone back.

"Less than five hours. Plenty of time to have breakfast before I deliver." Ke'Von put the pedal to the metal. Lyle passed the bottle, and Ke'Von drew a long pour into his throat.

The sunrise reflected in the side mirror. Ke'Von was tipsy. Biscuits and gravy would do him good before he dropped off his payload. He pulled into a diner and decided to treat Lyle to coffee, toast, and a couple of links of sausage.

"Thank you for the ride." Lyle pushed the plate away. "And the breakfast."

"It's my pleasure, young man. In an odd way, I felt like I spent time with my son." Ke'Von dropped a twenty on the check, and the two left the diner to finish the final leg of the journey.

Ke'Von opened the door to the cab and hoisted himself into his seat. Javad Nehwal reached around the driver's seat with a garrote and began to strangle Ke'Von. The thin wire dug into Ke'Von's neck, and his eyes bulged from the sockets. Ke'Von thrashed his legs and grasped behind his head, trying to free himself from the hulking grip of Javad. Then Ke'Von's body relaxed into death, and Javad dragged him into the back of the cab.

Javad fired up the rig and drove down the Pontchartrain Expressway, followed by Lyle and Floyd. The streets of the Central Business District of the French Quarter were still in the light drizzle. Javad turned the truck into the load bay of the F. Edward Hebert Federal Building. The lone security guard groggily asked for delivery papers. Javad handed him a clipboard through the window. Then Javad pointed the Sig Sauer M11-A1 pistol at the guard's head and shot him in the temple. Floyd came down the ramp and opened the gate. Lyle placed the dead security guard in a vehicle inside the garage. Javad eased the rig to the subterranean loading area.

Rohit Guzan provided Lyle with vital, real-time, hacked intelligence, giving him eyes and ears. From hundreds of miles away, Guzan deftly shifted cameras, silenced alarms, and created the fabricated peaceful morning Lyle desired. Deliveries to the Federal Building weren't scheduled to begin until ten. The dead security guard started his shift at six and mostly read the paper until he was relieved at two in the afternoon. Employees entered the parking garage from a separate entrance. Lyle, Floyd, and Javad left the eighteen-wheeler in the loading dock and bided their time.

The streets of Maestri Place were teeming with traffic around the art deco F. Edward Hebert Federal Building. The sun winked, drying the puddles left by the early-morning rain. New Orleans was waking to the first day of July. Shopkeepers swept the sidewalk, and vendors handed over bagels and hot coffee. Employees settled in front of their desks and checked e-mails and Facebook.

Lyle observed the drones of humanity from an empty office on the fortieth floor of One Shell Square, the highest building in New Orleans. He watched over the Federal Building from above and the normalcy of the day's proceedings. He held the radio transmitter in the palm of his hand.

"Do you want the honors?" He handed the transmitter to Elroy Floyd.

Floyd dialed the number. The C-4 under Ke'Von's truck detonated, igniting the eleven thousand gallons of ethanol. The floor beneath them rumbled from the blast. Blocks away, flames screamed out of the windows and the Federal Building rocked. The south face of the building peeled away from the main edifice, creating a landslide to the street below. A woman at the top of the building who was wearing pink dangled and fell into the smoking rumble, her colorful blouse a stark contrast to the destruction.

A few miles away at the FBI offices in New Orleans, Bruno called Jeremy to the window. They saw the smoke billowing in the distance. Jeremy turned on the television; the firsthand reports and images of the destruction were being transmitted. He looked at Bruno. "I want every freeway and street road cut off. This is Lyle. Get helicopters in the air."

"What are we looking for, Jeremy?" Bruno asked.

"I'm not sure. Get their pictures out and describe them as suspects." Jeremy threw on his jacket.

"We don't know Lyle did this."

"We don't know he didn't. If law enforcement is looking for anyone, it might as well be him."

THE MADELINE SESSIONS:
JULY 1
ARLINGTON, VIRGINIA

Early sessions of hypnosis were possible now that Madeline had graduated. Diego began the now-familiar process of relaxing Madeline into a deep state of suggestion. Dr. Smalling and Dr. Osaka paid careful attention to the distinct mannerisms that transformed the anxious and unsure Madeline into the proud and defiant Wanikiya.

Dr. Osaka noticed the changes first. Wanikiya's shoulders would normally broaden, but they did not this time. Diego struggled to wake Madeline. Her eyelids twitched rapidly, and her jaw jerked in a sideways motion. Her eyes slowly opened, dark and brooding. She remained still, her eyes trailing across the room and studying each person present. Salome made contact. "Where is Wanikiya?"

"She is not here."

Dr. Osaka steadied his voice and worked through Salome. "With whom am I speaking?"

"I am Aashiyra." She spoke with a distinct British accent. "He is here."

"Who is here?" ask Dr. Osaka.

"He is known as Kroni, but he has many faces."

Dr. Osaka searched for the next question. "Kroni is here. What does Kroni want?"

"He seeks to destroy the one who can change the destiny of humanity."

"Who is the one who can change the destiny of humanity?"

"We are here to warn her of Kroni."

"Who is 'we'?"

"There are many of us. We are all here. We will not be free until the chain is unbroken."

"What chain?"

"The chain of death."

Blood dripped from Madeline's nose and ears. She began to shake violently in the chair, and she held her hands to her head, pulling at her hair. A shattering yell split the air. "He is upon us. He is coming for her!"

"For whom is he coming?"

"Madeline!" She slumped in the chair. Dr. Smalling and Dr. Osaka laid Madeline down to the carpet. Sophia called an ambulance as Raphael got an emergency alert on his phone that the F. Edward Hebert Federal Building in New Orleans had just been bombed.

JULY 1
GULF OF MEXICO

T he smoke from the Federal Building still engulfed the New Orleans skyline. Helicopters flew in and out of the deadly cloud, transmitting pictures of the destruction for the world to see. Lyle and Sadie sat at the edge of the trawler, the warm waters of the Gulf of Mexico spraying occasionally into their faces. The great nets lowered into the waters and dragged for shrimp, another day of work for the *Family Affair*.

Javad and Elroy cast their lines into the waters, hoping to snag a grouper, drum, or fluke. The captain of the *Family Affair* permitted the bumbling tourists to avoid the high cost of chartering a vessel and allowed them to come aboard for a modest fee. His high school children manned the nets and the day's catch. The captain saved the money for their college education.

The boat trawled the waters until night fell. The *Family Affair* pulled alongside a coral-blue speedboat. Lyle explained that they had friends in the area and they wanted to take Sadie for a ride in their new thirty-nine foot Top Gun Unlimited Cigarette boat.

Sadie Davil wished the others well. "Where will you find me after Washington?" Davil hated parting with Lyle.

"We will meet in Mumbai as we have planned." Lyle helped Sadie into the swift craft, and she went off into the night for her assignment in Houston.

Javad and Floyd loitered at the stern as Lyle climbed the ladder to visit the captain.

"Did you have a good day?" The weathered man chewed on the stub of a cigar.

"Oh, we had a blast."

The captain turned the craft and headed home. "Did you boys catch any fish?" The cigar hung on his lip like it was glued there.

"They caught a few." Lyle reached around the captain, grabbed the back of his head, and twisted. The neck cracked, and the captain's head fell limp toward his chest. Then Javad plunged a knife into the teenager's side and twisted, ripping the lungs and the heart. Elroy blasted the brother in the temple with his pistol, and they threw the crew to the sharks in the Gulf of Mexico.

Lyle took the wheel and changed the course of the *Family Affair*. New Orleans was not an option. They would seek the dark craggy inlets of the Mississippi coastline.

The FBI building was filled with press and agents still scrambling to assemble details of the bombing. A lady wouldn't swear, but she thought she saw Lyle at the diner. Now late reports had come in that the shrimping trawler *Family Affair* was late to port. A fellow ship reported seeing the ship heading east. "Call the general. Get the Arapaho in the air," Jeremy instructed Bruno.

"Where do you want them to look?" Bruno asked.

"Along the shoreline. Into Alabama and Mississippi. Into the gulf. Have the air force send a reconnaissance plan deep into the gulf in case they are headed to Colombia. We might not be able to find them, but we can sure find that big-ass fishing boat."

WEDNESDAY, JULY 2
PASCAGOULA, MISSISSIPPI

E lroy Floyd shone the floodlight onto the black waters; in the light the eyes of the alligators in the water glowed red. They monitored their movement. Lyle eased the grand vessel into the estuary and glided to the shabby dock. Javad threw the line to a woman built like a refrigerator with a head. Dhayna Bescond ran a terrorist camp in the swamps of Mississippi. She secured the rope and escorted the men to the camp.

Bescond offered the men a lukewarm pot of beans. The small camp harbored ten terrorists, each being sculpted for a different mission. Inside Bescond's tent, pictures of the Brooklyn Bridge, the Sears Tower, and the University of Phoenix Stadium, which was hosting the 2015 Super Bowl, dangled as future targets. Photographs of Barack Obama, John Kerry, and CIA director John Brennan showed the targeted faces of an assassin's bullet.

"The van has the weapons and explosives you requested. Credit cards and identification are in the black duffel bag on the driver's seat." Bescond handed Lyle the keys to the van.

"Compensation will be wired to your account." Floyd spoke for Lyle, who walked the camp.

They heard the rotors of the helicopters first, and the camp scrambled. The lights blinded the men emerging from their tents. The machine guns fired into the sky toward the swirling lights. Flares from the choppers ignited, bringing daylight to the shadows of the forest. The mercenaries loaded the shoulder-held surface-to-air missiles and fired, the smoke blasting backward as the projectiles slammed into the chopper. The blades of the army Arapaho whacked the trees, sending wooden shrapnel into the camp. Rangers fell from the sky as the helicopter slammed into the ground, the fireball streaking skyward, a match to the kindling of the forest.

Hand grenades rolled into the camp, blasting holes and providing cover for the rangers. Lyle hurried to the van, Floyd in tow. They screeched away from the camp, weaving their way in the darkness down a dirt road, headlights off.

Javad stood shoulder to shoulder with Bescond, firing rounds at the advancing soldiers. Bescond took a round to the neck, blood spraying onto her dog tags and camouflage. Javad retreated to the swamps and entered the creek, wading to the far embankment, the camp engulfed in flames and the staccato of battle rattling behind him.

Javad's height allowed him to walk in the water, remaining stealthy, head above the surface. He held the machine gun high over his head. He never saw the gator but felt the eighty teeth sink into his side. He dropped the rifle as he was dragged under the water, the fourteen-foot, 900-pound gator spinning him to the bottom. Javad flailed in the silt as his lungs filled with water. The gator released his prey after Javad drowned at the bottom of the creek. He floated dead on top of the water, a waiting midnight snack, and the gator devoured Javad's carcass in the shallows.

The soldiers set the perimeter. The terrorist camp had been destroyed. Jeremy absorbed the cost. Two rangers and the pilot of the Arapaho were dead, leaving behind their widowed wives and children.

Bruno reported to Jeremy. "They're not here."

"They were here." Jeremy rubbed the soil on his hands. "We found the shrimp boat. I know they were here."

"Officers. You should see this," a soldier reported.

Bruno and Jeremy walked to the edge of the creek. Javad's severed head floated in the waters, held afloat by twigs and leaves, bobbing. "I knew they were here. There's one. Where are the others?"

JULY 4
WASHINGTON, DC

Raphael flipped the burgers and adorned them with American cheese. He laid the buns on the grill to mark them and make them toasty. He rolled the dogs. "Sophia, do you have the onions and pickles?"

"They're already on the table."

"Burgers and dogs will be ready in two minutes."

Oliver observed his dad with the tongs and the spatula. It was nice that the Fourth of July was on a Friday. It gave his parents a nice three-day weekend. "When can we shoot off the fireworks?" Oliver salivated at the thought.

"We will shoot off a few after lunch." Raphael winked.

Oliver held the box of illegal fireworks Raphael had invested in on the ski trip to Pennsylvania. Oliver studied the box. Should they try Atomic Warlord or Bling in a Box? Nuclear Sunrise or Crackin' Skulls? Oliver brought a box to his dad as Raphael plated the burgers. "I want to try this one." The box said it was five hundred grams and twelve shots of the completely addictive The Chronic.

"Give me that!" Raphael handed his curious son a dog and told him to go eat.

Mackenzie stopped by, bedazzled in red, white, and blue. Sophia thought it was cute that Austin came by to say hi to Madeline. They played cornhole and threw a Frisbee. Oliver talked Dad into setting off a few rounds of bottle rockets and firecrackers. Oliver was enamored with the sparklers.

"Would you like to see the fireworks with me tonight, Madeline?" Austin asked Madeline as he threw a beanbag. It slid past the hole.

"I am sorry, Austin." Madeline's attempt went wide right. "We've been invited to the National Cathedral."

"OK. How about a movie sometime?" Austin asked with no expectations.

"Sure. That sounds fun." Madeline picked up the beanbags and placed them into the basket. Austin was really nice, but he stirred nothing in her heart.

After dinner Raphael made sure the coals in the grill were dead, and the Deschampses piled into the car. They passed the Key Bridge Marriot, the location of Madeline's prom-night episode. All held their collective breaths, making sure not to whisper of that frightful evening. Across the Key Bridge and into Georgetown, the University's spirals towered over the Potomac. The traffic was light, and they took a left on Wisconsin Avenue and climbed up the hill to the top of Washington, DC. The neo-Gothic church stood alone and proud at the crest of Mount Saint Alban, providing a view that spanned 360 degrees. On a clear day, a visitor could see for several miles.

The gargoyles and grotesque statues eyed them from above as Madeline walked the grounds.

"Hello, Madeline!" The distinct voice of Father Salvatore Moutinho called from the arched doorway. "Hello to all the Deschampses. Welcome to my house."

"You live here? Where is your bedroom?" Oliver craned his neck to the top of the great church.

Moutinho laughed. "I do not actually live in the cathedral. My residence, however, is on the grounds." Moutinho waved them forward. "In fact, my residence is very close, and there is something I believe you will find very—how do they say?—cool."

The Deschampses followed the father to the northwest corner. "Your eyes are much better than mine, but if you look very high…" Oliver followed Moutinho's finger.

"Darth Vader!" Oliver exclaimed.

Raphael nodded approval, knowing the priest had captured the young man's attention for the rest of the day.

Inside, the light splintered through the cathedral's stained glass, creating a prism of color that bounced off the safety nets.

"Why so much construction, Father?" Sophia asked, marveling at the building she had until now neglected to visit.

"If you recall, Virginia had its very own earthquake, and it affected many buildings in Washington, including the cathedral and the Washington Monument."

Little old women in purple hats and gowns shuffled tourists through the caverns of the cathedral, pointing out the flying buttresses that balanced the walls and allowed the vaulted ceilings. The tomb of President Woodrow Wilson was on display, and an authentic rock from the moon was embedded in the Space Window. But Sophia's eyes were on a different window.

"That one is quite beautiful." Then Sophia gazed to the west; the late-afternoon sun was spraying the deep hues of red and purple of the stained glass over the balcony.

"That is the north rose window, Sophia. Many consider it to be one of the finest works of stained glass in the world." Moutinho stood shoulder to shoulder with Sophia in admiration, pointing out other ecletic pieces such as the window of Robert E. Lee and Stonewall Jackson, Moses, and the mural of the burial of Joseph of Arimathea.

Oliver stood tall at the pulpit, orating for the masses to hear. "Our first reading will be—"

"Oliver!" Raphael whispered-screamed. "Get down from there!"

Sophia's face flamed a bright red as Oliver reluctantly removed himself from the altar and into his father's arm jail.

The Deschampses walked the length of the nave, the flags of nations and states raised in unison. Moutinho pressed for the elevator, and the small compartment arrived. As they exited, the world around them opened high into the towers of Saint Peter and Saint Paul. Elevated above the world, they found the perfect spot to watch the fireworks that would explode below them.

"Thank you, Father Moutinho. This is wonderful." Madeline hugged the priest. "I want to thank you for all you have done for me and my family."

"My dear Madeline. Oftentimes in life we need the help and love of another. It is the way God would like it to be."

"This would be a great place to see the moon," Madeline noted.

"Your mother has told me of your love of the moon." He smiled at her. "I will see when the next full moon will come. We will watch it from here."

"I would like that very much, Father."

JULY 5
WASHINGTON, DC

The ruddy, rugged, handsome face was trusted by the people. Gaston Milner, a member of the US Senate for twenty years, connected like oxygen to the brain of the American political machine. His outward aura of leadership, patriotism, and family values belied his devious and anonymous backstabbing and blackmailing, exposing every weakness of the already anemic Congress and Senate. There in the deep pockets of his Armani suits lay the sacred votes of the American people, which he traded at his whim, shifting the government ever so slightly to the edge of its own destruction. Guiding it into conflict and helping the world to despise the very nation he represented. To the nation he was America's backbone. To the elite of **ORBIS**, he was known as the Dirty White Boy.

Milner slipped his assigned Secret Service agent at the bustling restaurant and entered the single handicap stall, leaving the ice in his glass to soak in the bourbon of his Manhattan on the table. He closed the door and washed his hands, Rohit Guzan behind him in the mirror.

Milner handed Guzan a slip of paper. "Send the money to this account. The arrangements you asked for have been made."

"My employer is very grateful." Guzan accepted the slip aligned with the ORBIS account.

"Your employer is all over the news. He is being hunted by the entire criminal justice system." Milner wiped his face with a paper towel. "He's hotter than Megan Fox in underwear."

"He will complete the mission he designed, and you can put the keys into your war machines and turn them onto high volume. The American public will seek retribution, and you shall spearhead its revenge all the way to the White House."

"And kill all the sand niggers I want." Milner blew his nose into the towel. "An alternate identification has been fabricated for this Floyd. Backstories tie him to a new group emerging from Syria. A group called ISIS. You will be contacted to confirm the date, but it will be in early October. Your man will be instructed to enter the US Capitol from the south entrance. We have a man who will make arrangements to allow him into the building. He will receive appropriate paperwork from Senator Rueben van Gaal's office. I hate that guy." Milner made sure his hair was perfect. "From there it is up to your man."

"Surely, there will be more than one guard at the south entrance."

"That is true, but you spoke of a diversion. Their attention will be elsewhere." Milner looked at Guzan.

"I have that arranged," Guzan assured the senator. "Video will surely note your guard and his failures. Those failures may lead back to you."

Milner opened the door. "We have a plan to eliminate him." He returned to his booth to an awaiting filet mignon.

Guzan walked down Fourteenth Street on a humid summer night, hiding in plain sight. He contacted Lyle and confirmed that everything was going according to plan.

JULY 7
ATLANTA, GEORGIA

B randon Lyle opened the door and walked into Chick-fil-A. He noticed the pudgy redhead behind the counter working the first register immediately. He had known this day would come. It was part of the plan. She would call him Victor. He waited his turn in line, the mother ahead of him struggling with her child's order. Evelyn Cahill handed the woman her sweet tea and sack of food. Kuyt stepped to the register.

"I will have a number one with a Coke." Victor tried to make eye contact with Evelyn.

In her sugary work voice, Evelyn asked the customer for the $8 and change. She looked up and froze. "Oh my God! You're here." Her face turned as red as her hair. Radiance Bancora watched the meeting, surprised that Victor Kuyt really existed. She was happy for Evelyn.

Evelyn poured the drink and handed it to Lyle.

"Do you have time for lunch?" he asked, sipping on the Coke.

"I thought you weren't going to be here until next week." Evelyn wondered how she looked.

"I couldn't wait to see you," Lyle lied.

"I can't sit with you right now. But I get off at three." Evelyn thought he was more handsome in person. His hair was longer, and his beard was full and sexy. Much had changed since he'd first gotten out of the navy, except for those crystal-blue eyes.

"I'll be here at three. It's great to finally meet you in person. I can't wait to get to know you better." Lyle gazed at Evelyn with bright cheery eyes that hid his deceit.

Her heart was pounding. "Meet me at Nero's. It's a bar on North Avenue. At four." Her mind was racing. "I want to change."

"I'll be there." Lyle left. On the way out he threw his sandwich and waffle fries into the trash and kept the Coke.

The Atlanta humidity was oppressive. Lyle slicked his growing hair back in the bathroom at Nero's. He found an open barstool and ordered a Fat Tire.

Evelyn snuck up behind him. "Hey, you!"

Lyle turned, and they fell into an embrace. He noticed her teased hair and low-cut shirt that did nothing for her oversize carnival breasts. Her jeans grabbed her snugly, highlighting her camel toe and accentuating her pronounced FUPA.

"Would you like a beer?" Lyle motioned to the bartender.

"Boy, would I." Evelyn settled in next to him. "I'll have a Miller Lite."

They toasted to their first meeting and sloshed their way through the afternoon and into the late evening with shots and beers, Lyle astonished by how many nachos and mozzarella sticks Evelyn could pack away.

"What happened to your tooth?" Evelyn stuck her finger into his mouth. He jerked his head back.

Lyle laughed it off. "A terrible broom accident in New Orleans."

"When were you in New Orleans?" Evelyn had been texting him the whole time.

"The navy sent me there to receive my final papers," Lyle feigned.

"Where are you staying, Victor?" Evelyn poked.

"With a friend from Los Angeles. He lives on Joseph Bone Boulevard."

"Joseph Boone. Not Bone." Evelyn cracked up.

"A Freudian slip." Lyle and Evelyn each tossed back another shot of Fireball. "I don't know how long I will be welcome there with his wife and kids," Lyle lied.

"I would say you should stay with me, but I am not that kind of girl. At least not on the first night." The whiskey slurred her words.

"Last call!" The bartender turned up the lights. Lyle asked for the bill and peeled off a couple of hundred-dollar bills, leaving the difference.

"You've got a lot of money." Evelyn noticed Lyle's wad.

"I haven't had a chance to open a bank account."

It had been forever since a man had paid for Evelyn's drinks.

"May I walk you to your car?"

"Certainly." Evelyn climbed down from the barstool, Lyle steadying her. He escorted her to her car, and she invited him to sit with her for a few more moments. Lyle obliged.

"I had a really good time, Victor. It feels like I've known you all my life," Evelyn spilled. "We have been kind of dating for almost five months." Evelyn reached over and stuck her tongue in Lyle's mouth, unable to contain herself any longer. She blew him in the passenger seat, knowing she had more to give of herself to the man she loved.

JULY 7
ODESSA, TEXAS

TEEN MISSING FROM FIREWORKS DISPLAY
Odessa American

The Odessa Police Department is posting a missing-persons report for Irina Goldstein, sixteen years of age. Irina was last seen at McKinney Park with a group from Temple Beth El. The teens were at the park to watch the fireworks for the Fourth of July festivities. Irina and two friends went to the portable toilets, and the friends thought Irina went back to sit with the group, but she never reappeared.

Irina was last seen wearing a One Direction T-shirt and a pair of khaki Old Navy shorts and flip-flops. Irina is five feet five inches tall and weighs 140 pounds. She has light brown, shoulder-length hair and brown eyes.

A white van was seen speeding away from McKinney Park shortly after the disappearance was reported.

If you have any information on Irina's whereabouts, the white van, or her disappearance, please call the Odessa Police Department at 432-555-4987.

THE MADELINE SESSIONS:
JULY 9
ARLINGTON, VIRGINIA

"I won't allow it! No more! You saw what happened the other day. This is going to kill her," Sophia protested to Dr. Smalling and Dr. Osaka.

"It's not going to kill her, Sophia. It's going to save her," Dr. Smalling insisted.

"How about the blood rushing from her nose and ears?" Sophia asked.

Raphael put his arm around his wife.

"We witnessed a traumatic event while Madeline was under hypnosis," Dr. Osaka noted.

"I'll say." Sophia was irate. "What the hell did happen in there?"

"We don't know. That's why we have to continue the therapy. It's possible that the personality we spoke to last, Aashiyra, had a vision or dream that caused the anxiety. These personalities have their own memories and visions, but it is Madeline's body that is reacting to their pain."

"Wanikiya. Aashiyra. How many other people are inside Madeline?" Sophia questioned.

"MPD often shows several different personalities."

"Christ." Sophia's will had eroded.

"Let the doctors continue," Raphael said, trying to console Sophia. "I don't see any other way."

Sophia nodded. "OK."

Diego put Madeline into a deep, relaxed state. Everyone wondered who would show up to the session. Diego brought Wanikiya to the group. "Good morning, Wanikiya. When we last spoke, Samuel had returned from the hunting trip with Chayton, and the elder had given permission for Samuel to court you. How did that go?"

The tepee collapsed in the middle of the day. The children ran, and the tepee began to move like a brown, painted ghost. Samuel came from the horses and pulled the tepee off Big John, who crawled in the dirt. Big John returned from Fort Laramie, but not with tools or supplies. He came with whiskey, drowning his pain, crying for Emmy Lou. Big John spent his days by her grave and his nights in the tent with the bottle. Harriet, Samuel, and Angus prayed for him, chided him, and consoled him, but he was lost to all of us. Harriet smashed his bottles, but Big John would steal away in the night and return in a week's time with more. Angus wanted him to leave the village, but he had become part of our family. We could not turn our backs on him.

The warriors passed through the village. Hundreds rode north to meet Crazy Horse and the Sundance alliance the Lakota and Sitting Bull had formed with the Cheyenne. Chayton and Shadow left the village with Angus and many other young braves and joined the force, anxious to repel the advances of the Seventh Cavalry into the Lakota territory of Montana. The women filled their sacks with jerky and dried fruits and filled their bladders with water. Samuel saddled the horses, and the men sharpened their spears and arrows, their bows taut and ready for the fight for which they had trained. The children chased the horses into the woods, shouting encouragement to their heroes as the women held their emotions to themselves, fearful that their children would be slain in war.

The days had grown long, and the sun stayed in the sky. Samuel and I would take long walks in the woods, picking wild mushrooms and berries. We swam in the river and raced to the rocks. Samuel found a part of the river that was deep, and he taught me to dive. He taught me of the great poets and writers: Shakespeare, Emily Brontë, Dostoyevsky, and the Americans Mark Twain and Thoreau and the spooky Edgar Allan Poe. I entertained him with the legends of Iktomi, the socially inappropriate trickster of Lakota legend whose lewd comments and sophomoric pranks landed him in hot water. I also told him of the truly dangerous Double Face, Hestovatohkeo'o, the monster with a second face on the back of his head. If you connected eyes with his second face, you would be murdered by the brute.

We hiked into the mountains and looked to the east and the Great Plains of Lakota, level, endless, and exposed. We climbed toward the sun, short of breath, our legs aching and shoulders burning. We looked west to watch the sun fall from the sky, the earth spiking, mountains forging into the heavens, only contained by the umbrella of the sky.

The moon, round and full, filled the eastern sky with a bright, white glow. Samuel took my hand, and we walked to the lake at the base of Bear Mountain. We pushed the canoe into the water, the last rays of the sun slipping into the night. The pale radiance of the moonlight shimmered across the gentle ripples of the lake. We paddled into the heart of the lake.

"I will soon climb the mountain, alone, to see my destiny," I explained to Samuel about my vision quest.

"What do you think you will find?" he asked.

"That is for the creator to tell. The elders have told me that many have begun the journey with their own visions, only to be enlightened as to their true destination."

"Do you believe I will play a part in your destiny?" Samuel asked me.

I turned in the canoe to face him. "Surely, you have changed the direction of my life. I can only hope that you play a large role in what the creator has designed for me."

Samuel rested his paddle. "It has been a long time since I have swum at night."

The waters passed us, warm and dark. I stood in the canoe and removed my tunic, naked before him. I dived into the waters. Samuel raced to remove his clothing and joined me in the moonlight. We swam, only able to separate the darkness of the sky and the water by the light of the moon. We faced each other, our feet touching under the water. I could see the whole of his face, his long hair swept back and drenched. His colorful eyes of the universe captured a single ray of light in the dark center. His mouth stayed below the level of the water, and he moved to me. Our arms wrapped around each other, our legs entwined as our mouths met for the first time. We kissed as we sank into the water, both of us willing to drown to capture that moment in time, but to the surface we rose and gasped for the air. My hands felt his back and his chest as he treaded water, keeping us both afloat. My legs wrapped around his hips, and he ran his hands through my wet hair, his mouth finding my neck. He tried to enter me, but I said no. We would have to wait until we were married. Samuel asked if we could marry tomorrow. We had talked of marriage many times. I began to shiver in the black water. Samuel pushed me back into the canoe, and I pulled him in. He began to pull his pants to his leg. I moved toward him and laid him back, gently so as not to capsize the canoe. Our bodies warmed as we pushed together, his hands soothing my back and neck. I pressed against him, my breasts rubbing his chest, his tongue finding mine. I could wait no longer. I reached down and put him inside of me. He was sturdy, and I pushed down on him, my body on fire. His lips suckled my neck and breasts as I filled the sky with my songs of pleasure. I leaned back, exposing myself to the man I loved, my hips grinding into his flesh, scratching his chest. His warmth filled me, and I knew my life had changed. I was no longer a girl, and I understood the naughty laughter of the elder woman to be true.

We did not return until the first rays of the sun had appeared over the plains. I knew Samuel in a way that we had not previously explored. I slipped into my tent, knowing there was but a moment's time to sleep. I lay on my mattress and closed my eyes, pretending not to notice the open eye of Laughing Maid.

Sophia adjusted herself uncomfortably in her chair, everyone silent from the awkward confession of the Native American girl.

JULY 14
SARASOTA, FLORIDA

The heart of summer was beginning to bore Riverview High School rising senior Deandre Mikel. His job at Dairy Queen sucked. Flipping burgers and making Blizzards for screaming brats wasn't his thing. But it put gas in the car and paid for his cell phone. Deandre stretched out on his bed, knowing his brother and parents wouldn't be home for at least an hour.

He typed "hot blond teen" into the search engine and decided which page he would peruse today. "Hot teen Chloe masturbates with her wand." No. He had seen that. "Hot blond teen seduces older neighbor." Nope. Not his thing. "Hot blond double penetration." Deandre had seen that. "Hot blond teen gets creamy cumshot." Deandre decided to check this one out. He tapped the screen, and the video loaded.

A very sexy and young blonde pranced around in her underwear and then fell to her knees. A guy sat in the chair before her, and she unbuttoned his belt and pulled down his zipper. She pulled out his member and started to perform fellatio. Deandre was just getting excited when he recognized the girl in the video. She'd gone to high school with him. It was the girl who'd disappeared during the school year. It was Yael Almeida. Deandre put his pants back on and sat on the bed, wondering what to do.

A few hours later an embarrassed Deandre and his father walked into the Sarasota Police Department, and Deandre showed the officer the video with Yael Almeida.

JULY 16
ATLANTA, GEORGIA

Lyle spotted the headlines of the *Atlanta Journal-Constitution*. He stopped for a moment to read the article. Four boys playing on the beach in Gaza were killed when an Israeli missile exploded on the beach. Israel and Gaza were at it again. *This little event should set off something quite explosive,* Lyle thought to himself hopefully. Lyle loved it when humans killed themselves over religion. *Nasty irony,* he thought to himself and smiled.

Lyle sipped his latte and read the article by Bayleigh Debuchy that provided an update on the Horace Ford trial. No plea deal was made, and they were going to trial. *Excellent,* he thought to himself. He slipped into the drugstore and bought Evelyn a card. She had given him a key to her apartment and invited him to stay there as long as he would like.

JULY 18
ATLANTA, GEORGIA

Lyle opened a bottle of sauvignon blanc and had the table cleaned and set for dinner as he watched Evelyn dragged her lard ass into the apartment. Evelyn was stunned. She had never seen the apartment so clean. Handsome, a great lover, and clean. What had she done to deserve such a man?

"Victor? You didn't have to do all this." She kissed him on the lips and dropped her bag to the floor.

"I thought it was only fitting that I made some dinner for the breadwinner." Lyle turned the sea scallops and dipped the angelhair pasta into the boiling water.

"How did you know I loved scallops?" Evelyn breathed deeply, absorbing the aroma of the shellfish and the delectable beurre blanc simmering in the saucepan.

"A lucky guess." Lyle had never seen Evelyn show a dislike of anything she could shove into her mouth.

"Did you watch the news today?"

"I did not," Lyle lied.

"Malaysian flight seventeen left Amsterdam for Kuala Lumpur." Evelyn scratched her head. "Where is Kuala Lumpur?"

"It is in Southeast Asia." Lyle strained the shallots from the sauce.

"Yesterday it crashed over a remote region in Ukraine, killing two hundred ninety-eight people." Evelyn snagged a bag of Doritos.

"Dinner should be ready in a few minutes," Lyle reminded her.

"I know. I'm just famished." Evelyn crunched on the triangular snacks. She turned on the television, and Lyle could hear the pundits pondering the fate of the aircraft. "Ukraine and Russian separatists are blaming one another for the attacks."

Lyle smirked, knowing the hatred humanity possessed. This powder keg of a region would soon be a volatile hotbed of death. Lyle remembered fondly what the *Lusitania* had done for the cause almost a century ago. Twelve hundred passengers and crew sank to the bottom of the Atlantic after being torpedoed by a German U-boat, an act that ultimately began World War I. *That was a good day,* Lyle recounted. That whole part of the world was boiling. It was just a matter of time.

Lyle plated the pasta and laid the scallops carefully on top, drizzling them with the buttery flavor from the pan. He brought them to the table. Evelyn switched the news to a rerun of *Here Comes Honey Boo Boo* and shoved a few Doritos onto the side of her plate.

JULY 19
ATLANTA, GEORGIA

Lyle opened the laptop and clicked on Internet Explorer, bringing him to the MSN home page. Russian separatists refused to let officials recover the bodies from the Malaysian Airlines crash, enraging officials from around the globe. Videos of the dead littered the Internet, Russian rebels laughing around their remains as they looted the luggage of the dead. *Outstanding,* Lyle thought to himself as he sipped Earl Grey tea.

Lyle clicked on another page. Joep Lange, a dedicated HIV/AIDS researcher, had died on board along with one hundred other AIDS scientists. Double bonus. The virus was a key component in the destruction of humanity. This collateral damage should prevent any progress on a cure for years. This was turning into a great week. He added a touch of sugar to the tea.

Atlanta was beyond hot this afternoon. He would buy himself a vanilla bean Frappuccino with a pump of cinnamon dulce de leche. Yum!

JULY 20

Elroy chauffeured Lyle around Atlanta, listening to news radio on WSB 95.5 FM. ISIS, the Islamic State in Iraq, had killed at least twenty-seven in Bagdad. This included a suicide bombing that had killed nine.

"Now that's commitment, Elroy!" Lyle smiled in the rearview mirror.

Lyle loved suicide bombers. Right at the top of the list. "People killing people. That's what it is all about." Then the reporter detailed the story of a New York City police officer who'd choked a six-foot-three-inch, 350-pound man for selling loose cigarettes from a bench. What? Was the guy going to run away? Lyle loved the failures of the empowered. Especially when they killed their own. Power and vanity. The real war came in the form of the self-righteous. How much sweeter the day was becoming.

JULY 21
ATLANTA GEORGIA

Lyle rolled Evelyn over and hammered away at her from behind. It was repulsive to watch her on top. She smelled of her work, and having sex while facing her was like making love to a waffle fry. He raised his arm and walloped her ass, leaving his full pink handprint embedded on her fleshy, pale haunches. She shivered in delight and squealed like a sow when he yanked her hair violently, wrapping his fingers around her neck and squeezing tight, choking her. Lyle finished out of duty as opposed to desire. Evelyn rolled her flaccid, pale skin across the bed and cozied next to Lyle. He shifted and pursed his lips to hers.

"You are fabulous." Lyle offered. The sight of her disgusted him. He knew she wanted more, and he eyed the clock radio hoping she would shower and go to her low-level food-industry job at Chick-fil-A. "Stay," he whispered in her wax-filled ear, testing reverse psychology.

"I will be late for work," Evelyn chortled.

"They won't fire you."

"I have been late four times since you got to Atlanta, and I've been written up once." Evelyn's shoulders slumped as she sat naked on the edge of the bed. She lit up a Marlboro and puffed. The crack of her ass folded over the sheets like a turnover. "Not that it hasn't been worth every second." She worked her way over to Lyle again.

"Well, I don't want to be the reason you lose your job." He eyed the time.

Evelyn stood and headed to the bathroom to shower. To Lyle, she looked like a walking manatee.

Lyle searched the sheets for the remote and clicked the television on. He turned on the morning news show *Java and Grits* with Natasha Ha.

The conflict in Israel and Gaza was heating up. Each side was firing missiles at the other. Israel had killed seventy-three Palestinians already. Israeli forces were hunting for tunnels built into the country. The violence was escalating, just as Lyle had hoped, polarizing the world as it picked sides. Lyle loved division. The legion was doing a great job.

Natasha Ha continued the report. "The Italian navy rescued more than eighteen hundred refugees but conceded that as many as five hundred have died in six months fleeing Africa from violence, poverty, and disease, using the porous borders of chaos-torn Libya. Forty refugees drowned yesterday as their boat capsized from overcrowding. Thousands have taken to the seas in wooden boats in an attempt to cross the Mediterranean to the boot of Italy's southern shores. Italy has received more than seventy thousand refugees and has no place for them to go, and the Italian government is seeking help from the European Union on where and how to place the influx of humanity."

Excellent, thought Lyle to himself as he pulled the blanket up to his chest. Evelyn kept the apartment far too cold.

The reporter continued, "We will be back after this with breaking news of an arrest in New Orleans in connection to the bombing of the Federal Building and new, chilling video of the bomber
taken months before the attack."

Evelyn walked naked out of the shower, killing Lyle's buzz. She
put on some skintight panties that displayed her crater-size cellu-
lite. She needed a trim. She loaded herself into her polyester uniform pants and shirt. Evelyn searched frantically for her name tag.
Lyle snared it of the bureau and handed it to her along with her
sun- glasses and Chick-fil-A ball cap.

"What would I do without you?" She stuck her tongue practi-
cally down his throat.

Lyle held the embrace just long enough to make it believable. "I
will miss you today."

"I will miss you, too." Evelyn was so happy she had found Victor.
She pulled the door tight just as the commercial ended. Lyle focused on the news report.

"Welcome back to the *Java and Grits* morning report. I am
Natasha Ha. The FBI has arrested Rahman Mesbah, a cleric from
the mosque Masjid Al-Islam in New Orleans, in connection with
the bombing of the Federal Building that killed three hundred
twenty-seven. Mesbah was charged with operating an Islamic terrorist cell and conspiring with bomber Ke'Von Keshi. The FBI has
had the mosque under surveillance, and agents reported a meeting
between Mesbah and Ke'Von in May. Recent developments in the
investigation of the bombing led the FBI to Ke'Von's cell phone.
Forensics was able to gather data off the SIM card of the badly damaged phone, including an ominous quote from Thomas Jefferson:
'The tree of liberty must be refreshed from time to time with the
blood of patriots and tyrants.' Federal agents consider this to be the
smoking gun along with this chilling video taking in March by a
patron at the Bayou Club in Lafourche Parish on Mardi Gras." Lyle
watched as the rolled the video.

"They are going to kill all of you!" Ke'Von had yelled. "You are all going to die! Your government is going to send you all to your death!" Natasha Ha started talking to all the paid experts and getting their commentary. Lyle salivated over his victory and what he had put in motion: fear.

JULY 24
WASHINGTON, DC

J eremy had been called to Washington to brief his superiors and select members of the Senate and Homeland Security on developments in the search for Brandon Lyle. Senator Gaston Milner had been chiefly critical of the performance of the FBI. Alexander Khan, Alcott, and Bruno Sommer spent the morning in the hot seat and were currently wallowing at the piano bar. Jeremy sat on the stool with Bruno, Khan opting to sit in front of the bartender and a bottle of Lagavulin 16. Jeremy played quietly as the afternoon sun reflected onto the keys.

"You play well." Sommer sipped his whiskey. "Where did you learn?"

"I never had any formal lessons. I've just always been able to play. That and the guitar. The harmonica. Other instruments. They just come naturally."

"That's quite a gift."

"Not really. I only seem to play when I'm sad or frustrated. The chords are full of music but absent of soul."

"You know, we've been going after Lyle for half the year. Do you have anyone?"

"What do you mean 'anyone'?" Jeremy picked out some chords.

"Do you have a girlfriend or something?"

"No girlfriend." Jeremy plucked at the low notes on the scale. "Never had one, in fact."

"Never?" Sommer seemed surprised.

"I guess I've been looking for the right girl. Just haven't found her. I can see her in my head—just can't seem to put her in front of me."

"Well, you can't wait forever. There are some pretty girls over there at the bar. They're kind of checking you out. Musicians get all the girls. FBI and a musician. That's a lethal combination."

"You're a good man, Bruno Sommer." Jeremy stood from the piano and removed his glasses, revealing eyes that folded all the colors of the universe into one. "I am going to call it a day. I just got my ass kicked all day by Senator Milner."

"OK, partner."

JULY 24
ATLANTA, GEORGIA

Lyle adjusted the fan, trying to quell the heat. Evelyn stripped down to her underwear, much to Lyle's dismay, her sweaty thighs dripping sweat onto the couch. She thumbed through the mail, bemoaning the bills and checking her balance on her bank phone app. She rubbed her hands through her hair, frustrated at her finances. Lyle shoved his hand in his pockets and placed four Franklins on the table.

"Victor. You don't have to do that!" She jumped off the couch and hugged him with one arm, pulling the wedgie out of her butt with the other.

"We're a team, right?"

"I love you, Victor." Evelyn had never felt so hopeful in her life. She would do anything for Victor Kuyt.

"I love you too." It pained him, but it left his lips.

"What is this?" Evelyn shredded open the envelope from the State Court of Fulton County.

"Uh-oh. Looks like someone got jury duty. When do you report?"

Evelyn studied the small print on the document. "It looks like Thursday, August twenty-eighth. Well, that will give me plenty of time to check with Chick-fil-A."

"It is your civic duty." Lyle crinkled a smile.

"Do I get paid to do jury duty?" Evelyn looked at her stack of bills.

"Yes. It's something like $40 a day." Lyle stood in front of the fan, noticing Evelyn's flab.

"That's almost as much as I get at Chick-fil-A. I could use some time away from that joint."

"Well, maybe you'll get a long trial." Lyle winked at Evelyn. In his mind he saluted Rohit Guzan for a job well done.

THE MADELINE SESSIONS:
JULY 25
ARLINGTON, VIRGINIA

The heat of summer forced the village to move the tents into the forest. The women dragged the large posts and reassembled the tepees in the shade but farther from the river. Samuel grazed the horses and battled the sun and the bugs. The children drew colorful accounts of the day on the tepees, and Hair Storm helped them with the Lakota weave.

That evening Samuel, with the blessing of his mother, Harriet, entered the tent of the elder Appanoose. I waited in the tent for Samuel with Laughing Maid. Samuel had wanted to ask permission to take my hand in marriage from my father, Matoskah, but he had died in battle against the army many years ago. Samuel was nervous speaking with Appanoose and very nervous speaking with Laughing Maid.

"I wish to ask for the hand of the maiden, Wanikiya," Samuel said to the elder.

"The hand of the prestigious Wanikiya would require a substantial dowry," Appanoose explained.

"I have but a horse to give." Samuel reached into his pocket. "The only thing of value that I have to offer to Laughing Maid is this golden pocket watch that was my father's. It was made for him in Switzerland and bears his initials on the back."

Laughing Maid held the timepiece, turning it over and opening and closing the face. Laughing Maid asked Wanikiya to give Samuel a message. "From the moment you arrived in our village, I knew that my daughter had found the one she loved. I had prayed to Wakan Tanka that she would find such a strong man. As we learn in life, strength comes in many ways, and while you are not strong as a warrior, your heart is strong. I cannot accept the watch that was your father's, nor do I need horses or things of value. I have my family, and my daughter has found the man she will need and love. I welcome you to our family, and may you have many children." Wanikiya blushed, and Harriet hugged Laughing Maid.

"Samuel, you have chosen wisely. May your seed bear fruit, and may you choose your next wife with the same success." Appanoose smiled.

Samuel, confused, expressed to Appanoose that he wanted only one wife, though he was entitled to many.

Samuel wished to share the news of his marriage with Big John, but he lay in his tent, asleep from drink. Angus had traveled with the warriors to Montana, so he sat with the drunken Big John and played his guitar to me. We shared a pipe, and I tried to sing, which made both of us laugh like children.

The following day the warriors returned triumphant. A great victory over the army at Little Bighorn. Chayton and Shadow returned with Angus and many other braves, the war paint still on their faces and the courage still in their hearts. Chayton told of the many thousand warriors who assembled under Sitting Bull and followed Crazy Horse in fighting the two armies near the river and on the bluffs, encircling the enemy and driving them into submission. Chayton told them of how Lieutenant Colonel George Custer fired upon the women and children of the village, killing several, and the plan of taking the unarmed children as hostages in an attempt to quell the battle by bartering for their lives. Chayton reveled when Custer was knocked from his horse and then shot several times, falling in the line of battle.

Angus retreated to his tent and sat with Samuel, Big John, and me, and recounted his perception of the engagement. "Chayton tells the truth." His voice was somber. "The armies attacked from two directions, one approaching the village and firing with their guns. Little ones lay on the ground, dead and bleeding. Women lay on other children, victims of the army bullets, covering the children from the slaughter. The warriors waited in the trees and attacked when the armies pushed in, driving them back to the bluff. The army circled, but the warriors were so many. They rode around them in a circle that became smaller as the dead piled up. The warriors attacked with clubs, hatchets, and spears. They knifed the soldiers where they stood and then stripped the dead of their clothing, mutilating their bodies in hatred and anger. The bleeding and injured cried from the field, and the warriors responded with their spears, putting them down like horses. Toward the end, the soldiers put their own guns to their heads and blasted holes in their skulls." Angus began to weep, consoled by his brother.

"The army will be back, and they will be more prepared. The Sioux and the Cheyenne have won a victory. They can paint their faces to hide from Wakan Tanka, but they cannot hide from the army. They will let more die, but then more and more will be sacrificed until the tribes are outnumbered and either surrender or are exterminated."

Angus had seen the true nature of battle, and it had left him hollow.

That night the village celebrated the victory. Chayton and Shadow boasted of the power of the tribes and praised the names of Sitting Bull and Crazy Horse, invincible youth, and the promise of victory and freedom.

Samuel and I rose early and hiked into the Black Hills. It was as any normal day as we gathered beets, carrots, turnips, and onions. Samuel picked a flower and handed it to me. I told him of my love, and he showed me his with his kiss. We sat in the shade and shared the fresh berries, just picked. I told him how Laughing Maid had already begun to make a dress for the wedding. How the other women of the village planned to decorate and how wonderful it was that Harriet was a central part of the festival.

I told him that I had not bled after the night on the lake. Samuel seemed perplexed, and I told him that I was with child. Great joy crossed his face, and we danced together in the shade of the forest.

We began our journey back to the village, holding hands and talking of the future and whether our child would be a boy or a girl, discussing names. Samuel said if it was a girl, we should name her Girl Who Sprang from Lake. I said if it was a boy, we should name him Boy with Quick Trigger. He chased me, and I fell to the ground with him on top of me laughing. We brought ourselves to our feet, and the two men stood silently in the trees. One was an Indian scout, bearing the markings of the Crow, the enemy of the Sioux. The other wore the dark blue uniform of the US Army, his piercing blue eyes fixed upon my gaze. Samuel said they were "crystal blue, like the water that surrounds the islands." His fair, scraggly beard and blond, dirty hair fell below his hat. He smiled an evil smile, exposing a missing upper-front-left tooth. I whispered to Samuel, "Hestovatohkeo'o. Double Face." Samuel reached into the basket and placed his hand on the six-shot Colt revolver Big John had promised to take everywhere, pointing the barrel to the edge of the basket. The Crow, a single feather extending from his US Army hat, wearing the coat of an officer and bearing a rifle of the infantry, spoke quietly to his partner. The white man's blue eyes never left me. The two men took two steps back and disappeared into the maze of the forest.

Samuel and I reported the sighting to Appanoose and Chayton. Chayton surmised that they were deserters not looking for trouble. Appanoose felt they were scouts, seeking a village such as ours. More war was rising on the horizon. It was the first night in many seasons that I did not think of Samuel. That night I had terrible visions of the man with evil, crystal-blue eyes. The eyes of Double Face. And I had stared into the back of his head. He was coming for me. He was coming to murder me.

SUNDAY, JULY 27
BRADY, TEXAS

Levi packed the bowl with a pinch of the tight bud he had scored. He flicked his lighter, placed the flame to the pot, and sucked the smoke through the tube. Levi held the drag in, expanding his lungs until he coughed uncontrollably. He handed the bong to Bo.

Levi poured the Budweiser down his throat, cooling his fiery chest. Bo wheezed in the lawn chair under the mobile home's awning. There wasn't much to do in Brady, Texas, during a heat wave. "Go give the bitch some water."

"I had to feed her this morning," Bo complained.

"She ain't no good to us dead." Levi's head got light, and his eyes glazed over. "That's good shit."

"Damn good." Bo passed Levi the bottle of cheap, rotgut whiskey. "She ain't no good to nobody. Worthless Jew."

"Well, the Brotherhood wants to make an example of her," Levi rationalized through his bloodshot eyes.

"Well, the Brotherhood ain't gotta watch the bitch all the time. We should just kill her now." Bo laid his head back in the morning sun, his buzz scrambling his brain. Levi struggled out of the lawn chair and grabbed a bucket. He turned on the spigot and filled the bucket with lukewarm summer water. He opened the trailer door and set it inside. Irina Goldstein kneeled before the bucket with hands tied behind her back and lapped the water.

"I got an idea, Levi. You still have the girl's phone? We might just make a name for ourselves with the Brotherhood."

Levi listened intently to Bo, a wide grin crossing his face.

Levi and Bo spent a couple of hours pulling the rods and carving out the hole. Levi squirted the lighter fluid on the charcoal in the pit and set it ablaze. Bo entered the trailer and approached Irina. "Come on, you little Jew whore." He untied her bonds. "Get those clothes off." Irina struggled. Bo ripped her shirt and forced it off her shoulders. "Unless you want to end up in a hole in the desert, take off your goddamned clothes." Irina stripped naked. Bo escorted her out of the trailer.

Levi held the ten-foot metal bar against his shoulder. "Damn, you're even uglier naked."

Bo lined Irina up against the pole, and Levi tied her hands behind it. He bent down and tied her ankles, fusing them to the bottom of the pole. Bo removed an apple from his pocket and shined it on his jeans. "Open your mouth." Irina refused. "Open your mouth!" Levi pulled her hair, slamming her head into the pole. Irina opened her mouth, and Bo shoved the apple in between her teeth. "Now, don't drop that."

Bo and Levi forced Irina onto her knees, the pole teetering on her back. Levi kicked her to the ground. Irina's naked body lay in the dust, the apple still in her mouth. Levi and Bo picked up the ends of the pole and placed them in the spit jack, over the burning coals. Levi pulled Irina's phone from his pocket and photographed

Irina nude, hog-tied on a pole and roasting with an apple in her mouth.

Later that evening, Bo and Levi went to a friend who had a computer and uploaded the picture of Irina to the Brotherhood of Aryan Defenders website. Irina was nude, hog-tied, and cooking with an apple in her mouth over the white-hot charcoal. They labeled the picture *Texas Bar B Jew*.

JULY 28
ATLANTA, GEORGIA

E lroy Floyd hung a left onto Auburn Avenue. The radio commentator Fabian Zhirkov offered his opinion. "While the United States focuses its attention on Ukraine and the conflict in Israel and Gaza, another part of the world has been at war for decades. It is not a country but a continent. There are very few African nations that are not at war. Libya, Chad, Nigeria, Sudan, Ethiopia, Ghana, the Congo, and Egypt all have their own internal crises. President Obama instantly approved a quarter of a billion dollars to help Israel with its Iron Dome. We sent one hundred men from specialized forces and a few Osprey to the Congo to apprehend Joseph Kony, the ruthless warlord. Does this seem disproportionate? Why are the lives of one nation more valuable than those of another? The simple answer is money and race. Americans feel they owe something to the Jews from World War II, while the Muslim world is our sworn enemy. No matter how many innocent women and children die in United Nations shelters from the Israeli missiles, you do not see the American public protesting on Pennsylvania Avenue. The death toll in Palestine is climbing to two thousand, and while I mourn all those lost in the throngs of war, Israel has lost only three civilians and some fifty soldiers. This is a preposterous mismatch, and the United States has chosen to side with the bully. We have slapped Vladimir Putin on the wrist for his nation's support of the Russian rebels in Ukraine, too cowardly to stick up for the two hundred ninety-eight innocent victims aboard Malaysian Airlines flight MH17. The world press has brought those international conflicts to the front pages, yet the fickle American public will not take a stand. They will pick up their remotes and turn to another channel that takes them far, far away from the real world we live in. Then the press will find the next shocking world event that will entertain the public for fifteen minutes, and we will switch the channel again. Wake up, America! Your chickens are going to come home to roost. While you are playing on your iPhones and surfing the Internet, the world is changing. There is an evil in the world, and the most powerful nation in the world has lost its religion. I applaud those who care and reach out to help the starving and the misplaced refugees of the world. There are the health-care personnel who stand in the jungles and work for the victims of Ebola, stepping in for the untrained shaman trying to heal the deadly disease with burnt applewood, honey, and secret prayers. But there are not enough people in the world who care. And it starts right here in America. I hope you listened today. This is Fabian Zhirkov."

"What do you think about that, boss?" Floyd passed in front of the Georgia Dome in the sweltering humidity, which was so hot you would shove a Rocket Pop in your underwear to stay cool.

"It is a time when God has lost control," Lyle boasted from the backseat. "The war shall be over soon. We are everywhere. We have been here through all of time. Stoking the fires of hatred. Feeding into humans' fiery distrust of one another. Humankind is rusted and corroded, the legacy of Adam when he ate the apple.

The poison changed the destiny of humanity, God's new angels, ordained to protect the universe from the master. They began pure and open but now exist corrupted, ordained to serve in hell."

"Then why all the fuss over this one girl?" Floyd persisted. "Why not just blow some more shit up? There's a lot you can do with four sticks of dynamite and a lot of hate."

Lyle appreciated Floyd's narrow vision. "What I smell is a dove. Committed to change and peace. The complexity is an antidote to the poison. God has sent her back to earth since the beginning, hoping to change the fortune of humanity. She is pure and dangerous. She carries the gift of pure love. It is the thing I must destroy, for it can destroy me. She can swallow my master's dream of annihilating the universe, sending light back to darkness. I have found her in Nanking and Jakarta. Mongolia and Cambodia. And I have found her again."

Lyle closed his eyes, and his dream took him back to the trenches. Today was a special celebration, the one hundredth anniversary of the commencement of World War I. This led to the death of almost thirty million people worldwide. He thought of the voice on the radio. Palestine and Israel. The sand niggers against the Red Sea pedestrians. With a little luck, someone just might drop the bomb.

"Did you hear the government might be bringing some of these Ebola people here to Atlanta?" Floyd turned up "Cop Killer" by Ice-T.

"No good deed goes unpunished, my friend." This perplexed the dim Floyd. "No amount of hatred and war can remove all of humanity from the earth. That is the genius of my master. Humanity has been weakened by the apple. Not just its soul but its body. That is the danger of the girl. She is pure. She strengthens them. That's why she and her kind must be eliminated. The ones we can't get to kill themselves in war become devastated by the evolutionary game changer of disease. The incurable viruses that will whittle away the great masses that escape the carnage. We will leave the earth ravaged and scorched, and the rest will fight alone against cancer, Ebola, starvation, and plagues that will decimate humanity. I don't have to kill them all. They will do it for me. All seven billion of these low creatures."

AUGUST 2, SOMEWHERE

Colt and Harlow creaked down the steps into the basement. Celia knew it was them just by their footsteps and goofy cackles.

"Girl, we are going to miss you around here." Colt's twang reflected no anguish.

"Where are we going?" Celia recoiled against the dryer. "Please take me home! Please! I will do anything!"

"You've already done everything, girl," Colt sputtered perversely. "Harlow, you tie her hands."

"No! Don't kill me! No! Please let me stay, Colt." Celia slobbered through the fear.

"We aren't going to kill you, Celia." Harlow took the small pieces of rope and tied Celia's hands behind her back. "We are selling you."

"And we are going to make a lot of money off you." Colt held Celia's arm straight and filled the syringed with Versed. He found her vein and plunged the needle in, drawing back a bit of blood and then sending the sedative on its course. Celia fell into Harlow's arms, and Colt applied a blindfold. They loaded her into the back of his paint truck and headed south.

AUGUST 3
SARASOTA, FLORIDA

Ciro Costa had worked the docks of Manatee County Port Authority for forty-five years. He walked the detectives through the giant vessels and far into the shade where the barges sat secure, waiting to take their unwanted cargo to be dumped unceremoniously and clandestinely into the Gulf of Mexico.

"Where are we heading, Mr. Costa?" The heat was getting to the older detective.

"It is right this way." Ciro waved for them to keep going.

They climbed aboard the unprotected barge and were halted by the stench. Both detectives covered their faces. Ciro asked them to climb onto the mountainous pile of refuse, surging forward like a wildcat on a mountain. They reached the apex and worked their way down the backside of the trash pile.

"Why were you up here again?" The second detective tried not to slip while climbing with one hand.

"I hope you do not judge me, officers." Ciro's smile was as broken as his English. "My job is to work near the barges. They take them to the ocean full and bring them back empty. There are so many people here in America who have nothing. Sometimes they come to Ciro and ask if they can look at the things others throw away."

"So you bring a bunch of trash pickers here to rummage through this shit?"

"You can say what you like, but many people have found treasures for their lives. Bicycles for their children. Pots and pans to cook with. Chairs and couches and frames for the beds their children sleep on."

"I get the picture." The detective looked at his partner. "I suppose if they are going to use it, what's the harm?"

Ciro eased down to the deck of the barge and stood next to the round, waist-high metal container. The detective slid the top to the side and saw the foot sticking out of the sludge. The grease had coagulated around the ankle. The other detective called Florida CSI to remove the folded body of Yael Almeida.

THE MADELINE SESSIONS: AUGUST 4 ARLINGTON, VIRGINIA

I found Samuel in the fields with the horses. He knew I would be leaving in the morning to begin my vision quest. He was worried for me. He brought the group of horses around.

"I call this one Colossus." Samuel rubbed the horse's nose and gave him a slice of apple.

"Why do you call him Colossus?" I asked.

"Because he is so big." Samuel smacked the horse on its behind and sent him back to the pack.

"He is no bigger than the others."

"He is much bigger in some places." I smacked him on his behind, but he made me laugh. I was concerned about leaving the village for two nights.

"Have you decided where you will go?" Samuel asked me.

I told him I would climb Bear Mountain and commune with Wakan Tanka as close to the heavens as I could. My body was already feeling weak. I had shared with no one that I was with child. The ritual of spending many days in the sweat lodge, purifying my soul, had drained me physically. That evening our families shared a great feast of buffalo stew. I gorged myself, knowing I would be fasting for two days. My trepidation did not allow me to sleep well, and the vision quest required one to be awake. One didn't know when one's destiny would be served.

The medicine man came to my tent with the first rays of the sun. I could feel Samuel's eyes upon me as I began my journey to the base of Bear Mountain. I crossed the creeks and climbed through the Black Hills on my journey. Small birds pecking at the ground for food. The deer leaping the logs in the forest. I stayed quiet as I saw the brown bear cub. It wrestled with some vines, but I crept along, knowing its mother was close-by.

I came across the lake at the base of the mountain where Samuel and I canoed at night, my thoughts taking me to our next adventure on the water. The hunters had taught me the trail, and I took my first steps toward the crest. I was a good climber and found myself looking west to the mountains, my first dreams taking me on a journey to the west, discovering what lay beyond our village. The sun followed my every move. With no food and water, I had become very hungry, but more so thirsty. I was careful not to drink too much as the water was all I had for two days.

I followed the unworn path. At times it was steep, and I pulled on the bushes to bring me higher. I looked back to the east. I could not see my village but knew it lay just at the edge of the forest. The sky was clear, and I looked to the south, wondering if I could see Fort Laramie. I thought of Big John and the pain he endured. The loss of his wife and his baby had taken him to a dark place, fueled by the whiskey of the white man.

I thought of Harriet and her strength. Of the many things she had taught the village. How she had learned to wear the colorful robes of the tribe and how she shared her dresses of the West with the women. I hoped to love my child with the love she bestowed upon her children. Her fair face had become weathered in the year she had spent at the village. I believed the village had taught her that women were strong.

My tracks moved higher, and I thought of Angus, still a boy, yet doing the things of a man. That someday he would be a great leader and father, like his own. I marveled at his skill with a bow and a knife and prayed that he would never have to use them in war.

I thought of the baby I carried inside me. Laughing Maid would soon know, if she did not suspect already. I imagined a boy and considered what name we should bestow upon him. I imagined a girl and how she would love her father, as I did mine.

Mostly, I thought of Samuel and the joy he had brought to my heart. Our wedding would be soon, and plans to make our own tent had begun to be made. I had never dreamed of leaving the village, but Samuel had taught me of the world that lay beyond the horizon. Places I had only dreamed of seeing—he had promised to take me to them. I did not fear the future. I yearned for the world.

I arrived at the top well before the sun fell from the sky. I laid my blanket in an even spot and fell to my knees. I prayed to Wakan Tanka to show me the way. To enlighten me as to my purpose. The wind blew chilly at the top of the mountain. I shivered but remained focused on my prayer.

The sun disappeared, and the temperature dropped. I pulled the buffalo skin over me and tried to focus on my quest. I could hear things in the night. A fox? A bird? A wolf? Samuel had given me a knife to protect myself. I walked the perimeter of the peak, my knife exposed and waiting to slay the bandit. I moved back to my blanket, sure it was the wind rustling the leaves of the bushes.

I could not see in the darkness, and my hunger consumed me. My eyes felt heavy, and I struggled to keep them open. I reached for the stars and counted them by directions in the sky. The air was clear, and I quickly lost count. My stomach churned for food, but I dismissed my hunger and played games in my head to occupy my desire for nourishment. I petted my stomach and told the baby that upon my return I would feast.

The moon moved over the sky and now glowed over my head. I breathed deeply. I remained on my knees in prayer as I dared not lie on the blanket. The wind blew some dirt into my hair. I passed the time by shouting to the moon and singing the songs of my village as loud as I could. No one was there to hear me.

My shoulders slumped, and my back curved, but I remained awake as the sun's first rays beamed over the plains. I found the energy to stand and look east, stretching my arms as far as I could and rejoicing at the splendor that is our world and the beauty of the land we live in.

My hunger raged inside me. I took some water for the baby. With the sun came the heat. I was becoming weak and frustrated that my vision had not come to me. There was no dream—only hunger.

My mind was not filled with spirits or revelations. My soul felt hollow and my belly empty.

I thought I was dreaming. The purple and orange rays of the sun bled over the tops of the mountains to the west, bouncing its image across the lakes and ponds. Nightfall was upon me, and I licked my skin for the salt that it gave me. I knelt and prayed that tonight I would cry for the dream.

The world above me began to spin. Fire streaked across the sky. The moon, a half crescent, melted and then re-formed. I looked at the stars, and they took me into the universe. I leaped from star to star, flying to each new place in an instant, riding my buffalo, my guide. We raced the eagles and trampled on the clouds. The children followed me closely. I slowed my buffalo so as not to leave them behind. They followed me wherever I went. We crossed oceans and streams and climbed mountains and entered cities.

The dream took me to a vast field. Our Indian nation and the eyes of many other nations stood with me in the meadow. They sought my direction and guidance. The souls of the oppressed yearned for their freedom. A wise old man stood in the grass, alone. I walked to the center of the field with my bull at my side. I told him war had to end. That the world could live in harmony no matter the color of the people's skin and no matter whether they were men or women. He held out his arm, his fist closed. He opened his hand and shone the most truthful light. I had seen my vision quest. I had seen the truth, and the people would follow me to the light.

The cries of freedom rang from the multitudes behind me, our arms raised at the hope of a new world. I turned to thank the spirit that had shown me my way, but he had turned his back, exposing the face of Hestovatohkeo'o. Double Face had found his way into my quest. I turned, and the people I had gathered from around the world turned to ashes in the field. I stood alone with his evil face on top of the mountain, having seen my future and my death.

I left the mountain in the darkness, picking my way step by step through the tears, crashing and sliding. I still remained high on the mountain when the sun came. I moved more rapidly but continued to fall. My body was weak. My skin bled from my arms and knees. The blood dripped into my eyes from the scratches on my face.

Disoriented, I followed the edges of the lake. I sipped the waters and splashed them upon me. I passed through the hills and woods. I could see the village, but the village would disappear. My strength was gone. I began to crawl. My mind was as weak as my body, and I would only hear the stories of Samuel finding me in the woods and bringing me back to the village.

AUGUST 9
ATLANTA, GEORGIA

E velyn snored like a beast on the couch, interrupting the late news. If he didn't need her, he would have strangled her right then and there. The first reports were streaming in from a small suburb of Saint Louis, Missouri. A white police officer had shot an unarmed black teenager in the middle of the street. Flowers in the middle of the street marked the slain youth's death.

The impoverished and oppressed of Ferguson were the fuse of America, and the powder keg had just been lit with an officer's bullet. The fever of Atlanta burned silently, waiting to erupt in Savannah Gabriel. And the storm surrounding Eric Garner loomed in New York City, destined to escalate to a category-five frenzy if the officer wasn't convicted.

AUGUST 10
DURANGO, COLORADO

Andres grabbed Ilana by the hair and held her against the couch. He drove his knee into her abdomen, taking her breath. He ripped off the duct tape and slapped it over her mouth. He rolled her over by her hair and tightly wrapped her wrists behind her back with the same duct tape. Vincente filled a Playmate cooler with a combination of bottled water, Mountain Dew, and Coors in a can. He threw the last of the ice cubes from the freezer into the cooler and grabbed a bag of Cool Ranch Doritos.

They dragged Ilana into the garage and stuffed her behind the seats of the pickup truck with the cooler next to her head. They backed out into the cool summer night and headed south to Houston, Texas, with their cargo estimated to return a fee of $10,000.

AUGUST
SOMEWHERE

The side of Lila's face hit the floor of the Winnebago. She could see the wrinkly ankles of a woman wearing a housecoat and holding the old man's shotgun. Lila tried to scurry to her feet, but her ankles were bound. She wanted to scream, but she was gagged. The other girl was thrown on top of her, causing Lila to lose her breath. The two captives engaged each other's eyes. It was only the second time she had seen the girl who knocked on the walls. She was frightened but gained strength from Lila's defiance. Lila still didn't know her name.

The engine cranked, and the old man turned on the radio. The old woman sliced an apple on the kitchenette table but offered the girls nothing. "How long is this going to take?" she muttered while slurping on the slice.

"Should be there by sundown." The driver hummed to Waylon Jennings.

"Are we going to stop in Memphis?" The rifle lay in the woman's lap.

The old man turned and shot the woman a look. "No stops today. But by the end of the day, we will have that money you need for the deck you want."

"That will be nice. Sitting on a deck in the evening will be very nice." The old woman crossed her wrinkly ankles. She peeked over the kitchenette table at the two girls tied up on the floor of the RV. "I remember the girls who furnished the living room. They weren't nearly as pretty."

AUGUST 11
CEDAR CITY, UTAH

HIKER MISSING

*I ron County Today*The Iron County Sheriff's Office has posted a missing persons report for Sui Sterling, seventeen years of age. Sui was last spotted at a gas station near Cedar Canyon. Sui was scheduled to meet friends at eleven in the morning and never arrived. Sui was driving her mother's 2012 silver Chevy Impala, and the vehicle was found of the shoulder of Interstate 15 with a flat tire.

Sui is five feet four inches tall and weighs 109 pounds. Sui has short black hair and brown eyes. She was last seen wearing black sunglasses and black climbing shorts, long white socks, and a short-sleeved gray T-shirt.

If you have any information on the disappearance of Sui or her whereabouts, please call the Iron County Sheriff's Office at 438-555-2311.

AUGUST 12
ARLINGTON, VIRGINIA

Father Salvatore Moutinho met Madeline at the Starbucks in Ballston Common Mall. Madeline had yearned for the Pumpkin Spice Latte and added a Caramel Pecan Sticky Bun for good measure. Moutinho stuck with the Salted Caramel Mocha. "How are you feeling?" Moutinho scraped off a bit of the whipped cream and licked his finger.

"I feel all right." Madeline waited for the latte to cool.

"Just all right?"

"I have good days and bad days. I never feel like I did before." Madeline watched the people on the escalator. "Before all this."

"What do you feel?"

"I never feel completely relaxed. Like everything is going to be OK. It's like I'm always looking over my shoulder."

"Have the doctors explained everything that is happening to you?" Moutinho coaxed Madeline into telling him more.

"Yes. I believe so." Madeline tried the latte. "They said I have multiple personalities."

"That doesn't frighten you?" the priest asked.

Madeline thought for a second. "No. Not really. I don't feel them or anything. I don't talk to my different personalities. But my parents won't let me see the videotapes."

"Why?"

"They said now is not the time. The doctors agreed. They said there is still work left to do to find the root of my 'issues.'" Madeline made quotation marks with her hands.

"You parents feel it is best to not let you go to college in the fall. Are you OK with that?" Moutinho pinched a piece of Madeline's sticky bun.

"I guess I am. I haven't had an episode in quite some time, but I don't feel comfortable being far from home if it were to happen again." Madeline picked a pecan and sucked on the glaze. "What scares you, Father?"

Moutinho raised his eyebrows. "That's a tough one." He sipped his mocha.

"Not like in the movies. In real life."

The old man screwed up his mouth. "Hell." He brought Madeline's eyes to his. "Hell scares me."

"What do you mean?"

"Imagine feeling the worst, most terrible feeling you ever could every day. Physically, mentally, and emotionally, all wrapped up into one, and it happens every day."

"Kind of like my life." Madeline tried to lighten the priest's mood.

"There are no sticky buns in hell." Moutinho winked and then turned serious. "A place you can never leave. A place so awful, you would consider killing yourself, but you can't. Your body is already dead, but your soul has to endure an eternity of hell. That is my worst fear."

"Is that why you became a priest?"

"I suppose that is part of why. And I wanted to teach people the word of God. And if they listened they could avoid that terrible fate."

"Do people listen?" Madeline dipped a spoon into the froth of her latte.

"People claim to believe in God, but they really don't. They were taught when they were children to believe in God, but temptation turns them. Mostly, they don't believe in heaven and hell. So if there is no penalty for bad behavior, why worry? Religion is dead in the world. At least in America."

"How about all those people who go to church every Sunday?" Madeline challenged.

"I am not saying that everybody is a sinner, but those congregations are filled with hypocrites. They forget most of the sins they commit in a week's time. I am not talking about violent criminals."

"I didn't think you were." Madeline sipped the last of the Pumpkin Spice Latte and burped just a little bit.

"I am talking about thieves and adulterers. Liars and cheats. Racists and abusers. They are all sinners just the same. They come to church, sing the songs, put some money in the basket, and feel God has forgiven them for their week's transgressions, yet they never change. They may think of the things they have done and even confess them, yet they continue until they are caught."

"Caught?"

"By their wives. By their work. By the police. Everything is fine until they are caught. Then it is only 'one time,' and it will never happen again. And some have to repent and pay a penance."

"Like jail time?"

"Jail is easy. No one wants to go to hell."

AUGUST 13
EDNA, TEXAS

The plains of Texas were flaming hot and dry. Sweat dripped from their bald heads. Levi tied his T-shirt around his head to dam the sweat. Bo adjusted the gun stuck into his underwear. A van streaked toward the men, dust jetting from the back. Outside, Edna, Texas, was a lonely place.

Two men exited the van. The driver was large, muscular, and bald. The lanky passenger wore a nameless ball cap. Both holstered sidearms and bore the marks of the Brotherhood of Aryan Defenders.

"Did you bring the cargo?" the driver asked.

"She is here." Irina lay suffocating in the trunk of the racist's car.

"Where is she?" inquired the lanky one.

"In the trunk," offered the man with the T-shirt around his head.

"You idiot. Get her out of there." He moved to the trunk. "She could die."

"Isn't that why we are here? To kill the Jew bitch?" Levi cackled.

"We have different plans for her."

"That's not right," Bo protested. "Aren't we here to protect the white race from the people of Zion? That's what you said in your speech."

They pulled Irina from the trunk of the car. She was dehydrated and flushed. Welts covered her neck and arms. The driver removed the gag and gave her some water. "You beat her."

"She's just an animal." Levi seethed at the sight of Irina.

"She's as hot as a pepper," noted the lanky one.

"You can't find this donkey attractive," Bo protested.

"No. Law enforcement is looking for her." The driver glared at the young terrorists. "Her name is Irina Goldstein. You pinched her at some park in Odessa. She's young. Sixteen." The driver looked at the lanky one. "I'm sure she's a virgin."

"She's a Jew bitch. We should just kill her." The Iron Cross puffed across Bo's chest.

"I appreciate your fervor, my compatriot. I have different plans for this Jew. Hers will be a fate worse than death, I assure you." The driver poured water over Irina's face and soaked the front of the child. He put the gag back in her mouth. "Sadie will be in Houston in two days. We will meet her there." The driver and the lanky one put Irina Goldstein in the back of the van, leaving the two standing over the shallow grave they had dug in advance.

AUGUST 14
LAS VEGAS, NEVADA

Riyad opened the door and invited the young man and girl into room on the ninth-floor suite at the Cosmopolitan Las Vegas. "Hello. My name is Riyad." Riyad was dumpy, portly, and hairy. He slipped off his wedding ring surreptitiously and placed it on the bureau next to the flatscreen.

"Hello, my name is Nigel, and this is Shay." Shay sauntered into the room wearing high-cut jean shorts, boots, and a black halter top that ran across the top of her nipples. Her long blond hair flowed across her shoulders, and her makeup made her look eighteen. Shay went straight to the minibar, unscrewed the top of a miniature Grey Goose bottle, and downed the chilled delight. "Would you like to party a bit before we talk business?" Nigel inquired in his British accent.

"That's why you come to Vegas." Riyad showed his teeth from under his brushy mustache.

Nigel Baines dumped the cocaine onto the coffee table and spread it around with his Nevada driver's license, chopping it fine. Shay Bertrup grabbed another vodka and ignored Riyad's lascivious stare. "Shay loves the geek." He handed Shay a clipped straw from McDonald's, and she powered down the largest caterpillar of the cocaine lines. The drug blasted into her nose and raced into her bloodstream. She threw her head back, drawing in all of the powder.

"That was impressive. I don't want to do that much. It may affect me in a bad way." Riyad winked to indicate he was talking about his expected sexual performance.

"Do as much as you like, mate." Nigel shared the laugh. Riyad fumbled with the straw, clumsily snorting the coke.

"Don't mind if I do," Nigel said as Riyad passed him the straw. Nigel plowed through his share, wiped the table with his finger, and rubbed the remnants on his gums. "That will start your day." Riyad looked at the clock radio. It was nine in the evening, and the sun was slinking down over the western mountains. "Well, Riyad? Do you want to chitchat or talk business?"

Shay poked her finger at the table, scrounging any leftovers.

"I am not sure exactly how this works. This is my first time," Riyad confessed. Nigel repressed a giggle, wondering how many times he had heard that.

"Shay is the best. She's beautiful and young, as you can see. And she will do anything your heart desires." Nigel ogled his prize. Shay nipped at the vodka, her dying eyes unfazed.

"She is very beautiful." Riyad barely moved his eyes from Shay. He wanted her badly, and Nigel cashed in on Riyad's desire.

"You can have her for one hour for $500."

"Only one hour?" Riyad protested slightly.

"We do have other clients." Nigel lit a cigarette and felt the cocaine surge through his veins. "Do you have protection?"

"I do."

"Is she legal?" Riyad did not want to go to jail on the off chance that this venture went wrong.

"She is," Baines lied. Shay never flinched.

Riyad removed the roll from his pocket, peeled off five one-hundred-dollar bills, and handed them to Nigel. There was an uncomfortable silence as no one moved.

"I have to stay here, mate. Just in case any funny business comes about." Nigel turned Riyad's focus to the bedroom.

Riyad hesitated but took the fifteen-year-old Shay Bertrup by the hand and smeared his hairy, short body inside and outside of every part of her body for one hour.

AUGUST 15
HOUSTON, TEXAS

The dark waters of the Gulf of Mexico lapped against the Jacintoport terminal. Clouds shielded the light from space, offering an optimal night for Sadie Davil. The 125 acres of the Houston port were poorly guarded. Those employed to protect the vessels easily accepted payment to turn the other cheek.

Sadie idled in the obscure. Vehicles of all makes and models pulled to the ramp of the *Cathartidae Silentium*, the thirteen-ton chemical-supply ship bound for the Syrian port of Latakia via the Dominican Republic.

Envelopes of cash exchanged hands each time one of the children was boarded, their hands tied and mouths gagged. Little boys and girls. Some past puberty. Some not. Asians and whites. Blacks and Latinos. Christians, Jews, and Muslims. Some old enough to understand they were being sacrificed. All old enough to be scared. They were escorted up the ramp and then down into the bowels of the massive ship, piled upon one another as human cargo, their muffled cries muted by the assault rifles pressed to the smalls of their backs.

Harley sat nervously in the front of the paint truck. "Man, I just want to get this over with."

"No shit. This is a major operation."

Celia tried to loosen her restraints.

A knock on the window made the men jump. Colt rolled down his window.

"What is the password?" asked the masked gunman.

"Contritio." Colt butchered the pronunciation of the Latin word for destruction. The gate opened and let the van pass.

The narrow beam of a single flashlight guided the way. The van pulled around a warehouse to the hull of the supply ship. Harley and Colt craned to see the top of the colossal vessel. Another soldier of the night held his hands in the air, and they eased the van to a stop. He opened the sliding door. Celia's terrified eyes reflected back. The shadowy man pulled a knife and cut the ties from her ankles. Celia scrambled to leave the van and run. The shadow grasped her hair and shoved the rifle in her back. Celia was passed to another and made the trek up the ramp. The shadow handed Harley an envelope and shooed them along.

"Aren't you going to check it?" Colt asked Harley.

"Hell no! I'm getting out of here." Colt grabbed the envelope. It was the $10,000 they'd been promised.

Celia was dumped into the pile. Another body among hundreds. The guard forced her to squat. The cavern smelled of body odor and urine. Many of the captives sat in soiled pants or the vomit of others who had succumbed to the stench. The heat forced the odors to bloom. Celia shared the distraught visible in all of the lost faces. The grimaces of Irina Goldstein and Lila Chait, who kept her nameless friend close. The fear of Sui Sterling and Ilana Landreau.

"It is time to leave. Tell the well-paid captain to shove off," Davil instructed.

"Where are we going, Sadie?" the assistant asked.

"To the cradle of creation, my friend. We are bringing the chemicals back to Syria and giving them to the Islamic State. They will need them to defeat the world."

"And the other cargo?"

"We are feeding the lust of the hounds of hell." Davil boarded the *Cathartidae Silentium,* the "Silent Vulture," to ensure the arrival of its precious freight.

AUGUST 18
LOS ANGELES, CALIFORNIA

The news would never get a whiff of the deals the congressman had made. In the backrooms of Washington he brokered deals for his vote with energy developers, military programs, cable TV rights, abortion, voting precincts, and much more. The money swapped would total in the billions. Motta had traded his integrity for a prisoner trade involving three well-known international terrorists: Peter Benayoun, Lucia Cassano, and Guatram Blind. Somewhere Abel Sakai was laughing his balls off.

Congressman Motta sat alone on his boat. He opened a nice bottle of Syrah from Napa and enjoyed a couple of glasses while admiring his beautiful wife and children. He knew his sins would never be forgiven, not that they should have been. His inability to control his temptation had doomed his future. He had sold his soul. He spun the chamber, and the round blew through his temple and ricocheted off the wheel of the yacht as his body slumped in the captain's chair.

Lyle mused while reading the *Atlanta Journal-Constitution* that Danny "Trigger" Motta was not afraid to pull the trigger on what was best for California.

AUGUST 20
ATLANTA, GEORGIA

L yle heard the scream from Evelyn's kitchen. He turned the corner into the living room and saw her hands over her mouth. "What happened?"

"They killed him, Victor!" Evelyn sputtered through her fingers.

"Killed whom?" Lyle stepped in front of the tube.

"The journalist in Iraq. They beheaded him." The black-masked murderer stood over the balding journalist, a knife in his left hand. "These people are going to do this in America."

Lyle sat on the couch, bemused at the scene. Evelyn was terrified, and so were hundreds of millions of people around the world. Senator Gaston Milner and ORBIS had pulled it off. With the picture of a man in a mask holding a knife and the creation of a terrorist group no one had ever heard of six months ago, America could now convince the world to light up the war machines to rid the world of a few renegade terrorists from Syria. *Genius*, Lyle thought to himself. America wouldn't run to the aid of the people of Rwanda when hundreds floated dead down their rivers. They wouldn't enter Ukraine after the Malaysian flight was shot down, killing 298 innocent victims. They wouldn't enter Gaza and defend the children being blown up. But they were running to the desert to defend their oil and reposition themselves for the future attack of Iran, securing their presence in the region for the next century. Greed. One of the great sins! The trillions that would be conjured from the collapsing American budget would be spent on missiles and tanks and arming their sworn enemies in Syria. It would not go to the starving in Ethiopia or India. Not to the impoverished of Pakistan or Burundi. "Politics does make for strange bedfellows."

Lyle put his arms around Evelyn. So fragile and weak. That was why she would have to die. *In time,* he mused. She still had work to do. Work that would evoke another great sin: wrath.

AUGUST 21
FORT WAYNE, INDIANA

Huang sat nervously in the front row with a court-appointed attorney. Her parents sat on the other side of the aisle. The district attorney in Seattle had contacted the district attorney in Fort Wayne, Indiana, and a case for Huang had been opened. She had been placed in the temporary custody of Tangela Shaw, Huang's math teacher. Huang was fighting for her freedom. Her parents were fighting to have her returned to their custody, a hell to which Huang vowed she would not return.

Everyone stood as the judge entered the courtroom. He adjusted his glasses, and the entire room paused as he prepared to read his decision. "I have carefully reviewed all of the evidence presented to the court, including the psychological evaluations of all parties involved and the testimonies of Ms. Lodygin, her parents, and support persons. I have taken into consideration the home provided and loving environment that Mr. and Mrs. Lodygin have afforded Huang. They are exemplary members of the Fort Wayne community. Given the lack of physical evidence and the under-standing that there was no complaint of sexual abuse before Ms. Huang ran away, I have concluded that these are the acts of an impetuous teenager and that the parents are to retain custody of their daughter."

The cheers contradicted the moans and groans. A dazed Huang left the courtroom with her father's arm around her shoulders.

AUGUST 25
TWIN FALLS, IDAHO

Luther Bichman stood on the sidewalk in front of the Vera C. O'Leary Middle School in Twin Falls, Idaho, with his daughter, Maryna.

"This is where you are going to school, Maryna." Luther looked down at the bow in his daughter's hair.

"I don't have to go to school, Daddy. I can just stay with you." She smiled as she held his hand.

"You know I would love that. But you have to go to school. There is so much to learn. And you are real smart, Maryna. You are going to go to college someday." They headed in to register Maryna.

Luther stepped up to the counter in the office.

"Hello, how may I help you?" The woman with puffy blond hair had a smile as wide as the Snake River.

"I would like to put my daughter in school. She is going to be in seventh grade."

Maryna squeezed his hand really tight and glared crossly. "Eighth grade, Daddy."

"How quickly they grow up." Luther smiled at his mistake, and so did the woman.

"Don't I know it! I have two in college." She beamed proudly. "Are you new to the area?"

"We are. We just moved here."

"Well, here are some forms that I need you to fill out regarding her previous school. Then we can transfer her transcripts. These are some medical forms for the school nurse. For the medical forms I will need immunization records showing proof of shots for diphtheria, tetanus, polio, measles, mumps, Rubella, hepatitis B, and chicken pox. I will also need to copy your driver's license, and I will need a copy of her..." She looked at the happy girl.

"Maryna, and my name is Luther Bichman."

"It's nice to meet both of you. I will need a copy of her birth certificate or a passport if you have one. And lastly I will need proof of residency."

"What do you need for residence, ma'am?"

"A copy of your lease will do or a current utility bill. A voter-registration card will suffice." She stapled the documents together and handed them to Luther.

Luther and Maryna walked out of Vera C. O'Leary Middle School with registration papers in hand. They piled into Luther's 1997 Mazda Protegé with balding tires and a two-tone gray-and-blue paint job that he'd gotten off a friend for $750. Luther revved the engine and headed down the road. He pulled in to the Twin Falls Police Department.

"Why are we here, Daddy?"

"Because Daddy loves you and you need to go to school. You need to go someplace in this world."

"But the school is back there, Daddy." Maryna could feel the writing on the wall.

"You have to go home to Arkansas and go back to the school you were in." Luther's eyes filled with tears.

"Daddy, I love you. I don't want to go back." They cried and held each other close.

"I don't know about all this paperwork. I don't have what they need, and you can't fake this stuff. I am tired of trying to fake people out, Maryna."

"No one loves me there, Daddy." She sobbed into his chest.

"Just know that I will always love you. You are a very special young lady."

Luther and Maryna entered the police department, and he turned himself in and handed his daughter over to the authorities, ending the best three months of his daughter's short life. She had laughed and loved with her father, who loved her back.

AUGUST 26
ARLINGTON, VIRGINIA

D r. Smalling turned the air conditioner up and removed the jacket of her suit. The late-August Washington humidity stifled the room. Madeline Deschamps sat for a regular psychotherapy session. The heat was so oppressive that even Madeline had shunned the omnipresent hoodie.

"All of your classmates are going to college this week. Does this bother you?" Dr. Smalling inquired.

"Not really." Madeline fidgeted with her phone. "I am going to take some classes online to stay busy and not fall behind." She paused. "My parents are right. I need to get this all sorted out before I leave home for any period of time. For me and them."

"That's a good attitude, Madeline. How have your dreams been?"

"I haven't had a real episode, but I feel very"—Madeline crossed her legs—"nervous."

"Nervous? How?"

Madeline lowered her eyes. "I just don't feel like it is all over."

Dr. Smalling waited. "I don't think it is. I think we are close to finding the root of your anxiety. Very close."

"I just want it all to be over."

"I understand." Dr. Smalling rubbed Madeline's shoulder. "You seem to be doing well, Madeline." She turned the page of her notebook. "If you don't mind, I would like to sit with your parents for a few minutes.

"Thank you, Dr. Smalling," Madeline said.

Madeline exited Smalling's office. She smiled at her parents and felt the intense look of a woman sitting across the room. Dr. Smalling asked both Raphael and Sophia to join her in her office. The staring women rose and followed them.

"Raphael and Sophia," Dr. Smalling said, turning to the diminutive stranger, "I'd like you to meet Dr. Morgan Kim. She is a DNA expert from Johns Hopkins University." Raphael's hand engulfed Dr. Kim's. "I asked Dr. Kim to join to go over some interesting results that we stumbled upon." Dr. Smalling told everyone to sit. "Since we met Madeline early in the year, we have run multiple blood panels. These panels have been utilized in an effort to help Madeline and seek to diagnose a medical condition that might reveal the nature of her condition. We have looked for drugs and cancer, done standard biochemical analysis, and searched specifically for small tumors in her brain with MRIs, and all this has revealed little. We have checked her urine and lipids, and physically, Madeline is a very, very healthy young woman." Dr. Smalling removed her glasses and set them on her desk, wiping the sweat from her brow. "I would like to ask both of you to submit a sample of blood for a DNA test."

The blood drained from Raphael's and Sophia's faces. "Why?" they responded in unison.

Dr. Smalling glanced at Dr. Kim. "Somewhere along the way, one of the many blood tests was submitted for a DNA test. Those results were returned to Dr. Smalling," Kim informed the Deschampses.

"I, admittedly, am not a DNA expert, but I found some fascinating dynamics concerning Madeline's results. I called Dr. Kim in for a consult."

"You just said she was very healthy. What do you want from my daughter now?" Sophia protested.

"But she's not your daughter, is she, Mrs. Deschamps?" Dr. Kim had observed the genetic markers immediately.

Raphael and Sophia sat, stunned. Sophia broke the uncomfortable silence. "No. Madeline is adopted."

Raphael chimed in, "I don't understand what this had to do with our DNA or Madeline's."

"We wanted to sample your DNA and try to find similarities with Madeline's. Hers is very unique," Dr. Kim informed them.

"Unique in what way?"

"Madeline's DNA is an evolutionary game changer. A complete upgrade in the engineering of how our bodies and brains are structured and perform." Dr. Kim handed them the charts.

"An upgrade, like, with a computer?" Sophia mocked.

"In a way," Kim retorted.

"This means nothing to me. Madeline is just a girl. And yes, she is adopted, but it's not like we found her in some type of spaceship." Raphael handed the chart back to Dr. Kim.

"Who are the parents?" Kim pursued.

"We don't know. We had worked with the adoption agency for a year or two. Raphael and I had been married for about ten years, and we couldn't seem to get pregnant. The doctors put me on fertility medicines, but no one could figure out which one of us was the issue. We were working a lot, but I—we both," Sophia said, looking at Raphael, "wanted a child. We were very specific in the type of child we sought, given that we are an interracial couple. We wanted a child we felt the public would consider to be our own. The world is cruel enough concerning race. Madeline was going to have to answer questions about her father being black and her mother being white. We didn't want her to have to deal with questions about adoption. We wanted the child to be loved." Tears filled Sophia's eyes.

"I'm sure you have been terrific parents. I ask because I want to follow the bloodline."

"Madeline came to us through tragedy. Her parents were killed in a traffic accident. They were following a logging truck up a steep incline, and the logs broke free from the ties and slammed though the front of the windshield. The father died instantly, but the mother remained alive, with Madeline inside of her. Ambulances arrived, and they removed the mother from the car. She was barely alive. The EMTs performed an emergency Cesarean section and saved the child. That child is Madeline."

The room was silent as they digested the chilling story. "What do you mean that Madeline's DNA is an evolutionary game changer?" Sophia asked Dr. Kim.

"Every living organism is constructed by DNA. In these molecules are encoded the instructions for how we are to function and develop. Small evolutionary steps often take millions of years. For example, the difference between a human's DNA and a monkey's DNA is less than five percent. We know that we share similarities with our primate ancestors, but a shift in DNA allowed monkeys to evolve into humans."

"So why is Madeline's so much different?" Raphael continued.

"I just used the example that a monkey's DNA is roughly ninety-five percent like a human's. Yet that five percent is enough for there to be light-years between a living thing being a monkey or a human. A regular human DNA sample is roughly ninety-six percent of what Madeline's is. It is a scientific miracle." Kim remained astounded at the charts.

"Madeline doesn't have any superpowers. She is a good student, but she's no Einstein. I don't see her as being any worse or any better than the other kids her age." Sophia was skeptical.

"This is the first time we have seen anything like this. We do not know how it will manifest itself. May I ask you a question?" Kim moved closer to the Deschampses.

"Sure."

"How often has Madeline been sick growing up?" Kim surveyed.

"I don't know. Not often."

"Dr. Smalling and I did some research. Until this year, and the subsequent events of your daughter's MPD, Madeline had never missed a day of school."

"So? Others were honored for that at her graduation."

"Sophia, her genetic makeup is so secure that I doubt she will ever be sick a day in her life. Her immune system is a fortress. From her DNA we would see disease become a thing of the past. Humanity would become smarter, using more of its brain capacity, as well as healthier and, I believe, more keenly cognizant of other people and the environment in which they live. This increased awareness creates a freedom and understandng, providing answers to the fears instilled in our being. With this lack of fear, humanity can release those bonds. Madeline is the beginning of this transformation."

Raphael and Sophia held each other's hands tightly. "How is this possible, Dr. Kim?"

"Frankly, I don't know, Mr. and Mrs. Deschamps. I really have no idea. That's one of the reasons I was curious to find the biological parents. They may have been able to help map the DNA history of Madeline."

"Are there any other people that have a similar type of DNA? Like Madeline's?"

"Not that we are aware of. The science of DNA has come so far in the last generation. Mostly, that research has been focused on unlocking the mysteries of DNA and learning about how humans can benefit from the opened codes of the molecules and atoms. Scientists and doctors from around the world have been researching to find what Madeline has naturally. An evolving, almost perfect

DNA structure." Dr. Kim showed them a variety of color-coded and highlighted double helices and DNA origami, only confusing the Deschampses more.

"This is very hard to believe." Sophia put down the photographs and highlights. "It's all so scientific, and you have given me zero reason as to why Madeline should be so different."

"Let's put science aside. There are some things in the universe that, no matter how hard scientists and philosophers try to explain them, may simply not be explainable. Some of them have to be honored through faith. There are still questions unanswered by the world's elite about how the earth was even created. What amount of cosmic luck provided all the chemical elements in the middle of a solar system to even sustain life? And when I talk about 'life,' I am talking about algae. With time comes evolution. Twenty million years ago a new species emerged. It was called Hominidae and was a branch of the species from which the gibbons evolved. Six million years later orangutans became a part of a new species that walked mainly on two feet. Jump ahead in time," Dr. Kim said, grinning. "Eight million years after the orangutan came the chimpanzee. And four million years later the branch for *Homo sapiens* evolved."

"Thanks for the history lesson, Doctor, but what does this have to do with Madeline?" Sophia crossed her legs, miffed at the scientific jargon.

"That's exactly where we are heading, Mrs. Deschamps. Around two and a half million years ago, the brains of these earliest humans were about the size of chimpanzees', but there is a gene called SRGAP2 that plays a vital role in synaptic development. This is a gene not found in other animals. That gene perpetuates more rapid mapping in the frontal cortex, and over the next million years, the cranial cavity began to encephalize, or grow. We have been able to prove that each new generation of humans from that point used up to one hundred twenty-five thousand more neurons in their brains than their parents. Something miraculous happened two and a half million years ago, but we have never been able to watch or observe this quantum leap firsthand. That has changed with Madeline."

"Kids are always supposed to be smarter than their parents. You just mentioned that one hundred twenty-five thousand neurons more were used with each generation," Raphael conjectured.

"I did. If I were to compare Madeline's differential with that of the average kid her age and you, her parents, the mathematical improvement would be the equivalent of three million years."

The Deschampses sat, flabbergasted. Sophia shifted in her seat and raised an uneasy thought. "Dr. Kim. You mentioned that the last time scientists believe there was some 'miraculous' event was two and a half million years ago. Why did you use the word 'miraculous'?"

Dr. Kim hesitated. "As a scientist, I am not supposed to believe in coincidence. Only fact. Facts that can be fit into a justifiable theory. But I am a human also. And what happened two and a half million years ago makes no scientific sense. There was no way anyone could see that significant of an evolutionary advancement just occurring. I believe there are mysteries to this world that cannot be explained. That we are left enough bread crumbs to solve the mysteries we are supposed to solve and for others we have to have faith in the universe."

"And Madeline's mystery? Where in evolutionary science or faith in the universe does she fall, Dr. Kim?"

"As a scientist, I believe Madeline's DNA opens up a galaxy of doors in our attempt to understand humanity. As a human and a believer, I consulted several theologians at Catholic University and Cardinal O'Shaughnessy himself. They feel Madeline has a spiritual and chemical bond that could bear to the world an angel. A pure love. A love without fear. A child who bears no original sin. A soul who all humankind can love and who can cleanse the world of hatred. During Madeline's sessions under hypnosis, two personalities' subconsciouses and Madeline herself indicated there was someone in the world destined to harm her."

"Do you think there is a connection, Dr. Kim?" Sophia asked.

"I did read the files. Madeline carries something extraordinary inside her. Humankind fears change, and Madeline will change the world and what we know. There are those who would find Madeline to be very dangerous. It is my feeling that Madeline, or the lives that exist inside her, have been here before and that the danger is very real. Whether that enemy is humanity or a demon that has been vomited back to earth, Madeline's life is in danger."

AUGUST 28
ATLANTA, GEORGIA

Evelyn Cahill shuffled through the historic Fulton County Courthouse. Her hair was pulled back, and she'd squeezed on a pair of jeans and rummaged through the closet to find a semi-ironed blouse. It was as good as she was going to do. Victor had told her she would probably be there only a day, listening to a case for possession. "Ma'am, where do I go for jury duty?" Evelyn asked a woman in uniform. The woman instructed her to take a right at the end of the corridor and then enter the first room on the right. Evelyn thanked the woman and found a spot among the citizens of Atlanta.

Evelyn was called into the courtroom, where she and the others were sworn in by the bailiff.

Judge Charlotte Wilshire addressed the panel. "Thank you all for fulfilling your civic duty. You are part of what we call a venire, or a panel of potential jurors. I am going to poll the panel for anyone who may not be able to serve for hardship." Wilshire noted the blank faces. "Let's first verify that everyone is eighteen years old and an American citizen." Two members of the panel discussed their immigration status nervously with a member of the court and disappeared through a side door.

District Attorney Leo Gargano and Defense Attorney Eva Jo Diamond studied the panel carefully, observing body language and analyzing the personal responses and voice inflections.

"Is anyone a student who has exams?" None of them raised their hands. "Probably not, as school just started. Does anyone have a surgery scheduled in the next, say, two weeks?" A pair of elderly members raised their hands and spoke to a representative. "Does anyone have to care for small children or a member of the family in a full-time capacity?" Several took this opportunity to find their way off the panel. Evelyn hadn't heard a category into which she fell.

The judge asked if any member had been involved in a sexual assault or had a family member involved in a homicide. Evelyn answered no, but her heart sank. A murder? A sexual assault? She didn't need to be on a long trial. "Have you ever been associated with a racist group or organization?" Evelyn answered no, but it weighed heavily in her heart, knowing her father had strong feelings about the coloreds.

"Move to strike juror nine," Eva Jo petitioned the judge. Evelyn was curious why the black guy in the nice suit was dismissed.

"Move to strike juror fourteen," said Gargano. The elderly white lady grabbed her cane and exited.

"Move to strike juror sixty-two," Diamond whispered across the table to her assistant. The young black female was excused. Evelyn wondered why she wasn't sent home. She was young and female.

A few hours passed. After two dozen jurors were sent home for bias and implied bias and after the attorneys made preemptory challenges and arguments against the suggestions made, the panel was whittled down to twelve jurors and two alternates. Evelyn Cahill, juror number eighty-one, was asked to report to jury duty on Tuesday, September 2.

AUGUST 31
LAS VEGAS, NEVADA

Nigel tied the knot around his arm just above the elbow. His vein bulged, and Shay stuck the needle into the vein and plunged the syringe. He allowed her to snort a bit but wouldn't shoot her up. The needles left marks, and the johns didn't want to pay for a junkie. Shay chased the smack with warm gin.

"Get dressed. We have a client at the Mirage in thirty minutes." Nigel straightened his hair and pulled down the long sleeves of his shirt on this hundred-degree night.

"Not tonight, Nigel." Shay lay back on the floor. "I don't want to go."

"You have to go. It's your job. Now get up, you lazy bitch."

"Fuck you. I work every night of the week having sex with these losers. Give me a break."

"Then where do you think we are going to get the money for all the drugs you snort? You cost me hundreds of dollars a day. You're a freaking fiend. Now get off your ass and get dressed."

"No!"

Nigel grabbed the broom and wailed away at Shay's naked ass, careful not to spoil her fabulous young face. Shay screamed and ran through the kitchen, but Nigel whacked away. Shay tripped and fell to the ground, and Nigel pounced on top of her. "I will put you right back on the street, and you can turn twenty-five-dollar tricks twenty times a day sucking dicks in cars and in alleys."

"I'll go! I'll go!" Shay pleaded.

Nigel removed himself from her chest. Shay rolled over, beaten and bruised, and tried to put on something sexy. They had to go to the Mirage.

Shay dried her eyes in the front seat, just before the Mirage valet whisked the car away. The heroin's effect subsided, and she needed a drink to mellow her out. Nigel escorted her to the elevators en route to a room on the eighth floor.

"Do this trick, and I'll let you have the rest of the night off. I'll try to get $1,000 for three hours, but you have to know that there are multiple clients."

"How many is 'multiple'?" Shay didn't like having to do four or five guys in a row.

"I think there are four." Nigel knocked on the door.

Shay froze as the door swung open. Her father rushed toward her as the Las Vegas Police took Nigel Baines into custody.

"I am going to take you home, baby. I am taking you home."

SEPTEMBER 2
ATLANTA, GEORGIA

Evelyn came home frantic and found Victor making dinner and enjoying some wine. "I am so happy to be home. That place is a zoo. There are news trucks everywhere. They had to sneak the jurors out the back door, and now they are going to put us up in a hotel for the rest of the trial. Oh, Victor. I don't want to do this anymore. I want to be with you."

"My word. It's only been one day, Evelyn." Lyle laughed under his breath. Sequestered! What a bonus! "I can't believe they are going to make you stay in a hotel."

"I am in shock. I got the Horace Ford case. I won't see you until the trial is over. This is our last night together for a while." Evelyn pulled the tab on a can of Miller Lite and downed the malty beverage in two gulps.

"Horace Ford? Who is he?" Lyle feigned ignorance.

"I forget sometimes that you're not from Atlanta. He's a white guy who killed this black girl last year around this time."

"You can't think that way as a juror, Evelyn." Lyle brought her a fried pork chop and homemade macaroni and cheese.

"Think what way?" Evelyn picked up the chop and ate the edges without utensils.

"When you sat down, you said that Horace Ford killed some black girl. You can't assume he is guilty. That is why there is a trial."

"Victor. You should see what he did to that girl." Evelyn talked to him with her mouth full.

"Allegedly." Lyle put his arm around her flabby neck.

"He chopped her up after torturing her, Victor." Evelyn switched the news to the Home and Garden channel, where the host was chatting up the viewers on the best way to camouflage a garden hose.

"Allegedly." Lyle poked into her fat and made Evelyn giggle. "You have to hear both sides of the story. He may be innocent, you know."

"I don't know. He's an awfully creepy-looking dude."

"You can't judge a book by its cover. Besides, it's going to be impossible for him to get a fair trial."

"Why's that?" Evelyn took exception.

"Not because of you but because of the political pressure. After everything that happened in Ferguson, how do you think a white guy is going to fare in the murder trial of a black woman? The streets went bananas. Riots and tear gas and tanks. The system will do anything to avoid that again. This poor guy is a sacrificial lamb. I just think you have to hear the evidence."

Evelyn conceded. "You have a point. I will listen to the evidence. I sure don't want to send an innocent man to jail."

"You will have to vote with your heart, Evelyn." Lyle went to the kitchen and got her a spoon so she didn't shovel the mac and cheese into her mouth with her fingers. Lyle came back to the room and presented Evelyn with a small box, soft and plush on the outside.

Evelyn started to tremble. "It will give you something to think about besides Horace Ford's innocence."

Evelyn opened the box and removed the marquise-shaped diamond set in a thick gold band. "It is for the most amazing woman I have ever known. Will you marry me?"

"Oh! Victor! I will. I will."

SEPTEMBER 8
THE MEDITERRANEAN SEA

S adie Davil stood at the bow and let the warm late-summer wind drift through her hair. The *Cathartidae Silentium* had made ten knots for three weeks and steamed through the Strait of Gibraltar into the Alboran Sea, passing Tangier to the south. The keel split the waves of the Mediterranean. Through the night the captain would correct his course and steer south toward the island of Malta. The journey would take the chemical-supply ship north of the coast of Libya. Davil could not help but ruminate on Muammar Qaddafi and the excellent work he had done for the legion.

Sadie's moment of silence was interrupted by one of her team. "Why do you disturb me?"

"Another of the captives has perished. What should I do?"

"The same as the others. Throw them overboard for the sharks."

The henchmen dragged the emaciated remains of a young man and plopped them over the side to be churned by the screw or picked at by the crabs.

A tremendous bellow from the ship's horn shattered the night. All lights on the vessel went dark. The crew scrambled across the deck and took defensive positions around the vessel, arming themselves with assault rifles and submachine guns. Three airborne lights from the port were on course to intercept the *Cathartidae Silentium*. Davil moved below and armed herself with a German Heckler & Koch G41 assault rifle and two clips. She watched from the door as the beams drew closer.

Three CH-53E Super Stallion helicopters from the USS *San Antonio* transport circled the *Cathartidae Silentium*. One chopper freed a series of bright red flares that illuminated the sky.

"There," the officer said, spotting the flares. The captain of the destroyer USS *Stout* adjusted his course five degrees south-southeast at twenty-five knots.

"*Stout*, we are taking fire." The pilot of the Super Stallion plunged the helicopter to the ocean surface.

"Stallion, you are clear to return fire." The pilot brought the chopper to bow level and pointed the stern toward the ship. The rear gunner blasted the white-hot spotlight on the port side of the ship with his GAU-21 ramp-mounted machine gun. The other two Stallions followed suit and sprayed the stern of the *Silentium*, killing five on board.

Stallion one circled the bow, raining bullets from the window-mounted machine guns, clearing the deck.

"Stallion two, you are free to board." Stallion one gave the green light but kept a watchful eye, as did Stallion three astern. Stallion two hovered over the stern, and ropes dropped to the deck among the dead. Fourteen specially trained visit, board, search, and seizure team members rappelled and fast roped to the deck armed with MK18s or Mossberg 500 shotguns and Beretta M9 pistols. The team received fire from the upper deck area, forcing them to take cover. The team split up with five taking the port and five stalking starboard, night vision employed. Four stayed to hold the stern and establish communications with the *Stout*. The Stallions hovered over the ship and provided supplementary coverage.

The starboard team encroached slowly. A door swung open, and the team took fire. Bullets slashed past their heads, ricocheting off the metal. Navy specialist Sergio Lens rose from his crouched position and filled the combatant's center mass with a round from his Mossberg 500, blasting a baseball-size hole in his chest. The firefight engulfed the deck of the ship, but the crew was overmatched. The navy teams stepped carefully over the dead bodies. Lens threw a fragmentation grenade into the hatch. The explosion neutralized the doorway, and the starboard team entered and worked upward toward the bridge.

The VSBB team cautiously checked each corner, moving with prudence. Lens shifted to the opposite wall. The enemy rushed toward him. It was a sudden ambush. Lens drew his combat knife. Lens let the assailant into his body and slid around him, drawing the knife across his neck, causing blood to pour from the carotid artery. It spewed against the walls as the soldiers proceeded in their climb to the top of the craft.

A wave of relief arrived as they rendezvoused with the port squad. Lens confirmed his location with the stern. The bridge was oddly quiet. Lens positioned the nine other soldiers, ready to breach. He kicked open the door and rolled in a flash bang. The explosion stunned the room. Lens and crew rushed through the door. Four members of the bridge cowered with hands raised. The captain of the *Cathartidae Silentium* lay slumped over the helm, a victim of his own gun and greed.

Lens spotted the USS *Stout*. It was closing fast.

"We are the US Navy. We are boarding your ship to search for chemical weapons. Who speaks English?" Lens implored his new hostages.

"I speak English."

"I want you to stop the ship." The man staggered to his feet, still feeling the effects of the flash grenade. He leaned over the console, and the ship began to slow.

"Get on the intercom and tell everyone to drop their weapons." The man followed the instructions. Lens waved for the port crew to search the rest of the ship.

"Where are the chemical weapons?"

"I do not know about chemical weapons." The man returned to his knees.

Lens was amped up and wanted to slam the man with the butt of his rifle. He turned to his compatriot. "Handcuff the crew and assemble them on the deck. I want them facedown until we can debrief them on the *Stout*."

The seas were calm, and the *Stout* drew parallel with the *Cathartidae Silentium* flawlessly. A team of chemical weapons specialists boarded the *Silentium* and began inspecting the ship for its venomous cargo. The bow of the ship became a living graveyard of terrorists lying facedown with their hands zip tied behind their backs. The actual dead were tagged and bagged. Sadie Davil spit and kicked at her captors like a cougar being hauled to the zoo. The seamen threw her to the ground and violently wrestled her arms behind her back. Sadie moaned in excitement.

Lens triple-checked the lower levels of the ship, opening each door and securing each room. He yearned to shed some gear as the heat was stifling. Lens figured he was near the bow of the ship and its tremendous hull. He opened the door and stood aghast. "*Stout*, this is Lens. Send every available crew member to my location. We have human cargo."

The *Stout* set up an emergency medical tent on the stern of the ship and utilized every available space that could be mustered to aid the hostages of the *Cathartidae Silentium*. One by one they left the reek of the bow. Some could barely walk. Others suffered from dysentery. All were gaunt and pale. The spirit of life had left their seemingly vacuous eyes.

Celia Nair stepped to the deck and sucked in fresh sea air. The sailor put a blanket around her shoulders, but she removed it promptly, wanting to feel the breeze of freedom.

Ilana Landreau put her arms around the female officer and wouldn't let go. She asked for her mommy.

Sui Sterling answered questions for the doctor, putting on a brave face. She was delirious and drained. Sui was one of the first to receive counseling for her ordeal.

Irina Goldstein clenched the Star of David in her right hand and continued to pray. She was so terrified that she refused to take off the clothes she had on despite being soiled with urine and feces.

Lila Chait walked arm in arm onto the deck with the friend she had made during the horrifying ordeal. Lila had finally learned the girl's name. It was Hope.

SEPTEMBER 9
ATLANTA, GEORGIA

Late in the afternoon Lyle received the news from Rohit Guzan of the failed voyage of the *Cathartidae Silentium*. His blood boiled, and his eyes bulged from his head. He punched the walls and smashed the mirror into the bedpost, shards of glass littering the floor. His breath seethed from his lungs being on fire, his veins pumped to the surface of his skin, and the bile excreted out of his mouth and onto the floor.

A tiny rap on the door ceased Lyle's transformation. He breathed deeply, retracting the deadly tentacles, his mandible folding back into his human jaws. He stepped to the doorway and peered through the peephole. Lyle opened the door. The ancient hillbilly woman from 3B stood in the doorway, a measuring cup in her hand, her frail eyes straining to survey the destroyed apartment. "What can I do for you, ma'am?"

"I was hoping to borrow a cup of sugar. Is Evelyn here?" She pushed the plastic cup into Lyle's chest. "What is the matter with your eyes?" The blood coursed through Lyle's swelling red eyes, not yet retreated into their sockets.

"I am sorry. She is not. Come with me, and I will get the sugar." Lyle closed the door behind the woman and moved to the kitchen. He moved into the kitchenette as the frail woman observed the destruction. "Here you go, ma'am."

"I heard an awful racket coming from down here. Is everything OK?" The senior tried to ease her way past Lyle and the door.

"Everything is fine, ma'am. I received some bad news today from overseas. My close friend was involved in a boating accident near Greece." Lyle stared solemnly at the linoleum. "I guess I let my anger get the better of me."

The woman reached out to Lyle and put her arms around him, her cloud-white hair fine on his shirt. "I am so sorry to hear such news. I hope he or she will be OK. God be with you." The octogenarian hobbled slowly back to the door. Lyle wrapped his hands around her temples and twisted, the sugar bowl shattering on the floor. *Something else to clean up,* Lyle thought to himself as he folded the dead woman in half and stuffed her onto the top shelf of Evelyn's closet.

SEPTEMBER 11
ATLANTA GEORGIA

Lyle woke and celebrated that the pig was gone. He turned on the cable and found the History Channel, Discovery, and National Geographic. They were all running documentaries about 9/11, a national holiday for Seaman Brandon Lyle. He prayed to his master as video of American Airlines flight 11 slammed into the north tower of the World Trade Center.

He praised bin Laden, knowing that he sat on the altar in hell with Stalin, Hitler, Amin, Mao, and Pol Pot. He watched the towers smolder and the ants running in fear. He blessed the soldier Mohamed Atta, the assassin guiding the airborne missile and its occupants into the heart of humanity.

He remembered the world stopping around him, faces glued to the television. The tears that consumed the people around him in school that day and the constraint he had to muster not to cheer as the towers collapsed upon themselves, driving thousands into the rumble. The joy he felt in the subsequent days upon learning that his mentors had started a war.

Outside, police questioned residents of the apartment building about the disappearance of Deborah Soudani, the eighty-year-old woman. Lyle knew that if they ever did find her, they wouldn't find much.

THE MADELINE SESSIONS:
SEPTEMBER 1
ARLINGTON, VIRGINIA

Diego relaxed Madeline into a malleable state. The unmistakable aura of Wanikiya emerged. Sophia and Raphael observed with Dr. Smalling, Dr. Osaka, Salome, and the ubiquitous Father Salvatore Moutinho, an unexpected blessing in Madeline's saga.

Wanikiya asked for Samuel, a request Dr. Osaka could not fulfill. He encouraged Wanikiya to tell more of the tale of her love of Samuel and their child.

The sun moved in the sky, and the days began to shrink. The village had worked together over the summer and gathered many supplies. The medicine man called for a fierce winter, and we would be moving along the path of the buffalo soon. On this morning, the day Samuel and I were to be wed, the sun came over the plains in gilded rays of gold and lavender. I could feel the warmth on my face and the life in my belly. There was no sleep the previous evening—only the dream of what my and Samuel's future held in store.

Laughing Maid and the women from the village had spent weeks fashioning small gifts for the ceremony and clothes for the wedding. Harriet brought me into the tent and presented me with a new pair of moccasins she had crafted herself. It was apparent that the women had worked in harmony. Talutah brought many colored feathers for my hair, and Star whittled bracelets made from buffalo bone. Industrious and Laughing Maid had beaded and sown a magnificent dress of deer hide for me to wear. The white blossomed with the blue and orange beads that created the village and Bear Mountain, the place of my vision quest. On this special day I would be the envy of the village.

Samuel was presented a vest from the youth of the village made of sinew, beads, tanned hide, and threads. It bore the cross of his religion on the chest and the image of the buffalo, representing the union of our cultures. Singing Voice gifted us both with a count, painted on tanned hide, that detailed the year that Samuel and his family became one with the Lakota. I floated through the morning, blessed to share such a family, and on this day all would celebrate and cross a bold bridge uniting the Lakota with the white man.

The village shared our smiles on this special day. Even on this occasion, Samuel attended to the horses. He shared with me later that many of his thoughts were of his daddy, who was gone. Angus was out hunting in the mountains. Harriet and the women sang songs and laughed while preparing food for the night's celebration. Even Big John, who had been drinking since the river had taken Emmy Lou, came out of his tent and tuned his instruments, having prepared a special song for the wedding.

As the sun perched over our heads, the warriors rode into the village. On this, my blessed day, they would ride north and west to gather with Sitting Bull and Crazy Horse. The reconfigured

Seventh Cavalry, having been bludgeoned at Little Bighorn, had been reinforced with the Fifth Infantry and was moving east into the Black Hills. Lakota scouts reported that the US Army had assembled almost four thousand troops at Fort Abraham Lincoln, determined to execute the Manifest Destiny of the white settlers migrating through Indian Territory and settling the Pacific Northwest. We bid farewell to Chayton, Shadow, and the rest the braves, their spears sharpened and bows taut, fierce in defense of our right to live free.

I took a moment in the early afternoon to hike along the rising shores of the river. I had no specific destination, but my path lured me to the place where Emmy Lou had left us on that misty day. I recalled the blood of her womb on her skirt and the sorrow on her face, knowing that she would not extend life. The loss of hope. I prayed that she had found a place to be free. I kneeled on the cliff and watched as the currents sped past the rocks, her body floating and bobbing in the ripple. I prayed that Big John would find the courage to escape his loss and fear. I shared Samuel's memory of his father and the good deed he had done for the Lakota. I thought of the first time I saw his face, proud and full of conviction, and then of his presence, frail and human, the day before he passed. It was the face of many I had witnessed in my short life. The understanding that life itself was but a chapter and, while the body weakened, the soul and memory of your earthly deeds lived on, carrying your name.

I prayed for Angus—his love for wide-open spaces and his innate ability to hunt and provide. His skin was white, but his heart had always been Lakota. I prayed for Harriet and her strength. I thanked Wakan Tankan for giving her the wisdom to stay with the village and, selfishly, for encouraging her to allow Samuel to stay with me. For if it was a bridge we crossed with the Lakota and the white man, Harriet was the first to cross, sharing with the women the ways of the East and accepting in her heart our ways and vision.

Mostly, I prayed for Samuel and the kindness of his soul. He was no warrior and his heart did not bleed with anger, but his passion for all things beautiful touched me deep inside. His search for knowledge, truth, and freedom inspired the true essence of humanity. I dreamed of the day when our ship would arrive on the shores of China, and I would place my hand on the Great Wall. I dreamed of stepping into the temples of Japan and walking in bare feet in the Ganges River as the waters scurry to the Bay of Bengal. Of walking in the villages of Africa in the shadows of Mount Kilimanjaro, offering our hands in friendship and peace. For it was Samuel Knapp who would take me to the world. And in the world I would forge the love of all people for people.

My thoughts had taken me too many places and fostered many dreams. I heard the diminutive voice of Singing Bird calling for me in the distance. I hurried to find her, and she led me back to the village and to the tepee, where the women prepared me for my marriage.

As I emerged from the tent, the air was still. I looked to the east, and the moon was full and red. The medicine man called it the "blood moon," a premonition that the warriors would find the battle they sought.

I turned to the west. The skies above the mountains grew dark with rain. Our celebrations would have to be inside, but my heart stayed exhilarated.

Samuel came from the tent, his curly, long, brown hair still straight from a bath in the pond. He wore the gift of the vest proudly over his English shirt and donned a new pair of moccasins gifted to him from tribal elder Appanoose. His curious eyes flickered in the dwindling sunlight, the blue folding into green, yellow, brown, and orange. I felt his love. I could stare into those eyes for eternity.

Big John stood by him, his left arm around Samuel's shoulders, his right arm holding his guitar. He was proud and red from the whiskey. Harriet wore the dress of the Lakota, her eyes radiant and her hair pulled back and pinned with the feather of an eagle. The children danced in a circle to the delight of the pounding drums, as all gathered on the edge of the village. We stood at the opposite end of the forest, and four young braves stood in the place of the warriors who had left for battle. They extended the corners of the great blanket, each holding a corner in one hand and a spear in the other. Samuel and I walked under the blanket and stepped through the village to the forest. The medicine man was colored in festive paint and brightly adorned in feathers. He carried the spiritual ash wand, shaking it as we went, proclaiming to all who were witness that we had become one in marriage.

Samuel kissed me in front of the village, a custom the Lakota were not prepared for. Gasps came from the women and giggles from the children. The faux paus was quickly forgotten, and the celebration began in earnest. The blood moon rose high in the sky, its sanguine color seeping and the dark clouds of rain shadowing its edges.

Samuel and I stood together and received the well wishes of the entire village. One by one they adorned us with gifts they had created in honor of our love. Laughing Maid proudly escorted us to our new tepee, the flap open for all to enter. Laughing Maid reminded me of my duty to invite the village in so all could see. Singing Voice winked and said she might stay the night as the tepee was so new and clean. I explained that wasn't going to happen, and we giggled knowing what would.

A group of children ran from the river, shouting. At first we thought they might have seen a bear or a ram. Out of breath, the youth described to his mother a white boat coming up the river. It had a big red beacon, a US flag, and a man on the rail. Samuel whispered to me that he "didn't think they were there to deliver the mail" and ran to find Big John. The boys reported that it had a gun on the side of the craft.

We never saw the army in the shadows of the forest. The lightning began to splinter from the heavens, sharp and wicked. The air became dank, and the skies became the color of pitch. The rain whistled cold and hard into our faces as the men on their horses thundered into the village, raising their pistols and rifles into the air. The village ran for cover and the few weapons that remained in the tepee's. The warriors were gone, leaving mostly women, children, and elderly. The soldier on the horse lit the torch and headed into the heart of the village, igniting the tents, dense black smoke beaten back to earth by the wind and the rain. The soldiers moved in, shooting everyone in their path. The glistening saber of an officer rose high above his head and slashed Star to the ground, slicing her chest, while her infant, My Heart, rolled out of his blanket to the ground and under the hooves of the charging cavalry. Industrious, hoary and slow, was gunned down coming out of her smoldering tent. Hair Storm was roped and dragged to her death by the stampeding army.

One by one I saw my family and my village pillaged. Butterfly was the victim of a rifle butt to the head. Lootah, trying to loose an arrow, took a bullet to the stomach. Walks as She Thinks, old and frail, was knifed across the neck. Every time I turned to help, another of my people called. I searched for Samuel in the driving rain, but I found the deadly, pale blue eyes of Hestovatohkeo'o, the murderous Double Face, spotting me in the forest and haunting me in my dreams. The eyes that defiled me in the daylight of the forest filled with the excitement of death. He pulled the long blade from his waist and charged toward me. Samuel stood behind him in the grass, his father's rifle in his unsteady hands. Hestovatohkeo'o's knife reached around my neck, his scraggly beard scratching my cheek. I could feel his heart beating as his malevolent laugh mocked Samuel. He spit at Samuel, daring him to shoot, but Samuel could not take the shot as he shielded himself with my body.

Hestovatohkeo'o reached down and sliced the back of my heel, and I collapsed to the ground in agony. He charged as Samuel let loose a volley that missed high. He struggled to reload his rifle, and Hestovatohkeo'o filled Samuel's chest, unsheltered from the powder blast and the demon that pulled the trigger. He stood over Samuel, who tried desperately to reload. He whispered something to him as he knelt over his bleeding body. He put his finger on Samuel chest, driving the bullet deep into his heart. I tried to crawl to my husband. I heard Samuel's weak voice. Blood gurgled from his mouth. He cried to me, "Remember me, my love. I know I will miss you."

In the fray, Hestovatohkeo'o put me on the back of his horse. I wept as my village burned. They had killed us in our tepees and cut our women down. They had killed our babies and left others lying on the ground. Big John was too drunk to leave his burning tent. The last I saw of my village was Harriet crawling on her knees to her son, Samuel, and then, rising to defend him, being slain by the sword of an army lieutenant.

The heart of the forest was murky. I tried to kick, but my leg would not respond. I screamed into the night, but my calls went unanswered. Hestovatohkeo'o rode me into the Black Hills, the sacred ground of the Lakota, and charged to the height of the craggy rocks, a little closer to the clouds, on top of the world for his damaged master to see.

He laid me down and boasted of his victory, singing, prancing, and praying to his destructive lord. The rain had subsided, and he placed himself on top of me. He licked my face and spoke of demons into my ear. I felt the pain at first, but soon I became cold. I fought for the soul of my unborn child but lay paralyzed as he tore into my flesh and womb, shredding me like the wolf slays the sheep. My legs would not move, and my blood flowed freely in a stream over the edges of the rocks, cascading deep into the ravines of the Black Hills. Hestovatohkeo'o stood over me, gloating, the blood of my child dripping from the corners of his mouth. He left me there to rot, and I listened to the footsteps of the horse clatter away. The last thing I remember was trying to crawl—edge back to my village—but I could not move. I could only feel sorrow, for the loss of my Samuel and our child. The loss of the people I loved in the village. And then I felt the buzzards pecking at my body, nourishing themselves on my flesh.

Madeline laid her head back and closed her eyes as the blood poured from her nose and the corners of her eyes. Sophia screamed frantically as Dr. Smalling and Dr. Osaka attended to the exhausted child.

SEPTEMBER 16
ATLANTA, GEORGIA

BUSQUETS TESTIFIES

The Atlanta Journal-Constitution—Bayleigh Debuchy

At the Fulton County Courthouse today, testimony continued for the murder of Savannah Gabriel from prosecution
witnesses under questioning by District Attorney Leo Gargano.
Defendant Horace Ford sat quietly next to Defense Attorney Eva Jo
Diamond, wearing a brown suit and tie with a white shirt. At times
it appeared that Ford closed his eyes to take a nap during the testimony of Detective Lake Busquets.

Gargano led the witness through the process of collecting the
blood evidence against Mr. Ford, only to have Defense Attorney
Diamond discredit Busquets and the forensics team for failing to
follow procedure in handling and storing the samples. Busquets
confirmed that key DNA samples found in the back of Ford's 2006
Chevy Silverado could not identify Savannah Gabriel conclusively

but were "almost certainly" her blood. Diamond pounced on Busquets, reminding her and the jury that Mr. Ford "wasn't going to die by lethal injection" because the police and RTLIT CELL laboratories were "almost certain." Experts for both the defense and the prosecution confirmed that many of the key samples had been degraded and could not be definitively linked to Mr. Ford.

While the evidence against Mr. Ford mounts, Diamond was successfully able to refute additional testimony by experts about fingerprints, fiber samples, and hair and saliva remnants.

Diamond hammered away at Busquets, at one point asking Judge Charlotte Wilshire that several documents of the prosecution be ruled inadmissible because Busquets had testified, "We misfiled them but eventually found the missing document." The judge ruled that the misfiling of the documents was a "simple clerical error" and allowed the documents to remain in evidence, but clearly, the mood of the prosecution dimmed as the jury shifted uncomfortably in their seats.

Diamond's cross examination continued into the afternoon session and was able to get Busquets to admit that several documents and physical samples had been "misplaced" during processing, including several blood swatches that had been recovered from "under the seat of the analysts car," opening the door for Diamond to introduce police impropriety. Diamond was able to link Busquets to several derogatory statements about Mr. Ford and his prior conviction in the rape of Breanna Green and her desire to "get that son of a bitch."

Both Gargano and Diamond chose not to speak to the press after the day's testimony.

SEPTEMBER 17
ATLANTA, GEORGIA

Inside the courtroom, Judge Charlotte Wilshire listened carefully to the testimony of Fulton County coroner Igor Lambert. Lambert's testimony was accompanied by grizzly photographs of the dismemberment of Ms. Gabriel.

"Dr. Lambert, was the coroner's office able to determine how Savannah Gabriel died?" Gargano trained his gaze on the jury box.

"Savannah was tortured to death." Lambert heard the gasps of the jury.

"Objection," Diamond said. "Assumes facts in evidence."

"Dr. Lambert, what was the exact cause of death of Savannah Gabriel?" Gargano asked again.

"Ms. Green died as the result of several internal organs failing and shutting down her system."

Gargano trained his eyes on the defendant, Mr. Ford. "What made Ms. Gabriel's organs fail?"

"Ms. Gabriel's entire body was under a tremendous amount of physical stress. She suffered trauma around the eyes and cheeks, consistent with being beaten with fists. There is a dramatic contusion on top of her skull, the result of being struck with a blunt, flat object, consistent with a shovel."

"Were there any injuries to her body?" Gargano asked the forensic pathologist.

"Ms. Gabriel suffered from dozens of small, round, intense burns to her forearms and thighs."

"What do you think created those burns, Dr. Lambert?"

"I confirmed that they were created by a lit cigarette. Tobacco residue remained on the skin around the burns."

"How many of these burns were there, Doctor?"

"One hundred and seventy-two." The gallery groaned. Wilshire rapped her gavel on the bench, imploring the audience to remain quiet and threatening to remove them from the courtroom.

"Was there more evidence of torture?" Gargano pursued.

"Absolutely. Ms. Gabriel's wrists had ligature wounds, consistent with being tied or bound. The scars stretch into the bases of her hands." Lambert raised his right hand to show the jury. "This would indicate that she was bound at both wrists and hung upright."

"Were there other parts of her that suffered wounds?"

"Her back and buttocks had been slashed and torn."

"What do you believe caused those wounds?"

"It is impossible to be exact, but I believe that she was whipped, several times over several days."

"Whipped?"

"Yes. My best guess would be a bullwhip."

"How did you conclude that she was whipped several times over several days?"

"The differential in the healing process of several different sets of wounds."

Gargano paused for effect. "How many slash marks ripped into Savannah's back?"

"Well over three hundred."

"So he used Savannah to practice?"

"Objection." Diamond did not stand.

"Withdrawn." Gargano moved closer to the jury. "Would you agree that it is fair to say that Savannah Gabriel suffered?"

"Greatly."

"Were there any wounds of a sexual nature?"

"Yes. There were wounds to her vagina and anus."

"Describe those wounds for the jury, Dr. Lambert."

"Both the outer walls of the vagina and anus had been ruptured by the presence of a large foreign object."

"Not something human?"

"No. There were traces of an unidentified fluid. When the lab returned the analysis, it indicated the presence of motor oil." Lambert paused. "It is our belief that the victim was sexually assaulted with an oil filter. Similar to the one you would have replaced in your car."

"You mentioned in earlier testimony that Savannah ultimately died of internal organ failure. Is that true?"

"Yes."

"And that the torture had made her very weak. True?"

"Yes. The human body can only withstand so much abuse." Lambert sat passively.

"What ultimately killed Savannah Gabriel?"

"During the autopsy we noticed a distinct rectangular burn on Savannah's stomach and a subsequent entry wound into her abdomen. There were small scratches around this wound."

"How large was the wound?"

Lambert referred to his notes. "Five centimeters below the umbilicus."

"Doctor? I would be grateful, and I am sure the jury would be as well, if you were to speak in layman's terms for this segment of the testimony."

Lambert adjusted his glasses. "Of course." He continued, "Five centimeters below the belly button, there was a hole, approximately seven centimeters in diameter and focused in the middle of the burn perimeter, driving into the abdominal cavity."

Gargano jumped in with his question. "Doctor? What body parts lie in the abdominal cavity?"

"Inside the abdominal cavity, just below the entry wound, lie the small intestine, the bladder, and the appendix."

"Anything else in that vicinity of the body?" Gargano gauged the attention of the jury.

"Everything is interconnected. The large intestine, the stomach, the gallbladder, and the colon."

Gargano walked slowly and stood at the far end of the jury box. "What created this hole in Savannah's stomach, Dr. Lambert?"

"We found a rat buried inside Ms. Green's stomach."

The courtroom buzzed, and Judge Wilshire again sounded her gavel but did not admonish the gallery. Gargano remained still as the jury digested the testimony. Gently, he walked back to the witness-box. "How did a rat get inside Savannah Gabriel?"

"Our theory is based on medieval torture. A metal box is placed over the rat on the victim's stomach. The metal is heated up—say, with a lighter or torch—making the box oppressively hot and forcing the rat to try to escape. In this case, the only way the rat could escape was to burrow into Ms. Gabriel's stomach to seek relief from the heat."

"And what happened once the rat made its way inside of Ms. Gabriel?"

"The rat clawed and chewed its way through the small intestine and punctured the bladder. Subsequent internal bleeding, lack of medical attention, and physical exhaustion eventually killed Savannah Gabriel."

"Where did you find the rat?"

"The rat was found dead between the colon and the spleen."

"How did the rat die, Doctor?"

"The rat died from suffocation." Gargano encouraged Dr. Lambert to finish. "The rat was forced to stay inside of Ms. Gabriel. Someone held the metal box over her stomach, forcing the rat deeper inside of her."

Gargano let the testimony sink deep into the thoughts of the jury. "How did Savannah Gabriel arrive at the coroner's office?" Diamond stood to object. "I'm sorry. Let me rephrase. What was her physical state when you first saw Ms. Gabriel?"

"The first time I saw Ms. Gabriel, she was in a standard police body bag, lying on the examining table. When I opened the bag, it was obvious she had been dismembered."

"How was it so easy to make that observation?" Gargano pitched.

"Because her right arm was in the bottom of the bag."

"Tell the jury the process of analyzing a dismembered body."

For the first time Lambert shifted uncomfortably in the witness stand. "There really is no sensitive way to describe the process." Lambert took a gulp. "It's basically like a jigsaw puzzle. We take all the parts we have and put them where they were supposed to be. From there we start the autopsy."

Everyone felt queasy, but Gargano pushed. "How many different body parts did you have to 'put' back together?"

Lambert reviewed his notes. "Both hands were severed from the wrists. Six fingers were removed from the hands. Two have not been located. Both feet were removed at the ankles. Both legs were removed at the hip joint and both arms disengaged from the shoulder sockets." Lambert closed his folder. "The head was severed at the neck."

"Have you determined what type of," Gargano said, searching for the word, "instrument was used to sever these body parts?"

"A cleaver, or butcher knife."

"What size butcher knife, Dr. Lambert?"

"By the measurements taken, this knife had an eight-inch blade made from high-carbon steel."

"What method did the assailant use to assault the victim?"

"I don't understand the question," Lambert asserted.

"Did he slice into the victim's skin?"

"No. He chopped. He chopped through the skin and the muscle and hacked through the bone."

Gargano felt the tension in the room. He knew he had the jury in his lap. "I am done with the witness, Your Honor."

Eva Jo Diamond stood and approached the coroner. "Dr. Lambert. Did the detectives, sheriffs, police, or any law-enforcement official bring you a cleaver or butcher knife from the crime scene?"

"No."

"Did they bring you a bullwhip or anything comparable that could have caused the wounds to the victim's back?"

"No."

"Was a metal box consistent with the one you describe on the victim's stomach presented to you from the police?" Diamond made eye contact with the jury.

"No."

"I have no more questions for the witness."

Judge Wilshire waited for Gargano to redirect, but he remained in his seat. The jurors sat ashen in their seats after hearing the gruesome testimony of the coroner, Dr. Igor Lambert. All except juror number eighty-one, who made a mental note that while the mutilation of Savannah Gabriel was repugnant, they had not tied defendant Horace Ford to any weapon used in her torture or death.

SEPTEMBER 24
ARLINGTON, VIRGINIA

"In Madeline's past life or lives, she was murdered," Dr. Smalling explained to Sophia and Raphael. "This is consistent with the anxiety and the posttraumatic stress disorder in our original diagnosis. The hypnosis revealed the multiple personalities and that the trauma originated with the murders. In her dreams she sees the face of the man who committed these crimes. I have brought in a sketch artist, and I want Madeline to describe the man in her dreams. It's most likely she has details of the man as remnants of her dreams and the memories of her inner personalities. At the very least, it will be therapeutic, and we can ease Madeline's fear by running the sketch through the database and confirming that this person does not exist in her life currently. That the face in her dreams is just the memory of others and it is the memories that haunt her, not something tangible." Sophia and Raphael agreed. "I would like you to meet Tora Yebda. She works for the Arlington County Police Department."

The artist's sketch pad was almost as large as the woman. Her small stature belied her huge smile, and she made eye contact with Madeline instantly. Tora and Madeline retreated to a small room away from Dr. Smalling's office. Tora removed the number two pencil from her tackle box and flipped the cover page of the sketch pad over the spirals. "I have spoken to Dr. Smalling, and I know that the person we are going to draw scares you. I want you to be strong and try to remember as many details of this person's face as you can. Facing these fears will help you."

Madeline fidgeted in her seat. "Thank you."

"Let's start with the head. There are lots of shapes for a head." Tora pulled out a chart. "Is it an oblong shape? Heart shaped?" Tora moved her finger to each sketched head.

"It looks like this one." She pointed to the picture in the corner of the poster, and she felt her pulse increase.

"OK. A triangle-shaped head." Tora stroked the pencil across the paper, outlining the shape of the head on the rectangular paper. "Now the eyes." And another chart. "Does he have droopy eyes?" Madeline didn't hesitate and pointed at the thin, almond-shaped eyes.

Tora started sketching them in, but Madeline stopped her. "Closer together. And they are blue. Crystal blue. They sparkle with something evil inside them."

Tora clenched her cheeks as Madeline weakened with each dot of the pencil. "Today we are just going to work on shapes. I will note specific hair and eye colors, and when I go back to the station, I will work on the computer to bring this sucker to life." Tora was glad to see Madeline grin.

Madeline described the smallish Greek nose with a slight deviation that turned to the right. The thin lips. The pointed chin and narrow ears. The thin, high-arching eyebrows. The scraggly beard that was thin on the heart-shaped contours of the cheekbones and full below the jaw. And the shoulder-length, sandy-blond hair, dirty and tangled.

Tora held up the sketch pad and showed the image to Madeline. The blood in her veins iced, and she held her own hands so they wouldn't shake. "That's him." Madeline stayed transfixed by the sturdy image. Her nightmare was fleeting and vaporous, and this was a chance to freeze the semblance. "It's missing something."

"OK. What's that?" Tora laid the pad back onto the table.

"He is missing a front tooth."

SEPTEMBER 28
ATLANTA, GEORGIA

The attorneys prepared to make final arguments in the murder
case of Horace Ford.

"All rise," the bailiff called, and Judge Charlotte Wilshire walked
to the bench. The gallery and press settled, and the jurors took
their seats, physically tired and emotionally worn.

District Attorney Leo Gargano stood and approached the jury.
"I want to thank you for the service you have performed. Yet your
duty is not quite finished. As we finish the day, you will be asked
to convene and come to a conclusion about the guilt or innocence
of Horace Ford. I know that, from where I sit, we have presented a
Mount Everest of evidence to you, the jurors, that without a doubt
implicates Mr. Ford in the murder of Savannah Gabriel. We have
heard experts talk about the scientific nature of blood and DNA.
We have all learned about how blood is handled and how blood is
exposed and corroded and the likely odds that the blood found in
Mr. Ford's Chevy Silverado was the blood of Savannah Gabriel. We

have learned that fibers and hair from Mr. Ford found on Savannah Gabriel were misplaced or compromised. The defense will argue that some of the samples were tainted or mishandled and that somehow the mistakes of the police were a mask for a larger conspiracy to 'get' Mr. Ford. I simply ask you to use your common sense. Even if some samples were corroded or inconsistent, all experts agreed about the likelihood that these samples of hair, blood, and DNA came from Mr. Horace Ford. The odds that it could be from any other person in the world are one in five hundred sixty-five million. One in five hundred sixty-five million." Gargano paused. "Mr. Ford's criminal nature is not in argument. He served an all-too-short sentence for the rape and beating of Breanna Green. We know who this man is! He is a violent predator who will continue to hunt women as long as he is free to do so. He had the means. The motive. And the evidence clearly points the finger of guilt at Mr. Ford." Gargano placed the mutilated, dismembered photos of Savannah Gabriel on the easel for the jury and press to observe. "Make no mistake about it, members of the jury. This is a tragedy. It needs to stop here. The nightmare will continue forever for the family members of Savannah Gabriel. Give them the smallest piece of justice. The justice that the man who did this to her pays for his crime. We have shown you with the indisputable evidence that Horace Ford did this to Savannah Gabriel." He moved the easel right in front of the jury box. "Convict Horace Ford for the vicious murder of this young woman. He is guilty."

Gargano took a moment and looked into the eyes of each member of the jury. He turned and thanked Judge Wilshire and quietly sat at the attorney's table.

Horace Ford managed to keep his eyes open as Defense Attorney Eva Jo Diamond removed her glasses and set them on the table. She rose and approached the jury. "Horace Ford never stood a chance in this trial." Juror number eighty-one, Evelyn Cahill, sat straight up in her seat. Her fiancé, Victor Kuyt, had said the same thing to her the day she'd been assigned to it. Diamond continued. "Mr. Gargano has told you about the insurmountable evidence against my client. He has admitted that the police have made mistakes. He has admitted that the scientific evidence, the holy grail of such trials in the twenty-first century, is tainted. Ladies and gentlemen of the jury, this essential evidence is the key to exonerating clients such as mine. Not a week goes by where I don't read about a prisoner in the United States who is freed because DNA evidence exonerated him or her of a crime after twenty, thirty years in prison have been served. Earl Washington Jr. was sentenced in Virginia to death for rape and murder. He was pardoned in 2004, the victim of overzealous detectives who forced a confession from a man with an IQ of sixty-nine. Shareef Cousin, convicted on the testimony of one eyewitness with no actual physical evidence. Cousin was sixteen years old and placed on death row. Additional eyewitnesses testified that Cousin was playing basketball. His attorney entered evidence that showed Cousin was playing in the game at the time of the murder. Yet the jury convicted him of murder. Why? They were wrong. They trusted the police and the testimony of the detectives. They bought what the district attorney was selling. Someone had to be blamed, and the jury took the first sacrificial cow the police brought them. Are these isolated cases? Randall Dale Adams. Joseph Burrows. Gary Gauge. Anthony Porter. Ron Williamson. Those are just some of the men from the nineties. The list grows. Nathson Fields. Paul House. Daniel Wade Moore. Ronald Kitchen. The United Kingdom abolished the death penalty after Timothy Evans was wrongfully charged and convicted. They hung him by his neck only to have the real killer confess to the murder of his wife and daughter and a slew of other murders. Men sentenced wrongfully to their deaths! Do you want to be party to sending a man to his death by lethal injection on corrupted, tarnished samples of blood and DNA and a compromised and unscrupulous police department? Detective Busquets's shoddy and incompetent collection of evidence and the well-documented vendetta to put my client behind bars defines this unethical standard! Where are the uncorrupted samples of blood? The untainted microscopic fibers? Not once has the prosecution presented a simple fingerprint of my client. They presented fingerprints of my client from his Silverado. I bet they would find your fingerprints in your car," Diamond mocked. "Nor have they produced a murder weapon, much less any of the tools of torture. They just don't have anything to connect my client to the crime. No cleaver. No lash or bullwhip. No metal box. The black trash bag that contained the remains of Savannah Gabriel—Mr. Ford did possess that style of trash bag. So do I. And I am sure many of you have them in your closets and garages right now, ready to rake leaves as fall comes. The district attorney rightfully pointed out that the murder of Savannah Gabriel was a tragedy. It truly is. The only thing worse would be to send an innocent man to his death. Two wrongs don't make a right. My client paid for his crime. Don't make him pay for a crime he did not commit. As you deliberate, ask yourself about the innocent victims sent to death row by incompetent police work and insufficient evidence who were later exonerated or pardoned after spending most of their productive lives in prison. Or, God forbid, found innocent after they had already died by lethal injection."

Judge Charlotte Wilshire instructed the jury to take the weekend off but to start deliberations on September 29. She reminded each juror to check in his or her cell phone with the officer of the court, as there was to be no communication with the outside world during deliberations.

OCTOBER 1
ATLANTA, GEORGIA

E velyn was exhausted from arguing with the other members of the jury. She slid the magnetic key into the lock, and the signal turned green. She powered her shoulder into the door and plopped her purse onto the floor.

She missed Victor immensely but did like staying in the hotel. The bed was always made when she got back from court or deliberations, and she only needed to pick up the phone for room service, complimentary of the Fulton County taxpayers. Evelyn grabbed a Coke from the minibar and clicked the remote. CNN Headline News was on, and she reached for the remote to change the channel. The picture caption in the corner of the screen caught her eye. The newswoman was reporting on the continued search for suspected homegrown terrorist, Seaman Brandon Lyle. She had heard the chatter about the man who had blown up the Federal Building in New Orleans but had never seen his picture. Until now. Her heart sank, and a boulder of sadness sprouted in her stomach. The sailor wore his hair close, but there was no mistaking the crystal-blue eyes of her fiancé, Victor Kuyt.

Evelyn lay back on the bed, hands over her eyes. The most trying few weeks of her life, buoyed only by her love for Victor and the promise of the future they had together, unraveled in the time it took to tell the evening news. How could she marry a murderer? How could she turn him in? How could she tell Victor that inside her grew his child? It was a secret, she decided, that no one would ever know.

OCTOBER 2
WASHINGTON, DC

FBI agent Ingrid Suarez poured herself another cup of coffee. The cyber-crimes unit had been on overdrive trying to find Seaman Brandon Lyle by hunting computer expert Rohit Guzan. Under the umbrella of the National Cyber Investigative Joint Task Force, the FBI joined the CIA, Department of Defense, and Homeland Security to neutralize cyber-based crimes and terrorism. Three hours of sleep in the last forty-eight had not helped her mood.

A ruffled agent entered Ingrid's office. "I think I found something."

"What do you have?" Ingrid held the bar low, as they had been eluded by the slippery Guzan.

"A computer in Brooklyn recently tried to hack a flight leaving Liberia. We followed the domain name to the IP address. The IP address is associated with a Nicole Samedov."

"OK. That's really creepy. I will send a unit over there to check it out." Suarez stirred her coffee.

"There's more. We ran her name through the database, and Samedov's name popped up."

"Terrorism?"

"No. Prostitution. An arrest on the tenth of August. One of those high-priced types. A real looker. Runs with the Russian crowd when they're in New York. This group has strong connections to ORBIS."

"I don't think she is the type to hack an airline." Suarez rolled her eyes.

"No. NYPD released her on bail. Guess who bailed her out?"

"Too tired to play games," Suarez pleaded.

"Rohit Guzan. Paid cash, but he had to sign and print. I think Guzan is in New York shaking up with Samedov."

Suarez picked up the phone and dialed the New York field office.

OCTOBER 2
BROOKLYN

Guzan ran his fingers up Nicole's neck, finding her chin. He moved her waiting mouth to his and ran his tongue around her lips. Her leg reached over his, and his hand found her ass, slipping it under her panties. She rolled on top of him, their mouths never separating. She ground her hips into his, his body aware and waiting. Nicole raised her body over him and put her hands on his chest, kneading his shoulders and pinching his nipples. She reached down, pulled her T-shirt over her head, and loosened her blond mane. She rolled to one knee and reached down, descending her fingers into Guzan's boxers, deftly sliding them down his legs. She rubbed the outside of his penis with her vagina.

"FBI!" The door was smashed in, and armored personnel charged into the room. The red dot of the target finder seared into Guzan's forehead. "Don't move!"

An agent moved toward Samedov, still on top of Guzan. She rolled off him into the handcuffs, her panties still moist. Guzan sat up in the bed and eyed the computer on the dining room table. "Don't even think about it!" the agent warned Guzan. "Sit up slowly."

Guzan moved his legs over the side of the bed, his hands up. "Get down on your knees!" Guzan slowly sank to the floor but made a sudden move to the computer. It only took one shot to the temple, but the FBI riddled Rohit Guzan with a dozen holes as he tried to destroy his laptop.

"Get that thing to forensics. ASAP."

OCTOBER 2
WASHINGTON, DC

"I'll call Agent Alcott right away." Suarez hung up the phone and picked it right back up. "Alcott?"

"This is Alcott." Jeremy was turning in to FBI headquarters.

"Jeremy. Lyle's in Atlanta. Forensics was able to break the codes on Guzan's computer."

Alcott turned his car around and told Sommer to call for a plane out of Andrews Air Force Base. "Jeremy. There is something happening at Kennedy. Guzan has manipulated a JetBlue flight from Liberia to New York."

"Call the State Department and ground the flight."

"It's already in the air," Suarez reported.

"When does it land?" Alcott sped through the mall area of DC.

"In three hours."

"Get the jets in the air. Force that thing down in a field if you have to."

OCTOBER 2
ATLANTIC OCEAN

Two F-15 Eagles escorted JetBlue flight 125 from Liberia to New York City to an isolated air force landing at Hanscom Air Force Base in Lincoln, Massachusetts. The air base readied for the possibility of an explosion. The F-15s were equipped to blast the 747 from the sky if it deviated off course.

The pilot circled the airfield once and lowered the aircraft to a perfect landing. Bomb squads raced to the slowing plane, the emergency slides ejected from the edges. One by one, the air force staff helped passengers from the isolated plane onto the tarmac.

Bomb experts and dogs searched the plane inch by inch as the 275 people disembarked, loading onto buses and heading for the safety of the terminal.

Airman Shernell Abbott brought water for the children and blankets for the elderly. She noticed that all of them seemed to be under the weather. Several adults had fevers, and many ran to the bathroom with nausea. One mother complained of chest pains and coughed violently. She called for a medic. The medic examined a dozen of the passengers. He spoke to the commanding officer. The bomb wasn't on the plane. The passengers were the bomb. Each member of the plane was experiencing advanced stages of the Ebola virus. It had landed in the United States.

OCTOBER 3
ATLANTA, GEORGIA

J udge Charlotte Wilshire called the jury into the courtroom. She had received a note from the jury foreman. Eva Jo Diamond sat opposite District Attorney Leo Gargano. Police outside Fulton County Courthouse had created a half-mile perimeter. Protesters, news trucks, reporters, and rubberneckers filled the lawns and lined the sidewalks, wondering if the verdict in the trial of Horace Ford had been delivered.

"Mr. Foreman, what do you say?" Wilshire asked the leader of the twelve-member jury.

"Your Honor. We are hopelessly deadlocked." A murmur rushed through the gallery.

"Have you reconsidered this conclusion and attempted to address the dissenting member or members of the jury?" Wilshire tallied the votes.

"We have, Your Honor. At this point, I cannot see or find any way to sway the vote so that we have a unanimous verdict."

Wilshire mulled her options but knew there was only one legal direction she could take. "It is with deep regret that the case of the *State of Georgia v. Horace Ford* has been declared a mistrial."

The sight of Horace Ford smiling and hugging Eva Jo Diamond sent tremors through the courthouse. The galleries erupted in cat-calls and boos. Trash and debris were hurled at the barrister. The police arrested several and cleared the courthouse with alacrity. Reporters scurried to the trucks to beam the news to the world. Jury members were escorted to assigned police cars and brought to their homes.

Judge Charlotte Wilshire sat at her desk with District Attorney Leo Gargano. He sulked at the defeat and consoled the judge, knowing she had abided by the law. They could not understand why juror number eighty-one had steadfastly voted to acquit Horace Ford.

Evelyn thanked the officer for driving her home. He helped take her luggage from the trunk, but she told him she would be fine taking it up the stairs. She was anxious to see Victor, or whatever his name was, and fall into his arms. She still loved him.

Evelyn turned the key to the lock and entered the door. Lyle advanced upon her and pulled her by the hair. He put her on the bed and smacked her across the face. The wallop left an impression. He removed her shirt and punched her in the ribs, the cracking sound puncturing her lung. She screamed in horror as the man she loved beat her.

"Victor! Stop! What did I do?" Evelyn pleaded as the belt buckle welted her in the ass. The leather cracked against her legs, causing blood to flow and drip down her thigh.

"Pray to your God, and he will not reply. You disgusting swine. This city will burn, and in the flames your flesh shall roast along with that of the other sinners who will join us all in hell."

"You're crazy!" Evelyn tried to crawl and hide from the assault. "Are you on drugs?"

Lyle removed the knife from his belt and held it flush against her neck. He dug the tip in. Evelyn squealed. "Please don't! I'm pregnant!"

"I know. But you're no angel." He ran the tip of the blade down the bridge of Evelyn's nose. Lyle grabbed a handful of her thick red hair and pulled it back, exposing her pale neck. "You have done what I needed you to do. I don't need you anymore. You have started a war." Lyle ran the blade across her neck, the blood spurting across the room as the jugular pumped the life out of Evelyn Cahill.

Evelyn lay on her apartment floor, her dead baby inside her. Lyle, amused by the irony, hacked off her head and put it in Evelyn's suitcase. He dismembered her arms and legs, remembering to separate the feet and the hands. In a final detailed touch, he removed four of the ten fingers in an homage to Horace Ford. He piled the severed body parts on top of her head and zipped the suitcase shut.

Seaman Brandon Lyle called Elroy Floyd and told him to meet him at the apartment. He walked past Evelyn in the suitcase and whistled while he showered. He put on a pair of jeans, a leather jacket, and a new pair of biker boots.

Floyd sat on a Harley SuperLow with maroon markings. Next to him idled a Harley Iron 883. Lyle kicked his leg over the seat, and he and Elroy Floyd sped out of Atlanta, Georgia, just before it burned to the ground.

Radiance Bancora watched Victor Kuyt leave Evelyn's apartment building on a motorcycle. She thought that was odd, as they had been waiting to see each other for a month. She also thought it was odd that Evelyn wasn't answering her phone or texts. She knocked on the door but received no answer. Radiance figured she was exhausted and had decided to take a nap.

Later on Friday, as the sun set across the cities and towns of the United States, citizens gathered in town squares, on street corners, and in strip mall parking lots. Students rallied at Berkeley, Harvard, and Duke. At Grambling, Southern, and Alcorn State. Some came with signs protesting the verdict in the Savannah Gabriel murder trial. Others came with guns and knives. They came with broken bottles and Molotov cocktails. As the evening wore on and the skies of Los Angeles and the streets of San Francisco fell dark, the cities began to burn. Riot police in Detroit and Chicago, Philadelphia and Washington, New York City and Saint Louis clashed with protestors and rioters, driving them back with tear gas and water cannons. Gunfire filled the breezy air of Miami as police protected by riot gear and tanks traded blasts with angry citizens hunkered down on rooftops and barricaded around corners. Opportunists raced away from the violence, looted stores, and set fire to local businesses. Downtown Atlanta glowed from the interstate as the fashionable shops of Buckhead blazed in the balmy southern night. Atlanta burned as it had by Sherman's torch in 1864.

OCTOBER 4
ATLANTA, GEORGIA

Radiance tried Evelyn all night. She hoped that Evelyn was sleeping, because she sure wasn't. The air still smoldered from the fires, but the cloaked faces of the rioters and masked police shied from the sunlight. She tried Victor as well, but he didn't pick up either. It was strange that Victor had gone off on a motorcycle with another dude. Radiance always thought Victor was weird and antisocial. He was always on the phone and never left the apartment. He rarely acknowledged her when she was in the apartment. Radiance didn't even know that Victor had a friend in Atlanta. Radiance changed tactics and decided to call the cops.

The operator refused to file a missing persons report as Evelyn had not been missing for twenty-four hours. Radiance demanded to speak to her supervisor. She convinced the supervisor to send a squad car as an elderly woman had mysteriously disappeared from the same apartment building in recent weeks.

Radiance met the officer at Evelyn's apartment. "Whose apartment is this?" The officer took out his notepad.

"Her name is Evelyn Cahill. She just got off jury duty, and we were supposed to meet at her apartment, but she never returned my calls," Radiance detailed.

"Is it possible that she met someone else while waiting for you?"

"She has a boyfriend. But I saw him leave the apartment on a motorcycle with some other guy. Evelyn wasn't with them." Radiance offered.

"And what is this boyfriend's name?" the officer continued.

"His name is Victor Kuyt. He just got out of the navy. And he and Evelyn just got engaged." Radiance tapped her foot.

"Maybe the two lovebirds just went out of town," the officer surmised.

"I don't think so. Something is wrong." She texted Evelyn again.

"Ma'am. You said Evelyn was recently on jury duty?"

"Yes. The Horace Ford case."

The officer moved quickly to the squad car and called in the report. He asked for his commanding officer. He spoke into the radio. "Boss, this is Officer Emmanuel van Persie. I got a call to check on a missing person. The subject's name is Evelyn Cahill. A person of interest is her fiancé, Victor Kuyt. The reason I asked for you," Van Persie said, running Kuyt's name, "is that the woman was a jury member on the Horace Ford case."

"Jesus." The CO smelled trouble.

"And boss," van Persie said, watching the computer screen in the squad car, "I got a hit on the name Victor Kuyt. It's an alias for the terrorist Brandon Lyle. Christ!"

"I want you to seal off the door. I am going to get a warrant and call the FBI."

The blue lights of squad cars flashed in the quiet neighborhood. The black Chevy Suburban arrived, and Agents Jeremy Alcott and Bruno Sommer joined the Atlanta Police Department. Yellow crime-scene tape crisscrossed Evelyn's door.

"Did you locate the super?" Alcott asked van Persie.

"Yes. He's right here."

The superintendent opened Evelyn's door. Alcott drew his weapon and identified himself. He and Sommer cleared the corners and stood in the small apartment. A framed picture of Evelyn Cahill and her fiancé, Victor Kuyt, aka Brandon Lyle, rested on the coffee table, splattered with blood. Sommer followed the scene into the bedroom, the carpet soaked and the walls sprayed. Lyle had left a scribbled note in Evelyn's blood on the wall: *Omnium vestrum esse moriturum.*

"Bruno, it's been a while since I took Latin. What does that say?" Jeremy asked his partner.

"It says, 'All of you will die.'" Sommer looked at the suitcase leaking blood. "You want to open it?"

"Not really."

The detectives donned vinyl gloves and unzipped the suitcase. Evelyn's foot lay on top of the rest of her.

7:30 A.M., WEDNESDAY, OCTOBER 8 ARLINGTON, VIRGINIA

"Not too much jelly." Oliver watched as Sophia slathered the Welch's grape jelly onto his bread.

"How can there be too much jelly?" Sophia sucked the jelly off the knife and smiled.

"It squirts out of the bread and gets on my shirt."

Good point, Sophia thought. "OK, buddy. You are all set. Now hustle. You have to catch the bus." Sophia gave Oliver a big hug as he set forth on a usual day in unusual times.

Raphael watched the morning news and the updates on the deadly and worsening riots that plagued the country for another night. The angry faces of the oppressed shouted for equality and impartiality at the men behind the gas masks who wielded batons, carried pistols, and fired tear gas. Savannah Gabriel was the final straw in a long history of American injustice. Each night a spark would ignite the violence between the police and citizens in the streets. And the process of collecting the dead and injured on the streets would begin the following morning as America went dutifully to work, fashioning a false sense of normalcy.

Reports came in from Seattle and Denver. Milwaukee and Mobile. Charlotte and Cleveland. The fires raged, and the black smoke billowed. Presidential curfews were mandated nationwide but not abided.

Raphael kissed Sophia and told her he was going to take the metro as the rush hour traffic had become unbearable since the eight o'clock curfew that required all government buildings to close at five.

"I have got a five thirty conference at the firm. I should be home by seven thirty." Sophia turned to Madeline, eating a bowl of Rice Chex. "Madeline, what are your plans today?"

"Father Moutinho is picking me up at three. We are going to Starbucks and then to the cathedral. Tonight is the blood moon, and he is going to take me up to the observation deck."

"Won't that put you home after curfew?" Sophia dotted the lipstick.

"Maybe a little. But don't worry, Mom. The cathedral is in northwest. There are no riots in that part of the city. Besides, I'll be with a priest."

Good point, thought Sophia.

10:00 A.M.
ATLANTA, GEORGIA

"All two hundred seventy-five passengers were diagnosed with the Ebola virus," Alcott reported to Alexander Khan.

"How many people have been exposed?" Khan kept his back to the agent.

"Everyone at Hanscom has been placed in isolation at the airbase. No one is allowed to leave or enter. The CDC has sent forty-five doctors to work with the patients. With the passengers and the people exposed at Hanscom, the number is four hundred two exposed or with full-blown Ebola," Alcott detailed.

"It could have been much worse had they been allowed to matriculate into New York City."

"What else did Guzan's computer give us?" Khan asked.

"Evelyn Cahill was set up. Guzan got her on jury duty, and then Lyle did the rest," Sommer noted.

"Cyber hasn't been able to unlock everything on the computer," Alcott confessed.

"So there could still be more surprises?" Khan threw the folder onto the desk.

"Yes," Alcott admitted.

12:00 P.M., WEDNESDAY, OCTOBER 8

Lyle helped Elroy Floyd fill the legal satchel with standard military-issue M112, 1.25-pound blocks of C-4. Each piece, eleven inches long and two inches wide, settled like a deadly gold bar. The bricks fit snugly next to one another, covering the base of the case. Floyd inserted the detonators and started to place another layer in the large briefcase. Gently, they laid each brick until they reached the top. Floyd ensured that the briefcase would close.

"Forty bars of C-4. Fifty pounds." Elroy held the case to test its weight. "It's going to be hard to tote the bag without anyone noticing its weight."

"That's why you will have a dolly." Lyle pulled out replicas of the legal satchels and placed them three high on top of one another. He placed the facade of FBI binders on top of the C-4 in case a snoop were to investigate each satchel. "And our man on the inside will get us in. He will escort you to the Senate conference room where sixteen US senators and the director of Homeland Security will be waiting for these documents." The legion was everywhere. "You drop the briefcases in the office of Pennsylvania senator Vera Torres. Report that these are the FBI reports they had been expecting and take them to her right away." Lyle fondled the remote detonator. "You leave from the north security exit. As soon as I see you, I squeeze."

3:00 P.M.
ARLINGTON, VIRGINIA

Father Salvatore Moutinho noticed right away that Madeline wasn't wearing her telltale hoodie. Her hair was down, and the concealment of makeup had diminished. She wore a snug-fitting pair of jeans and a Native American top with a pair of dangling turquoise earrings.

"You look quite beautiful this afternoon, madam." Moutinho was impressed with the change.

"Dr. Smalling and I talked about the personalities inside me. I told her I was starting to feel more comfortable about the MPD and wasn't going to fight it anymore. I figured it would be peaceful for my soul. She told me the stories of Wanikiya. She was a strong woman. I want to be strong like her. I want to love like her. I want to get to know all of the personalities inside me. I think they can teach me a lot. And maybe I can learn to live with all of them and not be frightened or have any more 'episodes.'"

"That's a wonderful approach, Madeline. I am proud of you. Starbucks?" Moutinho smiled.

"Uh. Yeah. I've waited all day." Madeline smiled back, and Moutinho steered the long black Cadillac sedan onto Glebe Road.

3:30 P.M., WEDNESDAY, OCTOBER 8 ARLINGTON, VIRGINIA

Officer Paolo Velozo walked by sketch artist Tora Yebda's desk. They had worked on several cases, and it had been some time since he had said hello to the sketch artist. "Hi, Tora! What's up?" Velozo waited for his hug.

"Paolo! How have you been?" Tora stood and stretched her arms around his growing waistline.

"Better than those cops in DC. It's been five straight nights of riots. The whole country is at war."

"It's so sad, Paolo. It has to stop soon."

"I know. Fortunately, and unfortunately, the protests have mostly been in DC." Velozo pulled a sketch from underneath Tora's knapsack. "Who's this?"

Tora looked at the sketch. "This is a sketch I did for a girl who was having bad dreams. I kind of put it on the back burner. I should plug that into the PortraitPad."

"I have a few minutes. Would you mind doing that now? I think I recognize this guy." Velozo pulled up a chair.

Tora slid over and opened the PortraitPad program. She inserted the face and added the eyes, following her sketch from Madeline's description. Tora was always pleased when her sketch looked better than the computer's. "Take away the beard," Velozo said politely. Tora removed the scraggly beard, leaving the image fresh faced and clean. "Shorten the hair." Tora followed his command. "Shorter. Like a military crew cut." Tora complied. "This thing works in color, right?" Velozo pressed.

"Sure." Tora moved the mouse and added color.

"Make the eyes blue."

Tora stopped cold. "How did you know the eyes were blue?" She swiveled in her seat. "The girl said they were blue. Deathly blue or something." They turned to the computer screen. Both of their mouths dropped.

"Tora. That's Brandon Lyle."

4:00 P.M., WEDNESDAY, OCTOBER 8 ATLANTA, GEORGIA

B runo sat with Jeremy and their boss, Alexander Khan, at the FBI's Atlanta field office. They looked out the window over the ruined buildings of Atlanta, still smoldering from a fourth night of rioting.

"The governors of twenty-five states have called in the National Guard." Khan had spoken with the president of the United States earlier in the morning. "The chief is thinking of calling in the real army."

"That's the wrong move," Jeremy observed. "That will only escalate the situation."

"Maybe." Khan looked at the skyline. "In the meantime people are dying. More than twenty-five hundred have died in the violence that started Friday night. Protesters and police alike. Not to mention the businesses and homes that have been destroyed."

An agent rushed into the room. "Director Khan. Agent Alcott. Agent Sommer. This just came in from Arlington, Virginia." He handed them the computer-generated composite of Brandon Lyle.

"It's Brandon Lyle."

"Yes. But Arlington Police reported that a girl described him perfectly to a sketch artist."

"How long ago was this?"

"Last week."

Jeremy grabbed his coat. "I am taking the plane to DC. I need to talk to this girl."

"We don't know he is in DC," Khan protested. "We know he was in Atlanta just five days ago. He's probably still here."

"He never stays long once his work is done. Bruno will stay with you. I need to talk to this girl."

4:00 P.M.

WASHINGTON, DC

"Mrs. Deschamps, your meeting in conference room B is about to start."

Sophia thanked God for her secretary. "Thanks, Cindy." Sophia touched up her hair and made sure she had the proper files for the meeting. She grabbed her cell phone but turned it on vibrate. This meeting was vital, and she didn't want to be "that person."

Raphael walked to the Foggy Bottom metro station near the George Washington Hospital Center. The students filled the sidewalks, protest posters drawn near other students lying in the grass on a wonderful, clear fall afternoon. Raphael took off his coat and placed it over his arm that held his briefcase. He took inventory of the day and of the briefcase's contents. He need to review the LaManna Files and the activities of the Italian underworld boss. He checked for his phone and remembered it was safe in his briefcase. He headed down the escalator and waited for the Orange Line to pick him up and take him to the Ballston stop. Maybe he would even stop in the mall and get his wonderful wife a present.

4:45 P.M., WEDNESDAY, OCTOBER 8 FBI FLIGHT OVER NORTH CAROLINA

Jeremy Alcott sat in his seat on the FBI Learjet, which sped toward Washington in the skies of North Carolina. The emergency phone rang, and he picked up the call. "Alcott. It's Suarez."

"What do you have, Ingrid?"

"Cyber has unlocked a subset of superhidden files on Guzan's computer. Lyle has someone on the inside at the US Capitol."

"Oh God." Jeremy sat back in his seat.

"Jeremy, it gets worse. The target date is today." Suarez held the phone nervously.

"I'll call Khan. Go to code red and get everyone out of the Capitol." Jeremy wondered if the plane could go any faster.

CAPITOL HILL

E lroy Floyd walked through the intersection of Independence Avenue and First Street, Northeast, the Library of Congress on his right. He pulled the dolly behind him, wearing his official FBI cap, and official identification clipped to his jacket. He whistled while he walked and hauled the three legal satchels up to the south security entrance of the Capitol building.

Seaman Brandon Lyle sat on a park bench on the north side of the Capitol, reading the *Washington Post* and enjoying a latte, his sunglasses on. His windbreaker disguised the handheld remote detonator. He peaked over the top of the Style section to see if Floyd had exited.

Floyd made eye contact with the legion, the Capitol police officer pledging allegiance to hell. Floyd set his keys on the conveyor belt along with his cell phone. Regular Capitol police checked his firearm and another watched as the items passed through the X-ray. The legion deftly moved the dolly past conveyor belt and the metal detector. "This guy needs an escort. Senator Torres's office. "The legion volunteed. "I'll take him."

The other policeman didn't notice and continued to check in visitors and deliveries. Floyd was personally escorted by the House Chamber and through the nine-million-pound cast-iron dome. The officer pressed the button for the elevator door. Senator Gaston Milner exited but did not recognize Floyd, and the two conspirators stepped onto the elevator.

A hand stopped the door from closing. "The Capitol is on lockdown. I need everyone to leave the building except authorized personnel." Floyd waited for his escort.

"Hello, Commander. This will only take a second. These documents were being rushed to Senator Torres's office for the Homeland meeting. We'll be right out."

"Nope. Everyone goes now. Including Senator Torres and her meeting. She can get them once we analyze the threat."

Floyd and the escort stepped off the elevator and were shuffled to the north exit. Floyd donned his sunglasses and adjusted his FBI hat and dragged the dolly out of the US Capitol. The Capitol police corralled the occupants of the Capitol, including Floyd, into a segregated area a hundred yards from the entrance.

Lyle watched from the bench, knowing something had gone wrong. He watched as the Capitol emptied by the dozens. Exits from north, south, east, and west leaked lobbyists and secretaries. Senators and representatives were taken to the tunnels and evacuated underground. Emergency vehicle lights flooded Capitol Hill. Lyle saw Floyd being escorted to an area north of the Capitol. He pushed his hand into his windbreaker pocket and pulled the trigger of the remote control device. Elroy Floyd, a lover of the bomb, would have enjoyed going this way. His body disintegrated into a billion pieces, the bomb killing dozens in its immediate vicinity and maiming hundreds of others. Bystanders ran like hell for safety, including Brandon Lyle, who disappeared into the frightened crowd.

5:45 P.M.
ANDREWS AIR FORCE BASE

Alcott received the call on his cell. "Jeremy, there has been an explosion at the Capitol."

"Lyle," Alcott muttered under his breath. "Was anyone hurt? Did we get everybody out?"

"It's bad, Jeremy. There are dozens dead. The explosion happened on the north lawn as everyone was being evacuated. So many people were injured."

The FBI Learjet lowered its landing gear and touched down at Andrews Air Force Base.

"Senators and representatives?"

"No reports. They followed protocol and left in the tunnels." Jeremy could hear Suarez crying. "The building itself is intact." Alcott found no solace; the damage was done to flesh and bone, not mortar and wood.

"Thanks for the update, Suarez."

Alcott exited the plane to a waiting Chevy Suburban, its blue lights flashing. "Where do you want to go?" asked the driver.

"I want to go to this address in Arlington, Virginia. I need to talk to a Madeline Deschamps."

6:30 P.M.
ARLINGTON, VIRGINIA

The agents knocked on the door of the Deschampses' house. Oliver answered the door. "Hello. We are from the FBI. Is Madeline Deschamps available?" The agents showed identification.

"Dad?" Oliver was out of his league.

"Hello. I am Madeline's father. How may I help you?" Raphael wondered what had happened to Madeline now.

"Raphael Deschamps?" Alcott moved into the doorway.

"Yes."

"We have been trying to reach you all day. As well as Madeline and Sophia."

"Sophia's my wife. What is this all about?"

"In the last week or so your daughter gave a description of a man to a police sketch artist."

"Yes. She did," Raphael confirmed.

"That sketch found its way to my desk. Sir. Your daughter gave a perfect description of a terrorist known as Brandon Lyle. You may have heard of him."

"Yes. He's all over the news." Raphael watched the news coming from the Capitol out of the corner of his eye. "Madeline has had some severe anxiety. Isn't it possible she saw his picture on the television and became afraid? Gave his image to the artist?"

"It's possible. But Madeline described the man as missing his front tooth. That's something that has never appeared on television and a detail that we only just discovered." Alcott looked over at the television and his first images of the bombing. "Sir, it is imperative that I speak to Madeline. The tragedy at the Capitol? We believe it was the work of Brandon Lyle. Where is your daughter?"

"She is with Father Salvatore Moutinho. At the National Cathedral." Alcott turned and headed back to the Suburban. "I'll go with you." Raphael grabbed his jacket.

"Sir. Stay here. Curfew starts soon. You need to be with your son."

6:45 P.M.
WASHINGTON
NATIONAL CATHEDRAL,
WASHINGTON, DC

F ather Salvatore Moutinho led Madeline through the nave, dim-
ly lit because the facility was closed for the evening. They found
the elevator in the darkness. The up light cast an eerie red glow.
They boarded the elevator and squinted in the bright light. The
doors opened, and they stepped back into the gloom.

Moutinho and Madeline perched on the observatory deck of the
National Cathedral and watched the eastern horizon. "There! The
edges of the full moon, bright and hopeful." Moutinho pointed.
Madeline craned to catch the first phase of lunar eclipse. "Shortly,
the shadows of the earth will leak in front of the moon like blood
soaking into a towel."

"As your blood will drip onto the altar of your fabricated God." Brandon Lyle stepped into the moonlight from the dark corner. Madeline screamed and tried to run, but Father Salvatore Moutinho grabbed her with both arms and spun her toward Lyle. Lyle extended his right finger, and it extended into a sharp point. He sliced Madeline's cheek and took the blood into his mouth. "It is good to taste you again."

"Father! Why? I trusted you!" Madeline struggled to free herself.

"I am his shepherd, and I lead his lamb to slaughter." Moutinho observed as Lyle circled his prey. "He was going to find you. He only asked for my help. He smells you. Like a shark. He is patient and will never stop searching. Over thousands of miles and through time. He will always finds you. We are in a war for the soul of humanity. You are their most valuable weapon."

7:00 P.M.
WASHINGTON, DC

P rotesters gathered in the quadrants of the District of Columbia and other eastern cities. As night fell and the blood moon showed itself, the nation would brace for another night of violence with people behind barricades like rabid dogs. Afraid of themselves. Afraid of one another. Behind the ski masks and under the helmets were fathers, brothers, sisters, mothers, and children. There were freaks and perverts. Jokesters and the dull. Blacks, whites, gays, Latinos, Asians, dykes, whores, and prudes. Behind each side of the barricade were the brown, the yellow, the red, and the white, the atheists and the devoted. The teetotalers, pill poppers, dope smokers, coke snorters, needle pushers, cross-dressers, business owners, shopkeepers, hairdressers, college students, auto mechanics, and librarians. The weaves and the flattops, the bobs and the dreads, the curly and the straight. The round and the freckled, the fat and the thin, the healthy and the disabled.

Behind their masks and under the helmets, they were all human. Sometimes frail and weak, but human. Sometimes passionate and dutiful, but human. Humans in desperate need to find common ground and remove the blurred lines of their differenences and the fear that pitted them against themselves. Humans in need of a shining light of truth to guide them. In a nation measured by the word *freedom*, the crowds stood before one another for a sixth night, ready to kill one another.

7:15 P.M.

NATIONAL CATHEDRAL

Lyle skipped the elevator and dragged Madeline by the hair down the sandstone, curling stairs to the nave, Moutinho following closely. Lyle beat Madeline about the face, knocking her unconscious. He put her over his shoulder and began to dance before the Canterbury Pulpit and into the cross section of the great church, spinning the lifeless Madeline in his arms, thanking her for the memories and celebrating that he would dine on her womb as he had for eternity.

Lyle stepped onto the altar and twirled past the great organ. His arm swept the chalices from the altar and laid her on the marble below the mural of Christ seated at his throne. He turned and mocked the son of God, spitting at his feet.

Outside, Agent Jeremy Alcott and his driver found the grand wooden door of the eastern lower-level entrance open. He entered the Bethlehem Chapel and found a staircase that took him to the main level. The cathedral walls pressed against him, and he struggled to find his way in the dark. He paused for a moment and put on a pair of night-vision goggles. He moved into the nave, the world visible but for the cloudy, green haze of the goggles. He heard the gloating from the altar and watched as Lyle hurled obscene gestures. Alcott drew his gun and moved to a closer pillar. Lyle's skin peeled away from his face, and the three heads of the dragon rose from his neck. His hands turned to claws, and the deadly tail swiped at the floor. Lyle spoke with the voice of all the souls in hell screaming as he hovered over Madeline's still body. "I have followed you through time. I live in your dreams and stalk you in your life. I hunt for you eternity. I wait for you in the shadows as my armies destroy the earth."

The light from the altar allowed Alcott to remove the goggles. The image of the dragon disappeared, but the same evil readied to sacrifice the teenager. Jeremy motioned to the driver to focus on the idle Moutinho. Alcott stepped from the shadows. "FBI!"

Lyle recognized the amazing eyes that folded all the colors of the universe together. "I see you have come back to die...again!"

"No. I came back for my wife!"

Lyle stepped away from Madeline as the vapors rose from her body. The ghost of Wanikiya, still adorned with her crown of flowers, grand and tall, hovered over Madeline's body, protecting her from Lyle, the jaws of her skeleton snapping as the demon moved close to the girl. She was joined by Aashiyra, Baozhai, Ahuva, Constanza, Cassia, Rashidi, and Geneva, the victims of Belial over centuries, in a circle of light. Wanikiya immersed herself in Jeremy Alcott's eyes. Samuel Knapp's eyes.

Lyle moved swiftly to Alcott. "Your feeble God always believes someone as weak as you is going to defy me. I like the way things are. You are such a pest." Lyle reached for Alcott.

"That's the pot calling the kettle black." Jeremy fired his weapon; the bullet absorbed into Lyle's stomach with no effect. The driver appeared behind Lyle. "My God! It's the devil himself!"

"No. I just work for him." Lyle waved the sharp edges of the dragon's tail behind him and slit his throat, the agents head dangling from his shoulder.

7:45 P.M.

ATLANTA, GEORGIA

Outside the Fulton County Courthouse, the press prepared for a news conference being held by Defense Attorney Eva Jo Diamond. She stepped to the podium in the glare of the television lights and among the clatter of the photographers.

"America has been at war since the verdicts were read last Friday in Judge Wilshire's courtroom. My duty is to defend my client, but my conscience can find no rest as the cities of America burn. I have let pride infect my soul and have failed all of you in my duties as an officer of the court. I bear the burden, at least in part, for why the people of America prepare to battle one another again tonight." Diamond reached into her suit pocket and removed an envelope. "During the discovery phase of the investigation, I failed to turn over key evidence that would convict my client, Horace Ford." The live broadcast beamed the news across the globe and into every home and restaurant in America. Americans watched. "This would have been the proverbial smoking gun. It is a letter written by Savannah Gabriel, and it is soaked in her blood and bears his fingerprints. Horace Ford taunted that poor girl and asked her to write her last words. This is how the letter reads:

I know I will die tonight. I have looked the devil in the eye. I will be crucified for my race. I will die because I am a woman. I will die in the name of hatred and oppression. For every nation has this man among them. This man has become our world. I blame myself for the existence of this man. I blame you for the existence of this man. We are all to blame. We have been given the choice to accept each man as our brother, but we have allowed evil to feed our souls. We have failed God. We have failed one another. We could build, but we destroy. We could share, but we take. We could love, but we hate. Freedom is not the ability to do whatever you want. Freedom is the loss of fear. The ability to love. Humanity's world will end soon should we continue to travel this path. I forgive this man. Forgive one another. Live in peace among the citizens of the earth. Light the candles of love.

I have read Savannah's words over and over again. I accept my fate for my failures. Hear Savannah's words and stop the fighting. Tonight."

8:00 P.M.

NATIONAL CATHEDRAL

Lyle rubbed Jeremy's face into the sandstone. He picked him up over his head and slammed him into the hard marble floor. His body was breaking, but he stood and attacked. Lyle hovered over him, his nail emerging in a sharp point. "I am but a soldier. His army will rise, and he will ride his pale horse across the clouds and revel as humanity destroys itself. Your God is impotent. We have already won."

"I have my own army, motherfucker!" Alcott smashed Lyle in the face.

8:00 P.M.

ACROSS AMERICA

News of Eva Jo Diamond's press conference found its way through the radios and televisions, the cell phones and the Internet. People shared the revelation with one another, and they heard what Savannah Gabriel had to say.

Before a shot was fired or a canister of tear gas launched, people on both sides of the barricades removed their masks. Off came the helmets of the police and the handkerchiefs that swaddled the unrecognized. They dropped their batons in Boston and Nashville. They put away their knives in Los Angeles and New York City. They holstered their pistols in Chicago and Detroit. A woman in Washington held her candle to the sky, its small light igniting a millions souls. They held flashlights and flares, fire and cell phones, high into the sky for Savannah Gabriel. They shone spotlights and glow sticks into the night. The light of the world gathered in a beam, stretching into space, passing the blood moon, a beacon racing into the heavens.

God stood on a dark ledge of heaven, facing the uncreated backdrop of space, searching for inspiration. In the darkness a tiny ball glowed. A firefly of illumination, a small bolt of hope, swirled around his face. He snatched the light between his thumb and forefinger and fired it back toward Earth.

8:01 PM

NATIONAL CATHEDRAL

J eremy Alcott lay on the altar, battered and beaten, next to Madeline Deschamps and under the fading ghosts that had escaped from Madeline's soul. The apparitions diminished with each powerful blow of Brandon Lyle.

Lyle held the crucifix in his hand and stared at the exposed abdomen of Madeline. He raised the crucifx high over his head. The tremendous light filled the west rose window, showering the altar with the brilliant colors of the stained glass. Father Salvatore Moutinho covered his eyes, blinded by the light. He burst into flames as the colorful glass exploded, flooding the cathedral with God's bolt.

Waves of light pushed Lyle against the marble walls of the altar, pinning him to the throne of Christ, his skin melting and the rays piercing holes into his torso, sending the demon back to hell for eternity.

Samuel Knapp, his soul trapped in the body of Jeremy Alcott, felt the light touch of Wanikiya on his forehead. He opened his eyes, giving his wife of another life one last chance to see the eyes that folded all the colors of the universe into one. She pulled his soul from Jeremy's body and Samuel and Waniliya, released from the bonds of hell, held each other in a wedding dance over the altar as they evaporated into Heaven, illuminating God's path for Madeline and mankind to follow.

In remembrance of the flight crew and passengers of MH17. Every time we reach for the heavens, unnatural forces pull us back to earth.

"Love will win. Light will break through."
—Relative of an MH17 victim

Violence persists in the twenty-first century on our planet because of age, disability, race, gender, creed, and sexuality. God performs miracles every day, big and small. We must do our part and stop the violence. We're all human. We can do better.